"WE CAN HAVE I

Vost knew he had them hooked. "We make contact," he continued. "Show them what we can do, and then offer our services. We take the best offer. We can always change our minds if we want to.

"But we have to be careful. Takuda and the rest of DEST team may not like our little plan. We'll have to convince him that we're doing it his way. Make him think it's all his idea. We have to get the 'Mechs out of that DropShip, and we can't do it as long as he's got a guard there."

"We have slug pistols," said Collis Brank, looking up at Vost. "We could just do a job on them."

"Not a good plan, Brank. Have you ever seen what a laser rifle can do to an unarmored human body? No. We have to do it slowly. Just wait until we get those 'Mechs out of the ship, and then we'll see who's boss."

Vost looked up at the first stars beginning to appear in the darkening sky. "By the eyes of the dragon, this will be an adventure our children and grandchildren will sing about!"

FAR COUNTRY

Peter L. Rice

A ROC BOOK

ROC

Published by the Penguin Group
Penguin Books Ltd, 27 Wrights Lane, London W8 5TZ, England
Penguin Books USA Inc., 375 Hudson Street, New York, New York 10014, USA
Penguin Books Australia Ltd, Ringwood, Victoria, Australia
Penguin Books Canada Ltd, 10 Alcorn Avenue, Toronto, Ontario, Canada M4V 3B2
Penguin Books (NZ) Ltd, 182–190 Wairau Road, Auckland 10, New Zealand

Penguin Books Ltd, Registered Offices: Harmondsworth, Middlesex, England

First published in the USA by ROC, an imprint of New American Library,
a division of Penguin Books USA Inc. 1993
First published in Great Britain 1994
10 9 8 7 6 5 4 3 2 1

Series editor: Donna Ippolito
Cover: Boris Vallejo
Interior illustrations: Rick Harris
Mechanical drawings: Duane Loose

ROC Roc is a trademark of Penguin Books Ltd. BATTLETECH, FASA and the
distinctive BATTLETECH and FASA logos are trademarks of the FASA Corporation,
1026 W. Van Buren, Chicago, IL 60507

Printed in England by Clays Ltd, St Ives plc

PROLOGUE

9 November 2510
Salford, Draconis Combine

1

Roaring gusts of wind swept across the open landing area of Salford Station, carrying dense clouds of talcum-fine grit that attacked the troops, DropShips, and vehicles gathered at the spaceport. The grit drove under the wristbands and neck rings of the troopers' uniforms, mixing with perspiration to form a slurry that scoured away layers of flesh. The only way to avoid the blasting grit was to turn away; the only way to avoid the constant abrasion was to remain motionless. Because it was beneath the dignity of a battalion commander of the Draconis Combine Mustered Soldiery to turn away from clouds of grit, *Chu sa* Tokashio Hamata chose the second alternative.

It was not so for the other members of the battalion staff, however. Seeing them crouched beside a landing pad, their hoods pulled tight against the blasts, Hamata was sure that they were also watching him for the slightest sign of weakness. A samurai did not flinch from an armed enemy, much less an attack by mere dust. Neither did a battalion commander. Neither did a graduate of the Sun Zhang MechWarrior Academy. And Tokashio Hamata was all three of these. Facing into the approaching cone of dust, his only acknowledgment was the slightest squinting of his eyes.

The cloud passed over the landing pad, where the DropShips awaited boarding by the members of the 2452nd Battalion, Fifth Galedon Regulars. Along with its sister battalion, the 2452nd was loading for transshipment to Brailsford, a world only one jump away. Because of the so-called McAllister Rebellion, the Combine's military commanders had been taking the precaution of pulling troops away from the distant edge of Combine space. Hamata had known about the change for six months, ever since he'd first gotten wind of the orders in June of that year. Supporting the two combat battalions were a Heavy Engineer Battalion, the 262nd, and a combat medical support battalion.

Tokashio Hamata was not happy with the situation. His battalion's DropShips, all of them *Vulture* Class, were not being combat-loaded. The ships assigned to his unit were too big to take only a single company and too small to carry two. As a result, he'd had to break some of the companies up among the DropShips. They would all be under his command once they linked with the *Raiden,* the *Leviathan* Class JumpShip that would transport them across the stars, but they would be separated and scrambled during the transits to and from the JumpShip awaiting them in deep space. Deployment onto Brailsford would be equally confused. Hamata dreaded the thought of administrative movement. It always made the troops slip a bit.

Even though he'd been assured that Brailsford was a secure planet, there was always the nagging doubt. Having raised and trained the 2452nd himself, Hamata wanted to be able to hit his landing zone combat-ready. These troops were his children. He didn't want to see anything happen to them.

Another gust of wind scoured the landing area and Hamata squinted against it. The loading ramp trembled under his feet as a Chi-Ha armored personnel carrier ground its way slowly up the incline. The ramps, Hamata noted, were of the older style and not quite wide enough to take the new family of equipment. The driver was keeping the twenty-two-ton vehicle carefully centered on the yellow line painted down the middle of the ramp.

When Hamata noticed that the driver was a woman, his jaw tightened involuntarily. He understood that females of the Draconis Combine were not barred from any profession. He understood that the Combine needed every human resource at its disposal. But that didn't alter the fact that he preferred to have only men in his unit.

By careful manipulation of the personnel records he had managed to keep his fighting units almost pure. It was true that the support and administrative units included more women, but that couldn't be helped. There were even women in the headquarters as officers. As a samurai of ancient lineage, however, Hamata never felt comfortable seeing a woman carrying the *dai-sho*. It was an attitude that extended back in time more than a thousand years, so deeply ingrained in his psyche that he would probably never be able to overcome it. But enough of that, he told himself. It was the loading operation that demanded all his attention at the moment. As he dismissed the thoughts from his mind, another Chi-Ha APC rumbled past.

Down the line of *Vultures*, Hamata could see the last of his vehicles grinding through the gaping cargo doors in the ship fuselages. These were not the biggest DropShips available, yet even they dwarfed the battalion's armored vehicles. Hamata grimaced again. He was being forced, by orders, to leave most of his combat equipment behind. Those orders had informed him that he would receive pre-placed equipment once they reached Brailsford. He was authorized to carry only ten percent of his vehicles with him; the others he must leave on Salford for the replacement battalion, a group of green conscripts who would take his place in the garrison. Hamata had commandeered the newest vehicles, regardless of their tactical value. He wasn't going to leave his best equipment to draftees.

There were rumors and reports from within the Combine military about the new breed of weapon coming off the assembly lines. He'd seen pictures of these walking monsters, and he doubted whether any mechanized infantry battalion could ever hope to oppose them. Just one of the giants carried more long- and short-range fire power than his entire unit could deploy. Those monster machines would surely change the face of war, and Hamata wondered if he were young enough to make the change.

As the cargo doors swung shut all along the line, the loadmasters stepped onto the ramps and flashed the Clear signal to the control tower. Green lights winked on above the personnel access ports: time to load the last of the troops. Hamata turned toward the clump of staff officers, smiling inwardly to see the clump suddenly shatter like a group of chickens startled by a predator. Though he knew they'd been huddled behind the ramp for the past hour trying to be as inconspicuous as possible, his officers immediately began to behave as though they had many important things to do. It was, of course, a charade. The battalion's officers were, for the moment, irrelevant. The civilian crews of the DropShips were in charge of loading and storage, and the troops and equipment would be stowed where they wanted, regardless of anything the battalion staff said. It gave both commander and his staff a feeling of helplessness, but no one could do anything about it. When the Draconis Combine said that this was how it was to be, then so it was. There was no appeal.

Hamata herded the staff together and prodded them onto the DropShip *Hideyoshi Toyotomi*. The *Toyotomi* held the bulk of Headquarters and Headquarters Company for the 2452nd Battalion. As he too stepped through the personnel door, Hamata was amazed by the size of the ship's interior. The *Vulture* Class ships were nothing more than huge caverns with tie-down points for the heavy equipment. Between the tie-downs were tiers of pipe-rack bunks standing vertically against the outer hull.

This ship had obviously been designed to move the maximum amount of people and equipment from one point to another. The quarters were spartan, but the adjutant had made sure the staff got the best of what was available. Hamata had the good fortune to get a single room; all the others had to share with at least one other member of the battalion.

At the moment the loudspeakers in the immense bay were spewing forth a series of commands and information, but the words were lost in the continual echo. Whoever had designed the communications system must not have paid any attention to the acoustics of the place. Hamata wasn't worried about it, though. He'd heard it all before and knew the announcement was an alert to takeoff. He signaled those around him to find seats and buckle in. Takeoff would be abrupt, and any thing or person not secured would end up plastered against the after bulkhead or skewered on some sharp object. The staff scampered to their stations.

Hamata moved to his stateroom, climbing up a broad shaft to the upper decks. He activated the sliding door to his compartment, walked across to the bunk, and lay down. He snapped the restraining straps across his chest and thighs and waited for the blast of acceleration that would hurl the DropShip off the planet's surface and toward the JumpShip that waited fourteen days away in deep space.

The launch was just as Hamata expected. The *Hideyoshi Toyotomi* exploded off the ground under full power, the force of the liftoff pressing passengers down into their bunks and peeling lips back from teeth. It was a notable experience.

Less than an hour later the gravity had dropped to a constant point-nine gees, making it possible to move around the ship. Then had come a twenty-minute transition period of zero gravity while the DropShip crew computed the final vectors for marrying up with the JumpShip *Raiden*.

Hamata kept the restraining straps in place until the green gravitational light came on for the second time. Having previously experienced the sensation of weightlessness, he felt no great desire to do so again. But some members of his staff, especially the younger ones, eagerly released themselves and floated through the cargo bay, creating the normal number of accidents as some inexperienced floater came into sudden contact with an immovable pipe frame. The only person Hamata needed to consult was the battalion priest to learn the outcome of the omens for the trip. When those came back as "uneventful," there was nothing more to do.

The DropShip began to accelerate, establishing artificial gravity. Hamata waited until the green gravitational light showed that point-seven gees had been achieved within the cargo bay, then hit the quick release on his harness. He gently pried himself from the bed, letting his body and his mind adjust to the reduced gravitational force and the change in orientation.

As the omens had predicted, the trip was uneventful. The first seven days went peacefully by. Now that they were halfway to the JumpShip, there was another transitional period as the *Toyotomi* rotated to approach the starship stern first. The second half of the transit would be spent in deceleration, allowing the same point-seven gees of negative thrust to slow the *Toyotomi* as it neared the *Ruldun*. By the time the *Toyotomi* and the rest of the DropShip fleet reached the orbiting JumpShip, their velocity would have been reduced to no more than three kilometers per hour. The closing speed would be less than that of a walking man, making the ships easy pickings for the grappling arms sprung like grotesque appendages from the bow and stern of the JumpShip.

Another seven days passed without incident, bringing the DropShips to the *Leviathan* Class JumpShip. Like piglets maneuvering for a teat, they nuzzled toward their mother ship for security and sustenance. One by one the DropShips came alongside and attached themselves to the spine of the *Raiden*. Hamata, still strapped in his chair, noted the gentle thump as the JumpShip's docking ports captured his and the other ships. That the DropShip pilots were experienced was obvious; Hamata had been through much more violent dockings in his day.

Hamata would have very little time between the DropShip's docking and the jump to Brailsford; just enough for a quick inspection of the carriers as they locked on and possibly also for a brief meeting with the JumpShip commander. He had never met Wilson Hartwell, Master and Commander of the *Raiden,* but like any other commanding officer in the Draconis Combine, the man was sure to be highly professional.

Six billion years, more or less, before *Chu-sa* Tokashio Hamata loaded his battalion onto the DropShips and began his voyage to Brailsford, the universe had been born in a cataclysmic explosion. Since that time it had continued to expand at enormous speed. Man, a resident of the universe for only a very short period, had studied and hypothesized about how all this had happened and what it all meant. Men had made laws and rules that attempted to explain the event, and then had become convinced and complacent about what they had written. Everyone then assumed that because the theories had been stated and written, they must be true. Space was thought to be rational and reasonable. Of course, some cherished theories about speed were demolished when the speed of light was first detected in the last half of the twentieth century, but once destroyed and re-cast, the theories became laws again. There was no one, certainly no one in the scientific community of the Draconis Combine, who would question them.

One of the laws dealt with the theory of jump points. Once the zenith and nadir jump points had been mapped and declared safe, the entire scientific community agreed with the theory and went on to other matters. A slightly myopic but completely human attitude.

But the immense forces that ripped apart the original particle of cosmic matter were unaware of the requirements and laws established by humans. Time, space, and mass changed and grew. All three parameters were in flux, and at great speeds. Compared to human existence, however, those changes were incredibly slow. The one hundred thousand years since homo sapiens first emerged from the mists was a mere instant compared to the six billion years of the universe. The universe was, in fact, a fractured element, and the rifts and joints between the moving plates drifted across what humans called "empty" space. One of those cosmic rifts was now drifting through the Salford jump point. Anything encountering the rift would be hurled across great distances as though it were in a sixth dimension. If the object were very lucky, it would survive to find itself lost in an unknown place. Or perhaps if it were *unlucky* enough to survive, it would find itself in that unknown place. For once there, there would be no way for the voyagers to return.

On the bridge of the *Raiden,* Master and Commander Wilson Hartwell watched the console as the JumpShip approached its exit point. Once transition occurred there would be no navigational work. All the plotting had been done while the ship hung near their jump point in the Salford system. It was like opening a door and stepping through. You passed from one room to the other, even though the rooms might be thirty light years apart. It was just that simple. The computer did all the navigating and plotting long before jump took place. As long as the jump point was correctly plotted, there was nothing to do but wait. The numbers on the console scrolled downward, rapidly approaching the time-distance mark. Then the console registered zero, and the Draconis Combine JumpShip *Raiden* shuddered slightly as it dissolved into the no man's land known as hyperspace.

2

The jump through hyperspace was like opening a door to another room; step through and there you are. Even if the step takes you thirty light years away, it's as easy as that. The transition is only a few seconds long, but the human mind is almost incapable of understanding the process or appreciating the time. Hartwell had been through the door so many times that he responded differently to the sensation than did those who didn't do it for a living. He braced himself against his command chair and stared at the navigational compusystem console. The screen showed a digital, three-dimensional polar coordinate system of their location. Sol, the star around which Terra revolved, was considered the center of the universe, for the chart makers had had to start somewhere. They had used the plane described by the orbit of Terra as level, with Terran north being "up" and south being "down." After that it was easy. A vector and a positive or negative number was all that was needed to determine a location in space.

With NAVSTAR coordinates and mapping, it was possible to get an accurate reading to within the nearest meter. Not that a JumpShip needed such accuracy. Once a jump was authorized, the coordinates of the final destination were plugged into the computer. The last digits would determine the jumping ship's exact exit point.

To make the jump, the ship began at a designated point

in the gravity well of the system, a point where all forces from the planets and the central star were reduced to absolute zero. With the coordinates of the next point already plotted, the ship rotated until the navigational heading was correct. The transitional authorization code was called up from the computer's memory. The JumpShip's Kearny-Fuchida drive sent a burst of energy plasma from the titanium-germanium alloy in its liquid helium bath to the field initiator. The energy produced the hyperspace field that was further amplified by the K-F drive itself. Like opening a door and stepping through into another room.

Hartwell watched the digital display of current/future location. The door opened, the ship stepped through. Then there was a sharp jolt as the threshold was crossed. There wasn't supposed to be a jolt, but it did happen occasionally that something in the doorway could cause an accident. Unfortunately, JumpShips had limited meteoric shielding to protect them from such an event.

The shudder increased. Hartwell grasped the arms of the command chair to keep from being hurled across the bridge. The navigation officer was not so lucky. He'd been lounging at his station, one leg thrown over the arm of his chair. He'd disregarded the first shudder with veteran aplomb; the second one caught his attention. With the *Raiden*'s bridge at zero gravity, there was nothing to drop into for support.

The navigator scrambled for his seat, but the forces were too great and too sudden. Hartwell saw a look of surprise and then fear flash across the navigator's face as the man's body hurled past the command chair. The navigator opened his mouth to scream, but whether it was in fear or a call for help, no one would ever know. Before he could draw a breath into his lungs, the man's body had struck the environmental control console and literally come apart on impact. The upper torso was ripped from the hip girdle and continued to spin away toward the cargo access doors. The legs lodged between the life support and internal security panels.

The environmental specialist, Fourth Officer Maria Savoyard, had just stepped through the access port from her quarters when the second jolt wrenched the *Raiden*. Not a seasoned veteran of jumps, she'd taken the first shudder as only a warning. It had not completely prepared her for the second event, but she was much better off than the wise and experienced navigator. By wrapping both arms around the emergency operation and override wheel next to the door, she kept herself from flying completely across the starship's wide bridge. It also saved her in another way.

By tripping the emergency override system, she froze the door in the open position. Had she not done so, the airtight door would have slid shut, just as all other doors and ports were doing on the *Raiden*. With thousands of kilograms per square centimeter behind the doors, there was nothing—certainly nothing human—that could have prevented complete closure. She hung on, gasping for breath.

Hartwell had no time to mourn the death of the navigator or to worry about the fate of the environmental specialist. While his body fought the violent bucking of his ship, his mind tried to make sense of what was happening. The master console by his command chair was going wild. The engineering lights that monitored the major functions of the power system flashed a phalanx of emergency red. The navigational and polar coordinate readouts were going crazy. Vector numbers flashed across the screen: 2753 . . . 9829 . . . 0080 . . . 1513. They came so fast and were so divergent that he couldn't comprehend them. The range reader flashed 0000000.0000000, and then went wild as it climbed to 9999999.9999999. The vector plot showed the same number: 9999999.9999999.

Hartwell felt his stomach churn and his mouth go dry. The *Raiden* was nowhere that was real.

Then the violence stopped as suddenly as it had begun.

Except for the panting, labored breathing of Savoyard, still wrapped around the emergency wheel, the bridge was silent. The forward viewscreen began to clear, showing myriad stars against the black void of space. The cameras swept across the emptiness, programmed to find and lock on to the nearest star system. The search had begun.

Hartwell called up a report from engineering and got the bad news all at once. The helium containment vessel for the K-F system showed major damage; helium was leaking into the access passageways. Worse still was news from the fusion power core. The containment bottle for the nuclear reactor was also damaged. The JumpShip *Raiden* was not in good shape.

The rest of the command crew slid into the weightlessness of the bridge, floating in, pushing off from the access shafts to drift across to their stations. Hartwell, meanwhile, turned to the comunication consoles and began to deal with the hysterical DropShip captains.

Like everything else not weighted down the hips and trunk of the unfortunate navigator began to float as well, drawn by the eddies and currents created by the movements of the passing command staff. A yeoman quietly corralled the pieces and herded them into a solid-waste disposal chute. Savoyard tentatively released her grip on the door control and moved toward her chair. Hartwell silently pointed her to the navigation station; her regular place at environmental control still showed the stains of the unfortunate navigator.

The *Raiden* would never make another jump; that much was obvious to Hartwell. Both the K-F drive power system and the fusion core had been damaged and were leaking containment. In addition, the surge of energy that had been part of the force that had thrown the ship off course had burned out most of the control and communications systems. The pulse continued to attack modules within the ship. The self-diagnostic and automated repair procedures carried the surge with them as they probed the vessel. Each time the crew checked or attempted to repair, the pulse was there to disrupt and destroy. The loss of the internal gyrostabilizers was the final blow.

Shortly after exiting from jump, Hartwell made the decision to abandon the *Raiden*. The only question was how long the ship would remain habitable, and that was dependent on its structural integrity. Hartwell could have extended the *Raiden*'s life by casting off the DropShips, but that would have been unconscionable. There was no place for the DropShips to go, at least no place known to be as safe. For a while at least, the JumpShip still had the sensors to locate a planet in whatever system they'd hit, a planet where the humans now huddled in varying levels of panic in their carriers might find haven.

The hyperspace transition had also played havoc with the electronics of most of the DropShips. Many would be unable to navigate the necessary interstellar distances to a safe haven. They would have to be ferried close to a planet before they could be cast off.

This became Hartwell's mission. Find a planet and get the *Raiden* as close as possible, transfer his crew to one of the attached ships or the *Raiden*'s small lifeboat, and cast off for their new home.

The third day after exiting from jump, the scanner had positively identified two habitable locations. One was a large planet and the other a huge moon. Hartwell chose the planet, but he kept a solid reference on the moon as an alternative. Day six of the transit toward the planet was Hartwell's target. If the *Raiden* could make it that long, the DropShips would have a good chance of navigating the rest of the distance. Events, however, conspired against the *Raiden,* her passengers, and her crew.

Late on day five, the JumpShip's fusion core reached critical, and they had to scram the plant. It was a simple process of merely venting the whole core clear of the hull. This reduced all power within the ship to emergency cells only. There were enough of those to maintain life support and command function for a period of fourteen days, but many had been damaged during the misjump.

Crew members crawling through the access passages detected structural failings. Two of the techs entered crawl space 23B/886 and never came out the other end. A life-sense scan detected no heartbeats or respiration within the passage, and the climate of the tube was indicated as a toxic environment. Both ends of the compartment were sealed shut and bonded.

Another structural failure was detected on the JumpShip's spine. The flaw was working its way down the skin of the ship, rupturing the access passage that connected the docking collars. No crew movement was possible between the DropShips unless the individual making the move was in complete life gear.

Then the life support, structural integrity, and engineering panels on the bridge flashed red, every panic light coming on. Indeed, the rosy hue from so much red light gave the bridge the almost cozy look of light from a campfire. But those who knew what was happening didn't find the effect either cozy or comforting. Instead, the bridge crew took the precaution of donning their life support gear. The *Raiden* lurched violently, spilling people and equipment throughout the DropShips. More emergency lights blinked on but never blinked off. The spinal rupture raced down the surface of the ship. Hartwell hit the emergency evacuation signal.

The emergency signal shrilled down the long, now-vacant corridor. Doors that had not been secured hissed shut. The preprogrammed un-docking procedures went into effect. DropShips were cast off whether they were ready to depart or not. Within minutes the bridge was clear. Hartwell was the last to leave, then he thrust himself down the passage toward his lifeboat station. As he pushed in, he made a quick count of the other people inside. They were a crowd of huddled figures swathed in life suits, their masks closed down and locked. The door snapped shut followed by a sibilant hiss as the lifeboat pressurized, and then the docking collar released. The thrusting jets pushed the boat clear of the tumbling ship.

Hartwell watched out the side vision port as the boat got clear. The *Vulture* DropShips were also breaking free. Most of them were safe, but one had become caught by its own collar, which had become twisted out of shape by the spinal rupture. The ship was firing its main thrusters in a desperate attempt to break clear, but to no avail. The blast of the jets only drove the ship deeper and deeper into the collar, wrenching the oculus into a useless wreck. The DropShip would never get free. Hartwell saw the DropShip's frantic thrashing become more and more violent, a snared animal trying to break clear of the trap. The force was too much for the skin of the ship. Hartwell saw the first rupture in the fuselage. Tiny at first, it suddenly split down the wing root from the trailing edge all the way to the cargo door. A cloud of moisture blasted from the hull, instantaneously freezing in the void. Bodies spewed out as well.

The DropShips began to drop away, headed toward the surface of the planet. The onboard computers had been given the coordinates of the surface, and they would head for that point even without control by the human crew. The computers might not pick out the best landing zone, but they would get the ship down. Four of the ships were clumped together. They would land close enough to be able to support one another on the ground. The other ships fanned out, the side of one of the fleeing *Vulture*s brushing the hull of another. Locked together and out of control, they tumbled downward. Hartwell watched them go and hoped that both crews were dead. A two-day fall, with no chance of survival, was more than he cared to even contemplate.

The space around the *Raiden* cleared of the departing ships. Watching from his lifeboat, the Master and Commander held his position near his vessel until he saw no further signs of movement. Then he was startled to see the sail used to collect solar energy to fuel the JumpShip's K-F drive suddenly deployed. Some impulse in the dying computer had decided that it was time to start re-charging the drive. The great sail would mark the ship for eternity. Some latent surge in the pulse had burned off all the absorptive material, and the fabric shone white. Then Hartwell turned his lifeboat and followed the DropShips and the rest of the lifeboats in their unforeseen journey toward the blue orb waiting in the distance.

Part I

November 7, 3056
Salford, Draconis Combine

3

The *Scout* Class JumpShip *Telendine* held position in its
designated space at the rim of the control area. The control station that hung clear of the jump point had directed
the ship there as soon as it had emerged from its jump
into the system. The master of the vessel, Reston Bannin,
had been fuming ever since. For fourteen days the
Telendine had hung there recharging its propulsion system; he was ready to go but still had been issued no clearance, and he still had no cargo.

Or no cargo aboard ship, that is. Waiting for him right
now on the surface of Salford was a DropShip packed
bulkhead to bulkhead, deck to overhead, with valuable
cholobara wine from the planet Shibukawa. Cholobara
was a delicate and short-lived beverage of amazing po-
tency. Not only was the natural alcoholic content more
than twice that of normal wine, but the cholobara fruit
was also an amazing aphrodisiac. Both features made demand for the brew astronomical. But the wine would only
maintain its aphrodisiac qualities for a period of just
under two months. That made speedy transport a priority
for those who wanted the profits that the wine's dated
amphorae commanded. Bannin should have had the cargo
loaded and ready for transport to the planet Hartshill as
soon as the K-F drive was recharged, but he'd been held
in orbit instead.

A *Scout* Class starship like the *Telendine* was too inefficient to carry bulk cargo. The few still in use by the Draconis Combine military served to carry single DropShips of high military priority. In the civilian world *Scout*s were used for valuable single cargoes, one-DropShip loads like Bannin's cargo of cholobara. Bannin had bought the *Telendine* at auction precisely for the purpose of making these high-profit runs. And now he was stuck with his cargo going bad on the surface and no clearance to jump.

"Message from station," said First Mate Elizabeth Hoond as she looked up from the companel. "They want another report on our readiness status."

"Tell them to refer to my report of three hours ago," snapped Bannin. "Tell them that I've been waiting here, fully charged, for the last four days, and they know it. Tell them that if they don't give me clearance to take cargo and depart, I'll report their dereliction to planet control." Bannin began to heave himself from his command chair, scattering bread crumbs that instantly formed a zero-G cloud that floated behind him as he moved. He'd been in almost constant residence in the command chair ever since the K-F drive was recharged and ready to go. He had a day cabin just off the bridge, but like most ship commanders, he preferred to live on the bridge when he was operational. And when Reston Bannin lived somewhere, he really lived there. He took his meals there and he slept there; he never moved except for absolute necessities. The remnants of the last three meals were splattered across his ample belly.

Hoond watched her Master and Commander, waiting for the spasm of anger to pass. She had served with Bannin for years, and she knew what would happen now. Bannin would froth and fume for a few moments before subsiding again into acquiescence. She watched as the commander made to lift his bulk from his chair, only to sink back again immediately. His countenance changed from the flush of anger to pale fear. Had Hoond sent the message as stated there would have been an equally abrupt reply from the station. The result would probably have been for Bannin to spend another fourteen days in orbit.

"Just tell them we're ready," he sighed, settling into the command chair once more.

"Message sent, sir," noted Hoond as she turned back to the console. She'd known what the message would be even before Bannin spoke again, and she had keyed in their current status. The message flashed across the seventy kilometers to the station. "They're sending again." First Mate Hoond watched the panel as the message scrolled across the screen. "Cargo approaching from Salford. We have jump coordinates and clearance to depart. Priority One."

"Priority One? Why Priority One? We've been hanging here for days, and now we get a Priority One departure order. Why don't those people ever get it right?" Bannin tapped the master control on the arm of the command chair and the message appeared. He scanned down the text, most of which was administrative garbage concerning account numbers and other administrivia.

His onboard computers would have a fine time digesting the material, which would of course be turned over to the appropriate bureaus of the Draconis Combine and ComStar. That was how the various Great Houses kept track of all the ships operating throughout the Inner Sphere. It was how they could tell if there were any unauthorized expeditions. And if there was one thing the leaders of the Draconis Combine did not like it was unauthorized visitors to its star systems. Such occurrences could only mean activity by pirates or black marketeers—or worse. At the time Bannin had bought the *Telendine,* he had carefully considered the choice between legitimate operations or entering that shadow world of pirate jump points and black market dealings. The profits from illegal trading were enormous, but the risks were equally high. Bannin liked the thought of credits building up in secret accounts, but he didn't like the thought of what the Draconis Combine would do to him if he got caught. The stories of what had happened to others who'd been arrested for such crimes were enough to make a strong man's blood run cold, and Reston Bannin was not a strong man.

As he reached the end of the message, his face went purple with rage. "What!" he shouted. "What is this nonsense? Military cargo? I've been given military cargo?" Bannin pounded the arm of the command chair in frustration. Damn them to hell! he thought, rueing the day he had ever signed a contract with the government of the Draconis Combine. He knew that, legally, they had every right to commandeer his ship, but that didn't mean he had to like it.

"They're sending a hold on the Priority One," said Hoond in an even voice. "And coordinates for a new destination." She knew it was no use showing any emotion; Bannin would have enough for both of them. "Looks like they're sending us to the middle of nowhere," she said almost to herself, then noted that they'd be receiving sealed orders for additional jumps after the first.

Reston Bannin burrowed down into the command chair and clamped his jaws shut tight. He would remain that way until the hold on the ship's departure was lifted. He was still sitting in exactly the same position three hours later when the JumpShip's docking collar locked the *Leopard* Class DropShip to its side. He was still in the same position when the skipper of the DropShip reported to the bridge of the *Telendine*.

Reston Bannin was good and ready for the unfortunate skipper. He'd had plenty of time to prepare his speech to the junior commander about the inefficiency of the Draconis Combine, about the temerity of the military in general, and about the overblown egos of the people in the control station. The tirade would be a work of art. It would start abruptly, become soft and mellifluous, then end in a high-pitched scream. It would be a beautiful

piece of rhetoric, not giving the battered skipper the least
opportunity to interrupt or to answer.

Unfortunately the speech was never given. When
Parker Davud, the DropShip captain, floated onto the
bridge of the *Telendine,* it was with an air calculated to
send Bannin over the edge. Following close behind him
was a Draconis Combine *sho-sa* in full combat gear. The
great speech died on Bannin's lips. He was fully capable
of chewing out a pilot, but hadn't nearly enough spine to
take on a member of the combine's regular military as
well. But then the appearance of the third man onto the
bridge almost gave him the courage. Seeing that the man
was obviously both a 'Mech pilot and a mercenary,
Bannin squirmed in anger. MechWarriors were bad
enough with their insufferable arrogance, but mercenaries
made Bannin's skin crawl. He bit his lip. "Welcome
aboard the *Telendine,*" he said. "The jump points have
been plotted and laid in. We can make the transit at
once."

"Whatever you say, boss," replied the pilot. "Ready
when you are." The comment was casual, not at all the attitude a DropShip pilot should have toward a JumpShip
master. He thumbed toward the *sho-sa.* "This here's the
man with the say-so I go with him."

"I have noted your ship, Master Bannin," said the
sho-sa. "I am Yubari Takuda of the Draconis Elite Strike
Team 6654. I am in command of this mission and in
charge of the Vost Lance until they arrive at their destination. Please assign an appropriate officer to escort me on
an inspection of your ship. Pilot Parker Davud and Mister
Garber Vost will remain in the DropShip and await my
return."

Bannin squirmed deeper into his command chair. He
could escort Takuda as was proper, but the JumpShip
master had no intention of showing that much courtesy. He
could assign Elizabeth Hoond, but she was even more
necessary to the bridge than Bannin. The job fell to the
third officer on board, even though he was more a war-

rant officer than a real one. Bannin pressed the companel. "Mr. Jacobs to the bridge." He turned to Takuda. "My engineer will escort you while my first officer and I prepare for departure."

If Takuda was aware of the insult he did not show it. "I will be honored by assistance from your fine engineer," he said smoothly.

Jacobs appeared on the bridge moments later, still wearing his utility belt and wiping his hands on a rag. He was surprised to see the conclave around Bannin's chair. "Ready when you are, Reston," he said. "What's going on?"

"You will escort *Sho-sa* Takuda through the *Telendine*. Show him everything. Take as long as he needs. The *Sho-sa* is a DEST officer so there is nothing he does not know." Bannin added a slight sneer to the last comment.

"I will be honored by your expertise," said Takuda to Jacobs. "I am sure that our inspection of the ship will be most thorough." He turned again to Bannin. "Many thanks for your hospitality, Commander." Takuda made a slight bow from the waist.

Four hours later Jacobs reported from engineering that the inspection was complete. At almost the same moment, the space station released the *Telendine* from its imprisonment. Reston Bannin had not moved from his command seat, and he gave the command to get the ship going even before Hoond could finish repeating the message. Warning klaxons sounded through the diminutive hull of the JumpShip as the thrusters maneuvered the ship toward the hypothetical, mathematical point from which it would make its interstellar jump through hyperspace. The ship steadied for a moment as it rotated onto the correct heading. Then it stepped forward and through the door.

The reaction was almost instantaneous. First a slight shudder as the ship made the transition to K-F drive, then another more jarring shock. The sensors on the bridge exploded in a shower of sparks. Hoond, crouched over the navigational console, had just enough time to raise her hands to her face to protect her eyes from the surge. Both she and Bannin were strapped into their seats, secure against a possible accident, but even with their restraints they thrashed about from the impact.

As the smoke cleared from the bridge, the foul air drawn swiftly away by the fans of the life support system, warning lights flashed from every station. The automatic crash sirens howled out of control. The overhead lumenpanels died as power was diverted to stabilization thrusters. The battle lanterns replaced the departing light with a soft glow.

Hoond removed her hands from her face and studied the navigation console. "Current speed seven hundred thousand kilometers," she reported.

"What? We can't be going that fast."

"Yes, sir. I know that. But that's what's being shown."

"Where are we?"

"I have no idea. Transferring readouts to your station." Hoond fingered a pressure-activated switch on the arm of her chair.

The information was transferred immediately to the sponson-mounted monitor beside Bannin. He saw the numbers glowing serenely from the screen. He saw them but did not comprehend, could not comprehend, the information they represented. The speed of the *Telendine* was as the navigator had reported: the ship was tumbling through space at a velocity of more than seven hundred thousand kilometers per hour. The polar grid coordinate readout was nothing but a series of nines. Bannin stared at the numbers, his mind numb. Commanders of starships did not have to know everything, only where to look in their ship's computer information banks to find the answers. But right now Bannin lacked enough information even to ask an intelligent question. Indeed, he was afraid to ask anything for fear that the answer would be even more confusing than the information he already possessed.

"Sensors report a habitable planet," remarked Hoond.

"There's something in orbit around it. Something metallic. I'm not sure, but the readings match a deployed JumpShip sail. It's bigger than we are." She was scanning the rapidly approaching star and its associated cluster of satellites. She continued to study the monitor, the green glow of the light giving her face a deathly pallor. "We're going too fast. There's no way we can approach it safely. Window of opportunity for maneuvering is passed. We'll have to abandon and take our chances in getting the boat down to the planet." She turned toward Bannin when he made no reply. Her commander was still staring at the monitor, his face a mask of fear and doubt.

Hoond looked back to her own station, saw the numbers representing the point of no return scrolling downward with alarming rapidity. "We'll have to abandon now, sir." There was still no answer from the command chair. She turned back and reached down between her legs to grasp the red emergency override handle. Bracing her feet, she pulled upward with surprising force. The response was instantaneous. All the battle lanterns on the bridge blinked out and came back on. The sliding doors that had closed on impact with the cosmic anomaly slid open. There was a rush of escaping air as the *Telendine*'s life support system began to compensate for the vagaries of pressure. The loudspeakers welded to the corners of each compartment blared their pre-recorded warning: "Now hear this. Now hear this. Abandon ship. Abandon ship. This is no drill. This is no drill. Abandon ship. Abandon ship."

Hoond glanced back at her station. A series of red lights glowed along the arm of her chair. She depressed each in sequence, waiting until the light changed to green before going on to the next. The buttons represented the escape sequence that would implant the *Telendine*'s current coordinates (as if they meant anything) as well as the azimuth and range to the nearest habitable planet into the lifeboat and the docked DropShip. The sequence also released those same two smaller vessels from the

JumpShip. With the panel showing all green, Hoond cut away from her station and moved toward the ship's immobilized commander. Gently, she uncoupled the restraining harness and got him out of the chair. The man didn't fight or resist; it was like directing a somnambulist.

The corridor to the lifeboat station glowed red from the emergency lighting. It didn't take long to reach the tiny escape shuttle, where Jacobs was already in place in the command seat. According to standard operating procedure, the first crew member into the shuttle took the command chair. There was no precedence in an emergency. Hoond buckled the still docile Bannin into an open seat and took her position beside Jacobs. Together they went down the escape check list. The door slid shut. Jacobs thumbed the thrusters, and the *Telendine II* slid gently away from the stricken mother ship.

As they cleared the hull, they could see the DropShip fighting to get free of the docking collar, which had been warped by the violence of the impact and the subsequent gyrations. Under full thruster power as it struggled to break free, the DropShip suddenly ripped its way clear with a final lurch and then tumbled away from the *Telendine*.

Jacobs let the escape shuttle hang for a moment as he waited for the DropShip to steady itself in a flurry of thruster fire onto a parallel course. Then he opened the thruster engines, and the *Telendine II* began its journey toward the unknown blue orb that was the only safe haven for the tiny crew and anyone else who had survived inside the DropShip.

4

Parker Davud gripped the controls of his DropShip with such force that his knuckles went dead white while the blue orb hanging against the blackness of eternity grew larger with alarming speed. The velocity indicator on his panel told him that their speed was well above safe entry velocity. This was going to be a hairy landing—assuming there would be any landing at all. If he didn't do it right, the DropShip could hit the atmosphere and flip off into space like a stone skipping across the surface of a pond. That was what would happen if Davud played it too safe. And if he were too bold, if he took the DropShip in at too great an angle, it would burn up as it passed through the atmosphere. The approach would have to be right on the money. There would be no second chance.

And that was because of their approach speed and the structural damage to the ship. The struggle to break free from the gyrating carrier had warped the DropShip's keel and ridgepole. At that very moment, the life support panel was showing that the hull was bleeding oxygen at kilograms per second. That wasn't an immediate problem because the ship carried hundreds of kilograms in reserve, but there'd be no time for a second pass if the first one failed. Davud could seal the bridge compartment and let the cargo bay bleed. They would let him survive, but wouldn't make the troops very happy.

Although life support concerns were a nagging concern

for the future, they were unimportant to the hazardous present. Davud nosed the ship down slightly to keep the planet's expanding rim just at the edge of the viewer, but the screen blanked out occasionally as the forward thrusters fired repeatedly in response to his commands to reduce velocity. With Davud diverting fuel from the wing tanks to the forward holding area, the DropShip shuddered as the thrusters fired again. Warning lights showed the level of fuel available, while the graph showing current rate of use indicated that nothing would be left for a final push. He cross-fed fuel from the maneuvering jets in the after section to compensate for the increased expenditure forward.

Off to the right Davud was aware of the lifeboat expelled by the *Telendine*, but its existence had little meaning to him. He didn't care what happened to it or its occupants as long as they didn't interfere with his approach vector. The lifeboat was so small that the DropShip could run over it with hardly a noticeable bump, but if it became entangled in some important part of the ship, the task of landing might become impossible. He hunched over the controls and watched the panels in front of him.

He knew that the ship's instruments had been damaged by whatever the *Telendine* had hit during its transition through hyperspace. Even though the numbers were going crazy, he'd been trained to trust instruments rather than his sight or his senses. Without an "up" or "down" in space, the instruments were the only consistent reference point a DropShip pilot had. Davud winced slightly as a companel screen to his right erupted in a shower of sparks, filling the flight deck with the acrid scent of burned insulation and ozone. Meanwhile, life support in the cargo bay was rapidly falling to a warning, if not critical, level. Davud concentrated on the remaining micronavigational screen.

Inside the cargo bay Vost and his men had finally gotten the four 'Mechs and the *Phoenix Hawk* LAM under control. They'd managed to secure the two *Locust* 'Mechs against the after bulkhead, which had held them relatively stable during the pummeling immediately after the misjump. The other two 'Mechs, a *Javelin* and a *Panther*, had come partially free from their storage along the bay's lateral perimeter. The *Panther*'s right arm had broken the restraining shackle holding it against the exterior bulkhead, and even the hydraulics had not slowed its thrashing. Vost had had to climb over the scaffolding that composed much of the bay's interior to reach the 'Mech's cockpit, where he'd clapped on his neurohelmet, and fired up the machine to get it under control. If not for people being hurled across the bay, that task should have presented few problems.

DEST commander Yubari Takuda had braced himself at the rear of the cargo bay, just outside the door to his stateroom, and snapped on the safety tackles. From there he could see and direct the members of his four DEST sections as they wrestled with the hurtling objects. It was an interesting problem.

An object in weightlessness was easy to move and control, but that didn't mean the object had no mass, that it was like a balloon. It wasn't. Just because an object was weightless did not deprive it of mass. Even when weightless, a five-hundred kilogram weapons pack still had a mass of five hundred kilograms. With the DropShip constantly decelerating, the free objects in the cargo bay were "falling" toward the front of the ship. They weren't falling very fast, but they still had enough momentum to crush the unwary. Takuda hung in his place in the aperture, snapping orders and warnings into his headset. The DEST team members were so well-trained that they responded instantly to his curt commands.

The mercenary 'Mech pilots and their small technical support team were concentrating on their 'Mechs and any objects that came near them; the rest of the flying objects were left to the responsibility of the DEST members. That meant Takuda's people had to control not only their own materiel, but also the spare parts containers hurtling toward the forward bulkhead. They could have let them fly, but Takuda knew that the DropShip's skin had been ruptured. He could hear the sibilant hiss of the escaping atmosphere. The thought of a steel box crashing into the bulkhead was not very reassuring.

The DropShip shuddered violently, threatening to tear loose all the newly secured equipment. Takuda at first felt the strain of the harness against his legs and chest, but the strain began to relax even though the shuddering increased. He was also aware of a growing sensation of heat. Throwing a glance toward the small vision port near the personnel access door, he saw that the ship's exterior had begun to glow with the heat of re-entry. Takuda was not an ostentatiously religious man, but he said a short, silent prayer for himself and his team. To die in service to the Draconis Combine was an honorable death, but he knew that he had more to offer than merely becoming an unknown cinder in some unknown and forgotten corner of this galaxy.

While these thoughts passed through Takuda's mind, the glow of the ship's outer skin increased, and with it the heat inside the cargo bay. He saw his Talon Sergeant, *Gun-so* George Bustoo, recoil from the side of the DropShip as the heat penetrated his insulated combat suit. Takuda's own forehead and back were beginning to perspire. Hot air dried his mouth; he forced himself to breathe through his nose as much as possible. With the DropShip now shuddering and bucking as violently as a bull, he would have been helpless except for the safety straps.

On the bridge of the doomed DropShip, Parker Davud continued to fight the controls. The instruments exploded in sparkling fountains as system after system overloaded, overheated, and died. This was seat-of-the-pants flying now, and Davud had to strain every muscle to keep the hurtling tonnage in a manageable configuration. He could see the approaching ground through the occasional gaps in the glare that swept across the forward view panel. There was no way to choose the best landing site; this would be a one-pass, dead-stick landing. Just above the edge of the panel he saw an opening in the thick vegetation below. It wasn't nearly big enough to handle the *Leopard* Class DropShip, but it was the only one in sight. Davud pulled back hard on the control column, at the same time yawing the ship right and left to help bleed off speed.

With every fiber in his body concentrated on getting the ship to the ground as close to one piece as possible, Davud temporarily stopped breathing. There was simply no energy left for it. His heart may have stopped as well. But his brain, his arms, his legs, and his hands did not. As the DropShip careened over the treetops, the lofty branches whipping against the underside of the fuselage, her captain extended the control flaps and began his landing flare. The nose of the DropShip rose. Speed and lift vanished. The nose dropped for the last time, and pilot Parker Davud watched as the trees at the end of the grassy area rushed toward him. Then the belly of the ship struck the soft ground and the ship plowed in. The nose buried itself for an instant, threatening to flip the ship over on its back. Then the lifting body shape took control and the nose came horizontal, cutting a furrow in the ground and into the trees. It came to a stop.

Davud looked around the steaming cockpit. Smoke hung thickly in the small space, and there was an occasional eruption of sparks as if one of the dying instruments were protesting this abrupt landing. Looking up at the checklist printed on the overhead above his seat, he began to go systematically down through the landing and shut-down procedure, reading aloud the command and then carrying out the order. It was completely superfluous, but he had done it so many times that it was unthinkable not to do it now. The checklist complete, Davud unsnapped the quick release on his harness and stood up. Only then did he realize how tense he'd been. His knees buckled under his weight and he fell heavily against the master panel console.

In the rear of the smoldering DropShip the personnel access doors had opened in response to Davud's checklist procedure. Pouring through them were the DEST members, their weapons locked, loaded, and ready. This was an alien planet, or what could be an alien planet, and they were going to be ready for anything.

As they dropped to the ground, the team quickly spread out, twenty meters apart, taking up a fighting stance. Silence. Not a bird, not an animal, not a person, not a bug. Nothing. Silence. Then a terrible, rushing, thundering whirlwind. The DEST commandos dropped to the ground and turned to face this unexpected and unknown attack. In a blaze of light an object crashed through the tops of the trees whence they had come and plowed into the ground along the same path they had just followed. It burrowed through the ground, expelling great clods of dirt and sod as it burrowed ever closer to the DropShip. It stopped a scant hundred meters short of the ship, a smoking tower of dirt, roots, and small trees.

Takuda felt his heart pounding in his chest, then suddenly he began to laugh. The monster that had attacked him from behind was the lifeboat from the *Telendine*. He walked toward the fuming pile and was mildly surprised when he saw a figure emerge from the steam. He recognized Mark Jacobs, the DropShip's chief engineer. Behind him came the navigator, Elizabeth Hoond, supporting the *Telendine*'s Master and Commander on her arm. They were a bedraggled trio, and Takuda thought they looked worse than he did. At least so he hoped.

Takuda assumed command. While in space, he'd deferred to either Davud or Bannin, but with solid ground now under their feet, he was the one in charge. The first priority was to organize the mercenaries and other survivors into salvage crews and to care for any wounded. Next they would have to establish security around the perimeter. His own troops responded immediately to his orders, but Vost's mercenaries did not accept his authority. The mercs were under his control only until the time he delivered them to their new commander. Now they wanted to know what right he had to give them orders now. They also wanted to know if they were still on the Kurita payroll. The fierce looks on the faces of Takuda's armed men stifled those protests almost at birth, but the DEST commander knew they would surface again.

Who was paying for what was an interesting question he would have to think about. Meanwhile, he also had to meet with Bannin.

Takuda approached the JumpShip crew, where they were huddled with Parker Davud under the belly of the DropShip. Only Jacobs rose deferentially on his approach. Davud had collapsed against the hull of the ship, and Hoond was still dealing with the seemingly catatonic Bannin. Takuda came to a halt at Bannin's feet. "Where are we?" he asked, more abruptly than he would have liked, but seeing no reason to dance around the subject. Bannin raised his head and stared through the DEST commander. "Where are we?" Takuda repeated harshly.

"Where? Where?" mumbled Bannin. "We could be anywhere. My instruments are all fried. They didn't tell me anything." He shrugged and then waved helplessly toward the silent forest beyond. "We're not anywhere that's real, that's for sure. For all I know, we could be in one of those parallel universes the futurists are always inventing out of their warped imaginations."

"Same's true of my instruments," put in Davud. He reached up and patted the wrinkled metal of the cooling DropShip. "I don't know where we are, either. But wherever it is, one thing's for sure—it's forever."

5

Night crept in on the strange, marooned group. Single campfires emerged from the gloom like vague, one-eyed monsters. Chewing silently on some emergency rations, Takuda sat alone by his own fire. Then he looked up at the unfamiliar sky and realized that it had been only a few hours since he'd completed his inspection of the *Telendine* back at Salford, confident that he was heading toward a known destination in a known universe. Now he was somewhere else, and had not the faintest idea where. His universe, his known, concrete, real universe, had disappeared in a single jolt. He was a man with no past, only a present and an unknown future. If he had any future at all.

Dawn came, and *Sho-sa* Yubari Takuda shook himself and stretched his legs. During a near sleepless night, he had struggled with the question of whether they should even go on any longer. But his very soul rebelled at the question. Of course they should go on—of course *he* should go on. Seppuku was an honorable end for a warrior, but it was not acceptable as an escape from responsibility. And Takuda was now responsible for the lives of the twelve members of his Draconis Elite Strike Team as well as those of the eleven mercenaries and the four crew members of the DropShip and JumpShip. All told, twenty-seven people who would have to learn to live out their lives in harmony.

Takuda made a quick mental review of his own team. The headquarters included himself, his aide, *So-cho* Saitan Yura, and *Gun-so* George Bustoe. They had been with him for years and would follow his orders to the death. Under normal conditions so would the whole team, but Takuda thought their present situation could hardly be classified as normal.

The three operational sections of the team were all headed by *Gun-so,* Talon Sergeants, of considerable experience. Shawn Arsenault, leader of the first section, spent slightly too much time worrying about his appearance, but he was unflappable and cheerful. Emmerdean Knyte, the second section leader, was intelligent and introspective. He could have and should have been an officer, the type of man who showed quiet leadership by example. He was another one who would take all things as they came. Ariake Sanae led the weapons team. She was as upright as any commander could wish, but had a tendency to be hidebound on questions of religion. She had no sense of humor, and except in matters military, had no use for Knyte.

The mercenaries Takuda knew less well. He'd had direct contact only with Garber Vost, their leader, and the man was everything Takuda most despised in life. Vost was a braggart who treated the other 'Mech pilots with only slightly veiled disdain. Holly Goodall, the only female MechWarrior among them, he treated with open contempt. Why she had joined the mercenary unit was a mystery, but Takuda knew that Mech Warriors, particularly the mercenary variety, were a breed unto themselves. Of the technicians who served the merc unit, Takuda knew only that they were six in number, half of them female. All seemed to pay the mercenary leader special attention.

The ship crews were another unknown. Parker Davud, the DropShip pilot, was certainly a professional of the highest order. To be able to land his ship with virtually no controls and then to keep it from breaking up on impact was evidence enough. That he was slightly casual with command structure was understandable; DropShip pilots were like that. Bannin, the Master and Commander of the JumpShip, rated much lower. The man had fallen apart during the crisis, and Takuda could expect little of him now. The navigator and engineer of the JumpShip were better, but they were ciphers as far as what they could contribute to the future.

The divergent group would have to work together to survive. It was certainly not the group Takuda would have chosen if he'd had the choice, but they were what fate had handed him. He rose to his feet and surveyed the area. The various camping areas reflected the attitudes of the members. The DEST areas were almost invisible among the grass and bushes that dotted the open area. Takuda was sure the weapons of each section were unlimbered and deployed. The mercenary camp, on the other hand, was a hive of activity, completely visible to inspection by any alien who might be hiding in the distant trees. The pilot group had not moved from under the crumpled wing of the DropShip.

As Vost left the mercenary camp and came toward Takuda, the *sho-sa* felt rather than saw Yura and Bustoe of the headquarters section approaching from his rear. They would, he knew, remain at a respectful distance, out of range of all but the most strident voices, but ready to lend silent, and well-armed, support. "Well, Major," said Vost, using the universal ranking system rather than the traditional Kurita ranks, "we seem to find ourselves in strange circumstances."

Takuda gazed serenely at the other man. He had learned from vast experience that silence was often the best reply. He also knew that Vost would continue with his pre-programmed speech no matter what was said in return. He was correct.

"The situation has changed since yesterday, or when-

ever it was. My men and I were employed by the
Draconis Combine as a complete lance. We were to participate in an action you people did not feel qualified to
perform. My contract states that we would be paid half
our fee upon signing and half on completion of the mission. You people were responsible for our safe insertion
and extraction. As I see it, you have not fulfilled your
part of the contract. What do you say to that?"

"I have no knowledge of the complete contract," replied Takuda in a level voice. "I was given my own mission regarding your lance." This was not totally true, of
course. He had been charged not only with the mercenaries' insertion, but in seeing that they completed their mission. The DropShip contained the documentation and the
money to pay Vost once his lance had completed their
work. But Vost was not to know this in advance, and as
far as Takuda was concerned, his own orders were still in
effect. Disclosing his knowledge would have an unfortunate effect on harmony.

"Well, I have my copy of the contract," said Vost,
reaching inside his vest. Takuda felt the slight stiffening
of his vigilant men, then felt them relax when the mercenary pulled out a scroll instead of a weapon.

"I have no need to read your copy, Pilot Vost. I assume
that you are telling me the truth. But I do not see that the
situation has changed that radically."

"Well, I say the contract is now void, and the rest of
my people agree."

"You vote on issues?" Takuda raised a quizzical eye-
brow.

"We don't vote. But I do listen to what they have to
say."

Takuda smiled. What Vost really had said was that he
told his people what he wanted them to say and then they
said it. It was an interesting form of leadership. "Well,
then, and what do your people have to say?"

"First, the contract is null and we're on our own. Since
you failed to deliver us to our destination, we have no

further need of you or your DEST team. That also makes your authority here superfluous. We are perfectly able to direct ourselves. Your people can disband and join my technicians."

"Disband?"

"They are useless, are they not? This is not a combat situation. What we need are people who know how to work. My techs are just the ones to do it. We can teach your people how to survive."

"Mr. Vost, my team consists not only of highly skilled assault troops, but all are 'Mech qualified. What's more, each one has been trained to survive alone in any type of environment. That persuades me to believe that survival depends on maintaining our current structure," replied Takuda.

"With you in charge, you mean."

So that's the problem, thought Takuda. What rankled Vost was the question of command structure. Takuda was beginning to feel better. At least he knew what was happening.

"So, if you're in charge," continued Vost, "what do you plan to do about the women?"

"I didn't know we had to do anything about the women."

"That's your real problem, Major." Vost had a sneer on his face that Takuda had seen before when civilians wanted to patronize a member of the military. "We're here forever," said Vost. He placed his fists on his hips and threw out his chest. "And forever is something you will have to understand. If we're going to survive at all, we will have to deal out the women to the best men. Which should be done immediately."

"I don't understand the 'we' in your statement."

"We. The ones in charge. You and me. And maybe Bannin, although I think he's going to be useless. You and me."

"What about the women?"

"What about the women? The women will do as they're told, of course."

"Really? In the Draconis Combine we do not treat women as chattel."

"We're not in the Draconis Combine anymore, Major. This is somewhere else, and our long-term survival is at stake." Vost shook his head. "Remember what Bannin said last night? We're not anywhere. This is all new. It's a new world, Major. Get with it, man."

Takuda had no answer. Vost was right about one thing. This was a new world and a new situation. Everything the *sho-sa* had ever known had come to a complete and abrupt end. There was no Combine to whom he must answer, to whom he could answer. There was no one above him as there had always been. His entire life had been built on a hierarchy of people, each one answering to an authority a step above and each one responsible to those a step below. Well, the step below remained, but the one above had vanished.

Of one thing he was sure, though. These mercenaries were incapable of rising above self-interest. The sole reason they'd been hired for their mission was because they possessed a Land-Air 'Mech, a piece of equipment that would have been invaluable to the reconnaissance aspects of their mission. LAMs had become as rare as they were valuable because no one in the Inner Sphere produced these machines any longer. The mercenaries had also been chosen because they would be expendable if their mission failed.

"I will think about it," was all Takuda would say. "We shall see."

"You bet we will," said Vost. "And we'll see about it pretty quick."

The situation changed slightly later that day. Takuda had sent out patrols to see what the woods had to offer, and the scouts had reported an abundance of what looked like edible fruit. They had not been bold enough to try any of them, but had brought back a significant pile of various types. The last patrol in, the one from Knyte's section, brought even more interesting news. Knyte reported that Horg and Holland, the two members of his section who had gone into the woods, had made contact with a large animal. Holland had taken a shot at it, but had missed. The animal had vanished into the woods, leaving almost no trail. But it had cried out at them as it fled. And the cry had sounded almost human.

6

The next three days were spent in directed activity. Not only had the survivors discovered a source of possible nourishment in the lush vegetation, but they had also established the possibility of a sapient life form on the planet. The human-like cry from the animal encountered that first afternoon remained a mystery, however. None of the survivors had encountered the animal since, although some of the patrols had seen tracks. The markings were those of a gigantic bird, which seemed to indicate the distinct possibility of two different animals. There were the ones who sounded like humans and the ones shaped like birds.

The food problem was partially solved by a thorough examination of the forest and some tentative experimentation. The examination revealed that some of the fruits had been partially eaten. Based on the theory that a human should be able to eat the same food that doesn't kill other beings, Takuda decided to taste the fruits in hopes of encouraging the others to do so. He chose a large, smooth-skinned yellow one, and consumed all but the greasy gray seeds. The others watched and waited, and when they saw that Takuda survived to see the next morning, the rest also ate of the yellow fruit.

A feeling of tension continued to exist just below the surface of activity and sense of accomplishment. The mercenaries and the DEST members became even more suspicious of one another, but splits were beginning to occur along other lines as well.

Garber Vost watched the members of his mercenary lance as they lounged around the camp area. He was mildly amused at how their various attitudes toward life were reflected in the way they maintained their own kits. As was to be expected, Brian Seagroves, the LAM pilot, had the most sumptuous area. Brian liked things, especially those things money could buy. He'd been the toughest negotiator when Vost was first forming the lance, perfectly willing to hold out to prove how much more valuable he was than any other member of the lance. He had also insisted on being paid most of his money up front, C-bills which he spent on pretty toys. His sleeping bag bore the label of a prominent outfitter on New Samarkand, a name recognized throughout the Inner Sphere. So did his hiking boots, combat vest, and cooking utensils. They marked him as a man who had money and who knew how to spend it. He had also managed to buy an additional mosquito net and frame from Kendall Pesht. Now his area had taken on an air of safari opulence.

Pesht, on the other hand, lived in the open air. Now that he had sold his mosquito net, his sleeping area was the only one unprotected from the swarms of famished insects that invaded the camp at night. The result was that he had to huddle inside his flimsy bag the entire time, but his face showed where his efforts were not totally successful. Pesht, the *Javelin* pilot, wanted to be everybody's friend. He was like a small dog, yapping and scampering around the feet of the people who really mattered. He was especially that way with Vost, who used him as a tool when necessary. The man had probably sold his mosquito net to Seagroves to curry favor, but Vost knew Brian would not remember it as a favor. Pesht had lost the net with no advantage gained.

Collis Brank, one of the *Locust* pilots, was a schemer. The man always had some plan in the works, mostly nefarious, but he could be counted on to rat on anyone else if it were to his advantage. Brank was an excellent source of information about what was going on in the lance, and Vost was careful to always reward the information with favors.

Holly Goodall was the other *Locust* pilot. She was the dangerous one within the lance, even though hers was a light 'Mech that posed no threat to Vost's control. She was such a directed wench. She kept her 'Mech in perfect trim and was always trying to upgrade the various systems. That would have been fine if she were a man, but it was strange in a woman. Vost was a little sensitive about women MechWarriors in general, and Goodall only reinforced that feeling. He had let her join the lance purely to fill out the ranks with the 'Mechs required by the contract. She was so tough. Most of the time she dressed in her MechWarrior's vest and shorts, skimpy attire that always created a tumultuous stirring in him. It was a good thing he had Michelle Guardine as one of his techs. He needed something to relieve the tension.

By and large Sagiri Johnson had chosen a competent body of technical people. Johnson had been with Vost for two years, the only other survivor of Vost's first lance. Underos Yaputl and Iliomoso Panda, despite a tendency to gripe at times, would do as they were told. The other techs, Tami Wilson and Fiona Sabine, were too smart to be good stooges. Not only that, but they were showing a tendency to listen to Goodall. Vost flexed his shoulders under his combat vest and ran his hand through his thick sandy-colored hair. He'd be able to deal with those two when the time came; he always had been.

Vost waved nonchalantly toward Collis Brank, who jumped to his feet and sidled over to where Vost was standing. The *Locust* pilot always sidled, then always hovered close enough to talk in whispers, even when it wasn't required. "What's the skinny?" he asked in a hoarse whisper as he sidled up to Vost.

Vost stepped back to put a little space between him and

the hunched figure. "Just wanted to talk," replied Vost. "Just wanted to see how you were getting along. You generally know the skinny before I do."

"I don't like the attitude of those DEST guys. They want to run the whole show."

"Of course. Combine troops always think they're supposed to be in charge. But I'd be a little careful about saying bad things about DEST. They have a reputation, and even if its overblown, it's close enough to the truth."

"They're not superhumans," whined the little man.

"They may not be superhuman," Vost said, "but they're still damn good. Be careful what you say. Be careful what you *think* when you're around them."

There were a few moments of silence between the two men. Vost let Brank do his own thinking for a while, waiting for the little man to come up with the right answer. "They've got all the weapons right now," Brank said finally. "We have our sidearms, but all the heavy fire power is theirs. That's too bad."

"Too bad we don't have the 'Mechs out," Vost said after the briefest pause. "That would change things. Then we'd be in charge, and they'd have to dance to our tune."

"We ought to be in charge anyway," interjected Brank. "They don't really have anything to do now. There's no one around to fight."

"That's not what they'd say. Who knows if this bit about human-like aliens and giant birds in the forest isn't designed to scare us and make them important. Except for worrying about that, what do they really have to do? Takuda sits there like some dictator, telling us we have to prepare to defend ourselves. Defend ourselves from what? What we really need is to get our lives organized. We've got to figure out how we're going to survive. And you know what survival means."

Brank had no idea what survival meant, except for more food and a place to live. He knew that Vost was expecting an answer, and that the answer should be profound, but he just couldn't think of anything. All he could do was hum in acquiescence and hope that Vost would give him a clue. Luckily for his stalled thinking process, Holly Goodall took this opportunity to stroll across his field of vision. That triggered a response. "The women." It was almost a question.

"You got that right." Vost was quick to take the lead. "We've got to deal out the women. If we're going to survive, there has to be someone to carry on. We've got to divide up the women."

"But there are only four of them." It was almost a whine. Brank was making a quick survey to see if he would get one, and if he did, which one it would be.

"You're forgetting the two with DEST."

"The major wouldn't like that. He would have something to say about it."

"Not if the 'Mechs were out, he wouldn't. We'd get the women over his dead body, and that could be arranged." Vost gave Brank a meaningful glance and was rewarded with a sly grin. "Those two over there are in top physical condition. They'd also probably snap the neck of any man who looks cross-eyed at them, but it could be fun trying to tame them. I bet you could have quite a time with one of them, don't you?"

Sho-sa Yubari Takuda watched the two 'Mech pilots deep in conversation. He couldn't hear what they were saying, but he could guess. The whole situation was uncomfortable for him. Trying to be the ultimate leader was something Takuda had never had to deal with. He didn't want to be the ultimate, but he saw no alternative. Vost certainly wanted to be top dog, but Takuda didn't believe the man could represent the best interests of the whole group. As for Reston Bannin, he was a dead loss; the man hadn't done a thing since they'd left the JumpShip. That left Parker Davud, but Takuda suspected that the DropShip pilot would resist any attempt to make him the leader.

That left the job to Takuda. As long as the DEST members remained cohesive, he would remain in charge. But this situation was as new to them as to the others, so he couldn't be sure what they would do. DEST members were chosen because they were intelligent, not because they followed orders blindly. Sooner or later each one would make up his own mind about the situation. Takuda didn't want to be a dictator. He believed that a benevolent autocracy was the best form of government. Wasn't that why it was the form of government in the Draconis Combine?

Johan Miranda, the junior member of the weapons team, rose from the grass nearby and approached Takuda. He stopped at a respectful distance and waited for his commander to acknowledge his presence. Takuda wondered mildly how long that deference would last. He nodded to the *joto hei* to approach.

"Most honorable *Sho-sa*," said Miranda, bowing ever so slightly at the waist. The sergeant was carrying his sniper rifle. Equipped with a low-light scope and aural sensors, it was said the weapon could see a gnat at a hundred meters. Miranda was a very good shot with the rifle; he couldn't have become a member of DEST otherwise. And Takuda knew that Miranda was good even by DEST standards.

"Speak, *Joto hei* Miranda."

"Perhaps I could be of some assistance." The young sergeant glanced toward the pair of 'Mech pilots still standing near their camp.

For a moment Takuda feared that the sergeant was going to suggest some target practice. That might temporarily solve some of their problems, but if they resorted to solving problems by assassination, the whole camp could become crisscrossed with gunfire. "Speak."

"I have been scanning the camp for sound, and there are some interesting events." Miranda paused to see if he could continue. When Takuda made no comment, he went on. "Someone has mentioned deploying the 'Mechs from the DropShip."

Takuda noticed that the *joto hei* did not reveal who had said it or where he had heard the information. The major nodded. "Thank you for the information, *Joto hei.* I will ponder it. You are dismissed." The sergeant made another, shallow bow and returned to his position in the grass.

"*So-cho,*" said Takuda. The call was not a shout, but Takuda had trained his voice to carry when necessary. The young sergeant-major rose from his position some fifty meters away and hurried to his commander.

"*So-cho,*" said Takuda when the sergeant came to attention before him, "there is some possibility that the DropShip may be in danger. See to it that a guard is placed on the ship."

The sergeant-major saluted, did a smart about-face, and went off to talk to the members of the nearest DEST section.

7

The lush, dripping, pungent growth hung silent and threatening in the still air. Each step by the members of the patrol sank deeply into the ground, leaving indentations that slowly filled with dark water. It was like moving in a soundproof room. Beyond their limited field of vision came soft plopping noises like the sound of fat, gray-green slugs dropping onto a wet sponge. *Joto hei* Andi Holland, the point of the patrol, made herself stop thinking about what might be making the sounds so she could deal with what she could see. Behind her she felt rather than saw the other members of the patrol.

Directly behind was *Gun-so* Emmanuel Knyte, the section and patrol leader; behind him was *Go-cho* Swalen Horg. Holland was the lowest-ranking member of the patrol, but that was not what had made her the point. All three rotated through the position, each one taking the duty for no more than twenty minutes at a time. Being lead was an exhausting business, and no one could stand the strain for too long. As fatigue began to take over, Holland began to hear and see things that weren't there. More important, she began to not see and not hear things that were.

The three members of the section had been on many patrols before, but this one was different. Most patrols operated in relation to a known enemy. Even if they didn't know where the enemy was, they usually knew what they might have to face and it was real. This time, however, they didn't know what was out there. The whole team had been trained for possible alien contact especially for this mission, but the specter of having to face the real thing raised the tension level to the point where no one could take the lead for very long. Holland had been on point for almost her full term; she knew she was getting tired. She raised her hand to halt the patrol while she sank into a kneeling position. She used the muzzle of her Nakajama laser rifle to part the foliage at the level of her face.

With a range of visibility a mere two meters or less, Holland wondered why she was armed with a weapon that was effective against human targets at three hundred meters. Here in the thick woods she would have preferred a slug-throwing cone rifle or even one of the pistols carried by the mercenary patrol.

That there was a mercenary patrol in the woods was both surprising and obvious. It was surprising because Holland had heard the argument between *Sho-sa* Takuda and Garber Vost over whether to send out a mercenary patrol at all. When the *sho-sa* had suggested that the mercenaries go out, Vost simply ignored him. When the DEST commander ordered the mercenaries to go on patrol, Vost had immediately responded with a heated protest. From what Holland had heard, it was not so much that Vost didn't want his people to go, it was just that he didn't want to be told they had to go. That, to Holland, seemed like an infantile attitude. She understood the necessity for order and respect. People did what they were told to do, especially when they had a leader of the *sho-sa*'s rank and stature.

Trying to turn a group of 'Mech pilots and technicians into a reconnaissance patrol was another matter. Even though they were filling out a necessary slot in the patrol scheme, Holland thought their chances of finding anything that didn't want to be found was virtually zero. They couldn't keep their mouths shut, constantly shouting to each other as they thrashed through the foliage. Two days ago Takuda had had to send Knyte's section back into the forest to extricate three mercenary technicians from a deep pit. The trio had stood at the bottom of the pit, howling like banshees and firing their slug pistols into the air to attract attention. That they could have used half that energy to climb out of the pit was not worth pointing out. If nothing else, the mercenaries provided the DEST members with endless stories and amusement.

Holland could hear them now, howling in pain, or surprise, or just to keep themselves amused. The muzzle of her rifle parted the foliage.

Two glowing red circles stared back at her from the opaque greenness beyond. She froze. The unblinking red circles stared back. They were a full twenty centimeters apart, and the face they were attached to must have been huge. Holland had a great imagination, quite possibly more than she needed, and the thought of the beast beyond filled her with both curiosity and dread, but mostly curiosity.

The red eyes moved, quite possibly closer. Curiosity ended. Holland pulled the trigger, and the power pack over the breech vibrated slightly as power poured through the crystals. There was a brilliant flash of light and steam as the unseen shaft of laser light struck something wet and solid. The red eyes fled in opposite directions like frantic rockets. Holland leaped back on her heels and sat down heavily in the soft ground. She was up in an instant, thrusting the barrel into the foliage.

Inside the dark cave beyond her position she could see the dissipating steam and the soft glow of burning leaves. There was nothing else. Whatever had been there was gone now. Holland felt slightly foolish and a little frustrated. She hadn't meant to shoot at it, had done so purely out of reflex. She sank to a crouch.

There in front of her, almost beneath her own foot, was a print, the print of a giant bird. It was like so many she had seen, like so many seen by other members of her patrol and the rest, that she hardly paid more than passing interest. But then she looked again. The print was absolutely fresh. There was hardly a drop of water in the bottom, and the sides of the depression were crisp and clean. Whatever had made the print had been there just moments ago. Holland motioned Knyte to her side and silently pointed to the track. Knyte waved his hand, and the patrol crept cautiously forward. Horg, the trailing member of the group, remained hunkered down facing the rear.

Every muscle tense, her eyes straining to pierce the foliated darkness, her ears discriminating among all the sounds in the forest, Holland moved with glacial slowness. Everything seemed strange and forbidding. Not knowing whether it was menace or hospitality to the front of her, it paid to be careful. Another track, and another, and another, each as fresh or fresher than the last. She rose to move, her eyes searching far ahead, but she got no further.

Knyte's hand came down firmly on her shoulder, rendering her motionless. She pulled back gently, replacing her foot in its previous track. Knyte had been watching the ground rather than the foliage. Now he leaned forward and pointed with the muzzle of his rifle. There, just discernible in the forest duff, was a thin line of different ground cover. He prodded the surface just beyond the line, and the forest floor collapsed in a fountain of wood chips, decayed roots, and random leaves. The gaping hole stood revealed.

Andi Holland waited until she had her heart under control and then looked into what could have been her new home. The pit was a meter square and better than two meters deep; deep enough to cause bodily harm, perhaps not grievous, but certainly some.

Knyte motioned Horg up to his position. While Holland was examining the pit and the way around it, Emmerdean had sensed something else. He pointed into the foliage on the left and indicated what he wanted Horg to do. The man nodded, then moved off into the darkness silent as a shadow. Knyte tapped Holland on the back and communicated that she should remain still. Without obviously pointing, he indicated where she should watch. Holland settled back on her heels and searched the green gloom ahead.

Swalen Horg, squat and solid, drifted into the leaves. He waited while the motion caused by his departure from the patrol's trail became still. When he couldn't hear anything but the sounds of the forest, he moved on. Knyte had indicated a target some ten meters ahead. Horg was to flank the position and attempt to come in from the rear. He had done such a drill a hundred times, probably even more than that. Continuing to creep away from the patrol until he was clear, he then turned to parallel the route. After twenty meters he turned again. Unconsciously counting steps, he reached a position ahead of the patrol. He turned again and began to creep silently, slowly, toward the unseen target.

He lifted each foot high in the air, balancing his weight on the grounded foot. With the toe pointed down, he slowly lowered the foot until it made contact with the soft soil. Ever so slowly he lowered the foot until it was down, feeling through the sole of his boot for any stick, leaf, or void that might reveal his position. Once the ground was confirmed as safe, he slowly shifted his weight to the new foot and repeated the process. It was an infinitely slow way to travel through the woods, but it was a noiseless one.

Ahead Horg saw a darkening in the surrounding undergrowth. He froze, hardly daring to breathe. It was a giant, feathered figure. With the same infinite care he raised the laser rifle. Horg didn't want to shoot the thing in the back; that was against all the training they'd been given in preparation for the mission. He tapped the side of the rifle. Just enough to attract the attention of the figure. The reaction was spectacular.

As Horg watched, the figure rose to its full one-and-a-half meter height. It was a ball on a pair of long, skinny legs. It spun to face him, revealing a long, ovoid body with two huge eyes centered over a short beak. The animal shrieked an almost human scream. It leaped backward in surprise almost as great as Horg's own. He, too, stumbled back, but recovered quickly and brought the laser rifle to his shoulder. The alien pressed back into the suddenly unyielding brush. The shriek continued. Horg depressed the trigger until all the slack was out and the détente of the trigger seer was fully engaged. If the thing moved, Horg would blow a hole through its hairy body; of that he was quite sure.

The alien gave another shriek, but this one was more than a cry of terror. It was a warbled wail that rattled and clucked. Horg held his fire. The cry came again, more muted now, more intelligible. "Please shoot not," it seemed to say. "Please shoot not." Horg relaxed the tension on the trigger. Not all the way, but just enough to keep the weapon from going off by chance. He listened more carefully.

"Please not shoot do. I your friend want to be." The figure whimpered softly and raised its hands to cover its eyes.

8

Horg lowered the laser rifle to waist-height and stared at the figure in front of him. He couldn't tell if the thing were a bird or a something else. Certainly the feet looked like a bird's. It was the body that made him stare.

The ovoid body was slung between extremely long legs in such a way that its horizontal axis was the long one. The eyes were the most fascinating part of the alien. The creature had elongated eye slits that extended from the side of the skull to the front, almost joining over the short beak that extended from below the face. The eyes had double pupils, one facing directly out and away from the skull and the other facing generally forward. The ears, or what should have been ears, had been reduced to mere vestigial openings on the top of the skull behind and above the eyes.

The rearward-bending knees were admirably adapted to movement within the swamp, Horg noted, allowing the alien to place each foot carefully into the uneven or treacherously soft ground. The long lower leg above the claws had broad, webbed phlanges that now stood out wide as though in surprise. The lower claws showed the same minor webbing as well. An interesting beast.

Horg was not the most articulate member of either his section or the DEST team in general, which perhaps made him the best person to make initial contact. There was nothing wrong with his mind: it was just that he was

careful about what he said and how he said it. Still holding the laser rifle with his right hand, he gestured toward
himself with his left thumb. "Swalen Horg," he said in a
firm, commanding voice.

He also said it with the sure and certain knowledge that
the alien would understand. Everyone knew that if you
spoke to someone who didn't understand your language,
you should speak slowly, and loudly, and wave your
arms. No one was so stupid that they couldn't understand
that. "Swalen Horg," he said, a little more loudly and
with a more violent hand gesture.

The alien continued to huddle against the foliage, but
he became more relaxed. "Dakodo I am." The alien
waved his hand with the same gesture Horg had used.

Swalen Horg's plan for dealing with the alien had not
been based on being able to speak to it in any mutually
understandable language. Now that he was confronted
with one alien who seemed actually able to speak, Horg
had no idea what to say next. There were so many possibilities, he didn't know where to begin. He had a whole
history of who he was, and where he came from, and
what he was doing here, and . . . He stood open-mouthed.
The muzzle of the rifle slowly dropped toward the
ground.

"Name my Dakodo is. I Tetatae am." The voice was
high and chirping with strength on the hard sounds, the
sibilant sounds almost lost. Dakodo watched the blank
expression on the face of the human with the rifle. He
concentrated on what he was trying to say. "My name
Dakodo," he said slowly. "I am Tetatae." Dakodo had to
think hard before he spoke. The sentence structure he
used was fine when dealing with his own kind, but a
straight transliteration, a word for word substitution, did
not work for humans.

Dakodo stared at Horg, the skin between his double
eyes wrinkling with the effort of thought. "You fell from
sky like the others," he said, half question, half statement.

"We came from Salford," said Horg, still confused about what to say or ask. "I think we had an accident. *Sho-sa* Takuda says we are here forever." It was the only thing Horg could think of. "I want to go home." That came out almost as an afterthought. Horg was surprised that he had said it at all. A wave of loneliness swept over him. His eyes blurred momentarily.

Ever since he'd been recruited into the special forces, Horg had considered the DEST his home, the members his family. Now, suddenly, he thought of what he had left behind, the people and places he knew. It suddenly hit him with full force that he would never ever see any of them again. He knew some people would think of him occasionally, but the memories would eventually fade and he would cease to exist.

There was an old legend that you existed as long as someone remembered your name. That was immortality. That was why there were graveyards with the names of people written in stone above their last resting places. But Horg, and all the others on that JumpShip, would have no resting place. They had vanished into the vastness of space. They would be listed "missing and overdue" on some log, and then their names would be filed in a vast computer memory and forgotten. It did not occur to Horg that perhaps the computer memory assured immortality.

"Horg. This is Knyte. Report." The tiny speaker set against the left mastoid in Horg's combat helmet snapped the soldier back to reality. His eyes cleared.

"Horg here. I have made contact with the . . . the . . . the person we were looking for." Horg didn't know what else to say. "He can talk," was the only other comment he could think of.

"On the way," came the reply from the team leader.

Dakodo had been chattering away all this time, but Horg had not been listening. Now he became aware of the strange chirping sounds from the Tetatae. It was hard to understand what he was saying and he concentrated on the noise. Slowly the words began to come through. The

Tetatae was saying something about where he lived and what he did. It would all have to be repeated when Knyte and Holland arrived.

When they did, the four of them squatted in a circle. Each member of the patrol questioned the Tetatae in his own way. Horg lapsed more and more into silence, quietly, methodically processing the information they were getting. Knyte questioned Dakodo in an orderly manner, examining each statement as it was given, using each as a lead to the next question. Holland just blurted out any question that came to mind. She was so full of inquiry the words seemed to fairly bubble out of her. Knyte would let her go on for a while and then get back on the track of what he wanted to know.

As they questioned the alien, they became aware of other movement in the gloom of the forest. That there were others out there, watching their movements and actions, was obvious. Dakodo showed that he knew it too. At first the humans were on guard, but as the questioning continued, they began to feel safer. They were aware of the unseen presence, but it seemed more inquisitive than hostile. And they could hear, occasionally, a soft chirping.

Even before Dakodo started to tell his story, Knyte had decided that they would have to take the alien back to the camp, but he wasn't sure how they would do it. Here was a link with the planet beyond the small circle they had explored on their own. This odd, bird-like creature could be the path to their own future. Knyte wondered, just in passing, if the two species would be able to inter-breed. Impossible, he thought, the idea vanishing as quickly as it had come. The alien answered all their questions; it was an interesting if incomplete story.

Dakodo was an elder in a small tribe of Tetatae who occupied this section of the forest. There were other tribes in the area, but they were separated by some significant distances. Knyte tried to understand how far, and he questioned Dakodo on the subject, but the Tetatae could not answer the questions. Like many humans, Knyte thought of distance in terms of linear measure. Dakodo thought of it in terms of how long it took to get from one place to another. The tribes were four to six days apart, but how far that was did not matter. What was important to Dakodo was that he had to carry or find food for four days if he were to make the journey to another tribe. What was the importance of linear distance?

The real question was how Dakodo came to speak their language. As Knyte listened he began to hear word patterns and vocabulary that were archaic. The language the alien spoke had been learned, he said, from the others who dropped from the sky.

"The others? What others?" asked Knyte. The three patrol members leaned forward, almost threatening the Tetatae. Knyte was tempted to put the laser rifle to his head, forcing the creature to give the right answers. He didn't care that there were others in the forest. All his thoughts were concentrated on this one question. What others?

"Long ago," said Dakodo slowly, concentrating on the words so that these humans could understand, "they from the sky dropped like you. This was long before my other's other's other's other came to the tribe. They in the valley fell, and there was great thunder. They came, they say, from the home in the new star that appeared in the sky then. That is what we of them say. They were not good for the Tetatae, and many died. That is why we were afraid. Many of the tribe said we should not meet you, but there were others who said yes. Perhaps you would for us be better."

Dakodo looked at the three human faces staring at him, searching each one for a clue to the future. There were other humans, he knew, back at the place where the star had landed. They would have to be consulted as well. "Those who fell were very weak at first, and the Tetatae who live in the flatter lands without great trees tried to help them. They who fell took the help and then they hurt the Tetatae. They who fell had guns, great sticks that could reach out and kill. The Tetatae ran away from them. Later we were able to trade with them. Mostly it was food and the knowledge of what they could eat from the land, and river, and forest. We gave them the belts we wove, and they were happy. But now they force some of those from the lands without the great trees to work for them and to do as they are told. There is great sorrow among the Tetatae. But what can we do? They are so strong and the Tetatae are so weak. Soon they will drive us into the mountains and we will not be here ever again. They so strong are. They were the people of the dragon."

Holland sat back on her heels in surprise. "Like this?" she asked, reaching under her battle tunic and presenting the emblem of the Draconis Combine.

Dakodo took the emblem with his slender fingers. He turned it over in his palm and studied it carefully. "Yes," he said finally. "Just like this."

9

"Tôã téotêo," said Dakodo, directing his remark to the forest beyond.

There was no sound from the forest. The four grouped together in the tiny clearing were frozen as though time had stopped. Knyte, the leader of the patrol, the man who was supposed to make the decisions and direct the actions of the others, was as stunned and silent as a computer that had just been overloaded with information. He stared at the dragon symbol of the Draconis Combine in the hand of the Tetatae. His field of vision narrowed, the outside edges becoming dark. All he could see was the glowing red and gold emblem in the alien's soft palm. It mesmerized him, holding him transfixed. He felt lightheaded, dizzy, unconnected with the ground or anything else.

Slowly his mind fought back against the cloud. He struggled up from the depths of some unconscious universe to regain the light in the forest. His field of vision widened until he could see the tableau of the three other figures around him. He glanced into the eyes of the other members of his team. Holland's eyes were vibrating, the condition of nystagmus that occurred after a violent neurological shock. All three members of the team had certainly suffered that. Horg sat crumpled, slack-jawed, to his left. Knyte reached out and touched each, shaking them from their reverie. He looked straight at Dakodo. "You must come back with us," he said, his voice hoarse and strained. "*Sho-sa* Takuda must speak to you. You will come with us."

Dakodo nodded in agreement. He rose on his legs to his full height and turned to the circle of trees. "Tôã téotêo dâdã dêdê," he said to the blank wall of green. There was an answering chorus from the wall. "Dâdã, dâdã, dâdã," it echoed.

Horg rose and stepped menacingly toward the Tetatae. "What did you say?" he asked, thrusting the laser rifle toward the bird creature. Not sure where it would be most menacing to point it, he aimed it directly between the thing's eyes. "What did you say?"

"I told them I with you was going. I said I going with the people from the sky. They just repeated the word we use for what happening is now. That's all I did. It will be all right."

"You'd better be careful." Horg was threatening enough in real life. He was quite spectacular when he really wanted to sound nasty. Dakodo looked at him, his four pupils tracking toward the muzzle of the rifle until they were all congregated in the front of his eye slits. Horg couldn't tell if the alien had gotten the message, but the sight of the eyes virtually crossed in the front of his body was ludicrous. He began to laugh. The eyes returned to their normal positions.

Knyte touched Horg on the shoulder. "It's all right, Horg," he said. "I'm sure Dakodo won't try anything. He's been pretty good to us so far. He won't try to run. It'll be all right." Then Knyte laughed too, joined by Holland.

Dakodo looked at the three of them laughing. "That sound," he said. "I have not heard humans make that sound before. Is it a bad sound?"

"No, Dakodo," smiled Holland. "That is the sound we make when we are amused. When we find something that tickles us." She looked at Dakodo, but he didn't seem to comprehend. "Don't you know what 'funny' means?" The alien continued to stare. "I can see that you have a lot to learn about us. I'm surprised that you never heard the others laugh. They must be awfully serious. We laugh all the time."

"I watch you to see what this is," said Dakodo. He nodded his head, his whole body rocking back and forth on his long legs. He turned in the direction of the camp.

Knyte knew the path he had taken from the camp to reach the point where the encounter had taken place. The patrol had been planned as a deep sweep, designed to penetrate as far as possible into the forest and still return to the campsite before darkness engulfed their little world, a little world that had suddenly become much larger. He also knew the most direct path back to the site. Dakodo took neither of these.

The alien led the group, his long legs contracting against his body and then extending well forward to brush away the foliage before he put his six-toed foot onto the ground. Knyte saw that each of the two pairs of forward-reaching toes was matched by a single toe in the rear. These two groups of three were completely articulated and able to grasp objects independently. The large hands on the thin arms were of the same design. This system made the Tetatae exceptionally capable of manipulating objects.

Dakodo led in an essentially straight line along an almost invisible path, but he avoided the deep swamp areas and the steep, wooded ravines, pointing each out as he bypassed them.

They did not talk to each other as they moved, respectful of the forest around them. Good woodspeople did not talk when in the forest. They concentrated their efforts on their progress and thus had little time or interest in conversation. The fact that they moved in single file also had something to do with their silence.

Dakodo stopped them at the edge of one of the numerous swamps and pointed to the varicolored globes that hung from the trees. "Those you eat can," he said. He directed their gaze toward a cluster of waxy purple spheres. "Those you not eat. Make humans sick. Humans say they smell bad." He shook his body in what the humans had learned was something like a shrug.

Knyte responded to the remark. "We can eat many things. Is there anything in here that you cannot eat?"

Dakodo eyed him furtively. Then he decided that the human wanted the information just to know, not because he was looking for some way to hurt the Tetatae. This human, these humans, were not like the few others he had encountered; certainly not like the humans of legend and fable that the Tetatae used to terrify the young. He was glad that he had argued in favor of encountering these life forms. Other members of the tribe had warned against it, had said that no good could possibly come from such an encounter, but Dakodo had prevailed. "We try not eat from anything with a four-pointed leaf. That for us is bad sign. That is a truth for as long as I can remember. I do not know if all four-pointed things will hurt, but I stay away."

Dakodo picked some of the fruit, including a couple of the purple ones. They were, he noted, well thought of by the Tetatae, even if the humans couldn't seem to stomach them. Before long the patrol was burdened with a plethora of specimens.

The members of the patrol pondered the information. The forest hummed and twittered. The smooth surface of the swamp was broken by the occasional ripple as something beneath the glassy surface rose to feed on some unsuspecting insect that had wandered too close. Knyte hoped that whatever was doing the eating had a fondness for the mosquitoes that relished human blood. Around them they could hear the twittering and chirping of what could only be other Tetatae, those who were following Dakodo and the party. A raucous shout broke the stillness. Laughter followed.

"That's a mercenary patrol," said Horg. "I bet one of them fell into that pit. Maybe we should help."

"No," replied Holland. "Let them be. I've had enough

of them and their leader for the rest of my life. I don't even want to associate with them. Let's just stay here and let them go by."

"My sentiments completely," agreed Knyte. "Vost wants to be king." He drew himself up, placing his fists on his hips and thrusting out his chest. "I want all of you people to think of me as your god," he said. His pose and articulation were so close to that of Vost that the others laughed. "I am the person best qualified to lead you to my promised land," he continued. Holland and Horg grinned back.

The sounds from the other patrol grew louder and more hysterical as they crashed through the brush. The mercenaries were laughing so much that they couldn't possibly be aware of anything around them. The chattering from the hidden Tetatae grew louder as well. Dakodo cocked his head and listened to the noise close at hand.

"Ka dêdê!" he snapped to the unseen figures. "Ka dêdê!" He stepped to the ring of leaves behind the party and parted some of the branches with his hands. "Ka, ka, ka." He stepped back, shaking his head. "Some of the others have gone to meet your friends. I do not think that is a good idea. I told them, 'No, no, no.,' but they already gone."

"Damn," said Knyte in an even voice. "I think you were right. They don't want to meet the merc patrol. Can you get them back?"

"I not think so."

"Hope for the best. Maybe the mercs will deal with them calmly. I'll try and warn the mercs to expect visitors," Horg said, raising the boom mike to his lips.

His hope was shattered by a burst of weapon fire. Knyte recognized the sound of the slug pistols that all the mercenaries carried. There were shouts and the sounds of breaking foliage. Then more pistol shots. One of the slugs whined overhead, snapping branches as it continued into the darkness of the forest. A chorus of Tetatae voices erupted from the vegetation beyond. Dakodo listened.

"Dêdêdê! Dêdêdê! Dêdêdê!" he chattered to the unseen listeners. He turned back to the party. "Your friends have killed one of my others. They are very afraid. They do not know what to do. This is very bad. I have told them to run away. I hope they will." The Tetatae wrung his hands as he talked. "This is very bad. It is ka ka da."

"Can we get the body back?" asked Holland. She could see the pinched expression on the face of the Tetatae, could almost feel the pain in his eyes. "It's important, isn't it?" she asked, putting her hand on the arm of the alien.

"They have gone to try. But I not think it will work."

Another fusillade of pistol shots echoed through the forest. The patrol crouched instinctively against the surrounding trees. The soft snick of safeties being thumbed into the ready position was the only sound they made. More shots. Knyte reached up to pull the alien down to safety. He grasped the figure by the sloping shoulder and felt warm stickiness under his hand. Dakodo crumpled at his feet.

Knyte dragged the alien toward the sanctuary of the tree he was using for cover. Dakodo was conscious and tried to crawl in the direction Knyte was dragging. Holland pushed from behind, exposing her own body to the occasional random shots that still snapped above them. The long, thin legs that were so admirably made for moving through the forest were not as useful when it came to crawling. Obviously this was not a mode of travel for which the aliens were designed. Holland muttered something about this under her breath. The efforts of all three eventually got Dakodo under cover of the thick trunk of the tree.

Panting from the effort, the two humans and the wounded alien huddled together. The only sound from the forest was the soft plopping. The sounds of the other Tetatae had vanished. Even the soft hum of the insects and the bubbling from the swamp had become still. Holland glanced back to where she had left Horg squatting at the ready with his laser rifle. He was so well camouflaged that it was several moments before she could discern his motionless figure. Then the sounds of cheering broke the stillness. The mercenaries were headed back toward the camp with their prize. Holland hoped that it was only one prize. "Let's get going," she whispered. "We've got to get him to camp as soon as possible."

Knyte looked into the eyes of the Tetatae. "Can you travel all right?" he asked.

10

Another ripple of shots crackled through the trees. "I've had it," snarled Knyte. He snapped the boom mike down on his helmet. "Cease firing, you idiots," he shouted into the communicator. "You're shooting at us. The only dangerous thing in the forest is you. Cease fire!"

"Bull," came the answer over the headset, along with the continued popping of the merc's slug pistols. "There're a bunch of bastards all around us," continued the speaker. "We got one and the others tried to attack us. They're clever little devils. But we chased them off. I think I winged a couple."

"They're not dangerous," said Holland into her own mike. "They're friendly. Now you've scared them away. They were only trying to be friendly."

"Says you. They tried to attack us. What's the matter? You going soft? What's your boss going to say when he hears that kind of talk?" They all recognized the voice of Collis Brank, one of the 'Mech pilots. He would be sure to let everyone know that the DEST members were getting soft. Holland flushed at the thought. Her fingers closed tight on the hand grip of her laser rifle.

"We can be as hard as you like," said Knyte into his mike. "If you want a demonstration of our abilities, we could always stalk you right now. If you really want to know how good we are, just take a couple of more shots. We can deal with that."

There was a momentary silence while the threat sank in. Even the mercenaries had some brains. They knew enough to understand that they were raw meat against highly trained soldiers in the woods. "Oh, get off your high and mighty talk. We promise not to scare you guys anymore." There was soft laughter from within the shrouding foliage, then silence. A little later they heard the mercs moving off through the underbrush.

Knyte and Holland did what they could for the wounded alien. All DEST team members carried a personal medical pouch that contained a pain suppressant, bandages, clotting agent, and a kit that could seal puncture wounds and slashes up to fifty millimeters long. They applied the bandage to the graze on Dakodo's back, but they didn't use either the pain suppressant or the clotting agent. His blood was a clear yellow, and they were afraid of causing an unfortunate reaction.

While the two team members were working on the Tetatae, he closed his eyes and remained still. Holland took the opportunity to examine him more closely. The downy hair that covered most of his body was rich and softly iridescent. The colors changed as she watched, undertones of green and purple flowing beneath the down of the hair as though the roots were changing color rather than the strand itself. The color did not seem to be controlled by the light in the forest or how she moved. Instead it fluctuated based on the movement of her hands as well as what Knyte did with the bandages. She was careful not to press too hard, and once when Dakodo seemed to wince at her pressure, she was quick to back off.

As the ministration continued, Holland was aware that Horg had crept closer to the three. He was silent and alert, his infrared scanner trained on the woods around the patrol. "I think we should take them out," he said when close enough for his whisper to be heard.

"That might still be an overreaction," said Knyte, intent on his bandaging. "There is no death penalty for being slightly stupid."

"Dakodo is my friend," said Horg in a tone so matter-of-fact that the meaning was crystal clear.

Knyte saw a vendetta coming and moved to avert it. "They are mercenaries. They had no business shooting, but they just don't know any better. They were only doing what they do naturally. You can't really blame them for their actions. They are not thinking people when they are in the woods. They would do much better if they were in their machines. It'll be all right, Horg." It was the best he could think of at the time.

"He is my friend." Loyalty had been Horg's byword since he first had a philosophy of life, and that sense of loyalty had only been reinforced during his training with the Draconis Elite Strike Team. DEST training stressed loyalty to the section and to the team, and from there to the Draconis Combine as well. There was no greater trait than loyalty to one's comrades. It meant that they could count on you and you on them. When you ran into trouble, your DEST comrades would be there to get you out. They would sacrifice themselves for you, and you would do the same for them. That was how it worked. Dakodo had joined the section because Horg had talked to him. Now Dakodo was wounded, and Horg felt responsible. There was a debt to pay. Knyte saw what that debt would mean.

Dakodo staggered to his feet. He swayed slightly, and his ovoid body hung lower between the leg joints. He steadied himself, his hand on Holland's shoulder. She felt the warmth of his hand come through her battle vest. Knyte looked into the alien's eyes. "We'd better get going," he said. "Night's coming on, and I want to get back before it's so dark that someone could make a mistake. There's no telling what the others have said about what happened and how dangerous these people are. I wouldn't want to be mistaken for a hostile alien presence in the gloom."

It was slower going. The forest lost the light long before the grassy places. Now that Dakodo was injured, he was no longer able to move as fast. Knyte led, moving cautiously. The sun was almost at the level of the far trees when the patrol broke the cover of the forest. In all this time Dakodo had not said a word, obviously concentrating on staying awake and mobile. He was staggering severely by the time they reached the grass.

The camp was in an uproar as they approached. The mercenaries and the ship crew members were gathered around the open personnel door of the DropShip, and Knyte could hear their loud talk and laughter. The DEST members were completely hidden in their fighting positions, and he knew they had been spotted by someone. He heard the soft click of warning from the mastoid speaker inside his helmet. He also heard the all-clear as they were recognized. No one rose from a fighting position to welcome them, and they moved directly toward where the command had been constructed. *Sho-sa* Takuda came to meet them.

Takuda saw the bandages on the alien's back as the group approached. He issued a sharp order, which brought Saitan Yura hurrying forward with the team medical kit. The Tetatae, meanwhile, had collapsed between the two groups. Yura dropped to his knees, quickly ripping off the bandages that Knyte had applied so he could get a look at the wound. "Slug weapon," he said to no one in particular. "Not one of ours." He glanced toward the cluster of rowdy mercenaries.

"Stray bullet," said Knyte. He looked directly at Horg. "It wasn't intentional." The leader continued with his report of the patrol.

Takuda listened carefully and then turned to Horg. "You did not shoot." It was both a statement and a question. The *sho-sa* looked at his soldier and awaited an answer.

"It didn't seem right," said Horg. The *go-cho* stood looking into the eyes of his commander. "He was not going to hurt me or run away. It wasn't right."

"You did well, *Go-cho* Swalen Horg. You did well.

You were to make contact with the aliens if it were possible, and killing one of them would have done little except provide us with a specimen to examine. Now we have a real live one. You did well."

"I don't know what to do for this one," interrupted Yura. "I've tried the clotting agent on a bit of the wound, but it hasn't seemed to work. I think we're going to lose him."

In the falling light, Holland could see that the iridescence had gone from beneath the down-like hair. The brown color had lost its sheen as well and had taken on an ashen hue. Looking down at the curiously shrunken shape, she felt a slight choking in her throat and a feeling of rage that must have been how Horg had felt. Perhaps he was right; the mercs needed to be taught a lesson. Vost and Brank would be good candidates. She looked beyond her command group at the celebrating mercenaries.

"Give him a shot from this," said Takuda. He opened the medipack on his left thigh, took out the twelve stimulant syringes, and handed them to Yura. "We have more of them if necessary. Give him one, and if he doesn't respond, give him another. Keep doing it until they're gone or he's awake."

"You can't do that, sir," protested Bustoe. "Use of emergency medical equipment on non-Combine personnel is prohibited."

The five other DEST members who were clustered around the fallen Tetatae looked at Bustoe. What he said was absolutely correct, but his words suddenly brought home the truth of their situation. They would never again have to answer to anyone at Military Headquarters. "I will deal with it at the appropriate time," said Takuda. "But you are quite correct to raise the question, *Gun-so* Bustoe. Quite correct." Takuda nodded to Yura. "Proceed."

Bustoe was ready to give in. "The medicine is designed for human use only," he continued. "If we give it to this ... thing ... there will be none for us. It will be a terrible waste."

Yura broke open the packet of syringes and jabbed one directly into the wound. There was no response from the unconscious figure. He applied another, still no response. Another syringe was drained, and then another. It was only after Yura had forced the seventh one into the alien's prone body that the creature showed a slight quivering. A wave of iridescence swept outward from the point of the needle's insertion. On the eighth application the alien opened his eyes. "Têodê," he muttered.

Holland bent close to the beak to listen to what he said. "Tell us what to do," she implored. "What should we do?" Dakodo murmured something. "The purple," said Holland, looking up at the others gathered around. "It has to do with the purple."

Horg rummaged through his pack until he found the foul-smelling plant he'd been given at the swamp. "What do I do?" he asked.

"Break it open, Horg," said Holland. "Break it open and rub it on the wound."

Horg followed her instructions. The odor from the fruit nearly made him gag, and the others in the group turned away at the stench, but he persisted. An evil gray juice dripped from the putrid flesh of the innards, oozing down into the wound. The reaction was almost immediate. The fluid flowed along the crease left by the pistol slug. As it did, the wound changed color from the rawness of exposed flesh to a creamy, semi-liquid state. "Da," Dakodo said. "Dada."

The feeling of relief among them was palpable. Horg was especially glad; the alien would live, and he was happy for the first time since the friendly fire incident in the woods. He even smiled as Kendall Pesht made his way toward the command group. The mercenary pilot looked down at the recumbent Tetatae. "You got one too," he said. "They're not bad. You should try one.

Tastes a bit like chicken." He turned away from the DEST team and moved back toward his own.

Later that night Horg sat contemplating the unfamiliar stars. *Gun-so* Ariake Sanae sat beside him. Horg often went to her with his problems, and now he confided his feelings about the mercenaries. The two sat in silence. Finally Sanae turned to her friend, placing a hand gently his shoulder. "Perhaps you're right, Swalen Horg. You do have cause enough for a vendetta. You have cause, but be careful. The time is not yet."

11

The front ends of the broad cephatus leaves that formed the roofs of the Tetatae homes reflected the soft starlight filtering through the treetops. No sign of life moved over the beaten ground between the log buildings, for the entire tribe was gathered in the long nesting house, as they did whenever a momentous decision was required. Apart from the birthing season, the place was usually empty except for meetings of this kind.

The central council sat in a circle, with Hetman Totito and Dokaepi, the shaman and spiritual leader of the tribe, in the center. There were only eleven members of the council; one space was left vacant for the missing member. The long interior of the house was filled with the sounds of soft muttering as the tribe settled down to what would be a lengthy meeting.

Whenever a Tetatae tribe faced an important decision, all the members gathered to hear the discussion. The subject would be announced by the hetman, or leader of the tribe, and then each member of the council would have a chance to speak in turn. The order of the speakers was ordained by a tradition that extended back as far as any living member could remember. The newest member of the council spoke first, for he would also be the youngest member. The twelve Tetatae represented the twelve oldest members of the tribe, be they male or female, and when there was a vacancy, the oldest member not of the council automatically filled that space. That was the situation now, and the tribe waited for the hetman to announce the vacancy.

Vacancies occurred only on the death of a member of the council. Under normal circumstances that death would have been witnessed by the entire tribe. When a Tetatae felt the cold fingers of his own passing, he would announce it to the tribe. They would then take him to the nesting house, where he would be comforted by the tribe. The dying member would accept water but no food until he quietly passed away. Then they would carry his remains to a special place, where the individual was buried among flowers, herbs, and some items of his or her own making. Because there was little private property among the Tetatae, the graves did not contain much. There the body would rest for eternity.

The Tetatae's religious system was a loose one. They knew or felt the existence of a power greater than themselves, and they were sure that it resembled their own form. But they weren't quite sure of its might or how it would deal with the Tetatae after death. They believed in an existence after death, but seemed mostly uninterested in the details. Life would be an extension of the present, and that was good enough. They also had a concept that doing good while in this existence was a requirement for the good life beyond, which made it important for a Tetatae to serve the tribe in some way. Sitting on the council was considered a good thing, especially if the member conducted himself with the dignity deserving of the office.

Now the tribe gathered in the nesting house, the most important building in the tribal compound, to hear what the advisors would say. This meeting was all the more important because one of the council members was missing. The fact that the member had departed without the traditional notification was unusual; such an event had not occurred within the memory of any but the oldest of the council. With the average Tetatae life expectancy something like two hundred years, that was a long memory. But even the oldest members could not recall a time when any member of the council had died without the benefit of a proper burial.

As the last of the tribe settled into their assigned places, Totito rose from his position in the center of the circle and began to speak. He looked around the entire circle of elders, his eyes passing over the vacant place. "Councilor Dakodo," he said in a firm voice, "Please answer the call of the council." He waited for a moment and then made the call again. He repeated the call twelve times as was the tradition of the tribe. Twelve was an important number in the life of the Tetatae, for it had roots in their religion, the birth process, the government, and their own physical structure.

There was no response from the missing member, nor had anyone in the room expected there to be. Everyone knew that Dakodo had vanished into the tribe of humans. It was also known that the humans had taken a young Tetatae who would never return. It was a time of some confusion for the members.

Twelve times Totito scanned the circle of elders. Twelve times he called for Dakodo to take his place within the circle. Then he made the announcement, "The missing member of the tribe makes no response, and so shall we consign Dakodo to the past. Let the present continue."

"I will take the place of my missing brother," came a voice from among the assembly. "May I serve as well as the missing Dakodo, as he served in the place of Têkă, as she served in the place of Tatádî, as he served . . ." The tradition of the place on the council was defined by those who had held it, and the newest member of the council repeated the names of all those who had gone before. The list was more than twenty names long, and the other members of the council waited until the recitation had finished.

Then each in turn greeted the newest member, who remained standing outside the circle. They uttered the ritual words: "Welcome, Pōpae, who will serve in the place of the missing Dakodo, who served for Têkã, who served for Tatádî, who served . . ." The list continued through the full response. Each member of the council gave the acceptance reply.

Thus were the traditions of the Tetatae kept alive. They had no written language, so their culture and knowledge were passed down orally. This transmission, which started with the young at birth and continued until death claimed them, was a time-consuming process, but it meant the Tetatae did not enjoy the luxury of forgetting. When a society can write down its past, its people have the option of forgetting their own history. Once it is written, it is assumed to be saved. And if it is already saved, what reason is there for each member of the community to remember it?

With Pōpae accepted into the circle of elders, the council was able to begin discussing the situation. Totito announced the question before the meeting, as was his duty. The position of hetman within the tribe was separate from that of council member. The hetman was the administrative leader of the tribe, but he acted more as a moderator than an advisor. It was his duty to ask the question and later to enunciate the answer, but he had no say in the decision itself. His position was filled upon vacancy by the member of the tribe best qualified to perform the mundane, day-to-day functions of administrator. That member must be accepted by all, and the one who would become the new hetman was named as successor long before the event became necessary. In some cases the position was hereditary, but that was not a law. Totito had succeeded to the place of hetman upon the death of his grandfather, stepping past his father who did not even hold a position on the council.

This question was much more complex than the ones that usually occupied council discussions. A traditional meeting often had to do with matters of sending an envoy to another tribe, or the opening of a new field, or the necessity of moving the tribe to a new location, or, occasionally, the need to break the tribe into two bands.

The division of the tribe was, of course, a grave decision. The Tetatae made very little use of domesticated plants and none of animals, living mostly by harvesting the area's natural abundance. When the tribe became too large for the surrounding area to support, it was time to divide the group in two. Such an event only took place perhaps once every three hundred years, however, because the tribe's population growth was so slow. It was a momentous event, requiring the most serious discussion. The question now facing the tribe was at least equal, and possibly even more significant, than the division of the tribe. For many of those gathered in the nesting house, the question involved the tribe's very survival.

What, Totito had asked, should be the response of the tribe to the presence of these newly arrived humans, especially since they came so long after the others who had arrived in the time of legend? Having asked the question, he sat and awaited the council's response. The other Tetatae shifted their positions and waited; it would be a long discussion.

Pōpae, as the youngest and newest of the council of elders, spoke first. She began with a long history of the Tetatae from before the arrival of the other humans, explaining in detail how the plains dwellers had become two different tribes. She dwelt on the growth of the two groups. She told how the plains dwellers had continued to move several times each year, how they were able to survive but that they did not progress. She explained that they were the victims of nature, but how, through them, the religion of the Tetatae was fostered. She then went on to speak of the long traditions of the forest dwellers: how they had been able to develop a different way of life, how the log huts had come into being, how life had become better.

Then she began the long saga of the humans and their

dealings with the Tetatae. Although there was little good to say about the humans, she stressed that their association had been with the plains dwellers. She understood that many Tetatae had been killed by the humans, but that eventually the humans had come to understand that the Tetatae were able to speak. The plains dwellers had learned the language of the humans and communicated that they were not hostile. The attitude of the humans changed. They had stopped trying to destroy the Tetatae once they discovered that the Tetatae could speak and think. Now they exploited them for other purposes. The relationship with the humans had not been a good one for the Tetatae.

When Pŏpae finished, she sat down. The next most junior member of the council, Kâeto, stood and began his speech. He covered the same ground as the first speaker, relating the information almost verbatim. That was the tradition of council discussions. But this speaker took the story into greater detail. He said that the humans were a threat to the Tetatae and should be dealt with at once. He advocated, if only gently, that the Tetatae should consider violence. That was a subject and an attitude that was far from the nature of the tribal council, and there were ripples of comment in the darkness beyond the circle. He continued, becoming more and more strident as he spoke. The expression of emotion was quite rare for a Tetatae, and the listeners began to shift uneasily in their places. Pŏpae ended his dissertation with what amounted to a call to arms: "There is a time to shun the enemy. There is a time to flee the enemy. Now is the time to . . ." He sat down.

There was a long pause before the next speaker. Kâeto was young, at least in comparison to the other members of the council. He represented a new concept among the tribe, and it was a popular one. He stood for an active rather than a passive attitude. And his position was gaining ground.

The other speakers were more cautious. They were not

willing to fight the humans, especially with the example of what could happen when they did. They had no weapons, they had no organization. The speakers recalled the response of the tribes to other dangerous situations. In those cases the affected ones had always chosen to either shun the intruder or to move, or both. In all cases the tribe had survived. It was the correct response.

The sun was high in the sky by the time the last councilor had spoken. The urgency of the situation had shortened many of the speeches. Whereas a discussion to send envoys could occupy a week, this one had taken less than eighteen hours. When the last member of the elders had retaken his seat, Totito rose to his feet. "The elders have spoken," he said. "The tribe will shun the intruders and prepare to move away. We will watch them carefully, but we will not contact them again. We will have nothing more to do with them."

===== 12 =====

Dawn came to the humans as well. The DEST members
had huddled around the fallen Dakodo through the night,
fearing that he would not recover and unwilling to leave
him to the tender mercies of the mercs. It had been unnecessary for Takuda to give orders to mount a guard. His
men, especially those of Knyte's section, were voluntarily
spending their time with the alien. The commander left it
alone, but he too kept up surveillance from a distance. By
the time the first streaks of dawn were coloring the sky in
the east, the soft iridescence had returned to the under
hairs that covered the Tetatae's body.

Swalen Horg sat beside Dakodo's quiet form. Though
his head drooped, he was still facing the mercenary camp
and fully aware of his surroundings. Like all the DEST
members, Horg could be almost completely asleep yet
still be conscious of certain sounds. It was as though the
elite soldiers had a sensor system trained into them, one
that could simply filter out non-hostile noises and activity. Conversation, the activity of the campsite, the casual
movements of the others as they went about preparing a
meal, had no impact on the watcher. But let someone
strange approach him, let there be the sound of a piece of
machinery, perhaps the click of a weapon being changed
from safe to fire, and Hort would be fully awake. It was
that sixth sense that permitted DEST members to continue when they should have been exhausted beyond the

ability to function. A soldier, no matter how well-conditioned, could not remain awake for an entire, year-long tour of duty. The body demanded sleep, but survival in a hostile environment created another kind of demand. And so Horg slept as he stood guard over his friend.

The rays of the sun probed beneath his eyelids, and slowly he responded. The eyes came open, but he did not change his pose. The alien lay at his feet in the same position he had assumed the evening after they'd treated the wound with the purple fruit. Now Dakodo also moved. The eyes came open, and he looked at Horg. "My friend," said the alien. "There was no need to wait for me."

Horg looked at the still recumbent figure. "I know. But it felt right."

The sounds of the conversation brought many of the other DEST members to join them. They offered bits of their own food, which Dakodo refused. He accepted with relish some of the fruits and vegetables gathered the afternoon before, however. Takuda waited until it seemed that Dakodo was sated, then hunkered down beside the alien.

"There is much for you to tell us," he said. "We would be glad to listen if you are able." Takuda glanced at his people standing a respectful distance away, and noted that those on watch had not abandoned their posts. He looked back at the Tetatae and waited for a reply.

Dakodo settled himself into a more comfortable position, looked into the eyes of those around him, and began his story.

In typical Tetatae fashion, he began the tale at the beginning. Perhaps the species had developed some inherent trait that would not allow them to get to the point. Whatever the reason, he started at a place far back in the memory of his people.

The Tetatae, he said, had lived here on Kaetetôã since the beginning of time. In the alien language, the word Kaetetôã meant, literally, earth and sky. There was never a time when the Tetatae had not been here. And if there were, it was without a chronicle and so could not be part of the story. The Tetatae had originally lived on the plains that bordered the great river to the west. They were nomadic, living in a kinship society and finding sustenance on the land. Life was good: téo da.

The tribes had grown more and more numerous, splitting when necessary to survive. After many generations some had traveled so far from the birth tribe that they had come into contact with the deep woods. With much fear and trepidation, these tribes had penetrated the green darkness. To their surprise, however, they found that not only could they live in the woods, but that in many ways the living was easier. No longer must they face the constant necessity to move on because of overgrazing; there was enough natural food in the area to support each tribe. The tribes still occasionally found it necessary to divide on occasion, but not nearly as often. The survival rate of the young increased. Life was good.

Then, a long time ago in human terms, a blazing shower descended from the sky. Out of the shower came the first humans. After journeying through the dark sky, they had landed here and found the place to their liking. At first the Tetatae thought the visitors from the stars had come as a sign. They thought that these new creatures with their great power would lead the Tetatae to the dream land where food was always abundant and where harmony reigned among all things. But that was not to be.

No sooner had the humans reached the peaceful surface of the planet than they began to fight. When the visitors were not killing each other, they were killing the Tetatae, with many dead on all sides, much fire, much ruination. The Tetatae thought that soon all of them would go on to meet their ancestors, but then the intruders stopped the killing. And so it had remained except for an occasional spasm of violence.

The humans were very strange, Dakodo told them. They had divided the land of the grassy valley into what they now called their own. How and why they decided on these boundaries was comprehensible only to the humans, the dragon-carriers, but they seemed to place a great deal of importance on them. They also seemed to want what the others had, and were willing to fight over it. Why this should be was a continual source of bafflement to the Tetatae. There was more than enough for all, so it seemed to make no sense to fight over it. But then, human activity did not make much sense, the alien commented.

It had been disastrous for the Tetatae who lived in areas where the humans wanted to go. Even after discovering that the Tetatae could communicate with them, they killed the Tetatae wholesale and drove them from their lands. The Tetatae, unwilling to be driven far, hung onto the outskirts of the human settlements. That was when the humans discovered that the Tetatae could be domesticated and trained to do menial tasks. In that capacity many Tetatae continued to live within the settlements of the humans.

They were treated so poorly by the humans that at times the Tetatae slaves revolted. After brutally suppressing those revolts, the humans would punish all by resuming their general slaughter of the Tetatae. Once the rebels were destroyed, matters would return to normal, and the surviving Tetatae would be brought back to resume their menial positions.

More recently, the humans had become more antagonistic among themselves, although Dakodo admitted that he spoke from tales rather than from actual experience. There had been outbreaks of violence between the various groups and a greater and greater number of killings as the humans also began to push out toward the forest lands. The humans seemed to have the breeding habits of small rodents, and the only way they could control that problem was to kill each other. They had not yet learned the Tetatae process of having fewer offspring at greater intervals. But that was a human problem of no concern to the Tetatae except when it began to affect the tribes. That was why the members of his tribe were so unwilling to make contact with the humans who fell from the sky again. Better, many of them had said, to let the humans kill each other than to make contact.

While Dakodo was telling his tale, an event that took most of the daylight hours, the DEST members and some of the mercenaries would join or leave the circle as their duties required. Only Horg and Takuda had remained throughout the entire telling. The commander and the soldier sat side by side in silence, nodding occasionally but never interrupting. Dakodo finished his narrative by saying, "Like you in many ways are they, but also not. Wear they the ringed dragon as you and to it give honor. Like you they are. Of that I certain am."

"How long ago did they come here?" asked Takuda.

"Dakodo not know. When Kátêo was hetman of the tribe it was, then comes Díkáká, and then comes Totito, who hetman is now. Not know how long, but think you say five hundred years."

"Five hundred years?" interrupted Kendall Pesht, one of the mercenaries who had joined the circle as the story was ending. "That's impossible! They would all have died by now!"

"Get a grip on biology," snorted Andi Holland, who had also heard most of the story. "They'd survive if they had women with them." She looked pointedly at Pesht. "They'd survive if they treated the women well. That's something you need to learn."

"We treat our women the way they deserve to be treated," said Pesht. " 'Mech pilots get their pick, and the others take what's left. That's the way it's always been, the way it will be, and the way it should be."

Takuda sat in silence through this exchange. He didn't even hear the words. The story of other humans could be true, he thought. There were many cases of ships lost when something went wrong with the hyperspace field during a jump, and those who fell from the sky could be survivors of such an accident, just as his group was now. All the pieces of evidence pointed to that fact. Dakodo said the people of the other group had worn the dragon symbol of the Draconis Combine. And there had been that hulk of the other JumpShip they'd passed in their fall toward the planet. Both Reston Bannin and Parker Davud had commented on its existence. But Takuda could not understand why those previous survivors had taken to fighting. The Combine way, established by House Kurita, was one of harmony.

Then again, any group of humans would surely respond with violence if their survival were threatened. He knew the same could happen with his own little band if Garber Vost had his way, which Takuda intended to prevent no matter what it took. His survivors had made contact with friendly inhabitants. There was even the chance that they would be able to meet the other humans.

The link with the Tetatae could be advantageous, thought Takuda. The fact that other members of the tribe lived among the other humans meant he could learn more from them. It was easy to imagine how careless the human masters would in the presence of their servants, perhaps not even remembering their existence at times. He had seen that same attitude at various headquarters. While the military would take elaborate security measures to keep the recognized enemy away from its secrets, they would think nothing of leaving the most sensitive documents on the desks when the cleaning staff was around. It was the old saw about blending into the woodwork. The Tetatae were probably equally invisible when moving among the other humans in their enclaves.

13

While Takuda continued to question Dakodo, Kendall Pesht left the circle and made his way over to the mercenaries. He had heard enough to grasp the great possibilities opening to him, to all of them, and he needed to talk to Vost. By the time he got to his commander, however, he found that someone else had stolen his thunder. Except for one little bit of information, Michelle Guardine had already given most of the story to Vost. But the piece she'd missed was probably the most important of all.

"Think of it, Garber," said Pesht. "Just think of it. All this took place five hundred years ago. They've been trapped here ever since. Just think of the weapons they have. Or don't have."

"We need to find out more," said Vost, standing up and placing his hands on his hips. The pose made him look imperial, and he knew it. He gazed at the other members of the mercenary team, allowing the full impact of his commanding presence to register. The only one who didn't seem impressed was Holly Goodall; he'd have to be careful with her.

"Let's go see if we can pry some information out of that furry critter. And maybe even a decision out of Takuda. I know we can get the information, even if it means having to invite the little bugger to our camp for a heart-to-heart, but getting Takuda to do anything will be another matter."

The mercenaries surrounded the group of DEST members who were talking with Dakodo. Shawn Arsenault, leader of the first DEST section, looked across the circle and caught the eye of Johan Miranda. He blinked slowly and Miranda nodded; not a big nod, just a slight creasing of the neck. Both men rose and stepped back through the ring of mercs. Vost and Seagroves pushed forward to take their places.

Now the questioning of the Tetatae began in earnest. Unfortunately, Dakodo did not have much specific information about the human enclaves. He had been to them before, but only when very young. He'd gone to them with Díkáká on a mission from the tribe to the humans when the humans first came into the forest. There had been no resolution of the problem, and shortly after that the tribe had moved deeper into the forest. All Dakodo's other information had come second- or third-hand from other Tetatae and the occasional human who wandered too far into the forest. It was from those contacts that he had learned the language of the humans. The humans sent traders to the woods to search out various delicacies that grew there, and the Tetatae had been glad to harvest them for the humans. Supplying these items seemed to keep the humans calm, and a calm human was much better than an angry one.

According to Dakodo, there were three inhabited human areas. There had been more in the beginning, but conflicts among them had reduced their number through attrition and amalgamation. The exact organization was beyond the aliens' understanding or knowledge. That they were three in number was all he could say for certain.

Vost probed for more information about the settlements, or enclaves, as the Tetatae knew them. Each one, it seemed, was surrounded by an elaborate system of walls and ditches in various configurations. Great gates, normally barred at night, secured each settlement. Although there was general free access to the enclaves during the hours of daylight, there was no entry during the hours of darkness unless one had a special pass. Dakodo did not know how to obtain such a pass.

It was the state of the walls that intrigued Vost, but he was careful not to lead the alien with his questions. He wanted to be sure the answers given were the most accurate, not the ones he wanted to hear. It was usual in an interrogation—which this surely was, that the person being interrogated begins by telling the questioner what he wants to hear. With his most careful questioning, Vost drew out a picture of an elaborate defensive position designed to stop ground forces. But the forces they were designed to stop would have been primitive even five hundred years ago. It was obvious that none of the humans had much in the way of powerful vehicles, though Dakodo's limited knowledge provided no explanation for this fact. Meanwhile, Vost tried hard to keep his excitement under control. A plan was beginning to form in his mind, but he didn't want it to leak out too soon.

Brian Seagroves was more blunt with his questions. Seagroves was the pilot of the *Phoenix Hawk* LAM, and he was frustrated at not being able to fly. Land-Air 'Mechs were the ultimate fighting machine in the eyes of their pilots, and Seagroves fit the mold perfectly.

There were two things that Seagroves liked, that gave his life meaning, and one of them was flying. The sense of power he got from taking the LAM into the air was more than he could describe or even admit. Sitting in the cockpit, the thruster controls under his hands, feeling the surge of power through the command seat, watching the ground flash by beneath the swept-back wings at 900 kilometers per hour, was almost sensual. Flying and wealth. Seagroves wanted to be rich, so rich he'd never again need to think about money. That was what drove the LAM pilot.

"But they don't even fly." It was a question as well as a statement. "The humans don't fly. How can that be true? Everyone knows how to fly. It's the first thing we do."

Dakodo looked at Seagroves in surprise. "Of course they not. Bird fly; human on ground walk." The alien shook his head. "Only bird fly. No need others to fly."

Seagroves leaped to his feet. "Get out the LAM," he shouted. "We can rule the world!"

"That's enough, Seagroves," said Vost sternly. "Just hold your jets for a while. We need to think about this." If looks could kill, Seagroves would have been dead on the spot. Vost had been very careful not to tip his hand, and now this fool was going to blow the whole scheme.

"But don't you see? Don't you see? They don't know how to fly!" Seagroves was almost dancing with excitement. "We can have it all!"

"Seagroves! Sit down and be quiet or leave the area!" Vost rose to his feet, hands on his hips as he glared across the circle. "This is not the time or the place to discuss it."

Seagroves stood open-mouthed. Vost had burst his bubble. His shoulders dropped, his lower lip hung down, his hands dropped to his sides. He was a pillar of despair. Standing there in the fading light, he looked like a man bearing the weight of the whole world on his shoulders. He turned from the group and slunk away.

Vost scrambled to his feet and followed Pesht. Coming alongside the shambling LAM pilot, he took him by the elbow and spoke softly. "You're right about the LAM, of course. You know it and I know it, but we don't want the others to get the idea. You're LAM qualified, but don't forget that I am too. We understand the power it can give us.

"Think of it, a whole society ripe for the picking. Remember what that little guy said about the walls? Those walls are designed to keep out land vehicles. There are places you can go to see things like that, I've seen the pictures. With the 'Mechs out we can have it all. We can become bossman of the whole planet. It's not just us against the DEST cruds. We don't need them at all. But we have to play our cards right. If they get the idea that we want to take over, they just might decide to destroy

100 Peter L. Rice

our 'Mechs. That we cannot let happen. So be a little more reserved. Cool down."

Yubari Takuda watched the two 'Mech pilots merge with the deepening gloom. That they were scheming something was obvious, and any plan of theirs would surely not be in the best interests of him or his men. There was always the option of eliminating the mercenaries, one that remained viable as long as the DEST team maintained superior firepower. Until now, he'd rejected the idea because they needed their combined strength for the survival of all. The discovery of the other humans on the planet had changed the equation. The mercenaries were no longer so important to survival, but then again, neither was the DEST team.

He was also certain that any other humans living on this world would consider the newly arrived humans a great asset. He didn't plan to make any moves until he had more information about the others, however. From what Dakodo had said, there were three groups, or possibly more, living some distance away by the great river that flowed to the west. The Tetatae was not sure how far distant they were, seeming to lack the grasp humans had on time or distance. The Tetatae seemed to give the concept little importance. But somewhere to the west were the humans. Takuda knew they would have to make contact, but they would have to do it gently. There was no need to upset what sounded like an already delicate situation between the other humans.

Meanwhile, Garber Vost had called the other 'Mech pilots around him upon returning to the mercenary camp. They squatted in a tight group, the technicians standing behind in a reverential circle. His tone was conspiratorial. "It's unbelievable," he whispered. "We have the whole planet in our hands. Nothing like this has ever happened before. We've got to make contact with the humans. With our firepower, we can rule everything. According to that furry little beast, the enclaves have only the most primitive defenses. Like something from a thousand years ago. They'll be a push-over."

"There may be too many of them," Pesht said. "And they may have weapons we don't know about, even if they have to crawl across the ground to use them. There are some archaic weapons that could do a job on a 'Mech."

Vost was about to squash the little pilot but thought better of it. Not only was Pesht valuable to him because he was the *Javelin* pilot, but he also had a point. There was no use charging into a situation that could be as fraught with danger as with possibilities. But there had to be a way to profit from the situation—they were mercenaries, after all. That was the solution! "Mercenaries," said Vost, thinking aloud. "That's it. That's what we can do. We'll sell our services to the highest bidder." He sat back on his heels and chuckled.

This called for decisive action. He stood up and put his hands on his hips, again hoping to impress the others with his air of command. "We make contact," Vost said. "Show them what we can do, and then offer our services. We take the best offer. We can always change our minds if we want to." He raised his fist in a victory salute. "We can have it all!"

He looked down at his followers. "But we have to be careful," he continued in a softer voice. "Takuda and the rest of DEST team may not like our little plan. He thinks too much, too much by half. We'll have to convince him that we're doing it his way. Make him think it's all his idea. We have to get the 'Mechs out of that DropShip, and we can't do it as long as he's got a guard there."

"We have slug pistols," said Collis Brank, looking up at his leader. "We could just do a job on them."

"Not a good plan, Brank. There are times when your mouth overloads your brain. How do you expect to get close enough to get them all on the first shot? Have you ever seen what a laser rifle can do to an unarmored human body? Or do you want to become a specimen yourself?" He turned away from the seated pilot. "No. We have to do it slowly. Just wait until we get those 'Mechs out of the ship, and then we'll see who's boss." Vost threw his head back and looked up at the first stars beginning to appear in the darkening sky. "By the eyes of the dragon, this will be an adventure our children and grandchildren will sing about."

In the quiet of the camp that night, Dakodo rose from his nest. The stars twinkled in the sky overhead; there was hardly a breath of wind. With a stealthy softness born of instinct and much use, he stole silently from the camp.

14

Sho-sa Yubari Takuda sat with the other members of the DEST headquarters. He would have to send a patrol to make contact with the humans, a mission that would require sending the best. The Knyte section had made first contact with the aliens, and so by all rights he should send Arsenault and his team on this patrol. It was a matter of sharing the responsibility and the danger. But he didn't have as much confidence in Arsenault's people.

Roland Dupe, the number two man in the section, had a tendency to gripe. That wouldn't have been so bad in itself, for griping about duty was a time-honored tradition among soldiers. But Dupe had a nasty habit of complaining about almost anything, which he'd been doing since even before they'd landed on the planet. Takuda felt for Arsenault, who had to put up with it on a constant basis.

The other member of the team was Dana Lost. One of Lost's distinguishing characteristics was the desire to do anything for anyone—to the point of volunteering to do so. There was not a fighting position in the DEST perimeter that Lost had not helped build. He had worked on his own, then gone roaming the site looking for other jobs that needed doing. The problem was that Dana Lost was also opinionated and loud—and most of his opinions were wrong. He and Dupe were inseparable friends, but between one's griping and the other's opinions, they were constantly fighting. Rising above it all was Arsenault, serene and calm. Takuda decided to give them the assignment just to keep them out of trouble.

Since time immemorial, military organizations had tried to prevent the dangerous problem of idleness among soldiers. They usually solved it with uniforms loaded with brass as well as healthy doses of close-order drill to keep the troops well-occupied during the innumerable, interminable periods of boredom between combat.

Takuda discussed the plan with *So-cho* Saitan Yura. He would have preferred to have another officer in the headquarters section, someone of equal social standing, but the non-commissioned Yura was all he had. Having served the Draconis Combine for nearly forty years, the sergeant-major had seen commanders, policies, victory and defeat come and go, come and go. Nodding in agreement, Yura listened impassively to his commander explain the mission and the people he would send. Yubari Takuda hoped that the nod meant agreement with this particular decision, not agreement with ANY decision. Takuda rose, about to direct the sergeant to issue the orders, when Garber Vost suddenly made an appearance.

"I've been thinking, *Sho-sa,*" the mercenary said, "about the idea of contacting the humans to the west. I think we must do it as soon as possible."

Takuda could hardly suppress the smile that tugged on his lips. This was the first time the mercenary commander had addressed him by his Combine rank of *sho-sa* rather than that of "major." It was also the first time since they'd boarded the DropShip that Vost had spoken to Takuda with anything approaching deference. Something smelled, but Takuda was willing to let it play out. "You have an idea, Pilot Vost?"

"Well, we don't know how far it is to the humans. We could send out a foot patrol, but it could take days to get to them, and more days to get back. If the patrol ran into any trouble, which wouldn't surprise me from what that furry fellow had to say, we'd never be able to support them. We'd all have to go. There's also the problem of how much time the patrol would need. We don't have a clue how far away from each other these enclaves are, and it could take days to recon all of them."

"Yes," acknowledged Takuda. "Time is a problem." He had, in fact, come to much the same conclusion. The 'Mechs could cover the ground much faster, and the LAM, which was stored in the DropShip's overhead bay, would be faster still. But he didn't want the 'Mechs deployed, at least not yet.

"The LAM could make the trip out and back in less than a day." Vost could see that Takuda would never think of using the 'Mechs on his own; he would have to be prodded. That was the trouble with the Combine soldier's mindset, thought Vost. Once he'd been trained to react in a certain way, he could never change that set. No wonder the Draconis Combine was so desperate to hire mercenaries. It was only mercs who had the ability to think on the move.

"Yes," mused Takuda. "That is so. But I wonder about using a machine of such immense firepower around these people who have never seen one and certainly have never seen something that flies. It could be quite a shock."

Damn right it will, thought Vost. That's just what I want. "We could tell Seagroves to stay at high altitude. They might not even be aware of his presence. And even if they did see him, they wouldn't know what they were seeing. It could be worth a try."

"Can we get the LAM out of the DropShip? It's taken some damage, and I understand from Parker Davud that the hull has been wrenched. We'd have to cut the hull open, which would mean we'd never be able to fly it out."

We're never going to fly it out anyway, thought Vost. Get with the program, old man. We're here on this planet for eternity, just like the others, and we'd better make the best of it. And even if the DropShip could fly, there's no place to go.

"The sacrifice of the DropShip would probably be

worth it," Takuda was saying, "but I worry about the weapons. Having them is a temptation to use them. I wouldn't want that. I think your Pilot Seagroves might be tempted. Perhaps you could use someone else. Perhaps Pilot Goodall." Takuda knew that Vost was qualified on the LAM, but next to Seagroves, Vost was the last man he wanted over the enclaves.

Oh no, you don't, thought Vost. You're not going to mess up this plan like that. "Well, Goodall isn't LAM qualified," he said aloud. "As for the weapons, we could always activate the external default for the lasers. To use them the pilot would have to land to re-engage the system, which it would take two men to do. The LAM is stored in flight mode in the DropShip, so once he took it out he'd be on his way. We just default the weapons while it's still hanging."

Takuda did not quite trust Vost's suggestions, but this did seem like the best plan. The LAM could do in a few hours what it could take a foot patrol to do in a week or more. The information wouldn't be of the same detail and accuracy, but it would provide enough to make other decisions. "We'll do it," he said.

"Great! I'll get my people working on it at once."

Parker Davud was equally convinced that deploying the LAM was the best plan, but he didn't want to see his DropShip gutted like a piece of meat after slaughter. As long as the DropShip maintained its structural integrity, they'd always have at least the possibility—however far-fetched—of being able to fly out again. Besides, the DropShip was his, he owned it personally. He'd bought and paid for it from his earnings, money he'd taken significant risks to get in the first place. His profits from owning the DropShip had let him live in a way that others only dreamed of. Destruction of the ship would mean he could never hope to resume his former life. Yet, Davud knew there was no alternative.

Examination of the ship proved beyond a reasonable doubt that it would never fly again, even if they didn't cut it apart. Davud dreaded hearing the news, but he couldn't avoid it for long. Once Mark Jacobs, the JumpShip engineer, got a really good look at the wreckage, he consigned the DropShip to the breakers. "Your main spar looks like a corkscrew," he announced. "Not only that, but ribs seventeen, eighteen, and nineteen have been stressed beyond their rebound point. They're so brittle I'm surprised you got this thing to the ground. The lifeboat's problems are even worse. I guess I really did a job on it while augering in. There's not an aerodynamic surface left to it. It'll smoke, and fume, and burn, but it'll never fly. Same with yours." He thumped the side of the DropShip. "Oh, well. Easy come, easy go."

But cutting into the DropShip proved a more stubborn task than first imagined. Even using cutting torches from the maintenance compartment, it took quite a while to slice along the top of the hull. The torch had been designed for minor repair jobs, not for peeling away a section of hull. Jacobs finally suggested that laying cable along the surface and then superheating it with power from the fusion core might do the job more easily. It did, amid a shower of sparks that sprayed over everything. At last the nose of the LAM came clear of the hull.

Seagroves had, meanwhile, been in the cockpit checking the systems and circuits. The crash had so damaged the power couplings that three of them needed replacement. That was easy enough for the two minor ones, because replacement couplings were among the prescribed load list bins the technicians carried. The third coupling was a major, no-failure joint that could not be replaced out of stores. The no-failure joints were designed to last the life of the ship and were sealed into the systems. Seagroves became pessimistic when he got a red light for that system, but Jacobs, always the tinkerer, came up with a solution. By cross-feeding the neurofield control system with the inter-coolers, he was able to bypass the damaged piece. He patted his repair with justifiable pride. "There.

That should serve you for the life of the LAM, or yours. Whichever comes first."

Takuda and Vost climbed onto the back of the LAM so that the DEST commander could see the laser default system. They broke into the access panel and threw the switches that controlled the power feed to the weapons system. When Vost explained that the machine guns would still work, Takuda decided that leaving those active was probably a good idea. The short-range defense weapons might make a difference if the LAM ever got into trouble.

With the side of the DropShip split down to the ground, the entire cargo area was exposed. The rest of the 'Mechs stood mute against the bulkheads, forgotten toys awaiting some call from the future. The other pilots could not resist climbing into their cockpits to check circuits and servos. There were no orders to deploy as yet, but it looked like they might still get their chance. The pilots felt a surge of hope. Even Jacobs, whose training on a 'Mech had occurred so long ago, could feel the urge to break the machines free. It had been a decade since he'd last sat in his father's 'Mech, but the instinct was still there.

When the LAM was completely clear, Seagroves reported to Takuda and Vost. The DEST commander took the pilot aside. "You will be in a very delicate position, Mr. Seagroves. It is important that you make as little contact as possible with the humans. We don't know the situation, and we don't want to stumble into something that could overwhelm us. Be very careful. Stay as high as you can and still get some idea about what the enclaves are like. Just be careful."

Seagroves nodded. With the briefing over, he and Vost began the climb to the LAM cockpit. "Get low," said Vost. "Low enough that they can see you and you can see how they react. As far as contact goes, Takuda's right. We don't want to get committed until we have more information." Seagroves nodded agreement to these instructions as well.

The mercenaries and the DEST team stood clear as Seagroves fired up the LAM. The clouds of exhaust poured out of the ruptured hull, enveloping most of the ship in a ball of glowing smoke. Then in a shattering burst the LAM came free from the restraining shackles and raced across the landing zone. The last those on the site saw of it, the craft was in a vertical power climb. Seagroves was in his element at last.

15

Seagroves settled deeper into the ergonomically designed command seat of the LAM. It had been a long time since he'd felt the craft's raw strength under him, and he reveled in the power that vibrated through his being. It was wonderful. Above him the blue sky also seemed to vibrate with happiness. He thought about rolling the *Phoenix Hawk* over into a vertical dive over the campsite. Wouldn't that give those ground-bound slugs a thrill? But he thought better of it. He needed to test the control response. He needed to re-learn the process of flying. He pushed forward on the starboard control arm and brought the LAM to level flight.

The LAM's cockpit was crammed with levers, switches, gauges, and lights. The *Phoenix Hawk*, designed to fly like a bird and walk like a man, had the controls for both modes. A standard 'Mech was a complicated piece of equipment with control sticks for both hands. The joystick, which sat between the pilot's legs and was controlled by his right hand, took care of movement vector as well as the weapon aiming systems. The left hand controlled speed and gross balance. The neurohelmet, specifically designed to react to the nervous system of the pilot, responded with sighting and fine balance. On the dashboard in front of the pilot was the weapons targeting system, spectral analysis panel, sensor array, radar plot, I/R plot, and communications system.

The gauges and sensors that reported on the status of the 'Mech's various control systems were also laid out in convenient clusters. Dials and digital displays would indicate the status of heat buildup, a nasty problem for all 'Mechs, as well as the status of heat sinks, ammunition, fuel, lubrication temperature, and power output. Across the bottom of the panel, just above the pilot's knees, was a ground status sensor display, which was designed as a plot plan indicator readout much like a standard radar or I/R screen. But instead of showing specific objects, the plot showed the perceived condition of the ground in and around the 'Mech. Direct observation of the ground was a problem for a 'Mech pilot. The ground status sensor felt the ground even before the 'Mech placed its feet down, warning the pilot, both through the color of the display and a warning klaxon if necessary, about the solidity of the ground surface. Most pilots learned to sense the shifts in colors that rippled across the display. Really good pilots could make their 'Mechs run at very high speeds without consciously consulting the terrain sensors. Pilots who could do that commanded machines like the light *Locust* 'Mechs. Good peripheral vision and a fine sense of balance were what those required.

All the controls and sensors for a ground-bound 'Mech filled the normal cockpit. The *Phoenix Hawk* had all those as well as the controls for a flying weapons platform. Because the 'Mech had been designed to fulfill both functions, the controls remained in the cockpit. When the system was in flight mode, the normal joystick was locked in the neutral position and the controls for the *Hawk* were activated. The flight control system used dual control wands in much the same way that the ground system did. Instead of having the central control between the pilot's legs, the wand hinged from a bar that rose on the starboard side of the cockpit. The top of the bar was a hinged stick that dropped across the right leg, placed so that the pilot's right hand dropped naturally onto the bar. The back of the hand and the first joints held the stick under control, and there were five buttons for triggering the weapons with fingers and thumb. The left hand had a similar bar that maintained flight speed and engine power output.

On either side of the display were the readouts for the *Hawk* system. The designers had fought over which system should have the central position, and the designers of the *Phoenix* had eventually won. They had reasoned that the 'Mech would spend most of its time on the ground, and therefore the ground systems should have priority. Seagroves didn't agree. Even if he spent most of his time on the ground, he only came alive when he was in the air. That was living, that was power, that was reality. The designers were desk-bound gnomes who used their brains to solve problems. They hadn't asked a pilot what he wanted. And so they'd solved their design problems with calculators and computer graphics. So what if it all worked fine on their computer screens? Real life was different.

Seagroves let his eyes sweep over the dials and readouts. Every fifteen seconds his eyes made the sweep from upper left, across the top of the displays, down the right side, and then across the bottom to the starting point. It was not a conscious act, and there was no requirement that he understand what each dial represented. The systems had been placed on the panel so that all the indicator arrows pointed in the same direction to be green. All that the eye saw and the brain recorded was a mass of little wands pointing the same way. It didn't matter if the dial were upside down, cocked to the right, or cocked to the left. As long as the arrows were in the same direction, the Seagroves knew he had a good panel. As a trained and experienced pilot, his eyes made the sweep every fifteen seconds. Some pilots never got the routine, but most of those were buried by now, six feet under. There were old pilots and bold pilots, but there were no old, bold pilots. Seagroves was daring when he had to be, but he was as safety-conscious as the best of them. That was how a

LAM pilot became an experienced LAM pilot. Seagroves was experienced and intended to stay that way.

He rocked the LAM left and right, feeling the response and noting that the controls were a little sluggish when commanded to move left. He didn't know whether it was the LAM or his stiffness at the controls, but his subconscious noted the hitch in the movement, storing the information away for future reference. He would have to check the systems when he landed. Pitch and yaw controls were checked as well, and his eyes continued to make their sweep across the panel. Good board, good board, good board.

Seagroves had been slouching along at 450 kilometers per hour, headed west, ever since gaining level flight. The LAM was trimmed in a slight nose-up attitude and had been gaining altitude as it traversed the ground. The system check complete, he turned his attention to the mission. With the LAM's throttle forward, nose up, Seagroves brought it to an altitude of 10,000 meters, or 10 angels, at 900 kilometers per hour. He punched in the look-down sensor array and watched the screen blossom with ground configuration and infrared signatures. Three distinct targets appeared at once. Those were the enclaves he was looking for. He pointed the nose north and began his first sweep.

He remembered the instructions of both Takuda and Vost. The DEST commander wanted high reconnaissance only; Vost wanted him to get down and dirty. No sense committing the LAM to a low pass until he had some information. Seagroves reached forward and toggled the ground flight recorder. From now on, what he saw, it would see. What he did, it would record.

All three enclaves were as had initially been described by the furry alien. Great systems of moats and walls extended from the banks of the broad river to enclose the central, metropolitan areas. The northernmost enclave was laid out in a square system of roads with large central plazas at regular intervals. From 10 angels, Seagroves could see dots of green that indicated vegetation placed at regular intervals between the broad streets. At the center of the enclave stood a huge building, the roof reflecting red. The sensor display recorded a multi-storied building in a pagoda style reminiscent of some of the government buildings favored by the Draconis Combine. The structure, a castle, was surrounded by a broad park with a triple wall beyond. Very regular, very strong, very secure. Seagroves rolled the LAM away from that enclave and turned south along the west bank of the river.

The next settlement had the same wall and moat system guarding its eastern, landward, side. The configuration was different from the first one, but the extent of the works was identical. The roads within the final wall were not laid out in the four-square pattern of the first, but looked like a giant pond of water lilies, the centers of the flowers surrounded by looping roads that formed the petals. The flowers were laid out in concentric circles that surrounded and were surrounded by a larger pattern with a huge, central edifice. The scanner showed another multi-storied building, but unlike the castle in the earlier enclave, this building was lower and considerably more sprawling. The entire structure was surrounded by paired pillars that supported inverted arches. There were significant open spaces within the enclosure, and many of the gardens were set on the various roofs of the building itself. The central structure was a windowless dome in the geometrical center of the compound and the enclave.

The third enclave repeated the walls and moat, but the entire system was a jumble of defensive works. Any attacker would find himself in a defense system that made no apparent sense at all. Seagroves noted that there were portions of the moat that seemed to have silted over to form bright green marshes. Other portions were better maintained, and some of the walls were guarded by massive towers and outguards. Within the walls the look of the defenses was equally chaotic. The streets were laid out with no apparent geometrical pattern. They were short and broad and began and ended for no apparent reason. Many of the structures had no streets at all between them, just narrow alleys. There was no central building like those in the other enclaves, but several dominating structures instead. Each of the larger buildings had its own defense system of walls and moats, but like the ones that guarded the entire enclave, they showed various states of repair and construction. The situation here did not look too promising.

Seagroves continued south along the river for ten minutes and then turned the LAM back north. He had accomplished the mission according to Takuda's orders; now was the time to do what Vost wanted. He toggled off the ground flight recorder. From now on what he saw, only he would see. There would be no official record of his actions. He decoupled the entire flight record system, noting the inertial plot indicator readout for future reference. He would return to this spot, or close to it, before he reactivated the record. He could always claim a system malfunction if he got the plot a little off the mark. Systems were known to fail. Takuda would never know what happened. The DEST commander, like every other member of his strike team, was qualified to pilot a 'Mech, but he was not experienced in a LAM. Besides, the old fellow had other things to worry about.

Seagroves rolled the LAM into a split-S and took her down. This would be seat-of-the-pants flying at its best. With all the record-keeping systems deactivated, there would be no readouts in the cockpit. The pilot checked the weather and visibility: CAVU. Down he went.

The LAM leveled off at 200 meters and throttled down to 300 kilometers per hour. Seagroves saw no use in blasting across the terrain so fast that he couldn't see anything. Even at this speed he had to keep the LAM well nosed up to maintain control. The chaotic wall system of the southern enclave flashed beneath his wings, and he was over the city proper.

From the people down below Seagroves got the reaction that he'd expected: they either stood and gaped or ran for the protection of the buildings. Seagroves streaked across the sky, leaving behind a trail of excitement and awe. The northern section of wall passed beneath his wings. Nothing unexpected so far ... except.... Something among the jumble of streets and buildings had caught his attention. It was something he knew he should think about, but he couldn't get a clear image in his mind. He rolled the LAM over and made another pass above the roofs of the city. And now he knew! There was gold everywhere.

Seagroves felt his heart leap in his chest. It was gold. Of that there was no doubt. And it was all over the city. He felt the sweat spring from the palms of his hands. He started to shake. He looked for a place to set the LAM down. Just ahead was an opening among the buildings. He needed a bigger area to put the LAM down, but caution had fled. Seagroves pulled back on the control bar, reached forward to toggle the *Phoenix* system. He felt the shudder of the 'Mech's legs coming down. There was a jolt as the huge metal feet touched something solid.

16

Clouds of dust rose from around the LAM as it settled into the upright position. Seagroves squinted through the bubble screen of the cockpit to see what stood beyond. He could feel his heart racing; he was frantic to get outside. He pounded on the quick release of his harness, unaware that the clips had come free on the first stroke. Not wanting to waste time, he pushed the control bars out of his way and snapped open the cockpit emergency access hatch instead of dismounting through the normal rear opening and down the chain ladder. The coaxial cable connected to the neurohelmet nearly strangled him as he leaped up from his seat. Sinking back into his seat again, he disengaged the bayonet quick release.

The momentary obstacle made him pause. He put his hand to his chest and felt the racing staccato beat of his heart. Got to get myself under control, he thought. What if these people are armed? What if they start shooting? I'd better be more careful. He forced himself to breathe deeply. Ah, he thought, that's better. He let some of the dust clear from his vision screen.

There was the city. The building directly in front of the LAM was one of the more substantial structures he'd seen on his first two passes. The front had been slightly damaged by the exhaust gases of the LAM drive, and it was pockmarked where bits of rubble from the street had blown against it. The openings in the face of the building had probably been glazed, but the force of the landing blast as well as the debris had removed all of it. Blank openings stared back at the LAM pilot. Seagroves might have felt remorse at the damage he'd caused, but that was not the emotion that flooded through his body as he sat in the command chair. He could see the glint of gold even among the debris.

He leaned forward in his seat to get a better look, squinting through the settling dust at the bright points of light in every window. The window frame catches were of gold. Gold! GOLD! His mouth went dry. This must be the most important building in the entire enclave. The people must be so rich that they could secure their windows with latches of gold. He started to giggle. He looked again at the façade. It was beyond his comprehension.

The window latches *were* of gold. So were the knobs on the great doors that stood directly in front of the LAM. So were the hinges on the doors. And the door knockers. And the light fixtures on the walls. His eyes swept down the street. The street lamps were of gold. So were the sewer covers. This place was a dream come true. He was so busy cataloguing the wealth that he didn't notice the people beginning to gather in the streets.

At first it was only a few faces at the windows, the ones that had been blasted open as well as those that still had glass. Then there were figures at the doors, and finally there were people creeping out of the buildings and hugging the walls. Blank faces stared up at the towering piece of machinery that had descended on them without warning. Fear and awe were reflected in their eyes. No one approached the LAM.

At last Seagroves could stand the tension no longer. He had to get closer to the gold. The neurohelmet disconnected, he crawled out the port side of the cockpit emergency access hatch. It was only then that he became aware of the people standing in the small square, and only then because they began to scream.

The people shrank back from the LAM, pressing themselves against the sides of the buildings or back into the doorways. Windows slammed shut. That was when they began to scream, to cover their eyes with their hands and scream. Several fell unconscious to the pavement. Seagroves took only mild notice of the commotion he had obviously caused the citizens of this small enclave. He stood on the shoulder of the 'Mech, his hands dangling at his sides, and stared at the glow of the gold.

He was aware, vaguely at first and then more acutely, of a man standing directly in front of the LAM. There were others behind him, crouching and peering, but the man had obviously come to open communications. The man began to speak, mumbling indecipherable words at first, and then speaking more clearly. Or perhaps it was that Seagroves was listening more acutely. The words were spoken with a thick accent, but the pilot recognized it as his own tongue. He looked intently at the man.

"We welcome you to our homes. We see that you have come for us. We bless your presence."

"What was that?" asked Seagroves. "Where did you say I am?"

There was a cry from the crowd, followed by distant chatter. It was like a pebble sending out ripples across a pond when Seagroves spoke. The wave of comment and response swept away from the center. Someone called out to the spokesman from the rear, and he raised his hand in response. The chatter stilled in the same wave pattern. "This is Usugumo," the man said, speaking the word more clearly. He bowed deeply and looked up at Seagroves. "We are here to serve you in all that you desire."

Two hours later the LAM rose from the streets of Usugumo. Seagroves still couldn't really grasp what had happened. It was a dream. But it wasn't. The cockpit stowage boxes were filled with bits of gold he had been urged to collect from Usugumo. He must have picked up three hundred kilos of the stuff. Three hundred kilos. It was a fortune. He'd be able to buy anything he wanted. Another couple of hauls like this and he could retire. In two hours he'd made as much as a very successful 'Mech lance could make in a year. And he didn't have to share it with anyone.

That brought him back to reality. He would have to report on the mission to both Takuda and Vost, which meant having to explain a two-hour gap in his flight recorder. Engine malfunction would serve. Just to add face value to his tale, he set the LAM down in some open ground and stomped around for a while. That would serve to show that the 'Mech had actually gone down somewhere. Then he flew back to the DropShip crash site.

The report to Takuda, along with the flight record that had been preserved, was straight and to the point. There was not much Seagroves could add to the data that had been stored in the visual and sensor portions of the log. There was a printout of the possible number of heat sources and their supposed type. Lots of fossil fuel burners in all three locations as well. Takuda retired to study the log and contemplate the situation.

The report to Vost was quite different. Seagroves had only one enclave to tell about. The engine malfunction provided an excuse for the lack of information on the other areas. He tried to contain himself, but it was impossible. "They're so rich," he blurted out. "You wouldn't believe how rich they are. They just gave me this stuff." He thrust out a handful of the gold trinkets he'd taken.

Vost stared down at the cluster of gold objects. What Seagroves said made some sense. The Usugumo were certainly rich, but what about the others? They had to be equally rich. There was no need to commit the lance just yet. "Did you make a deal?' he asked Seagroves.

The LAM pilot gulped. No, he thought, I don't think I did. But I may have. I can't remember. "Certainly not," he said with emphasis. "I wouldn't do that." He wasn't nearly as sure as he sounded.

"Don't lie to me, Seagroves," said Vost, his mouth a thin line and his eyes on fire. "If I find out different, I'll skin you alive."

You'll never find out if I'm careful, thought Seagroves. He looked the mercenary commander in the eyes. "It's the truth," he said.

The meeting that night between Takuda and Vost was attended by all. Even those who should have been on watch had moved quietly to the outer edge of the circle marked by the firelight. The news of the enclaves and the gold was too important to keep quiet. It started with the mercenaries, but it spread quickly to the DEST team. The JumpShip and DropShip crews saw no reason why any of this should be secret, and by the time the two leaders met, it was common knowledge that Seagroves had landed in or near at least one of the enclaves. Takuda had heard the report, or at least bits of it, and he was fuming under his composed exterior by the time Vost made his appearance in answer to a polite, but firm, summons.

Takuda wasted no time explaining what he knew about the day's activity. There was no way for the DEST commander to know that Seagroves had disobeyed his orders based on Vost's command, nor could he know that Seagroves had exceeded even what the mercenary leader had asked. Both men were walking stiff-legged and tense when they met.

"We need to make contact with all the enclaves," concluded Takuda after summing up what he knew of the situation. "From the pictures I've seen of the defensive works around each, the three enclaves seem hostile toward one another. It's very puzzling to me. They are obviously from an ancient Draconis Combine ship—either a military expedition or a colonization mission that was lost some five hundred years ago. How could they have gone so wrong? How could they have spent five hundred years fighting? They had the chance to found the perfect bushido society."

"Who cares what they've been doing?" countered Vost. He was frustrated by the DEST commander's philosophical maunderings. "This is our chance. We can get in there and take over everything."

"Or we can help make peace. From what I've seen in the report, these people are quite primitive. We could make them come to terms with each other. We could be their teachers."

"Teachers? You're hopeless, Takuda. I don't want to be their teacher in a peaceful society. I want to run things! I say we should sell to the highest bidder, then go and stomp on the rest of them. That's what soldiers do!"

"That's what mercenaries do," said Takuda in a level voice. "That is not what soldiers do. Soldiers serve the Coordinator and the Draconis Combine. We fight when it is required, and we are prepared to die for the Dragon, but fighting is not our reason for being. Service is the reason we exist. Into our hands has been delivered the fighting power of the state, and we should not abuse that power."

"Are we going to make contact with the enclaves?" Vost was standing now, his hands on his hips. He was almost nose-to-nose with Takuda.

The DEST commander didn't budge. "Of course we are, Pilot Vost. It has been my intention ever since your pilot returned that we should make contact. According to him the enclaves are less than a hundred kilometers from here. We can send out ground patrols. They can make contact and be back in less than a week."

"And what are we supposed to do while all that's going on? Sit on our hands? Twiddle our thumbs?" Vost, unable to make Takuda wince, turned his back on the DEST commander. "I call for a vote right now. I say we break out the 'Mechs and make the best deal. Who's with me?"

There was a noticeable tensing among those gathered around the central fire. This conflict could result in the fracturing of their little society. But even the most insensitive members of the organization could hear the sibilant whisper of laser rifles being taken off safe. It was the DEST members who'd been assigned the watch, standing now just outside the rim of light thrown by the fire.

"Uhha," said Jacobs, clearing his throat and standing. "Perhaps the problem has more than one solution. What *Sho-sa* Takuda says about contact is quite correct. We need to do that. On the other hand, perhaps Pilot Vost is right and we should break out the 'Mechs." He nodded to both leaders in turn. "But it will take at least a week to free the 'Mechs, and if what *Sho-sa* Takuda has said is true, we can have the information by then."

"That's fine with me," snarled Vost. "Just as long as we have something going on while Takuda and his troops are fiddle-farting around."

"We will not be fiddle-farting around, Pilot Vost." It was as close as the DEST commander had come to visible anger. "Mr. Jacobs has a good idea. I will organize a patrol for tomorrow. You and Mr. Jacobs can prepare a plan to free the 'Mechs."

"We'll do more than just prepare a plan, Takuda. We'll have the 'Mechs out and ready by the time your little patrol is back."

17

Both Takuda and Vost were wrong in their estimations of the time needed for their respective tasks. The section contact patrol, headed by *Gun-so* Arsenault, was back in six days rather than the seven that had been allotted. That event had opposite effects on Takuda and Vost; one was happy, the other decidedly was not.

Vost's unhappy reaction had more to do with the difficulties in breaking out the other 'Mechs from the DropShip than the DEST patrol returning too soon, however. When they'd pried the LAM out, it had been with the single thought of freeing it from the strained hull of the DropShip. They'd paid little heed to the relative position of the rest of the 'Mechs in relation to the breach. Most of the cutting of the hull had been at the top along the main dorsal spar. The dross produced by the cutting, and the subsequent wrenching of the hull, had made an opening for the LAM, but it had pinned the other 'Mechs behind the slag. In the excitement of the original extraction, no one had thought to plan for the future.

The second problem had to do with the LAM's actual exit. Because they hadn't been able to cut an opening big enough for the LAM, which had been transported in the air configuration, to walk out of the DropShip, Seagroves had been forced to take it out as an air vehicle. The exhaust gases from the Allied AVRTech 125 jet propulsion system had vented straight into the hull of the DropShip, where they had played havoc with the interior. It would have been better if they had cut gas-escape ports into the opposite side of the hull, but there'd been no time for that.

The other 'Mech pilots had managed, in varying degrees, to protect their machines from the gases, but other equipment had suffered considerable damage.

The blast of the exhaust had been deflected downward onto the cargo deck by the opposite side of the hull, the force and heat annealing the portside cargo access doors. They wouldn't be doing any cutting on that side of the DropShip. The blast had continued into the base of the cargo bay, warping and melting part of the decking. Some of the gases had escaped into the lower holding compartments; the rest had penetrated into the open space of the main bay. The velocity and force of the jet propulsion exhaust had scattered anything not secured, as well as some things that were, against the starboard skin and braces.

Thus, it was not a matter of simply freeing up the 'Mechs and letting them climb out the opening cut for the LAM. Before they could release the 'Mechs, the work parties had to repair the damage done by the blast and cut free the refuse that was stuck to various portions of the interior. Vost's *Panther* was the 'Mech most buried. It had suffered some damage from the fiery exhaust, and all the systems would have to be checked and repaired before it could be activated. Vost insisted, however, that his 'Mech receive first priority for extraction.

For three days, Vost spent all his time in the *Panther*'s command seat. The hot gases had scored the cockpit glass, and Michelle Guardine had spent the whole time spread-eagled across the bubble using a grinding wheel to smooth the crazing and polish the surface. The ogive of the glass was made of high-low surface tension material that was both extremely tough and extremely fragile. The high surface tension of the wind screen made it virtually impervious to all but a direct hit, while the low surface tension of the interior of the glass would act as a shock

absorber. The brittle outer surface would break up the incoming round, but the softer inside would flex ever so
slightly to distribute the force of the hit over the entire
surface. If the outer skin, a mere two millimeters thick,
were scratched, the inner surface would lose its structural
integrity and collapse. Guardine had to be very careful to
use only the finest grit to polish away the marks on the
outside.

The work of clearing would have gone faster except
that the other 'Mech pilots spent the time on their own
vehicles. In a mercenary unit like Vost's, each warrior
was the actual owner of the 'Mech he piloted, even
though the group was under the nominal military command of the leader. It was very difficult, except in a tactical situation, for Vost to get all his people to work
toward a common goal. He tried to persuade, and then order, the other pilots and their techs to help out with the
Panther, but his efforts came to naught. Holly Goodall
was the first to tell him where to get off, and the other pilots quickly followed suit. Only Pesht, the *Javelin* pilot,
was willing to help, and even that was done more with an
eye to getting his *Javelin* free.

By the sixth day the *Panther* was almost out, and Vost
estimated that it would be only a few hours more before
the *Javelin* was also up and operational. As the work
neared completion, a plan began to solidify in his mind.
Until now, he'd been unable to doing anything about getting rid of the DEST team because his 'Mechs had been
inaccessible. Now, his first move was to mention to
Seagroves that one blast from the LAM's heavy lasers
could blow the DEST command bunker, by now a significant structure, into oblivion. Seagroves had demurred on
the grounds that attacking the headquarters would not do
any good. The heavy weapons section, commanded by
Ariake Sanae, would react and dismember his 'Mech with
a few well-aimed shots. Vost had nodded and smiled.
Things would be different, he said, when all the 'Mechs

were out. The conversation rested there, but the seed had been planted.

Late on the afternoon of the sixth day, Arsenault and his section patrol returned to camp, their appearance a surprise to all but Takuda, who had maintained contact with them through the secure-voice communicator in his headset. Before the patrol had set out, he and Arsenault had coordinated on time and frequency for transmissions. Most were carried out by laser line-of-sight light wave carrier. Radio, an archaic system, was only used as back-up. Takuda and Arsenault had decided on the older system because the mercenary unit's commlinks were laser primary. They would probably never think to use the radio back-up—and even if they did, the possibility of them finding the correct frequency was slight. In addition, all voice transmissions were scrambled so that even if someone located the transmission, he or she would have no idea what was being said. The line had remained secure.

Arsenault went immediately to report to Takuda, but he'd barely begun before members of the mercenary unit began to filter into the headquarters bunker. Takuda could have stopped the ingress, but decided against it. He knew that the information would get out soon enough, and he wanted to maintain an open relationship with the mercenaries. He let them in as Arsenault continued to talk.

The first part of Arsenault's report consisted of an overview of the patrol, the routes taken, and the terrain traversed. All of this was interesting to Takuda, who would have to plan any movement to the west, but it was deadly dull to the mercenaries. All they would need do was hop into their 'Mechs and travel like the wind. The mercenary technicians, on the other hand, took some interest because they would have to walk out.

Then came the part that Vost especially wanted to hear: the report on the enclaves and the possibility of making a deal with one of them. The report was short, sweet, and to the point. Arsenault said he'd obtained the information

by observation from a distance and via limited contact
with humans who had ventured away from the immediate
vicinity of the walled towns. Arsenault had done most of
the talking, acquiring some, but not very detailed, information.

There were three enclaves, he said. The one to the
north was called Osio, and seemed to be under complete
centralized control of a dictator. This was much like the
old Von Rohrs dynasty taken to the extreme. They were
a recognizable group, but they had all of the human attitudes of that long-dead dynasty. They hadn't had the experience, or did not assimilate the experience, of the
McAllister years. They hadn't learned anything.

The second was Amatukaze, a religious enclave that
had fallen back on the pure Shinto/Buddhist philosophy.
They were fundamentalists who regarded the other enclaves as heretical in the extreme. Where Osio wanted to
dominate, the Amatukaze would like to exterminate. This
was religion taken to the extreme.

The third was Usugumo, an enclave controlled by a
merchant oligarchy that had subverted everything to the
god of profit. They had the most money, but were dominated by a group of families who exploited everything
they touched.

Arsenault's listeners received the information with
varying degrees of enthusiasm. Vost was ecstatic. Takuda
was depressed. Vost now had a base from which to deal.
The militarists of Osio would be more than willing to buy
a weapons system that would make their dictatorship supreme. The fact that they were the Von Rohrs personified
made little difference to him. The only fly in that oint-
ment might be their possible desire to swallow up the
mercenaries into their rigid hierarchy. Definitely not an
appealing prospect.

The Amatukaze's hatred of the other two enclaves
would make them more than willing to see the others
crushed, and they would probably pay well to see it done.
But Vost had dealt with religious fanatics before, and

knew that once the mission was accomplished, they would expect him to continue to embrace their cause. That was fine with Vost, as long as the cause aligned with his interests, which, in this case, did not sound very likely.

The Usugumo group was a real possibility. They sounded amoral, willing to pay in cash for what they wanted. And Vost could use offers from the others as a base line for his dealings with them. The negotiations would be sweet. He rubbed his hands with prospective delight.

Takuda did not see it that way. He'd been thinking about the matter ever since hearing about the other humans from Dakodo. Here had been the perfect opportunity for a group of warriors to build the perfect bushido-based society far from the hurly burly of the Inner Sphere. They could have established the traditional samurai society of warriors and workers, taking all the traditions to their natural conclusion. But that was not what they had done. No, they had fractured their small society into hostile groups. He and the others would have to act as spiritual guides for the original humans, showing them back to the true way, the path of harmony.

He looked up at the circle of faces that surrounded him in the headquarters bunker. "We must move slowly," he said. "There is much that we can do here, but we must lead these people away from their hostility to the true path of harmony. We must become the moral exemplars they seem to have lacked. But we must go slowly. We must build a society that the Draconis Combine, should they ever find us, would be proud to call its own."

His statement was greeted by stunned silence. "Like hell we will," said Vost, who promptly turned on his heel and stomped out of the bunker.

18

Dawn came gray, as much because of the low-hanging clouds and misting rain as because of the mood in the camp. Even the campfires seemed unable to blaze brightly. Sodden, sullen, gray.

The weather matched Takuda's humor exactly. He sat in the earthen command bunker, pushed back into the corner farthest from the low opening. The darkest corner, to match his mood.

The events of the evening had come as a surprise. Not just Vost's reaction, which he should have expected. Even the reaction of the others should have been predictable. The one who had surprised Takuda most was himself. He had no idea what had made him suddenly proclaim the idea of serving as moral exemplars to the planet's inhabitants. The words coming out of his mouth had been a shock even to him. Never in his life had he thought of himself in that way. It was against his heredity and his training. He sat and thought about what had happened.

His musings were interrupted by *So-cho* Saitan Yura, who stood before him, waiting for the DEST commander to acknowledge his presence. But Takuda felt no pressing need to do so. He would acknowledge the senior sergeant when he was ready. If the sergeant's mission had been really urgent, the man would have announced himself. Takuda looked up and scrutinized the professional soldier.

Saitan Yura had spent his whole adult life in the forces

of the Draconis Combine. There was no way of telling how old he was, his face was as smooth as a young man's. Yet Takuda knew that some of the *so-cho*'s decorations dated from campaigns of forty years earlier. He had been in the service as long as Takuda had been alive. "Yes, *So-cho*. You wished to see me?"

"Pilot Vost has requested to speak to you."

"A request? Pilot Vost has never been so formal with me before. This must be important. Did he say anything to indicate what it might be?"

"No, *Sho-sa*," said Yura. "The lights burned late in the hull of the DropShip last night, but there were no sounds of working."

It was typical of the senior sergeant, thought Takuda, to offer information without comment. The mercenaries must have been talking, but the sergeant could not know that directly and so he would not venture a supposition. He gave only what he knew. "Is he waiting for me now?" Takuda asked.

"Yes, *Sho-sa*. He and the rest of his mercenaries are outside."

Takuda nodded. Rising to his feet, he felt the stiffness in his joints. It was hell getting old. Men of his culture were supposed to be able to sit in the lotus position for hours without discomfort, a feat Takuda had never been able to master. Even as a young man he'd found sitting in chairs much preferable to sitting cross-legged on the floor. He waited a moment for his joints to stop protesting. He was not going to let Vost see him hobbling.

The mercenary commander was waiting for Takuda, who could see that the meeting, called formally by Vost, was going to be confrontational. The mercenary leader had brought along all his people to add weight to whatever argument he was about to make. The *sho-sa* glanced around to see which of his own people were in the area. It would be an admission of weakness for him to call the whole team together, but he wouldn't mind having some support if needed.

Yura was still at his side, standing one pace to the rear and two to his left, where he would remain until released. The *so-cho* had sensed the strain in the air, and would support his commander. Clustered on top of the bunker were the three members of the team's heavy weapons section. *Gun-so* Ariake Sanae was demonstrating the correct method of field-stripping a Pleno-Hamata short-range missile launcher. The weapon had some distinctive characteristics that required special attention, but Takuda was sure that everyone in the heavy weapons section, as well as every other member of the DEST team, was completely familiar with those idiosyncrasies. Sanae had probably decided to hold the class on top of the command bunker for reasons that went well beyond training.

Gun-so Ariake Sanae was a mystery to her commander. Of all the people on his team she was the one about whom Takuda knew the least. That she was competent was not in doubt; no one could become a member of the DEST special forces who was not. But she remained an enigma. Tall, willowy, and with a face cut from alabaster, she seemed to exist in a world of her own. As far as Takuda knew, she had no close friends among the rest of the team, not even Andi Holland, who made friends with everyone. Sanae ran the heavy weapons section firmly, fairly and with high professional standards. She observed all the religious rituals with punctilious accuracy. And that was all Takuda knew. The other two members of the section had taken on some of her characteristics.

Because heavy weapons people seldom functioned as a team, they tended to be loners. Certainly *Gun-so* Ariake Sanae was. *Go-cho* Oite Inaduma, the team's antitank expert, also fit the mold. Even though he'd been decorated for bravery more than any member of the team, they had been more acts of individual heroism than sacrifice for another. Thus, Inaduma was a three-time recipient of the Bushido Blade, and had even been recommended for the Order of the Dragon, but had never been mentioned for the White Starburst. The Starburst was bestowed on those who saved the lives of other soldiers or civilians through their heroism. Inaduma was more likely to go it alone in combat, stalking armored fighting vehicles or 'Mechs for the sheer pleasure of it. Some would call that foolhardy rather than brave.

Joto hei Johan Miranda was the team sniper, and he had the sniper mentality. Once he had remained in an open field for twelve hours without moving in order to get a kill. Absolutely stationary even to the point of not emptying his bladder. Not only was the man a model of self-discipline, he was also the best marksman Takuda had ever seen. The stalking kill was his specialty, but he could fire on the move as well. Takuda had once seen Miranda shooting rats from the hip, hitting them through the eyes as the little beasts scampered from their nests. He'd done that, the man later explained, because hitting their bodies would have ruined the meat.

With his weapons people on the command bunker and Yura behind him, Takuda faced Garber Vost.

"I've been thinking about what you said yesterday," Vost began in his most polite and servile manner, "and you just may be right."

Takuda, braced for a fierce attack, was astonished by this abrupt change from the mercenary's usual sneering bravado. He recovered quickly, determined to remain on guard. He waited for the other shoe to drop.

"There is no reason why we should not be teachers to these people," continued Vost. "Not only do we have weapons that make us superior, but we also have the benefit of five hundred years of society's traditions, which these people obviously lack. That they have fragmented into warring enclaves is foolish. They would have been much better off working together in peace and harmony."

Takuda nodded but did not speak, sensing that Vost was planning to take this line of thought in another direction entirely. Another motive was lurking in there somewhere.

"Harmony is very important," said Vost, standing with

his hands clasped behind his back rather than in the usual hands-on-hips pose. "It is what we should all strive to achieve in our interpersonal relationships as well as in the greater relationships between cities and states. It is the most noble of all life's goals."

"I agree with you, Pilot Vost. Harmony is important, even though life also demands of us duty, honor, and loyalty. But, yes, harmony is a high ideal."

"If we are to teach harmony to the people of Osio, Amatukaze, and Usugumo, would it not be appropriate for harmony to exist among those who would lead the way?" Vost was smiling a soft, winsome smile, the very essence of what he spoke.

"A most noble thought, Pilot Vost."

"You should call me Garber, *Sho-sa* Takuda."

"Thank you, Pilot Vost." Takuda had no wish to encourage familiarity. Vost was quite familiar enough already. "I'm glad you have decided to support the wishes of the whole team in our dealings with the other humans. And the aliens as well." Takuda threw in the mention of the Tetatae to make sure Vost understood that more was at stake than just the enclaves. He saw Vost flinch at the mention of the Tetatae. Good, Takuda thought. Perhaps he will be a little off balance.

Vost hardly missed a beat. "And you agree that to achieve harmony we must do the greatest good for the greatest number. Yes?" Vost nodded as he spoke. It was an old rhetorical trick, and whether Vost was aware of doing it or not, he accomplished it to perfection. The first part of the trick came in telling the listener what he wanted to hear. This was accented by nodding the head in agreement with one's own statements.

"Good for the greatest number is important." Takuda knew the rhetorical tricks even if Vost did not. He cut to the point. "Where is this going?"

"If we are to do the greatest good for the greatest number, perhaps we should ask the number what they want. I suggest that the program you proposed yesterday be put forward along with any other proposals. Then we let the people who will be affected have their say in the matter."

"I agree," said Collis Brank, stepping forward. "I say we listen to all of it and then vote on what to do."

"And are there other matters on which we should take a vote, Pilot Vost?" Takuda's eyes narrowed; he could see the point of the meeting coming closer.

"Well, now that you mention it, yes. Perhaps we should decide, by vote, of course, who is to be the leader of this group."

"Do you have someone in mind?"

"I'd like to put forward the name of Reston Bannin."

"And I'd like to put forward the name of Garber Vost," interjected Brank.

"And of course your name as well, *Sho-sa* Takuda," said Vost with a smile.

"'And then all of us would stand for election," said Takuda. "Is that your plan? And then the new leader would tell us all what to do about the humans and the aliens. Is that it?"

"I think you've got it," said Vost. He put his hands on his hips.

It was a clever plan, thought Takuda. There were eleven members of the DEST team and only ten mercenaries. That would seem to assure Takuda's victory in any election. But the mercenaries had signed on with Vost because they believed their interests lay with him, so there was no reason to think that they wouldn't do so again. That would leave the decision in the hands of the ship crews. With Bannin's name in the pot, they might be assumed to go that way, but Takuda could not be sure. The crew members would be willing to vote, but hardly likely to want to throw their votes away on a sure loser. Vost would need only a couple of their votes to become the group's acknowledged leader. The mercenary had obviously been doing some politicking during the night and knew what kind of support he could muster.

"I say we take a vote right now," said Collis Brank. "Let's get it over with it so we can get on with other things."

Neatly done, thought Takuda. There would be no time for him to talk to the ship crews even if he were so inclined. They'd used the argument about harmony to trap him. Very neat. He couldn't think of any way to get out of the situation without establishing himself as a dictator. Though he didn't want to do that, he was equally unwilling to see Vost take absolute power in the group. Yura would say nothing to interfere with what was happening. Takuda was trapped, and he knew it.

"Like all good ideas," came the voice of Johan Miranda from the top of the command bunker, "your thoughts have much merit, Pilot Vost." Takuda turned to face the weapons team on the roof behind him. Was Miranda going to desert him? he wondered. "I would suggest," continued the team sniper, "that we all do some thinking about it. There is no need to make a decision immediately. Wouldn't you agree?" Miranda was sitting cross-legged in the dirt, a position that was not ostensibly very intimidating, yet a very stable one from which to shoot. The sniper cradled his Zeus heavy rifle in his lap, his meaning quite clear.

Vost looked startled by the comment. His hands dropped from his hips and he took a step backward into Brank, who had been sheltering behind him. "That's fine for now," he said with a soft snarl. "But it will happen sooner or later. Count on it."

=== 19 ===

Vost was angry, as angry as he had ever been in his life. He stomped his way back to the DropShip. Not even the soft cooing of Michelle Guardine, his current inamorata, could deflect his anger. He swept her aside with a wave of an arm, and she crept away bruised and chagrined. Meanwhile, Vost ground his teeth and plotted. The other mercenaries stood around at a respectful distance and waited for the inevitable explosion. "We'll just have to blow that bastard away," announced Vost. "We get the 'Mechs out of the blasted ship and just blow him and the rest of his team away."

Elizabeth Hoond, first mate of the abandoned JumpShip *Telendine*, inched forward from the circle. "I've been looking at the interior of the DropShip. Based on what we've done, and what needs to be done, we could have the 'Mechs out in about two days."

"We could blast our way out," interjected Kendall Pesht. The mood among the mercenaries was changing. They were beginning to see possibilities rather than problems.

"They'd hear us," said Hoond. "They have a guard posted all night, supposedly to protect us from the aliens. The guard would be sure to alert the others. 'Mechs don't blast anything without making some noise."

"So they hear us," said Vost. "So what? If we move quickly, we can have some or all the 'Mechs out of the hold before the DEST crud can react. The 'Mechs have I/R sensors. We can see in the dark."

"So can they," put in Collis Brank. "Infantry weapons in the hands of normal troops are hopeless against 'Mechs, but we're up against a DEST team. They're specially trained for anti-'Mech work. They love it. And they have special weapons for the job. Have you ever seen what well-handled infantry weapons can do to a 'Mech at close range?" Brank shuddered. "That SRM launcher they were working on today can fire infernos. And they've got 'em. I've seen them. The last thing I want is to be in any 'Mech that gets hit by an inferno."

The other pilots nodded agreement. Fire was one of a MechWarrior's great terrors. The thought of being trapped inside a 'Mech cockpit while the machine burned to death was every 'Mech pilot's nightmare. There were too many stories of pilots incinerated, too many stories that began, 'I had a friend who . . . ," then ended with how that someone had been unable to fight free of the flames and unable to eject because the fire had disabled the machine's ejection mechanism.

"Then we take out the SRMs," said Vost. "We've got to get the weapons people first. And Takuda. Decapitate the team. Get him, and the rest won't know what to do. By then we'll be out and running things. Blow them all away."

Vost folded his arms in contemplation of the thought. "Just think of it," he mused. "We take out the DEST team, and then we have it all. We can cut any deal we want with any of the enclaves. We go with the highest bidder. Not the strongest, but the one who gives us the most. We can run this place for as long as we want. We'll be so powerful, nothing can stop us. Tell 'em, Seagroves. Tell 'em about the enclaves. From a MechWarrior's point of view. What do we need to know about them?"

All heads turned toward Brian Seagroves. Of the mercenaries, he was the only one who had seen the enclaves, the only one who could speak with authority. The big man shuffled forward. At last he would be the center of attention, as he deserved. "They're weak," he said. "They have complex defensive works, but none of it means anything. Lots of walls and ditches. They don't even have abatis. The only thing their defenses are designed to stop are really weak ground forces. They don't have anything that can stop a 'Mech. We'd walk right through them. And they don't have anything that flies. Nothing. There's something in their culture, their legends, that says they mustn't fly. Maybe someone has tried it, but they don't permit it anymore. With the LAM and the *Panther*'s jump ability, we can scare hell out of anyone. We win every time."

"As long as none of the DEST gets involved," said Vost.

"So we take care of DEST." Seagroves was angry at being interrupted. This was his show, and he didn't need Vost interfering. Seagroves had already decided which enclave he was going to join: that of the Usugumo. They were the ones with the money, the gold. He didn't care about fighting for a bunch of militaristic types. He'd had enough of Takuda and the way his people followed orders. Hard to corrupt those stiff-necked types. The religious fanatics of Amatukaze were just as bad, rigid in another way. No, he'd go with Usugumo no matter what the others decided. And he didn't have to listen to Vost pontificate about making choices. "We go with the best offer. I'm done with people who don't understand the value of money." He turned on Vost and glared at him. "From what I saw, the merchants are in the most need. We go with them and be done with it."

Vost was surprised by this speech. Seagroves, usually so docile, was suddenly showing traits that could lead to problems down the road. He'd have to be more careful in dealing with the LAM pilot in the future. But he knew which button to push for Seagroves. Money was all the man cared for, a fact Vost would use to his own advantage. He waited now to see if Seagroves was done. When the LAM pilot said no more, the mercenary leader spoke again. "Pesht, Goodall, Brank. Check your 'Mechs. See what needs to be done to get them free. Not completely free. Just enough so that they can blast their way out of the cargo hold. Take your techs with you.

"Guardine, check my 'Mech. Make sure the jump packs are clear to fire. I can take the *Panther* out through the top of the opening. Seagroves, I've got a special job for you." He turned to the LAM pilot.

"You're the only one who's free right now," Vost said conspiratorially, taking Seagroves by the elbow in a show of brotherhood and good faith. "When all this goes down, you'll have to play the lead. We can't do anything without you." Vost saw Seagroves visibly swell at the compliment. This guy is so transparent, he thought. I can play him like a cheap harp. "When I give the word, you hit their command bunker with the lasers and the machine guns. Just blow it away."

"Without warning?" It was Goodall. She looked upset at the prospect.

"Hell, yes," snapped Vost. "It's them or us. This is no time to worry about niceties. We'll give them what they deserve. Do you think that slant-eyed Takuda would give us a chance if he thought he could get away with it? I don't trust him a bit."

"As a matter of fact," said Goodall stepping forward, "I do think he'd give us a chance. He's had plenty of time to take a whack at us, and he's certainly had call to do you. But he hasn't. I think he's an honorable man. I, for one, trust him." She didn't add the words, "more than I trust you," but the implication was there.

"You can believe any way you like, Holly," said Vost, not hiding the menace in his voice. "Just as long as you do as you're told and stay out of our way. If you get squeamish, close your eyes till it's over."

The teams broke up and began their tasks. Seagroves climbed onto the back of his *Phoenix Hawk* and began his first-level maintenance checks. Underos Yaputi, his tech-

nician, stood on the ground and called off the checklist as
Seagroves made the inspection. It was mostly sham.
Seagroves was actually reconnecting the laser controls,
broken before he had flown his first mission. He'd done
that on Takuda's command, and the weapons system had
not been reactivated since. There had been no need. Now,
however, the lasers had a mission, one, chuckled Seagroves to himself, that Takuda would find most interesting. Yaputi called off the list and Seagroves responded.
The pilot cleared the ammunition belts for the heavy machine guns. He was ready. All he needed to do was make
a slight torso twist and align the I/R sight on the command bunker. That would be easy

Inside the disintegrating hull of the DropShip, the other
'Mech pilots were also going about their work. Guardine
checked the jump packs on the back of the *Panther,* making sure they were fully charged and that the back-blast
area was as clear as possible. When Vost fired the 'Mech
out the top of the cargo bay, no one wanted any FOD.
Foreign Object Damage was a part of being a 'Mech pilot, but none of them was fool enough to ask for such an
accident. A steel box driven into a knee servo could
freeze a 'Mech in place at just the wrong time. Best to
keep the area as clear as possible.

Holly Goodall and Sagiri Johnson worked on her *Locust.* With the debris around the light 'Mech cleared
away, all that was left now was to release the holding
shackles. Johnson and Goodall worked in silence, each
one deep in his or her own thoughts. Working beside
them on the other *Locust,* Brank and Panda were equally
absorbed in freeing that 'Mech. Goodall and Johnson
moved to the opposite side of the *Locust.*

"What do you think of the plan?" Johnson said, almost
adding "Sir" to the question—an old habit that died hard.

"It's a plan," said Goodall with a shrug.

"I'm not crazy about the complete execution." Johnson's statement was absolutely noncommittal. Anyone

hearing it and not seeing the look in his eyes would have thought nothing of it.

"You mean murder?"

"That's not what I said."

"I know that's not what you said." Goodall's voice was low enough not to carry beyond them. "I just wonder what you meant."

Sagiri Johnson worked silently on the restraining shackle, applying himself diligently to the task of removing some microscopic speck of dirt in the release mechanism. It took quite a while. Goodall waited for him to finish. "I wasn't too pleased with the 'slant-eyed' comment," the technician said finally.

"That's typical Vost," Goodall said dryly. "He thinks he's superior because he's a MechWarrior, and because of his race, and because he's a man. Typical. Sorry, Sagiri. Present company excepted."

The technician smiled at this woman who could pilot a *Locust* with the best of the best. "Don't worry. I know what you mean. And I agree with what you said about Takuda. I like the guy, even if he's a little rigid. And I'm not saying that because I'm a man or because my mother was Oriental. I just like him."

"Well. He'll be dead by dawn if Vost has his way."

"I'm not real happy about that, either." Johnson gazed off into the depths of the cargo hold. "He doesn't need to die, and certainly not that way." The technician stared at nothing. "I'm not even sure it wouldn't be better for Vost to get it instead."

Goodall felt the tension in the cargo hold. They were talking treason. Treason of the worst kind. They had signed on with Vost because he was a leader who would get them the best deal. Now they were talking about changing sides. Was it for the better deal? Or was it because some honor in each of them had not been satisfied? Goodall looked directly into the eyes of her tech. "Do you want to warn Takuda?"

"Do you mean me or us?"

"I guess I mean us."

"Then, yes. I think we should warn him."

"Who does it?"

"You've got to stay with your 'Mech," Johnson said after a moment. "I'm the one who can get away without creating too much suspicion. Let me do it."

20

The dripping darkness added to the sense of espionage and secrecy. No wind blew across the open field where the diverse band of humans had camped, and the gentle, misting rain obscured the tall trees beyond, cloaking the encampment further in an air of conspiracy. Within the darkness, vague shapes moved stealthily on missions of equal urgency and secrecy, each one avoiding, as if by choreographed movement, the presence of the others. In the darkness beyond the circle of grass marking the camp zone, the forest teemed with a secret movement of its own, the Tetatae creeping closer and closer to the human zone.

Had the DEST guards been alert in their security positions on the perimeter, they would have sensed the advance of the Tetatae. But they were busy with other matters. The moment darkness had fallen, changing the gloom of daylight fading under low clouds to a stygian blackness, the DEST sections had begun to move. They did not move fast, and they did not move far, but began to gradually slip away from their established positions to rally around the command bunker.

Takuda had left his position as soon as it was full dark. He was gone before the glowing shape of the LAM pilot, seen through the I/R scanner, scrambled up the side of the LAM and took his place in the cockpit. George Bustoe, the DEST headquarters clerk, watched the glow of the internal power supply begin to flow into the 'Mech's control, propulsion, and weapons systems. He reported the activity to Takuda, who was shielded from the prying eyes of the LAM's I/R sensors. Not only was his form masked by the rising bulk of the bunker, but like every other member of the DEST team, he was wearing an I/R suppression suit.

The area where the human survivors were camped was several hundred meters wide by six kilometers long. The DropShip and the *Telendine*'s lifeboat had grounded at one end, just short of the trees that barred further passage. The security arrangements they'd established put the DEST headquarters some five hundred meters behind the DropShip hulk, with the two light sections spread out in a wide vee behind it. The weapons section had been separated from the others, held near the headquarters as a reserve force. Security for the DropShip had been provided by the mercenaries and the ship crews. Takuda had not deemed it the best possible arrangement, but the plan had suited the various personalities involved. Now the arrangement suddenly became an asset.

The topography of the area permitted anyone on the DropShip to see only the DEST command bunker. Even the LAM, positioned near the forward edge of the DropShip's port wing, could see only the DEST headquarters and the position of the western section. But it could not see both with the same accuracy. The result was that Brian Seagroves, sitting tense in the cockpit of his *Phoenix Hawk,* had a clear I/R signature from the command position, but only a faint blue blur from the section area. He could see the heat signature from the entrance of the headquarters, but Yura had made sure that the bunker's stove was going full bore. The heat that radiated from the mouth of the bunker virtually blocked out any faint I/R noise from the surrounding area. Even Bustoe, lying on the top of the bunker itself, was invisible. And anyone moving along the eastern side of the ridge that marked the center of the position would be equally hidden.

Takuda was in a quandary about the operation. If this had been a standard DEST mission, winning would have meant the elimination of every mercenary around the 'Mechs; they would leave no survivors. But this was not standard. Takuda had no desire to kill all the mercenaries. They had done nothing to earn such retribution. There had only been the report that Vost was planning to break the 'Mechs out of the hull and make a run for the enclaves. They'd also been warned that the LAM was to destroy the command bunker, but that seemed logical. Takuda would have done the same if given the opportunity. But he had no wish to destroy the 'Mechs and their pilots. Takuda knew only too well that he would need them in his dealings with the enclaves. Thus he had ordered his people to use non-deadly force. If deadly force became necessary, only Takuda would give the order.

The attacking force consisted of the two light teams commanded by Arsenault and Knyte. Sanae stayed at the CP with the heavy section. From there she would be able to direct the SRM, loaded with inferno missiles, at any heavy target that appeared. She also had Miranda and his heavy rifle available to eliminate individual targets. The heavy team was the only one armed with deadly weapons; the other DEST members were carrying tranq guns.

Approaching the starboard side of the DropShip, the DEST team fanned out. Takuda and the headquarters section were in the center, with Knyte and his section to the right, Arsenault and his to the left. They crept through the grass, scanning the target with their I/R sensor goggles. One glowing life form stood out clearly against the black of night. It was Reston Bannin, Master and Commander of the late JumpShip *Telendine,* standing guard. He was seated on the top of the DropShip, his legs dangling into the gaping wound that had been cut in the ship's side to release the LAM. His guard position was most awkward for the assaulting DEST.

Takuda signaled Knyte to take Bannin out of the equation. Holland moved silently to scale the nose of the DropShip. The rest of the DEST team watched her creep over the battered ogive and along the top of the hull. Perhaps it was some water on the hull or maybe a spot of lubricant left by one of the mercenaries during the cutting operation. Whatever it was, her felt-soled shoes suddenly made a noise. Not much of one, and not one that would have been noticed during normal activity. But on this night, with no wind to mask the sounds, the slight squeak of her boots on the titanium alloy skin screeched like a banshee. Bannin twisted to face her.

Before he could grasp the situation, before he could open his mouth to give the alarm, Holland reacted. In one swift gesture she brought the tranq rifle from its carry position on her back, leveled the weapon, and fired two quick shots. One would have been enough for the JumpShip skipper; the second was just insurance.

The soft thunk-thunk of the rifle echoed through the gaping cavity of the DropShip's cargo bay, unheard by the workers on the deck ten meters below. From his post on the outer skin, Reston Bannin had a momentary vision of a figure swathed in black, then his vision clouded and he lost control of his muscles. He reached out to brace himself against the skin of the ship, but his arms had lost their ability to respond. He toppled forward into the opening. Holland reached for him to stop his fall, but she was too far away. As if in slow motion, the body of the JumpShip skipper dropped onto the inner cargo deck of the ship. If the reports of the tranq rifle had passed unnoticed, the crash of the falling body did not.

As Bannin took his dive into the black hole of the cargo bay, Takuda signaled the rest of the DEST team forward. Up and running toward the jagged rent in the side of the DropShip, they carried their tranq guns at the ready. The weapons were best at extremely close ranges, and Takuda knew they would have to get inside the hull of the vessel to have any chance of subduing the mercenaries.

Inside the hull, the thud of the falling body was amplified as the sound rebounded from the metal interior. Vost, halfway up the right side of the *Panther,* froze as he reached for the next handhold. He'd seen the body dropping out the corner of his eye; the form of Reston Bannin now lay curled beside the left foot of his 'Mech. Then he heard the pounding feet of the charging DEST team. The game was up, and he knew it. "We're out of here!" he shouted as he scrambled toward the *Panther*'s cockpit. Below him the dark interior bloomed with light.

Iliomoso Panda was standing with his back to the jagged opening in the hull. He sensed rather than saw the DEST team charge across the open ground and under the wing of the DropShip. He had his Sternsnacht autopistol holstered on his right hip, and he drew it as he turned to face the darkness. Behind him the interior glazon lighting system flared into life, bathing the area around the opening in brilliant blue clarity. Panda saw a black figure silhouetted in the glare. Without hesitation, he drew the heavy pistol, raised it to face level, and fired. The flash of the pistol erased any remaining night vision the technician might have had. The dark figure went down.

Inside the cargo deck the MechWarriors were settling into the command seats of their 'Mechs. Hands raced in well-accustomed gestures across the master switches and toggles. The cockpit recorders, sensors, and displays bloomed to life. Down below, technicians drove heavy mauls into the last of the restraining shackles. The 'Mechs were free, but they still did not move. None of the pilots would engage their drive systems until the entire checklist was completed. Even if the pilot had just done a third-level diagnostic and maintenance check, he would follow the entire initiation sequence. There were no old, bold, pilots.

The DEST team came pouring through the gap in the hull, their tranq rifles discarded in favor of lasers. Seeing

Yura go down under the blast of a heavy pistol, Takuda knew that the mercenaries were playing for keeps. He, too, would have to up the ante. He warned his people to be careful, still hoping to avoid having a pile of dead when the attack was over. Then Arsenault and his team scrambled across the DropShip's starboard wing and rolled through the opening into the brilliant light of the cargo hold.

Inside the *Panther* Vost's cockpit instruments glowed green. Twisting the 'Mech's torso to the right, he searched for possible targets. With nothing but a PPC and an SRM launcher, it would be disastrous for him to fire in the confined space of the cargo hold. His weapons made the *Panther* a powerful 'Mech, but at ranges of only a few meters he'd have been better off with machine guns. He saw Pesht and his *Javelin* begin to move away from the bulkhead where the 'Mech had been secured. The *Javelin* was in the same situation as the *Panther.* Its heavy load of SRMs did not make it a good fighting machine in a confined space. But, like the *Panther,* it could jump clear of the area. The *Locust*s, however, would have to walk out.

One of the DEST team was slinking around the feet of the shuffling *Javelin,* a grapple rod for attacking the 'Mech in his hand. Vost thought momentarily of firing his PPC at the figure, then changed his mind. That was Pesht's problem. "Man at your feet," he warned. "Goodall. Brank. Get 'em with your machine guns."

Outside the DropShip, Seagroves saw the bloom of light and heard the warning. As he triggered the pair of medium lasers on the arms of his LAM, the command bunker erupted in a brilliant ball of white fire. That'll take care of you, Takuda, he thought. He smiled, but the smile vanished as an inferno missile arced out of the darkness and struck the ground at the feet of the *Phoenix Hawk.* He felt his heart jump. Outta here; that's what Vost had said. Sounds like a good idea, thought Seagroves. I'd rather be rich than dead. The twin Allied AVRTech 125 jump jets roared into life as another inferno slammed into the ground where the 'Mech had been. "Adios, suckers," whispered Seagroves as the *Phoenix Hawk* lifted into the air.

Inside the cargo area the streams of machine gun bullets crisscrossed the open area. Bodies, caught in the deadly hail, ricocheted off the bulkheads in a macabre dance. Holly Goodall swung her twin heavy machine guns across the white void, searching for targets. Centered in her cross hairs she saw the rigid shape of a DEST soldier. She squeezed the triggers, taking up the slack. But then she saw that it was Takuda. Making an instant decision, she continued to traverse instead of firing. To her right she saw Brank's *Locust* making a similar sweep through the cargo bay, his twin guns stopping on the same target. Without hesitation, Goodall swung her 'Mech's torso as far to the right as it would go, taking a step forward with her left leg to complete the traverse. The cockpit of the other *Locust* steadied in her targeting cross hairs. She punched the firing button.

Standing at the opening of the cargo bay, Vost knew there was nothing he could do here, and he'd only be cut to ribbons if he stayed. Firing the *Panther*'s jump jets, he rose up and out of the combat. On his secondary screen he saw his techs also making for the woods. Inside the cargo bay the recumbent body of Reston Bannin vaporized under the searing plasma of the *Panther*'s jump jets, then the 'Mech was clear of the DropShip. Vost hit the ground running, the *Javelin* right behind him. It had taken Pesht one step to center himself in the same opening, then he had fired the smaller Rawlings jets and lifted out after his commander.

The two 'Mechs made contact in the darkness outside. For a moment they contemplated going back to free the *Locust*s, but their calls brought no response. The lights in cargo hold blinked out. With the LAM already gaining altitude, Vost called Pesht to his side, and the two 'Mechs began lumbering westward toward the enclaves.

=== 21 ===

Parker Davud crept through the sudden stillness. He had sheltered in the access crawlway during the combat that had unexpectedly engulfed his DropShip. Not that it was much of a DropShip anymore, he thought—or that it was even his anymore. He wasn't quite sure why he had been in the crawlway between the flight deck and the main cargo area, but something had driven him there early in the evening. Perhaps, he thought, it was his unwillingness to participate in the Vost-Brank scheme to eliminate Takuda and the other DEST members.

The whole thing had seemed like a good idea when they'd first talked it out, but the more he thought about it, the less he wanted any part of it. He didn't care, one way or the other, who was to be the leader of their little society, but he couldn't accept violence as the means of choosing that person. Vost's idea of putting it to a vote was a good one, though Davud wasn't quite sure whom he'd vote for if it came to that. Vost had a lot of good ideas, but Takuda seemed an honorable man.

Now Davud lay in the access passage listening for the sounds that would tell him what was going on. He'd heard the roar of the jump jets when the 'Mechs had fired them in the cargo hold. The shock had been enough to make the derelict hulk of the DropShip tremble from top to bottom. Then had come a series of explosions from outside as well. Now there was silence. He strained to hear any sound of movement. When no one came, he continued to crawl toward the emergency lighting panel access port that hung at the end of the passage. With his hand resting on the switches, Davud paused for a moment, wondering if it was a good idea to illuminate the scene. He didn't know the situation, and light might just exacerbate an already potential disaster. He held his breath and threw the switches.

The soft, blue-green emergency lights flooded from the back-up illumination panels. Carefully raising his head, Davud scanned the cargo hold, but the lingering skeins of gossamer smoke gently eddying in the air made it hard to see much. That the cargo hold was a jumble of twisted frames and broken spars confused him at first. Smoking bales of unidentifiable debris were scattered across the deck and piled around the two 'Mechs that still stood forlornly against the rear bulkhead. Davud stared at the 'Mechs, trying to figure out what made them suddenly look different when they'd always looked identical to him before. Perhaps, he thought, it was only because he was viewing them from the new angle.

Then something moving on the deck drew his attention. He studied the area, trying to catch it again. Then he saw it. It was a man crawling ever so slowly across the metal plating. He was leaving a distinct trail of something dark and light behind him. Davud felt his stomach rise in his mouth, the bitter taste of his own gorge pressing against his teeth. The black trail was blood, the light stuff was the man's entrails.

Another man bent over the crawling figure. Davud saw that he, like the wounded man, was dressed from head to foot in black. Then he noticed other black-draped figures picking their way through the rubble. The DEST team held the cargo area.

Takuda straightened up from his position over Roland Dupe. There wasn't much he could do for him, even with the advanced medical systems they had with them. Dupe had been climbing one of the 'Mechs, using a grapple rod to reach a delicate arm joint or perhaps the jet propulsion unit that gave the 'Mech its jump capability. But the 'Mech had made its move before the DEST commando could plant his explosive charges. It had been a brave but foolhardy move on the part of Dupe, yet just the sort of action the man would try. All Takuda could do now was to make him as comfortable as possible.

He searched for the wounded man's personal medikit, which was normally strapped to the calf of a DEST member's inside right leg. But Takuda found no right leg, at least nothing where the medikit should have been. He would have searched the other leg, but it too was gone below the knee.

Roland Dupe squirmed on toward the opening in the hull of the DropShip, but Takuda reached down and restrained him. "It's all right, Dupe. You're safe here."

Dupe rolled over onto his back and stared blankly at his commander. Takuda could see the effort as he tried to focus. The man's eyes cleared and he looked up into those of Takuda kneeling beside him. He reached up and grasped the collar of the black battle suit. "I'm done," he gasped. "Isn't that the way it always is for me? I was just doing my job and the others didn't help. I'm always the one who gets it in the shorts."

Griping to the last, though Takuda. Yes, he mused, Roland Dupe was done. There was nothing anyone here could do for him. "You did well," he said. "No one could have done better."

Dupe shuddered as a wave of pain swept over him. Takuda could see that the wounds were not restricted to his legs alone. The man had been gutted like a perch, split from crotch to chin. His whole interior was pouring from what was left of his battle suit. The dying man put both hands on the collar of his commander. "Finish ... me," he gasped. "Finish me." He fell back against the metallic plating of the deck.

Takuda rose and stared, unseeing, at the fallen soldier.

156 Peter L. Rice

There was nothing he could do to help him, nothing he could do to ease the pain. He had syringes of anesthesia in his own medikit, but there was not enough painkiller in all of DEST to alleviate what Dupe was feeling. The wretched, twisted face looked up at him, the eyes silent and imploring. Without seeing, without even being fully aware of what he was doing, Takuda drew the needler pistol from the holster at the small of his back. Almost in slow motion he brought the weapon around and pointed it into the face of the wounded man. He could not fire. Dupe was lying on the plates, his back arched in pain, his eyes closed.

Then the eyes of the wounded man popped open and he saw his fate above him. For an instant he stared at the pistol, knew what was about to happen. A look of fear spread over the grimace of pain. Then he relaxed and looked into the face of his commander. Dupe smiled and nodded. Takuda squeezed the trigger, firing the entire clip.

Takuda stood for a moment at the side of the dead man. Around him was the chaos of a battle won, or at least a battle not lost. Two of the 'Mechs had escaped, but the two light *Locust*s were still in the cargo hold. His team had been hit hard, though. With Dupe now dead at his feet, that was three DEST members gone. Saitan Yura had died at the mouth of the cargo hold, taking a shot from a heavy slug pistol through the face. And Oite Inaduma had made one heroic charge too many with his antitank weapon. While rising, the LAM had hit the man with a random shot as he climbed out of the melee. And now Dupe was gone too. The wounded, including Takuda himself, would have to be attended to. The weight of leadership heavy on his shoulders, he holstered the pistol and moved away.

The DEST team, the surviving mercenary techs, and the two remaining crew members from the ships spent a night filled with tension, fear, and small alarms. They all expected the mercenary 'Mechs to return to finish the job.

There were two BattleMechs still within the cargo hold as well as the few remaining technicians who had failed or chosen not to flee when the others had made their break for freedom. With the heavy weapons section reduced, the defense against a 'Mech attack would have been desperate at best. But the 'Mechs never came.

There was also the hovering presence of the Tetatae, who the DEST members now had the time to discover lingering in the fringes of the heavy woods. There was no way of telling if they were hostile, friendly, or just observers, only that they were there. Takuda decided to keep a watch on them but to do nothing that would precipitate any kind of action. The Tetatae were still there when the first faint rays of the morning sun broke over the tops of the eastern trees. It promised to be a fine day with only a few puffy clouds from the front that had moved through the area.

In full daylight the situation was further revealed. Takuda still had nine DEST members but those three were wounded: Dana Lost, Swalen Horg, and himself. Mark Jacobs and Parker Davud of the ships' crew were still around, but Takuda didn't know how valuable they would be. Of the mercenaries, only Holly Goodall was uninjured. Now, there, thought Takuda, was an enigma. Goodall had warned them of the impending combat, and she had, by the evidence, taken care of one of the 'Mech pilots. The shattered cockpit of the *Locust* bore mute testimony to that. But he was not sure of her status now. Two technicians had also remained behind, but both might have escaped with the others had they not been wounded. Sagiri Johnson, the chief tech and, like Goodall, one of those who had passed the warning, had been injured by the jump-jet blast of one of the departing 'Mechs. Underos Yaputi carried a wound from a laser rifle in his right arm, although how he had come by it was a mystery. He might have been hit by a random burst from either the DEST team or the fleeing mercenaries, although Takuda had a tendency to discount random shots by his people. DEST members did not take random shots.

The major task before him now was to remove the two *Locust*s from the DropShip. If the mercenaries decided to come back and finish the job, the DEST team would need their own 'Mechs. The *Locust*s were not as powerful as either the *Panther* or the LAM, but they could hold their own against the *Javelin*. Working together, they could also provide a good fight for the *Panther*. The lasers had some range, and the speed enjoyed by the light 'Mechs could keep them relatively safe until it came to a showdown. But first Takuda would have to get them out of the ship.

Goodall proposed that someone among the survivors be trained to operate the *Locust*. Though all the EST members were qualified as 'Mech pilots, putting one of them into the cockpit would reduce the already strained fabric of the team. It would have to be someone else. Mark Jacobs became the volunteer. Takuda wasn't quite sure how that happened, but suddenly the little chief engineer was crawling into the *Locust*'s cockpit.

Another enigma, thought Takuda. The *Telendine*'s engineer had been more like a non-person to Takuda thus far. Jacobs had been polite and competent enough aboard the *Telendine*, but had simply faded into the background since the crash. Now he was volunteering to pilot a 'Mech. Takuda had no way of knowing that Jacobs' background included more than JumpShip engineering. In his youth the man had been trained as a 'Mech pilot by his father, but Jacobs' dream of becoming a MechWarrior died when his father's lance was destroyed in a long-forgotten battle. The sudden resurgence of that long-buried dream had propelled him, almost involuntarily, into the cockpit of the *Locust*. He didn't even seem to mind that they had to scrape the remains of Collis Brank off the inside of the cockpit and out of the neurohelmet.

By the end of the day the debris had been cleared from the legs of the *Locust,* and they were clear to move to the opening in the hull. Jacobs was all ready to pilot the *Locust* out of the cargo hold, but Takuda would not allow it. Even a DEST member without a neurohelmet would be a better pilot than Jacobs, he decided. The engineer gave up his position to Shawn Arsenault with a disgruntled look, but Takuda permitted him to ride inside the shattered ogive for the experience.

Holly Goodall went first in her *Locust,* talking through the process out loud. She moved slowly, carefully planting the feet of the *Locust* on the deck of the DropShip. Goodall paused at the mouth of the gaping rent in the skin of the ship. The opening was big enough for an experienced pilot to maneuver without difficulty, but Arsenault was not an experienced pilot. Goodall talked herself through the opening, planning to talk Shawn through his turn. That way he would have heard the instructions twice.

Goodall stepped through just as the last rays of the setting sun struck the top of the DropShip. She turned to face the opening as she began the instructions. With her face toward the DropShip and her back to the woods, she didn't see the Tetatae emerging from the forest.

═══ 22 ═══

The Tetatae had been in the forest for nearly a full twenty-four hours. They had arrived just after dusk the previous night, and had been watching the humans ever since. Observing the movement within the camp, they had immediately recognized it as dangerous. Hadn't enough of the tribe already seen enough humans in their killing frenzy? They understood the DEST team's stealthy movements as a precursor to violence. They knew that when humans fought, any Tetatae who got in the way would die—quickly and without remorse. Better, they decided, to observe and not become involved.

The double explosions of the jump-capable 'Mechs had scared them to the point of incoherence. So had the LAM's takeoff. Dakodo had seen the *Phoenix Hawk* when it had left the DropShip the first time, but none of the others were prepared for the violence of the event. Especially at night, the sight of a Mech rising from the ground was an awesome experience. When the jumping 'Mechs had come crashing back to the ground, the Tetatae became so terrified that some of them had scattered wildly and frantically trying to get away. Some had died as a result, for the 'Mech pilots had not cared where they placed the giant feet of their machines in their haste to escape the DropShip area.

It had been a night of terror, and the event would forever be remembered as such in the oral history of the tribe. The Tetatae had gathered up their dead and injured while continuing to watch the humans. The humans had not come after them as they had feared, but instead had moved closer and closer to the thing that fell from the sky with fire. Perhaps, said some of the Tetatae, the thing was preparing to leave. Dakodo said nothing to disabuse them of that hope. The humans would remain, he knew, and the Tetatae would have to deal with them.

And so the day had passed. Some of the humans stood around the hull of the thing that fell from the sky with fire while others went in and out of its belly. The Tetatae waited for something of importance to happen, but the humans only stood around and waited as well.

In the falling light that signaled an end to another day, the Tetatae saw the thing that was going to happen. It wasn't that the thing was going to fly, for the actions of the humans showed no sign of departure. They stood now in a half-circle around the opening in the hull and stared into its dark interior. There was excitement. They began to cheer.

Andi Holland was the first to see the aliens break the woodline. Goodall's *Locust* had just cleared the entrance and had turned to talk Arsenault through the opening. Holland was watching the process with some interest when she heard a noise in the woods behind them.

Though forest sounds had become almost background input for her, heard and qualified but not consciously registered, this was something different. As she turned to look, she saw the Tetatae coming out of the woods. They didn't emerge, they boiled. They were crowded together in a tight pack, those in front jostled forward by those in the rear. The front ones, reluctant to approach and yet forced forward, drifted to the outside of the gaggle, which eventually put others in the lead. Those who had been pushing the front members suddenly found themselves in the front ranks. Then they began to balk and resist the thrust from the rear. Those who had been in front, reluctant to approach, found themselves suddenly emboldened by their relative security. They pressed forward against the backs of the reluctant leaders.

Holland sounded the alarm in her lip mike and then dropped to one knee. She didn't want to shoot these little creatures, but if pressed, she would have to. She raised the rifle to her shoulder and aimed at the center of the boiling crowd of fur. The cross hairs of the laser sight steadied on the figure of Dakodo. She took up the slack in the trigger.

The Tetatae was moving toward her in a strange, crouched walk. Holland took a deep breath and then let half of it out, just as she had been trained to do on the rifle range. Then she paused. Dakodo was not behaving aggressively. His bobbing gait resembled that of a man who couldn't decide whether to advance on his feet or his knees. Holland let the sight drift over the others. All were doing the same thing, advancing with their bodies held low between their legs. She relaxed her finger and let her breath out with a hiss.

The mass of Tetatae advanced more and more slowly, spreading out to surround the shattered DropShip. The DEST team stood with their backs to the hulk, their weapons cradled at the waist, safeties off, but waiting. Takuda emerged from the center of the line to meet Dakodo, who now crept forward from the center of mass. With him were two other Tetatae whom Takuda had never seen.

The three Tetatae advanced, their eyes fixed on the *Locust* towering over them. They jabbered to each other and to Dakodo, who responded in turn. Takuda did not understand the words, but the tone of Dakodo's voice made them sound soothing. The Tetatae turned back to Takuda. "We are . . . we are . . . we are amazed," he said, staring up at the *Locust*. Holland had turned the 'Mech to face the crowd of Tetatae. "You may be the ones who will change everything. You are the ones."

Dakodo stepped back and drew the other two forward.

"These are Totito and Dokaepi, the leaders of our tribe. They are here to see the other humans, the ones I have spoken of. Now they find that you are quite different. You are what we have been waiting for since the others arrived so long ago. Now everything will be better. It will be as it was before they came."

Takuda was confused. The Tetatae were not hostile, but this was more than just awe at the size of the 'Mechs. The *Locust* was not a particularly impressive 'Mech, certainly not like either the *Panther* or the *Phoenix Hawk,* yet it was the one that had brought the Tetatae from the protection of the forest. Seeing the aliens and the 'Mech together, Takuda was suddenly struck by the similarity to the two-legged bird-like creatures of the woods. The *Locust* was a Tetatae grown to enormity and sheathed in metal.

Dakodo explained the situation as best he could. In the beginning, he said, the Tetatae had lived in the woods. They did not have a sense of what was good or bad, no sense of the malevolent. Things were just as they were. There were natural events that swept down upon the tribe: wild fire, great winds, storms of ice, but they were not thought of as punishment. Then came those who fell from the sky with fire. They brought harm to the Tetatae that could not be reconciled with the nature of things. The humans had taught the Tetatae that there was such a thing as an angry super-being. The Tetatae had believed this and assumed that the humans represented that.

Since then, the Tetatae had come to believe the legends taught by the humans: that there was an evil in their past and that there was a future. That was another concept that the Tetatae had never imagined. They had always been taught that as it was, so had it always been; as it was, so always it would be. The humans had proved that different. But with the establishment of a past and a future, as taught by the humans, there had to be a hope in the future that things would get better. That had become the new belief of the Tetatae. What that future would be no one had ever fully explained. Perhaps, said Dakodo, it required more generations that those that had passed in the five hundred years since the arrival of those who came with fire.

Now, according to Dokaepi, the shaman of the tribe, that time had come. The shape and size of the monsters that accompanied the new ones who came from the sky with fire showed that they had arrived to aid the Tetatae and show them the future. Dokaepi said that these humans were the ones to whom the Tetatae could turn in hope of a better life. The Tetatae would serve the humans who served the great symbols of their existence.

Dakodo's recitation finished, Takuda stood in silence. He had never faced the dilemma of being considered or treated like a deity. Commanders were sometimes allowed to make mistakes, but he doubted a deity enjoyed that luxury. When first they had crashed on this unknown world, he had struggled with the sudden prospect of wielding absolute command, but now he was confronted with the prospect of even more power. Not only he, but all the humans who were with him. Takuda was silently thankful that Vost was not here to hear this.

Takuda protested. Using Dakodo as his translator, Takuda registered his protest. He tried to explain that he and his group of humans were no better or worse than the others; that falling from the sky was an accident; that the 'Mechs were just machines that had no special symbolism to anyone or anything. But it was no use.

No, said Dakodo. Totito and Dokaepi were convinced that the opposite was true. There was no way that he or Takuda would be able to change that belief. The Tetatae believed that the *Locust*s with Takuda were the way of the future. The Tetatae were here to serve the 'Mechs and the humans they brought with them. The word of the humans would be absolute. If Takuda told them to go away, that is what they would do. But the status of the humans and their monoliths would remain unchanged.

"Don't you understand that we are just like the others?

Don't you understand that we are humans who can die?" asked Takuda. "I can show you the bodies of those who have fallen. I can show you the ones who have been injured."

"That," said Dakodo, "only I am able to understand. Others will not believe. To them you be supreme, even if all of you die. As long as the great beings remain, you will be special to them."

"I am a human," snapped Takuda. "No better or worse than any other human. Believe that."

"I do. But I cannot change what done. You human, but are special. You special to me in certain ways, and you special to them in other ways. So it is, and nothing you can do, not even killing us will change that."

Takuda was defeated. He and his motley troop of humans would become, had become, the leaders of the Tetatae. Perhaps, he thought, that would change in time, but for now he could do nothing about it. The problem of absolute power had returned with a vengeance. It was his fate, he decided, to be a leader, if not among men, then among the aliens who saw him as a god.

23

The warning sirens in the hold of the DropShip began to howl. Their screaming ululation struck into the marrow of those gathered near the shattered hull and even into the closed cockpits of the BattleMechs. Hands pressed against his ears, Parker Davud stepped through the access port into the hold and staggered to the rent in the side. He was yelling something, but the screech of the sirens drowned out the words. When the sirens stopped abruptly, Davud's voice was suddenly loud in the stillness. ". . . really close! The 'Mechs are really close! The sensors picked them up."

While the others had been involved in unraveling the philosophical conundrum of the status of the humans, the *Locust,* and the Tetatae, Davud had been on the flight deck of the DropShip. He had engaged what was left of the sensors after the crash, and began to search the distance. When the telltale blips of heat had appeared on the I/R screen, he'd tried to communicate with the DEST team and the 'Mechs, but the sending unit would not accept power. The siren had been his last resort. It did have a marvelous way of attracting attention.

"How close?" asked Takuda, his mind still assaulted by the sound.

"Can't get an accurate fix," replied Davud, "But they're close enough for me to get a solid impression."

"We're dead meat in the open like this," said Goodall

from her perch on the shoulder of the *Locust*. She had climbed out of the cockpit during the discussion. If the *Locust*'s appearance had powerfully affected the Tetatae, the appearance of a human from the side of the head of the alien deity had been a real shocker. Arsenault and Jacobs had also evacuated their cockpit.

Takuda looked around at the bare ground. Their defensive position, strong in its ability to deliver long-range fire against any attack from the woods, was suddenly vulnerable. Now the DropShip sat like the center ring on a dart board, an absolute magnet for any attack. Goodall was right. Standing in the open against three 'Mechs would only get everyone killed, including the Tetatae.

And the Tetatae were now a consideration in any plans. Takuda would have liked to tell everyone to die in place, but the Tetatae would do just that, and the DEST commander felt the extra weight of responsibility for the furry, helpless beings. This being a god was more than just a formal tea that led to philosophical discussion. This was the real thing. Along with absolute power came absolute responsibility.

Takuda was a qualified 'Mech pilot, but he hated the iron monsters. They gave you plenty of weapons and armor, but you also sacrificed individual flexibility. Not only that, you also became a bullet attractor for the other side. He much preferred the vulnerability of his own body to the loss of control that armor gave. That was why he'd decided to remain a lowly foot soldier, turning down the chance to command a 'Mech lance when the post had been offered many years before. He looked up at Goodall. "We'll have to leave the 'Mechs behind. They're too much of a liability. We can evade in the woods on foot."

Goodall glanced around the clearing. Abandoning 'Mechs was not something she was willing to do unless the situation was really desperate, and she didn't have that feeling just yet. Her 'Mech was clear of the DropShip, and she mentally calculated the time required to get the second *Locust* free. There was a chance, but someone would have to pilot the other 'Mech. "Parker," she said, turning to the DropShip Commander. "Do you still have power for the ship's weapon targeting array?"

Davud thought for a moment before answering. "I have power, but that won't help. You and Vost both know that the weapons themselves are out of commission."

"Vost won't know whether we've repaired the weapons or not. Just initiate the sequence. Vost will see the emission, and it may make him think twice. That will slow him down. Anything to make him stop and wonder." She looked down at Takuda. "I think we can save the 'Mechs. If someone can pilot the other one, I think we can at least get free. If we can get into the woods, we may have a chance."

"That's no good," said Takuda with a shrug. "I can't let Arsenault pilot the *Locust*. He's too valuable as a section leader. Can't afford to have a good man trapped in something he can't fight."

"I can do it." It was Jacobs. "At least I can try." He paused as his eyes met those of Takuda. "I can pilot a 'Mech. I've been trained. I can do it. It wasn't on one of these, but I understand how they work. I can do it. Really I can."

Takuda thought for a moment. Jacobs was a null as far as he was concerned, neither an asset nor a liability in the team's survival equation. If he were lost, the sum would not change. It was worth the gamble. "All right, Jacobs," he said. "If you think you can get the 'Mech free, try it. But remember," he said looking straight at Goodall, "we're not going to sacrifice ourselves for the 'Mechs. Understand that."

"Roger your last," said the pilot. The 'Mechs would be on their own. If they were to become part of the team, they would have to survive on their own merits. Goodall was sure that she could do it, but she wasn't so sure that Jacobs and the other *Locust* would do as well. All they could do was try. 'Mech pilots were individualistic in the extreme, and mercenary 'Mech pilots a step even beyond that. But Goodall felt the emotional draw to any other 'Mech. She would do her best to keep Jacobs alive. It was a challenge she was willing to accept. "We'll be right behind you, sir." The old habit of command slipped into place. Takuda was the boss now, and she'd follow his orders.

Jacobs was already in the command seat of the *Locust,* lifting one giant metal leg tentatively to clear the edge of the shattered hull. Arsenault was on the ground, helping Lost with his gear. The wounded man would need assistance if he were to clear the area before the heavy weapons began to shoot. Despite the heavy sedation they'd given him, he was whimpering from the pain. Lost, like the other wounded members of the group, would be a serious liability when the running started. He would be better as a shooter, but that would mean having to leave him behind if they had to make a run for it.

The foot of the *Locust* came down on the ground, and Jacobs shifted the 'Mech's weight to the outside leg. Gingerly, he lifted the other one and began to extract it. There was no way he could brace himself, for the *Locust* had no arms. "Brace yourself with the last bar," came the suggestion through the earpiece of his communicator. Goodall was giving as much help as she could. "Just hold it against the side of the ship. Don't push too hard or you'll bend the activator tube. Get the crystals out of alignment, and it'll be useless. Just enough to steady yourself. Gently now."

Jacobs rotated the *Locust*'s torso until the laser came in contact with the ship. That felt more stable, and he moved the inner leg again. He watched as the foot came almost clear of the side, but he couldn't get it quite over the lip. "Stop," came Goodall's voice over the commline. "Stop the leg." He obeyed. "Now activate the foot to swing it clear. Lock the foot in its full back position. Remember to unlock when you're clear. You don't want to put it down while frozen." Jacobs paused to absorb the instructions.

He was getting too much information too soon. He'd have to be careful.

Outside the hull of the DropShip, the DEST team was making final plans for evacuation. The real problem was the heavy equipment. With the heavy weapons section reduced to only two members, they had more than enough to carry. They'd broken up the loads among the unwounded DEST members, but that only gave them four more bearers. There was just too much; they'd have to leave something behind.

"Let us help you," said Dakodo. The Tetatae was still here, not a single one having made a move to flee. They stood there shuffling back and forth, watching the humans. Takuda had completely forgotten about them, assuming that they would already have headed for the woods. Now they intruded on his already busy brain. "We are small, but there are many of us," continued Dakodo. "Each one of us can carry something."

Takuda wanted to ask many questions: Where will you take it? How much can each of you carry? Will it all get to the right place at the right time? Will you damage it when you carry it? Too many questions; too little time. "Do it," he said.

Dakodo turned to the other two who standing with him. He rattled off a string of musical gibberish. There was a brief response from the others, followed by another stream of the same sort of stuff. The little Tetatae, the one who had been identified as Totito, turned to the tribe, gave a short command, and then the gaggle of Tetatae exploded into action.

They swept around Takuda like a wave of fur and feathers and beaks and legs. Before he could give an order, before he could even think about giving an order, the Tetatae were into the pile of equipment. As if by magic the stores vanished, carried toward the woods by an army of ants. There was nothing left for the DEST team to shoulder. Dakodo stood quiet amid the commotion, his eyes following the activity with benign indifference.

When quiet reigned once more, he was left with two of his brethren, who stood bobbing and silent behind him. "These will ride with your machines. They will show them where to go. There are holes in the hills that can hide them if necessary. This one is Potáet, and this one is Kaotôt." He turned to issue short commands to the two Tetatae, who still bobbed and nodded. Without hesitation each chose a *Locust* and scrambled up the leg to settle alongside the ear piece formed by the heavy machine gun mount.

It was time to go. In the distance the *Panther* was visible over the trees, suddenly respectful of the DropShip's fire control system. Overhead the LAM orbited just out of PPC range, waiting for an opening to develop. Takuda knew that sooner or later Vost and Seagroves would guess that the fire control system was a hoax and then they would move in for the kill. The last of the foot-mobile DEST members were nearing the woods, the wounded supported by Tetatae. Takuda signaled the *Locust*s to begin their withdrawal.

Jacobs went first, his 'Mech moving slowly as he mastered the controls. The 'Mech swayed wildly as he misjudged the terrain, and Takuda could see the Tetatae guide holding on with all four appendages while it chattered instructions at the confused pilot. The 'Mech steadied and continued to move. Then a burst of PPC fire from the *Panther* snapped overhead. Either Jacobs didn't notice or was unable to do anything about it. He continued on his way toward the trees at the foot of the gently sloping hill.

Goodall waited until he was almost clear, then she too began her retreat. She backed away, watching the movements of the *Panther* in her sensor screen while keeping track of the LAM with her eyes. She didn't worry about the *Panther*. Her *Locust* could move fast enough that the 'Mech wouldn't be a real danger until it closed to short range. The LAM was another problem entirely. With its speed, it could circle behind her and make a pass from the rear. Its triple lasers could rip the *Locust* apart with a few well-aimed shots. Even lucky hits would be enough to slow her down. As the LAM streaked away to begin the attack run, she craned her head to keep it in view. As it turned to make the attack, Goodall sprinted toward the woods. By moving perpendicular to the line of the attack, she hoped to give Seagroves the most difficult target possible.

The *Panther* PPC fired again, this time ripping into the shattered hull of the DropShip, which vibrated under the pounding. Goodall let the *Locust* drop below the line of the hull, using it as shielding. The PPC fired again, creating a fountain of incandescent sparks as the particles burned through the armor. A fire flashed into life in the abandoned cargo hold.

Looking back, Goodall saw that the LAM was making its attack, but she was not the target. Seagroves had either sensed or guessed that the other 'Mech was not under full control. He had changed his point of aim from the *Locust* in the open to the one partially hidden by the trees. Goodall sprinted down the hill to reach a range where she could defend the vulnerable Jacobs in his 'Mech. The Tetatae guide hung on, its body pounding against the armor on the hull.

The LAM screamed in for the attack.

24

Goodall crashed into the woods, her instinct and training keeping the *Locust* upright. The terrain analysis system flashed red, but she knew by the feel of the ground that she was all right. Branches whipped against the 'Mech's torso and legs; vines clutched at its feet. She kept going, breasting the forest out of the way in an attempt to reach Jacobs. The Tetatae pounded its beak against the ogive of the cockpit window, desperately trying to get her attention. She ignored him.

That was a mistake. Just as her deep terrain analyzer showed angry red across its entire spectrum, a ravine suddenly opened beneath her feet. She tried to draw the 'Mech's leg back, but the forward momentum was too great. The *Locust* toppled forward into the cut in the ground, the force of the fall burying the laser. Even secured by the restraining harness of the command seat, the fall was enough to create a violent shaking. Above the fallen 'Mech, the forest branches closed to hide the attack on the other 'Mech.

Jacobs was concentrating on keeping his *Locust* upright and under control. The Tetatae guide was equally active, gibbering in a nonstop flow of advice or condemnation; Jacobs couldn't tell the difference. The little alien had tapped the cockpit window so much that the rattle of its beak now seemed like no more than background noise, which he was tempted to disregard completely. The shattered main screen of the cockpit had not yet been repaired or replaced, and vision through the front was difficult. He leaned forward in the harness to peer through the hole that the laser and machine guns had blasted through the armored glass. With one eye he glared out at the green terrain that closed in all but the *Locust*'s upper hull.

The laser blast from the LAM came as a complete surprise, the foliage around him suddenly flashing into a cloud of steam as the column of aligned light vaporized leaves and branches. A warning light flashed angrily on the control panel, but Jacobs ignored it. It wasn't that he was either foolhardy or brave; he simply had no idea what it really meant. The Tetatae gripping the hull had a better idea. The little alien had seen the metal skin on the side of the vehicle glow red and then bubble away in a fiery foam. He didn't know whether that was supposed to happen, but the sight filled him with a sense of foreboding for the safety of his charge. The Tetatae beat on the side of the 'Mech to get the pilot's attention.

In the ravine, Goodall staggered to her feet in surroundings that had changed completely. Where a moment before the body of her *Locust* had been cruising through the forest above the tops of the trees, now she found that the *Locust* was not tall enough to see above the foliage. The sensors still recorded the presence of the LAM as it made its turn at the end of the attack run, but she couldn't get a visual fix. Around her the forest was green-gold with the light dappling through from above. She steadied the *Locust* and began to look for a place to climb out of the pit. The Tetatae guide tapped on the side of the hull. This time she looked over to see what it wanted.

The Tetatae stopped its frantic hammering, pleased that the human was at last responding to its entreaties. It pointed down slope through the trees to a place that looked darker than the surrounding area. The Tetatae pointed and nodded, pointed and nodded. It grew so animated that it released its arms from their hold on the hull. Goodall stared. It was the first time the alien had released its grip since they'd begun to move away from the DropShip.

Goodall eased the throttle forward and cautiously let the *Locust* move forward. The ground beneath her feet was soft and yielding, but the terrain sniffer gave no warning of calamity. She moved with greater speed, confident now that she could travel without difficulty. Sensing a greater feeling of security, the Tetatae grasped the hull with only one of its arms rather than with both. With the free one it continued to point to the dark place in the forest ahead. Then Goodall saw that the darkness was a cave set into the side of the ravine into which she had plunged.

Jacobs, meanwhile, felt his heart pounding in his chest, the flash of the lasers having taken him completely by surprise. It was difficult enough to keep the *Locust* under reasonable control; it just didn't seem fair that he had to get shot at as well. The constant chatter of the little Tetatae on the side of his cockpit was equally unnerving. He just wanted to be left alone to deal with the problems of piloting this giant machine. He didn't regret the decision to take over the *Locust*. The sense of power was undeniable. But why didn't they just leave him alone and let him drive?

The tops of the trees to his left were suddenly shredded, and Jacobs felt a hammering on the side of the 'Mech. He didn't understand what had happened, didn't understand that the *Panther*'s PPC had made a rattling hit at long range. The control panel flashed more red lights, and the Tetatae continued to chatter wildly. Sweat was pouring into his eyes from under the neurohelmet. Things were becoming more and more difficult. He eased the throttle forward and felt the *Locust* suddenly sink away. He pulled back, but it was too late.

The *Locust* crashed downward through the trees, completely out of control. Jacobs hung on as he was jolted back and forth in the command seat. Branches whipped by, then came another flash of steam as the LAM's lasers burned through more of the leaves. Jacobs could smell the pungent odor of charred wood seeping into the cockpit as he continued to jolt forward. The alien's eye appeared in the laser hole of the cockpit glass. The *Locust* came to a jarring halt. The eye in the hole disappeared.

Jacobs leaned forward against the harness to peer out at his surroundings. The surface of the trees, glaring green in the light of the risen sun, had gone. Instead Jacobs saw a dim green darkness. He had passed below the level of the vegetation into a steep valley that continued down and away before him. Twisting the 'Mech's torso to get a sweeping view, he saw that it was all the same. Just a green dankness that went on to the limit of visibility. The little Tetatae tapped cautiously on the side of the cockpit. Jacobs opened the access panel and craned his head out the side. The Tetatae was pointing toward something in the distance. A darker portion of the green blackness. Jacobs let the *Locust* slide forward as directed.

The green forest moved past the *Locust* in an even flow. The little Tetatae chirped away happily, tapping on the cockpit and pointing toward the goal. Jacobs saw other aliens drifting through the forest. They were carrying things that looked strangely familiar. Overhead there was a burst of steam and falling leaves. The foot-bound Tetatae scattered into the gloom. Then the mouth of a cave opened in front of him, and he understood what the Tetatae wanted. Safety was just ahead. Inside the cave he would be hidden from the LAM searching overhead. He turned gently to line the *Locust* up with the opening, then let the 'Mech move faster. He didn't want to get caught with sanctuary just in reach.

High above the trees, Seagroves banked the LAM for another pass at the BattleMech hidden beneath the foliage. He took the craft into a high hammerhead stall and rolled it over for a power dive. His other passes had been at a shallow angle, and he knew from the target's reaction that he hadn't scored a kill. This time he would come straight down, zero deflection, almost no intervening terrain. He let the cross hairs steady on the I/R signature. The target grew bigger and bigger in his sights. The warning klaxon began to scream, telling him that he was into the maneuver envelope for his dive. He held the LAM a few seconds longer, trusting to instinct and ability to save him as they always had. The target was huge. He triggered the triple laser battery, letting the light lasers fire first to burn off the foliage so that the large laser could strike the target. There was an explosion of stream as the moisture in the foliage vaporized under the impact of the searing aligned light. Then the large laser fired. There was a flash and the heat signature of the *Locust* vanished. A good kill.

Deep in the cave Jacobs felt the tension drift away from his body. There had been a terrible explosion as he entered, but he was safe. The little Tetatae scrambled down and chattered happily with his mates, who looked at him with significant awe. Jacobs would have followed his guide to the floor of the cave, but he couldn't get his knees to work; they had turned to jelly. He swung his legs over the side of the hull and took several deep breaths. Perspiration had soaked through his uniform, and he could smell the stale scent of fear rising from his body. He felt a chill, and shivered even in the comfortable warmth of the cave.

"Pilot Jacobs," came a voice from below, and when Jacobs looked over the side he saw the DEST commander looking up at him. "Are you all right?" Takuda's voice revealed genuine concern.

Jacobs nodded. He felt warmth returning to his limbs. "Yes, sir," he mumbled, and then again with more confidence, "Yes, sir. Had some problems, but we made it, him and me." He pointed toward where the little Tetatae was still surrounded by his mates.

"Good," said Takuda. "That's good. Goodall is safe too. She's in another cave some distance from here, but she's all right. From what I've heard, the only one missing is Parker Davud. Evidently he was still in the DropShip when we pulled out." Takuda shook his head. "I hope he got out all right." It went against the instincts of the DEST members to leave someone behind.

Moments later, the missing DropShip—or ex-DropShip—pilot made his way into the cave, led by a Tetatae. Davud was laughing and ebullient. He sat down at the feet of the silent *Locust* and smiled at those who crowded around him. "Well," he said, "the others won't find much of value in the DropShip. I vented the thruster fuel tanks before I left, and I scrammed the plant. They won't get any useful stuff from the ship. I'd love to see their faces when they start looking. The last I saw of the ship, that big 'Mech was pouring shots in through the broken flight deck like a lunatic. I think he was really pissed." He smiled at the DEST members around him, then his face went pale.

Davud jumped to his feet and pushed through the surprised throng. "What are they doing?" he asked in a strained voice, pointing toward a cluster of human wounded surrounded by a group of Tetatae. "Get them away from our people."

Takuda stepped forward. "They're helping, Parker. They're helping. Don't worry about it."

"But they're nothing but aliens. What do they know? What can they know?"

"They can know a great deal," said Takuda. "Don't let their shape or their language fool you. They've been here a lot longer than we have. They know what works."

"But not on humans."

"Perhaps. But they'll be careful. They've led us to safety, and we have no reason not to trust them now."

Parker Davud didn't look convinced. Doubt and mistrust were clear on his face. Takuda put his hand on the pilot's shoulder, a gesture that was as strange for him as the emotion that powered it. "We all have things to learn," he said in a soft voice. "We find ourselves in an alien situation or an alien world. We will have to adapt.

It will be an interesting problem. In the past, we've always considered anything not human, and even some humans, as a lower form of life, something to be exploited or killed at our convenience. In this world that will be different. We have to respect the lives of these beings even if we don't completely understand them. It will be the new way."

Part 2

RICK
HARRIS 9
3

25

Takuda was right. Everything about this situation was new and different. The humans were the ones who were the aliens. They had always believed one should change the environment to fit one's needs, seizing anything they wanted or needed and molding it to their requirements. Now it was the reverse. The Tetatae were the ones who fit the environment; the humans were the outsiders. Not only were they outsiders, they were also unable to change the surroundings to suit their desires. The humans did not have enough of anything to fill their needs. They could survive on their own for a while, but sooner or later they would exhaust their meager supplies. They would have to adapt or perish.

Takuda was one of the first to accept the reversal. He, who had been a member of a rigid hierarchy for his entire life, seemed to find it easiest to change. Perhaps it was the responsibility for the lives of the others that made him open to the necessity, perhaps it was in his nature. In either case, he listened to the words of Dakodo and the others and did what was necessary.

By the third day in the caves, the humans were well enough to travel. Takuda decided that it was time to act, even if there was no real plan. The mercenaries had been given three days of grace to deal with the enclaves, and it would take more days for his team to reach the river. They would have to move and move with purpose.

The Tetatae had been helpful during the recovery, feeding the humans and generally fussing over them at all times. There was something unnerving about having one of the little creatures squatting at your feet when you fell asleep, and even more unnerving to awaken with him still there. They seemed to have the ability to sleep with one eye socket closed and the other open and alert. Very weird. The humans got used to it, each one according to his nature. Andi Holland was the first, Dana Lost only grudgingly.

Before they could move, Takuda had to reorganize his team. The casualties suffered by the DEST members made it even more imperative that Jacobs improve his 'Mech piloting skills. Goodall worked with him throughout the hours of daylight and on into the hours of darkness to get him up to speed. She was sure that with enough training he would become a good pilot, but time was one thing they sorely lacked.

Under normal circumstances it would take weeks simply to master the maneuvering of the complicated machine. That was one of the functions of the neurohelmet. With the helmet linked to his brain, a MechWarrior could maintain fine balance without conscious thought. But no matter what Goodall and Jacobs did, they just couldn't get the helmet to work well for Jacobs. Perhaps it had been damaged in some indecipherable way, and that was what made it do strange things at the most unexpected times. Goodall simply didn't have weeks to train Jacobs.

The weapons systems were another problem. After mastering the machine, a pilot would normally be expected to spend additional time on the range. It was not so much that he had to learn to shoot, but that a MechWarrior had to become aware of the heat surges that the weapons transmitted to the 'Mech. Heat was the real killer of 'Mechs on the battlefield, and more than one pilot had ignored the climbing heat indicator at his own peril. In that way the *Locust* was in its element. The light 'Mech had enough heat sinks that it could bleed off all the heat it generated either by maneuver, or fire, or both combined. Goodall saw no reason why Jacobs had to be warned about heat. They'd save that subject for later discussion.

When the two pilots weren't maneuvering the 'Mech through the woods, they were talking about how a 'Mech worked. Goodall talked tactics and deployment of the 'Mech lance until she had Jacobs convinced that the 'Mech was the ruler of the battlefield. Then she had to turn around and teach him that the king of the battlefield was vulnerable as well. There were many things, she explained, that 'Mechs did poorly or could not do at all. She was adamant about fighting in towns; those were places that a 'Mech should avoid. Heavy vegetation and steep defiles were another hazard. 'Mechs liked open, rolling terrain, she told him—no steep defiles, no heavy woods, no buildings, and no infantry. Infantry could be deadly if not treated with respect, and 'Mech-proofed infantry like the DEST team should be avoided at all costs.

The two 'Mech pilots were supported by Sagiri Johnson and Underos Yaputi, the remaining techs. Technical support for the mercenary lance had been thin to begin with, and with only one tech for each 'Mech, the Takuda pilots had to do much of the work themselves. Jacobs was perfectly happy tinkering away on his machine with the help and direction of the two technicians, and Goodall was humble enough to wade into the grease and oil as required. Vost would never have gotten his hands dirty on a 'Mech, even his own, but the two pilots and two techs with Takuda were perfectly happy working together in the innards of one of the *Locust*s. They were even able to repair and replace the shattered windscreen on Jacobs' 'Mech. The Tetatae had shown the humans how to heat and bend a lovely clear crystal sheet found in veins in the caves. It wasn't as strong as the original material, and it would shatter in the most inconvenient way if struck by a heavy object, but Jacobs could at least see through it.

Organizing his team had turned out to be an even more

difficult task for Takuda. He made Parker Davud his aide in the headquarters section, which meant he could move George Bustoe into Arsenault's section. The heavy weapons section would have to operate a man short, for there was no way to replace Inaduma. Sanae would have to double as both section leader and antiarmor specialist. She was perfectly capable of handling the job, capable of any job requirement in any position within DEST, but the move would put a strain on the section's capabilities.

And so, after three days of rest and recuperation, Takuda took his troops toward the setting sun, the enclaves, and a tentative future. The foot troops moved first, the 'Mechs bringing up the rear. This allowed for security ahead, while Jacobs and Goodall continued to maneuver and train together. Jacobs learned as he went, and improved. The first day he toppled the *Locust* twice, the second day only once. On the third day he was able to maneuver without mishap even when putting the 'Mech into a run. That evening, as they bedded down the equipment, Jacobs emerged from the cockpit with a beatific smile across his face. He was doing what he'd always dreamed of.

The trek was difficult because of the terrain and the matériel carried, but it would have been impossible without the Tetatae bearers. As in the retreat from the DropShip, the Tetatae carried much of the excess equipment. They were superb at the job, carrying heavier loads than the humans expected and at greater speeds than even the unencumbered humans could manage.

The only problem with the Tetatae was their inveterate curiosity. At the end of the first day, Takuda was appalled at the condition of the cargo; every weapon, sensor device, and heavy missile had been disassembled. The pieces were piled in the center of a ring of chattering aliens who then passed various pieces around the circle. Takuda was sure that everything was lost. Certain that it would take days for the DEST members to reassemble the parts, he took Dakodo aside and commented on the problem. The little Tetatae was surprised at the DEST commander's concern, and he assured Takuda that all would be well. He gave a short command, and as if by a miracle, the Tetatae put it all back together.

By the fourth day of the trek, it became obvious that the enclaves were near. Areas that had obviously been cleared with a purpose rather than naturally began to fall across the line of march. At first Takuda chose to bypass them, but by the middle of the day they were too numerous to avoid. In any case, they were deserted or abandoned. Some had once had structures on their perimeter, but an examination showed that these had been unoccupied for some time. In some instances there were signs of violence. The DEST group proceeded with caution.

As the last rays of the sun sliced across the sky, turning the undersides of the clouds into puffy peach confections, the open, sweeping savanna appeared at the edge of the forest. The DEST members strung out along the verge and settled into hide positions. They all knew that this would be a cold camp. The enemy, or the possible enemy, was in sight. The 'Mechs remained two kilometers behind in hide locations of their own. The DEST members lifted their rangefinding binoculars and swept the ground. A quick look and then a detailed search from near to far, left to right to left.

To their wonderment, they discovered that a battle had been in progress here, though it appeared that the battle was over, at least for today. To the right a force was withdrawing to the north, dragging what equipment it could. The southern force showed no intention to pursue. The fight must have been a draw. Takuda tried to identify the equipment he saw, but it was impossible. It was not that the gear was too far away to see, for his binoculars were capable of 400 times magnification, with white light, I/R, and ultraviolet receptors. It was that he didn't understand what he saw.

That the forces were not using modern power sources was immediately obvious. In almost all cases, huge stacks pouring smoke rose from the centers of the vehicles. The nearest one, its stack thrusting out from the right side and belching fire, had a great, box-shaped housing on its back. As Takuda watched, the housing rotated slowly until a great gun with the diameter of a trash can pointed southward. The vehicle shuddered to a halt, and a moment later a great gush of flame roared from the muzzle of the gun. Takuda saw a huge black projectile arc across the intervening space between the two forces to smash into the ground and then bounce along toward the enemy. He could see figures scampering away from its path until the ball vanished into a clump of trees. Then the firing vehicle belched fire from its horizontal stack and began to waddle its way north.

The BattleMechs were nowhere to be seen, nor was there any evidence that they had ever been there. PPCs, lasers, and even short-range missiles would have made short work of anything Takuda could see. He was amazed. With all the technology these people must have brought with them, what he saw now was a throwback to earlier times. Davud flopped down next to his position and also scanned the field with his glasses. "I don't see much iron," he said.

Takuda blinked. Davud was right. He scanned the retreating vehicles again, paying particular attention to the tank-like engine that had fired the projectile. The cannon itself had the dark look of iron, but there was no other evidence of the material. Most of the external fixtures had the look of bronze and copper. That was impossible, of course, but then he remembered the enthusiasm of Seagroves and the rumors of what he had seen in Usugumo. Other metal on the wheels showed of brass and copper. But almost no iron. This was a strange society.

Darkness fell over the field. The soft glow of lights from the enclaves north and south reflected against the gathering banks of clouds. The field of battle lay dark and abandoned. Even the I/R sensors of the rangefinders could find no sign of life except for the soft glow cast by the debris of wrecked and burning vehicles. The combatants had all gone home for the evening. It was a strange war at best.

"I guess I don't understand these people," said Davud.

"Neither do I, but I think we'll have to make contact. It seems that our mercenary friends haven't made a deal yet. I didn't see the 'Mechs or any evidence of them. Maybe we still have time to make our case."

"Those mercs are going to be a tough group. They have the power and a head start on us." Davud crawled back into the deeper woods. "I'll get the group together. Do you want to talk to the pilots at the same time?"

"No," said Takuda. "We'll send out patrols first. I'll go back later and brief the pilots and the techs. We might want them for support later on."

26

Sanae and Miranda slipped silently through the tall grass that had earlier been the field of battle. The two Tetatae guides, one ahead, one behind, moved more boldly. They were, after all, indigenous to the area and their presence would excite little notice. The two DEST members were a different matter. Even though they were not in uniform, their equipment would attract immediate comment. They could have worn electronic suppression suits, but that would have been too obvious to any observer. Takuda had made the decision, based on the desires of the three patrols themselves, that they should not wear the suits. The infrared suppression suits were also abandoned for this mission.

Each of the patrols was to enter one of the three enclaves, make contact with the indigenous population, and determine the possible status of the mercenaries. To do that they would have to be as inconspicuous as possible. The Tetatae had helped describe what the enclave humans wore, and the patrols had agreed to go unarmored and virtually unarmed. There was no use carrying heavy weapons. If they were discovered they wouldn't have enough firepower to fight their way out. Stealth and blending were their only chances of survival.

Far to the north, Arsenault and Bustoe were making their way toward Osio. In the center, Knyte and Holland would attempt to penetrate the religious enclave of the

Amatukaze. Ariake Sanae and Johan Miranda had been assigned the southern enclave, the merchant society of the Usugumo. In full darkness they had slipped away from the base camp to begin the penetration.

The patrols would take three nights and two days to accomplish their missions. That was why the Tetatae had been assigned as guides. Not only would they be able to aid the patrols on the routes to and from the enclaves, but they would also be able to contact their brethren who lived in the cities. Daeka and Topi had volunteered to accompany Sanae and Miranda. They had previously acted as bearers for the heavy weapons section, and the four had developed an interesting rapport. The two Tetatae looked on their human counterparts with deep respect and almost love. The two humans reciprocated with affection for their almost pets. Most communications consisted of hand signals accompanied by chirps on the part of the Tetatae and single-syllable words by the humans.

The walls of Usugumo loomed above them in the darkness. They had covered slightly more than six kilometers in the trip from the camp to the enclave, and the patrol had encountered no signs of activity. Even the walls revealed few signs of life. The patrol remained in the darkness while Topi scouted ahead. Presently she returned, and with chirps and hand signs gave Sanae the information that this section of the wall had but a single guard, and he was asleep.

The outer glacis and covered way were unguarded and showed few signs of recent occupation. The counterscarp and escarp of the dry moat were equally unattended. It was an easy climb up the crumbling slope to the rampart and the wall walk below. The four patrol members dropped silently down inside the rampart and made their way to the access ramp. In a few moments they had left the defenses and the sleeping guard behind and had entered the twisting byways of the enclave. The first part of the mission was complete.

The streets were unlike anything Sanae or Miranda had

ever seen. Even in the poorest sections of the cities of the
Draconis Combine, a sense of order prevailed. This was
different. The avenues were narrow and twisting, blind allies leading nowhere. And dirty. Piles of refuse were everywhere, many of them housing life of their own. Most
of it was the rodent or lower animal type, but occasionally there was a clan of Tetatae. There were even humans
sleeping, or perhaps dead, lying beside the darkened
buildings. The patrol and its Tetatae guides moved
through the area as quickly as possible.

Ahead, the glare of lights drew them onward. Daeka
led the procession, for he knew where he was going in the
labyrinthine maze. He had been in the city once before,
but like all Tetatae, one time in an area was enough. In
addition, he knew someone in the city and was sure they
could use that individual's home as a safe house.

Daeka held up an arm to stop the patrol. Ahead was a
brilliant glare of light and the rumbling clamor of activity.
Sanae crept forward to see the street ablaze with light and
packed with humans busily going to and fro. The fact that
it was well after midnight did not seem to matter at all.
Sanae scrutinized the people she saw; prosperous business types at play. They wore rich furs and spectacular
colors, but there was something strange about their clothing. Sanae studied them, comparing them mentally with
others she had seen in the cities of the Combine. They
were different, but she couldn't put her finger on it. She
drifted back into the shadows and to the rest of the patrol.

An hour later the patrol was safe in the home of
Pikaete. The Tetatae was aged, so obviously old that even
Sanae and Miranda could see it. He hobbled around his
little domicile with the strained pain of those for whom
life has not been easy. Pikaete had been a house servant
to the humans for more than a hundred years, a valued re-
tainer who had filled the position of part pet, part confi-
dant, part servant. He was accepted among the Usugumo
as a kind of fixture, seen when he was wanted and unseen
at other times.

Pikaete knew the Usugumo enclave as well as Daeka and Topi knew their forest. His knowledge came from more than just having been there before, and it was of more than the physical structure. He understood the dynamics of the city, its personalities, its hurts, and its dreams. There were people within the enclave who were willing followers, and there were those who felt a deep unease at how life treated them. It wasn't only those who lacked the wealth, so openly displayed, who were ready for change. They certainly were, but some of those at or near the top of the food chain also believed there should be a better way. It was to these people that Pikaete would introduce the patrol.

Ariake Sanae was worried at first. The plan was for the patrols to stay one night at the residence of a Tetatae, and then move on, dressed in appropriate clothing, to some public hostelry. They were to watch and listen; direct contact was not part of the plan, had not been contemplated as part of the plan. But Pikaete was enthusiastic.

He and the two guides had talked through the entire night, their conversation becoming excited at times and at times conspiratorial. When Pikaete woke Sanae and Miranda the next morning, he had everything worked out. The patrol would move to the Polygon Falcon, a small but well-respected ryokan adjoining the main market area that Sanae had seen the night before. Once ensconced in the area, Pikaete would bring members of the Usugumo to meet the two humans. He had made a list of possible contacts, dividing them into a Must list, a Should list, and a Could list. At the top of the Must list was the name of Homma Sirayuki, the chief administrator of Usugumo.

The name meant nothing to Sanae, but the position made her heart beat slightly faster. Here was a prize for which she would risk everything. If she could bring his support back to Takuda, then the Usugumo might be willing to follow the dream of a better world. The fact that he was even on the list made the Usugumo a best bet.

She and Miranda discussed the possibilities later that

day as they settled into their room. The process of checking in had gone much better than Sanae could have hoped. Pikaete knew the Tetatae at the desk, and so they'd encountered little difficulty obtaining a room. The only other person about was a single human sitting in the corner of the front parlor reading a well-worn broadside. The man was surrounded by the scattered crumbs of tea cakes. The paper had rattled slightly and then resumed its crumpled shape. Except for that they had encountered no one who might take notice of their presence.

Late that night there came a soft knock on the door. Sanae and Miranda swept the remains of their meal into the armoire and prepared to meet their seventh guest of the day. The residents of the Usugumo had come calling, one at a time, throughout the hours of the early afternoon and into the evening. The two DEST members had no idea how many more they would have to meet, but to have one appear this late meant he must be important. The room cleaned for their guest, Miranda opened the door to a tall, distinguished, well-dressed elderly man. They exchanged bows, and Homma Sirayuki stepped into the small room with the air of a man accustomed to being honored. He turned to Miranda. "I am Hetman Sirayuki," he said with another bow. "You are the emissary of the other force?"

Miranda closed the door and indicated Ariake Sanae, who was seated at the small desk against the opposite wall. "I am one of them, but the person in charge here is my *Gun-so,* Ariake Sanae."

"In my world," said Sirayuki with a slight raising of the lip, "we do not often find men who are willing to follow the command of a female."

Miranda saw Sanae stiffen slightly. She made as if to speak, but Miranda gestured with his hand, holding her in place. "In my world," he said with a deep bow, "we have managed to overcome that archaic prejudice." The words came out with such smoothness that their thrust was almost unnoticed. The *joto hei* indicated a chair near Sanae.

"Therefore she will do all the speaking for us." Other interviews had been shared between the two soldiers, but Miranda wanted to make sure that Sirayuki would feel as nervous as possible. One of the keys to a successful interview was to make the interviewee uncomfortable. Miranda felt he had succeeded.

Sirayuki settled himself into the indicated chair, straightened the skirts of his flowing gown, and smiled unctuously at Sanae. "I have come to hear what you have to offer. I have already spoken with the other partnership, and we know what they can deliver. We were treated to a short demonstration yesterday and another one today. They have been unwilling to commit their entire force, and that is understandable, but you will have to offer a great deal more in order to be within the bidding." Sirayuki had been in negotiations before and he knew all the tricks; when uncomfortable, attack.

Direct negotiations were not within the parameters established for Sanae. She and Miranda were to observe and be prepared to make recommendations. She began to feel the danger of the situation. "There are many things my Lord Takuda can offer you and the Usugumo," she said smoothly. Elevating Takuda from a mere *sho-sa* to that of nobility had been easy; it just seemed to flow. "But Lord Takuda is not used to dealing with mere shonin. He would prefer to deal with a true samurai." When in doubt, attack.

The comment made Sirayuki flinch. Sanae saw it and knew. The hetman seemed to shrink perceptibly. He rubbed his hands to erase the film of perspiration that appeared unbidden.

27

Takuda spent the two days preparing for the confrontation he knew would come. He wasn't quite sure what to expect from the patrols he'd sent out, but he didn't have enough information about the enclaves to make even a tentative decision about the future. He felt a nagging doubt, one that grew every day, that there was more separation between the enclaves than he had first imagined. Dealing with three disparate societies was not what he had planned. Surely, he had thought, there must be some connection, however tenuous, with the heritage that he knew and understood. Now he feared that he'd been wrong.

With his skeleton force, Takuda made the best defensive preparations he could. The BattleMechs were kept well to the rear. Their long-range laser weapons were better in support than their twin machine gun armament could ever be close in. If it came to the point where the machine guns were important, the situation would be beyond salvation. The *Locust*s, their pilots and technicians, and the Tetatae who they'd adopted as extra help, were bedded down in a ravine three kilometers behind the edge of the woods. If needed, they could be in the front lines in something less than ten minutes.

The infantry were spread out across the edge of the woods with the two light teams on the flanks, the headquarters and heavy weapons in the center. Horg and Lost were alone on the flanks, Takuda and Parker Davud in the center. A team deploying seismic sensors were in the grasslands beyond the wood edge.

With six members of the unit on patrol, the others did all the digging. Here again the Tetatae proved invaluable. All the humans needed do was give some indication of what they wanted and the Tetatae set happily to work digging holes in the ground. In less time than it would have taken a Combine engineering unit to accomplish the task, the Tetatae had created complex underground tunnel systems. Indeed, it took some effort on Dakodo's part to get them to stop their burrowing.

The savanna that fell away from the forest toward the broad river beyond was filled both days with the activity of combat. Takuda watched the intricate ballet through his binoculars, intrigued by the equipment and weapons he saw.

The combatants were from Usugumo, moving from the south, and Amatukaze, approaching from the north. The forces deployed a kilometer apart without interference from the opposition. Then, as if by some unseen signal, they would come at each other. Takuda was able to identify simple missile and melee weapons on both sides of the lines. The long firearms, bulky and cumbersome, carried by blocks of men many ranks deep were used to cover the deployment and movement of small groups of individuals with better-looking, belt-fed devices. These infantry groups would feint and dodge at each other with little contact. The main battle was carried on by mechanized forces that acted like champions, moving forward as individuals to engage in single combat with the champions from the other side.

The champions were similar to the vehicles Takuda had seen on the first evening, great, steam-driven or internal combustion machines with slug-throwing weapons of various sizes and numbers. The Usugumo had a great boxy vehicle mounted on six wheels with a huge trash can protruding from its sloping snout. It would rumble slowly across the terrain until it reached a comfortable range, then it would stop, the cannon rising and falling as though sniffing the air for the enemy. It would freeze, and a moment later would come a cloud of smoke and a great cylinder of stone arcing from the gun toward the target. It wasn't very accurate, and a nimble opponent could easily dodge, but most of the targets were not nimble. When the stone came down on an unfortunate opponent, the results were spectacular. Takuda saw one vehicle, struck on the roof, break in half under the impact. An instant later there was a catastrophic explosion, probably caused by the rupture of the fuel cell. A huge cloud of flame and white smoke rose from the victim. No one emerged.

On the first full day the 'Mechs appeared off to the south. Takuda held his breath as he waited for them to discover his group, but they paid no attention to his presence. The *Panther* had stalked through the trees and paused. Then, with almost casual indifference, it had raised its right arm and fired the PPC at a champion from the north. The vehicle disintegrated under the blast. As if to even up the fight, it then fired the weapon at the Usugumo vehicle that had been engaged with it in combat. The demonstration over and the sides returned to equality, the *Panther* had departed.

After the end of battle each day the combatants would retreat from the field, dragging what vehicles they could. The only time Takuda saw actual blows exchanged between the infantry forces was when the Amatukaze tried to capture one of the Usugomo vehicles damaged close to their lines. The Usugumo rushed the robbers, deploying a block of infantry into a long line. There had been a roar of gunfire from the advancing force, returned by a ragged patter from the Amatukaze. Then the Amatukaze had retreated quickly like small children discovered in some prank. A cloud of sulfurous smoke drifted over the deserted field.

Late in the evening of the second day, Horg reported I/R blips coming from the north. An hour later he reported a second target. There were the patrols returning from Osio and Amatukaze. Takuda passed the word of their approach and notified Lost to be alert for the patrols.

Arsenault was the first into the headquarters burrow. After glancing around at the complex of tunnels and shafts, he lifted his eyes in amazement. Takuda had indicated the Tetatae as the architects, but did not wait for the second patrol to arrive before taking the *gun-so*'s report.

Arsenault told him that they had taken rooms in a small traveler's ryokan near one of the gates. The people they met had described life in Osio as a feudal system gone crazy. The samurai lords dominated everything, freely using their katana to enforce their control. Arsenault had seen at least two beheadings in the street when a lower member of the society had not been acceptably subservient to a lord. No one had said a word or even touched the body until well after the samurai had departed.

Some of the Osio they had met would be willing to throw off their shackles, but there are not many of these. The enclave was seething with unfocused unrest, but most of it was so sublimated that the immediate chances of a coup were scant.

Takuda considered the report. Working in Osio would take time, but seemed to hold out hope, given that time. Its people were nominally loyal but that loyalty might be quite brittle. There had been no mention of the presence of the mercenaries. That in itself was on the positive side of the equation.

Knyte and Holland appeared at the headquarters shortly after Arsenault had finished his report. After two days among the Amatukaze, they had nothing good to say about them. They were, said Holland, religious fanatics who hated the other enclaves as heretics. The whole concept of religion gone wild made Holland shudder. The Amatukaze dealt with the others because it was necessary for their survival, but they were engaged in a continuing war with the Usugumo over some liturgical slight the merchants had committed.

The possibility of the DEST group turning anyone they met was reported as being low to nonexistent. The populace was so indoctrinated by religious fervor that they would be probably totally unresponsive. Some of the younger people might be receptive, but even those should not be considered reliable.

Again, Takuda had to consider the implications that no one had even mentioned the mercenaries. This time it did not seem positive, the implication being that the mercs had made their decision to go with the Usugumo. Seagroves must have had more impact on Vost than anyone imagined. Now he had only to await the report of Sanae and Miranda.

Johan Miranda returned just before dawn, alone except for Topi. He was still in mundane dress, having left the Usugumo enclave so quickly that he hadn't bothered to change back into his uniform. His report came in a flood of disconnected statements.

Sanae had been captured by the Usugumo, and presumably turned over to Vost and his crew. There was no way of knowing what would happen to her, but Miranda was sure that the presence, if not the location, of the DEST group was known. Sanae had gone with Homma Sirayuki for a meeting with some of the important members of the enclave, but according to Daeka, it had been a trap. She had left instructions for Miranda to flee the city in such an event. He had disobeyed and spent time searching for her, but without success. Daeka and Pikaete had finally convinced him to return to Takuda for help.

The people in Usugumo had made contact with the mercenaries, reported Miranda, and evidently they were about to strike a deal. The 'Mechs would make their appearance on the battlefield under the control of the Usugumo very soon. Money was the driving force behind the Usugumo. There were those at the top of the pile, and there were those at the bottom. But either way, it was wealth everyone wanted. There would be plenty of ways to overthrow those at the top, but it would be difficult to convince them that a better society existed.

Takuda was faced with two problems, both of them immediate and imperative. By first light he could expect the mercs to attack from the Usugumo enclave. Even if they didn't know his exact location, they could make some assumptions. They would come looking for them, and they would probably have the support of the Usugumo ground troops. The infantry and vehicles would not be a problem, but he couldn't afford more casualties to his already weakened force.

The second problem was the capture of Sanae. It was a tradition among DEST not to leave people behind, not even the dead. Now one of his team had been captured. She would have to be rescued or at least returned as soon as possible. He turned to Emmerdean Knyte, who had reappeared in the headquarters unbidden almost as though he knew his presence would be required. "Knyte," ordered Takuda, "take your section with Miranda and Topi. Get Sanae." Knyte nodded and left.

That took care of the second problem. Now he must deal with the first, an imminent attack by the mercenaries. As far as Takuda could tell, he had two choices: fight the mercs where they were or run for the cover of the woods and ravines. If he chose the former, then Knyte and his section would know where to return, but there might not be anything left for them to come home to. If he ran, there was no assurance that the team would survive. He explained the problem to Parker Davud, hoping the former DropShip pilot might have some other ideas. He didn't, but Dakodo, listening to the discussion, did.

He had seen the *Locust* stumbling around under the trees at the first camp. He had seen Mark Jacobs falling down repeatedly during the march to the enclaves. Now he asked questions about what the 'Mechs could really see. Why not, he proposed, build a fake position and let the enemy 'Mechs literally stumble into it? Not only would it give Takuda the chance to do some damage, but it might also reduce the perceived value of the 'Mechs to their prospective employers.

Takuda considered the possibilities. He had seen the Tetatae in their digging frenzy, and they certainly were capable of excavating traps. It just might work, he thought, and it certainly was worth a try. He turned to Dakodo and gave his consent. They would fall back slightly into the woods, leaving I/R emitters behind. That would draw the mercenaries onto the position. The Tetatae would handle the construction of the traps.

28

"Kill her now and get it over with," said Elizabeth Hoond, her voice flat and strained. "We've got all the information out of her that we can."

"What information?" replied Vost. "We don't know anything except that Takuda is close by. And we knew that just from catching her. There's a lot more to get."

Hoond kicked viciously at the wooden table that held the pinioned body of Ariake Sanae. The DEST sergeant didn't respond. She was so deeply drugged that the pain from the wrist and ankle restraints didn't even penetrate. Hoond kicked again. "Look. She's so doped up now that we'll never get anything out of her. You didn't have to give her four shots. It just blacked her out."

"We weren't getting anything out of her before the shots, either. These DEST types can stand a lot of pain. The drugs at least got her to babble about some combat she'd seen. Something about wrecked vehicles."

"You just didn't like the screams." Hoond walked around the other side of the table so she could see Vost directly. "I thought you liked a little pain with your women. Or is it you just like women?"

"You knew the deal when you came with us. You have no rank better than either Fiona or Michelle. And if Tami Wilson wants some of the action, she's welcome to it as well. You knew that coming in." Juggling three women, and perhaps a fourth, was harder than he'd thought it would be. The two techs had been docile about the situation, but Hoond, the navigator of the ill-fated *Telendine* was a different matter. Perhaps it was because she was odd man out in the organization, with nothing really to do, that made her such a witch. Vost was sorry he'd decided to add her to his list.

"In any case, we've got enough." He stepped away from the table to gaze out the window that looked out over the early sun and the broad expanse of grasslands that stretched toward the distant forest. "You're the one with the navigation skills," he continued. "Use some of that to find out where Takuda and his people are. I'll deal with the rest of it."

Hoond left the unconscious sergeant to come alongside Vost. She took his hand in hers. "I'm sorry I snapped at you," she said, resting her head on his shoulder. He didn't draw away, and she held him tighter. "I think she's dangerous. We know she's talked to Sirayuki. After all, he's the one who gave her to us. I think he'll use that to cut a better deal. But aside from that, she may have talked with others. It's like a virus in the body. She and it need to be destroyed. Kill her now."

Vost turned to face her. "She's a danger only if we don't act. Find me Takuda, and we'll go stomp him. That's what will convince these people that we're the future. And an expensive future."

Hoond rested her head on his chest. "All right, Garber," she purred. "I find them, you stomp them. But then this one is mine."

"Done. Find them and she's yours."

It didn't take Elizabeth Hoond long to get a reasonable fix on Takuda and his group. She knew from the information Sanae had given to Sirayuki that they were between five to eight hours away by foot. The patrol had made it to the city in one night. She also knew that other contact patrols had been sent to the other enclaves. That put the DEST group somewhere north of the city and probably at the edge of the woods. The drugged reference to a battle gave her an even better fix. The forces of the Usugumo had been in contact with those of the Amatukaze. A few questions to the leaders of the Usugumo gave her the battle location. She had the Takuda force well located.

The sun was directly overhead when the BattleMechs fired up. They had made their headquarters in one of the deserted bastions of the outer wall, well separated from the rest of the defenses and outside the city proper. Seagroves and Pesht had wanted to be inside the enclave, but Vost had vetoed that idea at once. He was more interested in keeping the mercenaries separated from their possible employers until the deal was done. In any case, the bastion provided security.

The bastion, with its towering scarp and counterscarp, would keep all but the most insistent away from the 'Mechs. The walls were no problem for the two land 'Mechs, and Seagroves' LAM could also traverse them with ease. Being isolated had the advantage of adding mystery to their presence.

The operation against Takuda was to be a straight "brute force and ignorance" operation. Three 'Mechs against less than a dozen infantry would be a cake walk. Even a lance as weak as Vost's should be able to deal with them. Granted, Takuda's group had a short-range missile launcher, but how much did that count against the smothering fire that the *Javelin* could deliver at the same range? If Takuda's people had the temerity to open fire with their SRM, the *Javelin* would deluge the location with its own missiles. The counterfire radar on the right side of the *Javelin*'s head could plot the location of the launcher to within twenty-five meters, and even if its missiles didn't make a direct hit against the system, the dozen explosions in the area would probably make the enemy gunner very respectful. There would be no second shot. It was BF and I all the way.

Vost and Pesht blasted out of the bastion in boiling clouds of incandescent gas. They hunched down just outside the walls and began to make their way through the waist-high grass toward the scene of the previous day's combat. Seagroves would fly out later. Fuel for the air portion of the LAM was critical. He still had hours of flight time remaining, but the fuel he had scrounged at the DropShip would have to last until he could find a suitable local substitute. And that would have to wait until after they'd finalized the deal.

Pesht trotted out ahead of the medium *Panther,* and Vost had to call him back. He wanted to hold back the *Javelin*'s SRM armament until they'd located the targets. Vost was in the interesting position of having to lead with the medium and follow with the light 'Mech. In normal conditions the light *Javelin* would have been deployed in support of the two *Locust*s, with the *Panther* and the LAM as reserve. But Vost didn't have the two *Locust*s. No one did. Seagroves had reported a definite kill on one of them, and the other was damaged, at best. The finest technicians in the galaxy couldn't have jury-rigged the parts to build a functioning 'Mech, and Takuda did not have the finest techs available. Nor did he have the depot workshop such repair activity would require. The mercenary settled comfortably into the *Panther*'s command seat and let its easy gait across the savanna lull him into a feeling of euphoria.

The scattered trash of the battlefield littered the grasslands. Patches of burned, brittle stalks marked the death throes of some giant metallic beast. This was the site of the recent and continuing combats. He knew there would be no fighting here today, however. The Amatukaze and the Usugumo were observing a one-day truce. It had all been arranged. There were, however, observers from both enclaves somewhere among the patches of trees. This would be good sales promotion. Vost turned the pair of 'Mechs toward the forest.

The *Javelin* moved up to the left of the *Panther,* two hundred meters away and slightly behind. Vost noted the other 'Mech's position on the secondary screen as well as

on the heads-up display. He wiped the information from
the HUD, leaving nothing but targeting symbols. There
was no use having it cluttered with extraneous data. With
no other 'Mechs in the battle, the location and activity of
the allied 'Mechs would just get in the way. Vost pressed
forward on the throttle and felt the pressure against his
back as the *Panther* began to gain speed.

The Cat's Eye 5 targeting system swept the approaching wood line. No targets. Vost adjusted the sensor array
to I/R maximum. Under normal conditions the infrared
sensors were adjusted to react to the heat of a 'Mech
rather than a human. It was only in city fighting that the
presence of humans became a survival imperative. In restricted terrain, where the PNT-9R was even more dangerous than in the open, the shadowy presence of an
infantryman could spell the difference between a 'Mech's
survival and becoming a heap of glowing metal. The secondary screen showed the *Javelin* to the right rear as a
bright green, its IFF identification number across the top
of the image. Vost disregarded it.

Then, emerging from the background clutter of the forest to the front, Vost saw the soft glow of an I/R signature. A human. A human lurking in a hidden bunker right
on the edge of the woods. He let the cross hairs of the
PPC steady on the image. At this range he could blast
both bunker and the human to smithereens. His finger
tightened on the trigger. No, he thought, that would be
too easy. He lowered the 'Mech's right arm and acceler-
ated. Stomp the little beggar flat, he thought. That'll show
'em who's boss.

The *Panther* sprang into the air and came down on the
unmoving I/R image, its right leg extended stiff and
straight for the crushing blow. Just as the foot crashed
through the top of the surprisingly soft bunker roof, Vost
had a fleeting thought; the poor, stupid grunt had not
moved. The 'Mech's foot, a three- by six-meter slab of
articulated Maximilian armor, sank through the overhead

cover and kept on going down. And going and going. And then stopped dead.

The shock threw Vost against the restraining harness. The *Panther*'s right foot was caught in an eight-meter-deep pit, off balance. The 'Mech's impetus had carried it forward. Vost brought the left leg under the toppling 'Mech, but it stubbed its toe against the ground. He fought to get it free. The 'Mech continued forward, falling. Vost swung the left arm back, trying to twist the 'Mech free, trying to throw some weight onto the immobile left leg. It was no use.

With stately grandeur the *Panther* toppled forward into the scrub, the PPC driving itself into the soft earth. Then the cockpit struck, and Vost was thrown against his harness again. His feet came off the controls, his finger tightened on the firing buttons. The PPC roared to life. Great gouts of molten, incandescent, glowing dirt spewed out. The right shoulder of the thrashing 'Mech lurched backward, twisting the head face-down against the ground. Vost hung suspended by the harness as he fought to regain control.

By the time he got the *Panther* upright and functioning, the *Javelin* was into the forest verge. Vost shouted a warning over the commline, but it was too late. He had a momentary vision of the *Javelin* lurching forward, its legs enmeshed in a web of vines. A tree snapped upright, his secondary screen showing the legs of the 'Mech sideways. The *Javelin* broke free and staggered on.

"Where are they?" screamed Pesht into his communicator. "They're everywhere. I'm lost!"

Vost swept the area. There were I/R signatures scattered through the trees. More signatures than Takuda could possibly have men. It was a trap. The secondary screen glowed with the identification of the incoming LAM. A heavy laser strike vaporized the ground in front of the *Panther*, leaving smoldering branches and glowing earth. Vost looked around for the antagonist, but it was just the LAM arcing away. "Seagroves! I'll get you for that!"

"Sorry, boss. Thought it was one of them in front of you." There was a pause. Vost thought he heard a chuckle as the transmission ended. "I have no targets," came the next report from the LAM.

Vost saw another I/R blur. This time I'll get you, you little crud, he thought. The signature blinked. It was retreating into the deeper forest. The *Panther* sprang forward. There was a slight tug on the 'Mech's legs as it passed between two trees. Damn vines, thought Vost. Gotta be careful. Then he saw the log swinging toward the *Panther*'s torso. He braced himself, felt the shock as the wood struck home. This was madness. There were nothing but shadows to fight. "Pull back," he ordered over the commline. "We're out of here."

=== 29 ===

Remaining hidden in the patches of scrub outside the main gate of the Usugumo enclave, the four DEST members and the Tetatae watched the 'Mechs blast out of the bastion and stalk northward along the river. Knyte, Holland, Horg, Miranda, and Topi huddled as low as they could. The plan was to enter the enclave at dawn if possible, and they had moved from the DEST position and across the open ground as fast as they'd dared. But they hadn't been quick enough. By the time they reached the outskirts of the enclave, activity had begun at the gate and on the walls, forcing them to wait until traffic around the entrance became heavy enough for their entrance to pass unnoticed.

They'd decided to make their move just before noon, but a flurry of activity in the bastion housing the 'Mechs had driven them to cover again. Now, as the 'Mechs leaped out of their fortification, the team had their chance. The sudden explosion of the *Panther* and *Javelin*'s jump jets had scattered the stray pedestrians. In the confusion Knyte gave the word, and the five rose from their positions and joined the confused throng crowding toward the main gate.

The guards, who usually checked the identification all who passed through, were huddled in their gatehouse, peering through the vision slits at the settling dust. They waved the crowd of panicked people through the gate, the

DEST group getting past them without earning so much as a glance. The guards would become officious later, making up in arrogance their lack of attention earlier. But not now.

Topi got the four humans off the main street and into the back alleys as quickly as possible. Miranda was still in the mundane clothing he had worn during his sojourn in Usugumo, and Knyte and his section were dressed in the clothes they'd worn among Amatukaze. Now, they realized, the dress of the three enclaves was so strikingly different that they were immediately recognizable as outsiders. They scurried into an alley and huddled behind some crates.

They didn't have to wait long. A pair of civilian humans wearing the loose jackets and trousers favored by the lower class of Usugumo approached. As the pair passed the team's hiding place, Miranda stepped out in front of them and raised his hand. The two men stopped, beginning to utter protests at this unwarranted intrusion on their lives. What was this civilian doing trying to stop them? They never got a satisfactory answer. Their necks were broken before they hit the street, and their clothes were off a moment later.

The job finished, Knyte and Horg were already dressed in attire appropriate to the enclave before they noticed the small group of Tetatae children staring at them in open-eyed wonder. Then the little bird-like creatures fled before any explanation could be given. The team moved on, directed by Topi toward their goal.

The little alien trotted ahead, chirping to any of his kind that she encountered along the way. She nodded and bobbed as she went, sometimes stopping for more lengthy conversations with the adults. But it was from the children that she seemed to get most of her information. The adults occasionally made scolding sounds as the humans approached, snapping their beaks in the direction of the team. The children crowded around at a respectful distance, their eyes bulging wider than usual.

Topi directed the team through the streets, heading directly toward the highest point in the enclave. She finally stopped where an alley so narrow that they had to squeeze through sideways debouched onto a broad square. She hunkered down and gestured to Knyte, indicating a room on the second floor. She rattled off some words that the section leader didn't understand, but the little alien was quite insistent. Knyte made walking signs with his fingers, and she nodded. When he indicated that she should accompany the group, she shook her head violently. She would not enter the building.

Topi stood to her full height and let the DEST members crawl between her legs until they were all in front of her. She spoke to Horg, the last in the line of four, as he passed and made some guttural sound. It sounded like a benison, and Horg took it as such. Knyte indicated that Horg was to stay outside and guard their escape route. Then they were ready to move inside.

Knyte went first, stepping into the early afternoon sunlight that flooded the square. The building directly in front of them was an imposing structure of stone and gold. The edifice was apparently intended to dazzle and humble all who approached, but Knyte was too interested in deciphering its internal structure to be impressed. The broad double doors probably gave access to a central staircase that led to the second floor, he thought. That floor probably had a central corridor that ran the length of the building, with doors leading off to rooms on either side. Up the stairs and then down the hall toward the windows Topi had indicated. He made a mental map of the building just by looking at the exterior. The others were doing the same thing, coming to the same conclusions. Training and experience made a difference.

They plunged through the darkness of the entrance. The stairway was ahead in the light that poured through a broad window halfway up and above a landing. The stairs doubled back on themselves to reach the second floor. They started up, climbing slowly, as though they belonged there. They made the turn, two going up each side.

The transverse corridor was what they expected. They turned left, Miranda hanging back to cover the rear of the other three. The right hall was empty, but the one they chose had a uniformed guard. He raised his hand to stop them, but before he could utter a word, Knyte challenged him. "We're here for the prisoner. And why are you not at the door to her cell? You should be there and not wandering the hall. Go there at once, or I will report you immediately to your superior."

The guard stood open-mouthed at the challenge. It took him a moment to recover, to remember that he was at his assigned post, to recognize that the language used by the stranger was just as strange as his garb. He opened his mouth to speak, but it was too late. The thrust took him square in the throat, crushing his larynx. He tried to speak, tried to gasp, but there was nothing. He reached for the pistol in the holster on his right side, but he felt a hand grasp his wrist. He struggled. Then a red mist covered his eyes.

Knyte lowered the guard to the floor and lifted the heavy pistol from its holster. He motioned Miranda to stand guard while the others went down the corridor in swift strides. They came to the door of the suspected room. Knyte put his ear to the solid wooden door to listen, but he heard no clue as to who or what was beyond the portal. He motioned Holland to stand to one side of the door while he took the other. They brought their short-barreled laser rifles out from under their cloaks. He then nodded to Andi Holland.

She crept forward to try the knob, the solid gold heavy and rich under her fingers. She twisted it gently until it came against the stops; the door was locked. She stepped back and leveled her rifle at the lock plate below the knob. Knyte tapped her on the shoulder and bent to whisper. "Not the laser. The gold will only absorb and dissipate the heat, fusing the lock. Use the slug pistol."

"But the noise," whispered Holland. "Everyone will hear it."

"Can't be helped. We'll have to move fast."

She nodded, shifted the rifle to her left hand and took the heavy pistol from Knyte. Poetic justice that she use the guard's pistol to smash the lock. The report of the weapon was loud in the confines of the corridor. The golden lock plate, knob, and innards of the mechanism exploded under the hammering impact. The door swung inward.

Andi Holland was through the door before it reached its stops. She rolled to the right, ending her move in a crouch. Sunlight cascaded through the windows beyond, momentarily blinding her. Then she saw the table and the pinioned figure. She cleared the room with a quick glance; no use being surprised by someone else. Clear. She sprang to the table.

The figure of Ariake Sanae lay motionless. Holland bent over the body, listening for the sound of breathing while she felt Sanae's throat for a pulse. A yes to both; Sanae was still alive. She slashed at the bonds with her vibrodagger, the straps giving almost no resistance. Behind her she heard the high-pitched whine of a laser rifle and Knyte calling, "Faster, Andi. We've got company!" There was motion beside her and then Johan Miranda was there, sweeping the prostrate figure off the table and into his arms. He turned toward the door. Holland jumped in front of him and led the way into the corridor.

Knyte was waiting, a laser rifle in each hand. Holland saw the blast deflectors glow red as Knyte fired both weapons from the hip. She had a momentary vision—probably from some old vidisplay she'd seen as a youth—of hatted gunfighters moving down a street, weapons in their hands, firing from the hip. Then the vision was swept aside by reality.

As they moved down the hall, Miranda fired into the darkened corridor, the laser hits splashing golden minnows of slag from the walls. His shots were unhurried, first at one side, then the other, a machine doing its job. She trotted after him. Behind her she could hear the heavy steps of Knyte.

Miranda stopped shooting and led the way down the stairs, two at a time. Then they cleared the landing, with the others pounding along behind. Somewhere in the building a klaxon sprang to life, its shrill blasts echoing through the halls. From somewhere above came the sound of doors slamming. They didn't stop, didn't look back. Knyte fired up the stairs without taking aim.

At the foot of the stairs Holland saw silhouettes to the right. She sprayed laser shots at them and saw figures fall away from the mob. Then there was a flash of light and a roar. Something hummed past her head to rattle off the wall behind her. A cloud of acrid, pungent smoke that stank of decay swept over her. She kept going.

The square was blindingly bright. Holland paused, letting her eyes adjust. The others crowded behind her. Civilians were scattering across the bright stonework. There were other, uniformed types, who stood their ground. A sharp sound made Holland turn to her right. A lump of lead glanced off the stone pillar and howled away.

Then a horrible, shattering, screeching roar drew the attention of the party to the broad central street that led from the square. Rattling into the plaza came a strange machine, all lumps and knobs and exhaust stacks. The copper-bound wheels screeched pathetically as it turned toward the building. Guards scattered from in front of it, others ran toward it cheering. Emblazoned on the front slope in green and gold was the symbol of the Usugumo. The monstrosity shuddered to a halt in front of the group. Holland raised her laser rifle and let the cross hairs center on a vision slit.

The top of the hatch popped open and the head of Topi emerged. The little Tetatae bobbed out, waving her arms toward them. From somewhere to the rear came another roar and the howl of a ricochet. Topi ducked and looked behind. She waved her arms more enthusiastically. "Let's go!" shouted Knyte as he vaulted into the vehicle. "We can't run from this mob, but we can use this. Let's go!"

The team was no sooner on the vehicle, not yet even within its protective confines, before it shuddered into reverse. Holland heard shouts of terror and disbelief as the guards scattered away from the flailing wheels. Then the vehicle was moving forward, rumbling toward the main street and the gate beyond. It picked up speed going downslope, roaring past the gate guards as they raised their hands in protest.

Then they were out on the main road, still careening along, the vehicle lurching and banging as it went. Horg sat in the driver's seat, cursing at the unresponsive controls like one possessed. Inside the dark interior, the little team held on to whatever they could find that was not burning hot. Cradled among them was the unconscious form of Ariake Sanae.

30

Vost slammed his fist down on the mahogany table, making the teacup rattle. He hated sitting cross-legged; there was no way a man could be aggressive while sitting in the lotus position. And he wanted so much to be aggressive. He was angry enough at Hoond for her bungling of the Sanae affair, and now he had to deal with obstructionist bureaucrats. Didn't anyone have any brains or imagination? he wondered angrily.

He was faced with the impassive stares of Homma Sirayuki and the senior members of his council. They sat along one side of the long table, while he and the commandors of his 'Mech force occupied the other. Elizabeth Hoond was there, sullen over her loss of the prisoner and unsure of her position within the mercenary force. As neither a pilot nor a technician, she was beginning to doubt the wisdom of this alliance. Equally sullen, but for a different reason, was Kendall Pesht. The *Javelin* pilot had not yet recovered from the embarrassment of the recent action in the woods. His 'Mech had been trapped, snared, tripped, and generally humiliated by unseen infantry enemy. His only consolation was that Vost had suffered equal humiliation.

Seagroves was the only member of the mercenary force who did not seem to be pouting. The LAM pilot had slurped his tea with equanimity, sitting flat on the cushion with his legs straight out under the table. He had seemed oblivious to any of the discussion, casting bright stares at the serving girls who moved silently about the room. He had not mentioned his near-miss on the *Panther,* and Vost was sure that if the subject came up, the man would blame the "fog of war" for the accident. The mercenary struck on the table again. "You've got to understand the danger presented by those people in the woods," he said through clenched teeth. "If either of the other enclaves decides to deal with them, you people will have a real problem on your hands."

"It would seem to me, Honorable Commander," purred Sirayuki, "that it is you who has the problem. You were supposed to demonstrate the power of your giant beasts to deal with such a small and weak force. You have not done so. It is all very strange."

"We can go elsewhere, you know."

"That is perfectly within your right, Honorable Commander. But as you well know, we have already came to a working agreement with you."

"It's not me you've come to an agreement with," sneered Vost. "You have an agreement with Seagroves. He's the one who's done all the talking so far."

"That is quite true," nodded Sirayuki. "Your man who flies has been quite persuasive in his arguments. It is he who has the most special abilities, not you. Your strengths are very great, or so we have been led to believe, but it is the one who flies who is the most impressive."

Vost shook his head in frustration. "Shidosha Homma Sirayuki, you do not grasp the concept of the BattleMech or how to use it. I understand that you are amazed by the abilities of young Seagroves, here, but he is not the most powerful. Even he will admit that." From the look on Seagroves' face, Vost saw that this was not a good time to call for an answer. Seagroves might just argue the special value of the LAM.

"We now know the location of the other humans. In the first attack our navigator was not completely accurate.

But now we know. The problem is the woods. Our machines have difficulty maneuvering in the woods. But we could use the Usugumo infantry and tanks to flush them out. Then we could get at them. We must act quickly, for although they currently pose no real threat, they could be quite dangerous if they join with the Osio or the Amatukaze."

Sirayuki considered the situation. Certainly the 'Mechs had not done the job of destroying the enemy in the woods, a fact that had serious consequences not even these humans could fully understand. The Tetatae in the city had learned of the defeat, had even learned of the part their brethren had played in it. The residents of the sumaru, the mass of tetties huddled within Usugumo, had changed as a result. It was not yet any great change, just something in the air. Some of the human waste had caught the scent as well. It would be best, thought Sirayuki, if the problem could be solved quickly.

The act was agreed upon, but the plan took longer. Sirayuki had many objections, not the least of which was how to deal with the other enclaves while the Usugumo forces were out attacking the others. He was afraid, and justifiably so, that they might take advantage of the situation. He wanted the mercenaries to neutralize the opposing forces. And he wanted the mercenaries to use the LAM.

The psychological effect of the LAM would be more powerful than any real damage it could do. The members of the enclaves had a deep-seated fear of flight. Their legends said that although they themselves had come from the stars as voyagers, they must never fly. Their great star, a single, bright light that hung over the land in the night sky, was the beacon of their only home. They were, so said the legends, incapable of reaching that star and they must never try. They could do many things on the land, as they had proved over the last five hundred years. But flight—and there were some early legends that spoke of it—had only brought devastation to the people. They did not, could not, would never, fly. And now there were people here who could and did. Attack from above would be ruinous to the morale of the others.

Vost argued against it, knowing that the LAM was having a real fuel problem. It had refueled in the last encounter at the DropShip, but unless they could find a substitute for the KR-4, the LAM's endurance would be limited. That limit was great, but it was also finite. And a stroke against the other enclaves would bring that limit ever closer. The arguments for the strike were, however, too compelling, and in the end he had to give in. The strike and the move against Takuda's people were scheduled for the following morning.

The force moved out at dawn. The Usugumo were fully mechanized, even to the infantry. Those who could not fit into the carriers, great boxes on copper-bound wheels with twin exhaust stacks protruding from their backs, rode clinging to the sides of the fighting units. A cloud of choking gray fumes rose from the roaring, clanking vehicles. Great clouds of half-consumed oil blotted out the weak sun that attempted to pierce the low, thin clouds. The steam, blown or seeping from numerous joints in cooling systems, curled down and mixed with the ground fog that crept in from the river beyond. When they reached the gates, they swung open to the cheers of the crowds of people lining the streets. The column moved out.

The 'Mechs stayed in the bastion until the corps was well on its way. The pilots knew that they would be able to catch the column at their ease. The slow serpent would, they thought, take hours to reach the target area. But they had not counted on the speed that the giant machines could achieve once they were fully underway.

Internal combustion contraptions—and that was the best description for what the Usugumo had deployed—gain efficiency with the passing of time. Fuel and cooling water are expended, making the vehicle lighter. In addition, the pistons and cylinders heat up, getting better and better at what they do. Thus, the leaders of the column began to gain speed. By the end of the first half-hour the vanguard had reached fifty kilometers per hour. The column began to spread out as the heavier vehicles, with their lower power-to-weight ratio, dropped to the rear. Relief drivers, drawn from the riding infantry, were pressed into service. It became a race to reach the DEST group, almost like a carnival atmosphere.

The light vehicles reached the designated location first. They slowed to begin their deployment, but the lumbering heavies were close on their heels. Pressed forward by the fighting vehicles, the four-wheeled reconnaissance units careened across the field to make way for their fighting brethren. The light units were thrust aside to the left and front of the formation, the tanks spreading out as best they could to the right and rear. Unit cohesion was lost. Some of the tanks could not find their mates, but rather than slow and search, they pressed on toward the distant forest. The infantry, those still clinging to the sides, those who had not been flung from their perches when the vehicles first left the road, cheered and waved at the spectacle. Never in memory had they seen such a force go into action with so much speed and power. It was all the holidays they had ever experienced rolled into one.

Behind them, surprised by the speed of the ground forces and aghast at what they saw, the *Panther* and *Javelin* came up from the river. Vost tried to decipher what he was seeing. The neat squares, drawn on the map the night before, had vanished—assuming, of course, that they had ever existed. He searched the formation for the deploying infantry that was supposed to lead the heavies into the scrub. They were not there. Deep in the pit of his stomach, Vost felt the sour burn of impending disaster.

The bloody Usugumos weren't waiting for the 'Mechs. Vost was torn between the urge to stand back and watch the disaster and the need to move forward and become involved in what was sure to be a hopeless situation. He chose a midcourse between the two. He moved forward cautiously, waiting for disaster. It came, and came even more violently than he'd expected.

The leading forces of the Usugumo plunged into the fringe brush that marked the boundary between the savanna and the denser woods beyond. It was the point where Vost's 'Mechs had been trapped by the pits. Vost knew what to look for now, and he saw the telltale signs of disturbed earth. A great armored carrier, smoke streaming from its twin stacks, toppled forward into a pit, the rear wheels still above the level of the ground. A great cloud of flame and exhaust erupted from the seams between the slabs of copper and wooden sheeting that provided the armor. A fraction of a second later the seams had ruptured and the vehicle exploded. There were no apparent survivors of the incandescent hell.

Other vehicles, oblivious to the fate of those caught in the pits, kept going. The sheer weight of the attack would carry the forces at least to the heavier woods. There was a momentary flash and then an arcing light as a short-range missile launched, tracked, and found its mark. It was an easy shot. Compared to the speed of a 'Mech, the lumbering vehicles were virtually motionless. The missile struck square on the side of one, the velocity carrying the warhead through the wooden plating even before it could explode. The entire force of the detonation was contained within the hull of the vehicle. One moment the tank was there, the next it was a ball of flame rising over the scrub lands.

Two tanks further to the rear flashed into flying debris, then two more. Vost searched for the missiles, but could see no firing signature or smoke trail. Through the dust and steam and smoke he saw a shadowy giant stalking above the trees. A pair of giants. Vost glanced at his secondary screen. There, for all with eyes to see, were the blips of a pair of *Locust*s. They showed the FFI of the Vost lance, but they certainly were not on his side. He was about to give the order to engage the enemy 'Mechs when the blips drifted downward over the brow of a distant hill.

Vost ground his teeth. He'd been so sure that they'd destroyed the *Locust*s that he hadn't even bothered to change the FFI frequency. The forces of the Usugumo were now retreating across the savanna even faster than they'd charged. But Vost had more information this time. To take his 'Mechs into the trees to find and destroy the *Locust*s would require pushing past the retreating foot soldiers. Without the Usugumo infantry to deal with Takuda's people and their alien allies, it would be useless to press forward. It was time to call it a day. Again.

═══ 31 ═══

Seagroves held the wine goblet at arm's length and turned it gently in his fingers, letting the brilliance of the metal catch and reflect the flames of the hissing gas mantle. He brought the cup to his lips, letting the fragrance of the iridescent green brandy caress his nostrils. Cabolos was a taste it took some getting used to, but Seagroves was making significant progress. He liked being important, and he felt he was finally getting what he deserved.

He'd gotten his first inkling of what was here for the taking just after he'd first landed in the square of Usugumo. He smiled at the memory, How different that first encounter would have been if he'd known then what he knew now. But the past was past, and right now he was doing just fine. He let the cabolos roll over his palate. Still a little too sweet for his taste, but if this was what the residents of this planet thought was luxury, that was good enough for him.

From the hearth came the warmth of the fire his servant had built against the late summer chill. The day had been dim with low clouds, and at this hour the fog was sweeping in from the river. The dance and radiance of the flames gave a ruddy glow to the room, setting off the dull brilliance of the golden accoutrements. Every metal object in the room was of gold; Seagroves had seen to that. He loved the look and feel of the heavy metal. If it couldn't be of gold, he had told his hosts, he didn't want it made of any other metal. The grate that held the lumps of glowing coal was ceramic.

On the mahogany table that supported his feet were scattered piles of golden objects. They weren't what anyone on this planet would call art, since artistic items were usually made of the less plentiful iron. Brian Seagroves didn't care. He wanted gold, and it didn't matter to him what shape it came in. It was the gold that was important. He let another sip of cabolos slide down his throat.

There was a sharp knock at the door, followed almost immediately by the appearance of Elizabeth Hoond. Seagroves glanced up, his eyes dancing in the light of the gas lamps. Hoond looked grim to the point of fury, her brows knit together in a deep crease, her shoulders rigid with anger. Seagroves was mildly disturbed that she had not awaited permission to enter, but decided to say nothing. There would be plenty of opportunity to dig at Hoond. "Why so glum," he said with a smile, pushing the golden salver toward her. "Have some cabolos. It takes getting used to, but it's got a pretty good kick after one or two. You look like you could use some."

Hoond stalked into the room, slamming the door behind her. She reached for the crystal decanter and a goblet so roughly that some of the golden objects scattered across the table and rolled off to hit the floor. Without batting an eyelash, Hoond poured herself a glass and took a long draught of the iridescent brew. She drained the goblet, then poured herself another. "Is this all you plan to do tonight?" she asked venomously. "Just sit here and swill this stuff?"

"I'm not the only one doing the swilling," retorted Seagroves, lowering his feet to the floor and retrieving the fallen objects. "But, yes, if the truth be known, that's exactly what I plan to do. I'm just a minor cog in the great scheme of events. Just a technician with special abilities."

"Bull!" Hoond spat the word out as though it had physical force.

"Just because I've been recognized for my worth in this society is no reason for you or the others to be jealous. It's quite unseemly of you."

"Bull! And again bull! I don't know why they think you're so hot. You fly a LAM. A LAM! I'm the navigator of a starship that travels to and from worlds dozens of light years apart. I've been to the outer fringes of the known galaxy. I even have my license from the Intergalactic Mariners Union to serve as master of any vessel, any area. That's a far sight more important than the pilot of a stinking LAM."

"Tut, tut, my dear Elizabeth Hoond. You make too much of yourself. You may be able to navigate a JumpShip between any two known points, but you cannot fly. And that's what counts *here*. And I can. These silly, simple people have no concept of star travel. They have no idea of your high and mighty importance." Seagroves leaned across the table, almost into the face of the navigator. "But they understand what I do." There was ice in his voice. "And don't you ever forget it. To them I'm more powerful and important than Garber Vost. He may tell us what to do now, but if it ever comes down to a choice, I'm the one who'll be able to cut the better deal. They respect me. They love me."

"They worship that stupid LAM is all! It's got nothing to do with you. A mere accident of fate put you in this position. Remember, Vost can fly the LAM too. Just because these people had to abandon their JumpShip five hundred years ago, and just because they've come to revere it as some starry home of the gods and so don't fly, is no reason they should think of you as some kind of god." She poured herself another glass of cabolos. "We saw the wrecked ship when we entered this system. That's all it is. A wrecked ship. It's no mysterious home of the gods."

"Well, go ahead and try telling them that, and see how far you get. As for me, I'm perfectly happy here sur-

rounded by their ignorance. And I plan to push that ignorance as far as I can. You're just jealous."

"You certainly have had some luck." Hoond examined
the golden fixtures around the room. "You're getting
yourself quite a horde."

"You bet. These people don't understand its value. But
I do. I'm going to be the richest man in the galaxy when
this is over. So wealthy you won't even recognize me.
But don't worry, Lizzy, I'll pay attention to you, even if
Vost won't."

"Pig," she said in an even voice. Seagroves could see
that his comment had struck home. Hoond was not a
steady member of Vost's entourage. Seagroves didn't
know what status she craved, but she wasn't number one
to anybody. She certainly wasn't important to Sirayuki,
not even a little bit. In Usugumo, women were nothing
more than servants.

"I prefer the title 'Divine Lord,' or perhaps 'King of all
he envisions' to the term pig."

"What makes you think you'll ever be able to get off
this stinking planet and away from these stinking people?
Don't you get it? We're *stuck* here for eternity. What's all
that gold worth then?" Hoond poured herself another goblet of cabolos, draining the decanter, then set it back
down on the table with a solid thump. "We're all stuck
here forever. They'll plant our bones in the stinking muck
by the river and let us sink in. It's hopeless."

"No. I don't believe that. You've had too much
cabolos, and now I'll have to get more. On your way out
tell that little girl at the desk I need some. I've got plans
to make."

Elizabeth Hoond drained the last of her drink and stood
up. Staggered up. She had the momentary desire to throw
the goblet at Seagroves, but in her current condition she
was sure she'd miss. And what was the use? she thought.
Aside from the personal satisfaction of bouncing the thing
off his face, she'd gain nothing by the action. She turned
to the door. "Next time you come," said Seagroves as

Hoond put her hand on the knob, "you might try waiting for permission before barging in."

Hoond turned to the blurry figure in the chair. Stupid lout, she thought. Then she threw the goblet at the fuzzy pink circle above the body.

Seagroves dodged the spinning goblet. His comment about barging in was as much a warning to Hoond as to himself. There was no lock on the door, and that meant that anyone could enter this room at any time. It was not a good place to hide his cache of gold, a pile that seemed to be growing by the hour. He had removed his clothes from the wooden armoire in the corner, and was using it to store the bigger items he'd accumulated. He had contemplated tearing out the golden tubing that was used to bring the gas into his room, but had decided against it. The management of the hostelry might become suspicious about something like that. There were other ways to store it, and there were safer places.

Luckily, Seagroves had found a jeweler on one of the enclave's side streets who was willing to turn the objects Seagroves brought him into chains. The pilot had spent most of his considerable free time combing stores in search of accessories. The little jeweler had rubbed his head in disbelief when Seagroves approached him, but such was the reputation of the LAM pilot that no one questioned his actions. The people in the stores hadn't even asked payment for the things he took. This being a demigod was all right, Seagroves thought smugly. The first of the chains, which had arrived only today, were now wrapped around the pilot's neck. Vost had made a disparaging comment at the sight of them, but as far as Seagroves was concerned, the mercenary commander could stuff it. Seagroves was going to be rich.

Vost was losing it, in Seagroves' opinion. Sirayuki was paying less and less attention to the commander and more and more to him. Seagroves loved it. Vost was such a cocky bastard; it served him right to eat a little humble pie. All he'd ever done was boss everyone around. Now maybe he'd be a little less sure of himself. Sooner or later, thought Seagroves, Sirayuki would deal with him rather than Vost. Then things would be different.

The LAM pilot rose from his chair and moved to the door to listen for movement in the hall beyond. He heard the soft patter of the serving girl coming toward his room. Hoond had evidently told her to bring more cabolos. It was a sure sign of his new importance that Hoond would have remembered to give her the orders and another sign that the girl would respond so quickly. He was sitting in his chair when the servant entered and placed the full decanter on the table, retrieving the empty one as she left.

He checked for noise again, and hearing nothing, quietly opened the door. A soft glow of gaslight lit the end of the corridor where the concierge was stationed, but the jets in the hall had been turned down to almost nothing. The area clear, Seagroves picked up the heavy bag of gold he'd hidden in the closet, and silently padded down the hall away from the servant. He was headed toward the 'Mech bastion to add to the ever-growing stash of items he kept buried there. Sooner or later, he knew, he'd have to establish another, more secure horde. The only place left was in the storage bins of the LAM itself. The gold's extra weight might make the LAM a bit unstable in flight, but it would be safe there because the bins would only open to his palm print. For the moment, the bins would have to do. He wasn't worried. The future looked as bright as the gold itself.

The great thing about keeping the gold at the bastion was that no one would ever suspect its presence. The mercenary techs were now housed in inns like this one. Not as good, but comfortable nonetheless. He was in a better place than even Vost had managed to acquire, a fact that had made the mercenary commander grind his teeth. When Vost had mentioned it to Sirayuki, the smiling shidosha only tucked his hands into his sleeves and shrugged. There was nothing he could do about it, he had explained. It was all voluntary. The Usugumo guards who now patroled the bastion, outside but not inside, were totally accustomed to the comings and goings of the pilots. They would report his presence to no one.

32

Kendall Pesht stared down into the bottom of the cup and contemplated the dark bits of residue. The little eatery, a ryoriten, had advertised the beverage as ocha, but any resemblance to any tea that Pesht had ever tasted was cosmetic only. Pesht was not a connoisseur of tea by any stretch of the imagination, but he had the general concept. This stuff didn't even come close. He swished the dregs around and looked again. There were some, he knew, who claimed to be able to read the future in the pattern of the leaves. He wished right now that he was one of those.

Pesht looked up from his cup and scanned the other clients of the small eating place. They were a general mix of Usugumo's middle class inhabitants, reasonably well-off people but not members of the seven ruling oligarchies that Pesht now understood were the only ones rich enough to call the shots in the enclave. The *Javelin* pilot drummed his fingers on the table, impatient for the scheduled meeting to take place. Seeing that his contact was late, Pesht was contemplating leaving and forgetting the whole thing. He decided to give the other man a few minutes more, and nodded to the little girl who looked inquisitively toward him, the teapot in her hand.

He was halfway through his current cup when he became aware that the soft background noise of conversation had suddenly stilled. Glancing up, Pesht saw Homma Sirayuki passing through the seated diners. The shidosha walked with the practiced arrogance of one long accustomed to obeisance from those around him.

The manager of the restaurant scurried before him, trying to determine the lord's destination. He offered the leader of the Usugumo any number of places, but none seemed to satisfy the man. The manager was becoming frantic. Then his eyes settled on the small alcove occupied by the new human. Pesht could see the concern in the manager's eyes, the slight beading on the upper lip. The man did not want to offend this new person, nor did he want to incur the wrath of the shidosha. There was obvious relief on his face when Sirayuki settled onto a cushion opposite Pesht. He bowed and scraped and snapped his fingers at the serving girls. There was a flurry of activity as fresh tea was brought to the table. The ordinary cup that Pesht had been using was whisked away and replaced by a beautiful ceramic version. When Sirayuki made no indication that he wanted more, the manager shooed away the staff and left the two men in splendid isolation.

"I think you have a developing problem," said Pesht, keeping his voice low enough not to carry beyond the table. "You may have taken a dragon into your household." Pesht had originally thought of using the metaphor of a tiger, but then decided on the dragon, whose image was everywhere in Usugumo. Pesht knew that it was because the mythic animal was greatly revered by the people of the Draconis Combine. A fitting symbol for Sirayuki and the rest of his group, thought Pesht. Ugly, stupid, self-centered beasts.

Sirayuki stared at Pesht with hooded, unblinking eyes. The little rat-faced mercenary was right, but he wanted to hear what else he had to say before responding.

"He's now been involved in a pair of humiliating disasters," Pesht went on. "I'm not sure how much longer you'll be able to deal with him. And he has other problems and interests as well."

Sirayuki stirred slightly, the teacup held between both

his ample hands. He let the warmth of the liquid flow into his palms. "I do not understand how your organization functions," he said, his voice dreamy as if he were speaking to himself rather than his host. "There seems to be no visible hierarchy within your unit. This Garber Vost does the talking and gives the orders, but I see no apparent reason for his dominance. He is neither rich nor more powerful than the others. And what about the woman who sits by his side? I do not understand her function."

Pesht leaned back from the table, then remembered he was sitting on a cushion and there was no chair back for him to rest against. He hated sitting on cushions; there was no way to show superiority on a cushion. "The status of the woman is easy to explain," he said. "Vost is hitting on her."

"Hitting on her?" Sirayuki was becoming impatient.

"You'd have to know Vost. He'll chase anything female, and the chase is more fun than the capture. He's got the hots for Hoond, and she's holding out. At least holding out most of the time. That drives him crazy. She's along at the meetings because he wants to stroke her."

"I still don't understand," mused Sirayuki. "In our society, here and in the other cities as well, women have a special place. They exist to serve the men who lead." The shidosha waved his hand to indicate the whole dining room. "You see that all the serving people here are women. That is as it should be. The man is in charge of the place, and the women serve. Even the women eating here are to serve the men they accompany. Doesn't your Hoond understand that?"

"We're a little different from that. Hoond was an officer on the ship that brought us here." Pesht could see that both the concepts of *female officer* and *ship that brought us* were beyond Sirayuki's comprehension. "It doesn't really matter. We're different. Leave it at that. Anyway, that's our problem and not yours. You have the problem of dealing with us as a group or as individuals. And if you deal with us as a group, you want to deal with someone who can deliver. I think you're worried that Vost can't."

Pesht hoped that he was on the right track. Right or not, he'd have to press on; he was too committed to the action now. "I think you will have to find a way to deal with more than Vost. Some people in the city may not be completely enthusiastic about the situation."

Sirayuki knew that the little rat-faced man was absolutely correct. The leaders of the seven oligarchies had been decidedly cool at their last meeting. They'd been especially frosty when Sirayuki explained what the mercenaries wanted and how they were to be paid. It was obvious that the leaders of the oligarchies had made contact with at least one of the other mercenaries and were attempting to do better.

The shidosha was elected as leader of Usugumo by the votes of the seven oligarchy leaders. It was not required that one family hold the position, though the Hommas had held it for three generations. That they'd been able to hold on to the position for so long was a measure of their cleverness and their ability to split the other factions. But it wasn't cast in iron that it would continue so. Sirayuki had a son who could win the position, but the shidosha would have to be careful. "You have, perhaps, a solution in mind?"

Pesht saw the conversation turning to his advantage. It would have been hopeless if Sirayuki were unaware of the unrest in his own ranks. "Your people want to deal with someone who can deliver what has been promised. The 'Mech is a powerful weapon, and if used correctly could dominate our little world. So far that has not happened. The people on your council want to see something better."

"Who are these people you speak of? Do they have names? Do they have faces?"

"That's not really important. See, I'm on your side. I want to work with you. As far as I'm concerned, you're the one who has the power. What you need is someone who can deliver and show these stooges what really works. And if they give us any trouble, we have the power to snuff them."

"I'm still not sure what you want or how you want to do it. You must understand my position. I am very weak compared to the others. I have no voice on the council when it's time to make a decision. All I can do is propose a course of action, and then they decide. I am powerless."

"That's a crock. I've been asking around. You're the richest man in Usugumo. You may not have a vote, but you have the money to buy any votes you need. That's how you've maintained control all these years. You and your family."

"It is true that I am rich, but in wealth is also weakness. I can be overturned at any time."

"Another crock. You are the one who controls iron production here. I know that. Seagroves hasn't figured out that gold has little value and iron is everything. There's not much of it—maybe it's just that you've kept it rare—so you have the power. I've done my homework. That's why I'm dealing with you and not one of the other dweebs. Let's cut the bull and get to the bottom line."

Sirayuki saw that Pesht was not completely blind to the truth of the situation. How the man had found out about the iron mine was a mystery, though. He had concealed ownership through a series of dummy corporations and figurehead positions. He'd even managed to get one of the members of the council to serve on the board of directors of one of the dummies. Now, in less than a week, this little man had unraveled the carefully constructed façade. There had to be something he wanted. "And what, then, is the bottom line for you?" Sirayuki asked amiably.

Pesht leaned back. Damn cushion, he thought. The next meeting we'll be in chairs at a real table. He leaned forward, putting both elbows on the table. "I can bring the team with me. We can support you. We can tell the others that you're the only one we'll deal with. If they need a demonstration of what we can do, we'll snuff one of them. Not a secret assassination like you people use. I mean a straight walk into the room, blow away the target, and walk out. Bold as brass. Bold as any metal you want to choose. That'll show them who's boss. I can do it. I know what buttons to push on the others."

"What buttons, as you call them, and what do you get out of this?"

"Ha. What do I want? I want all of it when it's over. I can control everyone in the team. Seagroves is the easiest. All he wants is money, and he thinks gold is it. Keep a shower of the stuff headed in his direction and he'll do anything. The guy's myopic on the subject. Pay attention to him, give him gold, let him fly. He's a great big fluff ball. No problem.

"Vost is easy too. I've been with him for almost six months, and there's only one thing he wants: women. And the more the better. The idea that women are servants is right up his alley. He chases every woman he sees. When he landed here a couple of weeks ago, the first thing he did was to try to set himself up as the sperm bank for the group. He's a libido at full power. I think he'd rather run after women than pilot a 'Mech.

"The last one to deal with is Hoond. She's a typical, insecure woman. She's doing a man's job in a man's world. All you have to do is treat her like a man. Show her some respect. Listen to what she has to say. You don't have to do anything she suggests, just listen. That was the trouble with the female 'Mech jockey we had; Vost wouldn't listen to her. She left. Left and took one of the 'Mechs with her. Stupid move on both their parts. I wouldn't have left her behind. I'd have killed her first.

"Those are the buttons to push on them. The technicians will do what they're told. They take orders. All they want is to tinker with the 'Mechs and keep them running. As long as the pilots don't bend the 'Mechs too badly, they'll be happy."

"You still haven't told me what you want. You said 'all of it,' and I haven't heard the 'all' yet."

Pesht smiled and leaned even closer to Sirayuki. "I want to be the next shidosha. I know it's supposed to go to your son, but I want it. So adopt me. I know it's possible. It's time for a transfusion of some new blood into the system."

33

Pesht let his eyes sweep across the parlor of his suite one more time, wanting everything to be at its best. Not so much in order to impress his visitor with the opulence of the place, but because he wanted to strike a pose. The place had to look like somewhere an important person might live. The inn had given him a suite of three rooms, with the sitting room finished to Pesht's specifications. The low table and cushions had been replaced by one of more comfortable height, plus a half-dozen straight-backed chairs. Pesht had no idea where the management had procured the items, but suspected they'd had to special order them from some local carpenter. They still smelled of recent workmanship. Taking a chair that faced the door, he settled down to wait.

He was still sitting there a quarter of an hour later when a knock came at the door. He rose quickly, opened the door, then closed and bolted it as soon as his visitor had entered. He'd installed the bolt personally, for it was the only way to secure the entrance when he'd first occupied the room.

Locks and bolts, Pesht had noticed, were reserved for the houses and businesses of the leaders of the seven oligarchies and the shidosha. That was one of the ways to identify their property; it had locks. It was how Pesht had been able to trace the ownership of the iron mine to Sirayuki; every door and gate in the facilities surrounding the mine had locks on them. Interestingly, the door of the offices of the firm that nominally owned the mine did not. It was obviously bogus and of little value.

The visitor entered the room silently, taking the chair to which Pesht gestured him from across the table. Pesht poured two small cups of budoshu and waited for Subash Chi to begin his presentation. He was the sanyu, the high priest of the Amatukaze, who had traveled to this meeting in Usugumo at what was probably some risk.

The Usugumo and the Amatukaze were in a period of truce since before the strike against Takuda's people and their allies in the woods three days earlier. The fact that Vost had engineered a preemptive LAM strike against the forces of the Amatukaze as the attack was beginning had not seemed to damage the fabric of the truce. Among other things, Pesht hoped to find out just how stable the agreement was. "You had no trouble finding the place, I trust," he said to begin the conversation. His visitor nodded and smiled. "There have been many changes since I last spoke to your agent," continued Pesht. "There have been certain offers made on your part and the parts of others that must be considered."

Subash Chi sat straight and rigid in the chair, his eyes fixed directly on those of his host as he tried to gauge the other man's strengths and weaknesses. The tradition of the Amatukaze was one of constant conflict with the other enclaves. Antipathy had existed among the three since the beginning of recorded time, but the animosity of the Amatukaze was the strongest. The Osio and the Usugumo had drifted from the fivefold path. Each had paid nominal respect to the Amatukaze as the religious exemplars, but over time they had turned their backs on the true way. The Osio had become rigid in their thinking, allowing only members of the nobility to become leaders. They kept the peasants as underlings, a class whose sweat and blood supported those whom birth had placed above them. The Osio had lost all feeling for the good of the population, coming to accept power as the only absolute.

They were a worthless agglomeration without whom the land would be better off.

The Usugumo, on the other hand, had turned toward the motive of profit over the needs of the people. Through time they had gained control of the means of production and distribution. Despite the fact that they were a despicable lot, the Osio could not eliminate them completely because it would lead to the ruin of the others. Chi understood that it would be better to subjugate the Usugumo than to destroy them. The Amatukaze had been planning that subjugation for as long as he and any of the other sanyu could remember. Now this little man presented the best chance to accomplish that dream. The forces the man claimed to control could drive the Usugumo to their knees without the need to destroy the entire enclave. But it was important that Chi know what the man wanted in return. He waited now to learn just that.

"There is a great deal I can do for you, Chi," said Pesht when his guest made no reply. He watched as the silent priest lifted the cup of budoshu and let the liquid brush his lips. Pesht could smell the pungent aroma of the hot wine that rose from his own cup. He had ordered the best budoshu available, and he hoped the sanyu appreciated it.

"You have already done much for me. The budoshu is of a very fine variety, and the kashi is without peer. I am in your debt."

Pesht understood about debt and status. These people in the enclaves were sensitive to both. Sirayuki had been obviously concerned about losing status among his peers, which was the sticking point on the subject of the adoption. Pesht had let the matter stew for a while, and the shidosha had finally given in. The word had come earlier in the day, and now Pesht was euphoric about his own future. The sanyu would have to come up with a significant offer. The budoshu and kashi had been ordered before the event, but they probably would help the sanyu make his decision. The sanyu didn't have to know Pesht had ordered the stuff as a celebration for himself; let the priest continue to think of it as in his honor.

"In Amatukaze," began Chi, clearing his throat, "we have a distinct hierarchy. It takes a long time, for many a lifetime, to reach a level of sublime contemplation. The way is long and difficult, and only the most dedicated can make the journey. Many begin, but few will achieve the end desired." Chi let his words sink in. This visitor from beyond the stars, as he and the others claimed to be, needed to understand in detail how strict was the discipline among the Amatukaze. One of the many aspects that gave the Amatukaze superiority over the others was the severity of the training.

"You must understand, you must absorb, the concept of the five," continued the sanyu. "There is a fivefold path to enlightenment, and five pillars that hold up the truth. These things must be appreciated."

"Is this going to be a lecture on philosophy?" asked Pesht. "I've heard all this before from the first sanyu who talked to me. He was full of the same stuff. Frankly, Chi, I don't care a hoot for all that. I want to know what you want from me and what you'll give for that service. I'm not looking for some reward in the great beyond or in the distant future. I'm not interested in some inner peace. Get that straight from the start."

"But without inner peace there is nothing. All the worldly trappings of our existence pale in comparison to that which glows from within. That is why our junior bokushi wear only simple gowns, sleep on the floor, and eat plain rice. They must allow the inner light to grow. Simplicity is everything."

"Right. That's why your temple glows at night. That's why you wear the embroidered, bejeweled gowns. That's why you recognize fine budoshu and kashi when you have it. Don't give me that story about being simple and poor. Your idea of five is to have five courses at every meal, five wines with each course, and five layers of goosedown under you when you sleep. That's what the five is all about." Pesht was enjoying himself; this dealing from a strong position was not bad at all.

"There are ways," said the sanyu, clearing his voice and letting his eyes drop to the table. "There are ways. We could always validate you as being of a higher level. You could become a second level, a full sanyu."

"I'm not sure I want to be a priest. I think I'd like to be higher than that. Perhaps higher than you. What comes above you?"

"There is nothing above me. There are only the philosophers and great thinkers who have laid down the tenets of our religion."

"Then let me be one of those. I can tell all of you what to do. That sounds fair and just."

"That would give you a power that no one has ever had."

"Someone did. There was someone who established all the claptrap that you guys spout. Why do all those guys have to be dead? There was a time when they were alive or there wouldn't be any record."

"But they were people of great simplicity and strength. They were thinkers."

"So it's time for a non-thinker. Time for someone who acts. I can act. I can see to it that the Amatukaze become supreme. Maybe you people have been sitting on your backsides so long that you've lost the ability to really do anything. Look, Chi. I have the power to do something. Something that none of you have been able to do for five hundred years. Now's the time. Swallow your pride, or your face, or anything else, and go with it. Make me your supreme speaker. Then it will get done."

"I will have to think about it," said the sanyu, rising from his chair. "There are many aspects to consider. The future of the Amatukaze is at stake. Perhaps there is a way for us to arrange this matter."

Pesht escorted his guest to the door. There was no one in the corridor, and the sanyu departed unseen. Closing the door behind him, Pesht smiled.

"Do you think he bought your idea?" asked Seagroves, suddenly emerging from his hiding place in the bedroom.

"You heard it all? Do you believe that garbage about being simple and poor? I wanted to laugh in his face."

"I liked the bit about becoming the philosopher for the religion," said Seagroves as he swallowed what was left of the budoshu from one of the ceramic cups, then filled it again with the wine. "I can just see you as Confucius or something. If you get the top spot, what's in it for me?"

"What do you want? I can make you anything you desire. How about you sit at my right hand and speak for me. Think of it: the mouthpiece of a god."

"They don't really have god," said Seagroves. "They just have a bunch of dead people who said a bunch of things."

"Right. The only difference is that we'd be alive. Those guys were alive once, and they didn't take full advantage of it. I plan to make full use of the power. If people are going to sit at my feet and listen to me, you can be sure I'll tell them what I want. And they can jolly well jump when I say so. The only thing they'll have a chance to ask is 'how far' on the way up."

"What about the Osio? You were supposed to hear from them too."

"Creeps. That's all they are." Pesht poured the last of the wine into his cup. Trouble with these cups, he thought, was that they didn't hold enough. That's one thing he'd change, no matter where he went. He'd have big flagons. No use drinking something if you couldn't pour it down.

"The problem with the Osio," he said, "is that they're too servile. Nothing like a military system to breed servility. They promised me anything I wanted. Wanted to make me their O, their king. They said that it wouldn't be hard.

"I didn't talk to the boss. Maybe he would have offered something else. It didn't sound like he'd be willing to bite the bullet so I could get the job. Anyway, the other guys offered to bump him off. That wasn't the word they used, of course, but they said they'd get rid of the big O and put me in his place. Said I could have the job for life.

"There's only one thing wrong with bumping off the big O to make room for another. It could become habit-forming, know what I mean? How long before another of them got the idea that I could be eliminated just as easily and another stud put in my place? Or how long before one of you figured it out? I'd have to eliminate the whole lot of you just to keep myself alive. I don't think I want to rule like that. Not that I wouldn't be willing to eliminate some of you."

Seagroves looked at the *Javelin* pilot. Pesht drove the weakest of the three 'Mechs. There was no real reason why the little rat-faced man should be the one in charge. "I still like the deal I have here. This is where I started, and this is where I think I'll stay."

"I'll take that into consideration before I make a decision," said Pesht with a smile. "Don't worry, big fella. You are a definite and important part of my plans. But just think about it—if we go with the Amatukaze, you'll be an almost god."

34

Takuda awoke to the smell of coffee that drifted through the curtain into his underground sleeping area. He lay with his eyes closed in the darkness, letting the aroma kindle memories of other mornings and other places. He'd been introduced to coffee while in the home of someone not originally bred in the Draconis Combine, and become an instant convert. Tea, the Combine's traditional drink, had never had the same power over his olfactory sense. Now, he sat bolt upright, fully awake.

Ever since Bustoe had been sent to Arsenault's section, Takuda had been brewing his own morning beverage. He even looked forward to the task as one of those little things that let him slip from the prison of command to the freedom of domestic life. Now someone else was doing it for him again. It had to be one of the Tetatae. He rolled out of the cot and slipped his feet into his armored combat boots.

Crouched in the outer room was the Tetatae who had "adopted" the DEST commander. The figure was attentively watching the tiny personal cooker that each DEST member was issued. The glowing fuel tablet cast a blue-green light onto the creature's face. So intent was the Tetatae in waiting for the coffee to begin simmering, for the first, tiny bubbles to appear at the edges of the cup, that he was unaware of the presence of the master. Takuda stood silent and still, not wanting to break the concentration of the neophyte chef. Getting it just right was an almost religious stricture for Pita.

Seeing the first bubbles appear, Pita whisked the cup from the burner surface with an excited, happy gurgle. His sounds were immediately answered by others from beyond the blackout curtain. There were scurrying sounds, and then the tiny room was suddenly full of other Tetatae, all hopping and bobbing with excitement and happiness. The sound and movement stopped the moment they saw the DEST commander, however. With screeches of consternation, the horde of Tetatae scrambled backward through the curtain. Pita presented the cup of steaming coffee.

Takuda accepted the proffered mug and settled into one of the simple chairs that stood beside the equally simple desk. Both chairs and desk had been constructed for him by the Tetatae. He hadn't asked for them, just mentioned in passing one day that he hated the folding stool. That had been enough; the next day a chair and matching desk had appeared in the headquarters. They must have quizzed the other DEST members about the construction. The following day a second chair had appeared. The Tetatae were attentive to the desires of the commander, and equally attentive to the other humans.

They seemed to have no sense of hierarchy and command, treating all the humans the same—like gods. Each of the humans had started out as an object of fear, which then changed to nominal acceptance and tolerance. When the *Locust* 'Mechs had emerged from the DropShip, that attitude had changed to reverence; now the humans were literally objects of worship. All of them equally. The fact that Takuda was the commander was of no importance to the Tetatae. That he was a human was enough and all there was.

The business of equal worship bothered Takuda. Equality broke down the hierarchy of command, and the commander wondered if it was going to affect his ability to control his people in the future. The problem hadn't come up yet, but the future was unknown. He would have to watch the others.

The other humans had also acquired servants. At first a Tetatae would follow while one of the humans went about his duties. The little aliens were especially intrigued by the techs, who were able to open the skin of the great machines and dig through their innards. They had become disciples; more had followed. Now each of the humans had a personal entourage following him or her everywhere.

It had started with the Tetatae attending to their immediate needs, but it had become much more than that. Before long the Tetatae followers began rushing to serve the humans in every way. A human had only to make a chance remark and the little aliens would scurry to accomplish the mission. Takuda had once mentioned in passing that he liked the color and scent of the rose-hued drengkit flowers that grew near the command bunker. The following morning he awoke to find the surrounding area covered with arengkits that had been painstakingly transplanted during the night. It was too late to do anything about it now, but Takuda had been extra careful about casual comments after that.

Takuda's troops were not so delicate once they discovered their power over the aliens. Dana Lost was a particular offender. After being assigned a position among some large rocks on the edge of the forest, Lost had mentioned to his personal Tetatae that he didn't like having one particular, huge rock directly behind the position. When the Tetatae found that moving it was beyond his capabilities, he'd gone off to organize a large working party. After struggling with the outcropping for an entire day, the party had managed to remove the offending piece. No sooner was it done than Lost commented that he really would rather have it there after all. The Tetatae had organized a second working party and labored to put the outcropping back in place. They did such a fine job that not a trace remained of either the removal or replacement.

Lost had been just about to comment that, in reality, he would rather the rock were gone altogether when Swalen Horg, followed by his own entourage, happened on the scene. The encounter was not entirely a chance one, however. Horg had watched the removal of the rock and then its restoration. When it looked like Lost was about to have the Tetatae move the offending piece a second time, he'd decided to step in. Horg took Lost aside and mentioned in his normal, soft voice that it was not right to abuse the Tetatae's loyalty this way. Lost had rebuffed him, saying that it was fun to see the little beggars work. Horg had pointed out that if Lost continued, there might be serious repercussions. That wasn't exactly the word Horg had used, but he made it clear to Lost that behaving this way could lead to serious bodily harm. Lost had retired in a sulk, but the big rock stayed where it was.

Holly Goodall, the *Locust* 'Mech pilot, had come to Takuda with another problem. Like the rest of the DEST team, she had her following. Though she'd gone about her business as usual, it was becoming difficult to move the *Locust* from place to place because of the number of aliens who clustered around its feet. She'd mentioned the difficulty to Takuda, but that was the extent of it. Then one afternoon Goodall had come to Takuda followed by a Tetatae that was obviously an infant. Not just a juvenile, but a real infant. The little ball of fluff was probably no more than a year old.

"Sir," said Goodall, "I have become a mother. I had nothing to do with it, and I'm not really happy about it, but the Tetatae have decided that I should care for this child. What do I do now?"

Takuda was nonplussed. Nothing in his years within the ranks of the Draconis Combine military had prepared him for this. Members of the Combine military forces did reproduce; that was only natural. Commanders were trained to deal with such events. But when a human soldier had a child, everyone enjoyed a certain lead time in which to prepare for the event. To have someone simply hand over a child for adoption was not the part of the training, nor was dealing with an alien child. The Combine didn't deal with aliens; no one in the Inner Sphere ever had. Colonization usually meant the settlement of a planet by humans. Takuda considered the dilemma of involuntary motherhood to be beyond him. He took the question to Dakodo, Dokaepi, and Totito.

The shaman, tribal hetman, and Dakodo, who acted as the spokesman, met with Takuda in the latter's headquarters. Takuda explained the situation, beginning at the beginning and working up to the delivery of the child to Goodall. By the time the meeting took place, Emmerdean Knyte had also reported a child being "delivered" to his team. Both Goodall and Knyte were trying to handle the situation, but both wanted to be relieved of the responsibility. Takuda explained all this to the three Tetatae, who promised to take it to the full council and to the tribe.

But the Tetatae had problems of their own. The announcement of the new humans had spread through the woodland. Tetatae visiting from other bands had come calling to see with their own eyes. They had seen, talked, and departed. It was not long before the other tribes began to arrive, at first in small groups, with the most mobile and strongest among the early arrivals. Then had come the mass of the tribes, with hundreds of Tetatae now camped around the human position. By custom, the host tribe, that headed by Totito and Dokaepi, was required to provide food and shelter. It was a task well beyond their current capabilities.

When the council met to discuss the problem of the children, they invited Takuda to attend. That in itself was a signal honor. It would have been unusual enough for them to invite a Tetatae from another tribe to attend a council; the presence of an alien was unheard of. The humans and Tetatae had cohabited the planet for five hundred years, but this was the first time a human had ever attended a Tetatae council.

Takuda went with the expectation that he would be asked to speak, that he would be questioned about why the humans were there. That did not happen. In fact, Takuda never said a word. It all devolved on how the Tetatae conducted their council meeting.

Because the event was one of great formality, the Tetatae's customary long orations became even lengthier than usual. The youngest member of the council, Popae, was the first to speak. She outlined the traditions of the Tetatae from the very dawn of time. She spoke of the importance of the children of the Tetatae. She spoke of the importance of the education of the Tetatae. She spoke slowly so that Dakodo, who was translating for Takuda, would not fall behind. She spoke of the coming of the first humans five hundred years ago. She traced the development of that relationship stage by stage. She talked on and on.

Takuda found the history interesting if slightly long-winded, but it seemed interminable. He began to wonder when Popae would get to the point, when she would arrive at the question at hand. Finally, after nearly four hours of straight talk, she mentioned the children and the humans. Then she sat down. Now, thought Takuda, they would ask for his opinion. But they didn't. Another Tetatae councilor rose and began to speak. He outlined the traditions of the Tetatae from the very dawn of time. He spoke of the importance of the children of the Tetatae. He spoke of the importance of the education of the Tetatae. He spoke slowly so that Dakodo would not fall behind in the translation. He spoke of the coming of the first humans five hundred years ago. He traced the development of that relationship stage by stage. He talked on and on.

Takuda began to lose it after an hour. At the end of two hours his eyelids were sagging. By the end of the third he was drowning in the talk. And still the second man went on. When that councilor was finally done, another rose in his place and began all over again.

Takuda was not well-versed enough in the history and traditions of the Tetatae to understand that each of the speakers was describing different incidents and different tribesmen. He nodded off. Even his bushido training could not keep him awake for the eighteen hours of talk. The Tetatae had the advantage. They could shut down half their bodies while the other half remained alert. They were built for just this kind of marathon. In the end they made no decision that Takuda could determine, yet Dakodo assured him that no more Tetatae children would be delivered for adoption. The aliens would still continue to revere the humans, however; there was no way to change that. Takuda stumbled back to the headquarters bunker and collapsed into a profound sleep.

35

Takuda awoke to find an unfamiliar civilian waiting for him in the outer room of the bunker. The man was dressed in a long, dark gown, but was unadorned except for a five-petalled lotus pendant hanging from a massive iron chain around his neck. The petals were of different colors: pale white, clear, turquoise, iridescent, and one that glowed softly in the dim light of the underground bunker. The man bowed and introduced himself. "I am Hushiko Miburi. I am a resident of Amatukaze. Some among us have learned of your presence and would like to hear what you have to say. We know what is happening on our small world, and there is much grief here. We seek to achieve a harmony that the current situation has disrupted. We want to see harmony reestablished."

Takuda gestured the man onto one of the chairs in the headquarters. He had three of them now, a third having appeared unbidden in the same way as had the first two. Takuda made a mental note to tell Pita that he had all the chairs he needed. Otherwise, there'd soon be so many he wouldn't have room to move in the small cavern. Two cups of coffee, the last ones from the emergency packets, were served by the little alien. Takuda waved the Tetatae away and faced his visitor.

"Hushiko Miburi, I appreciate that you have come such a great distance to see me. I too am interested in establishing harmony in this small portion of the world. I fear, however, that our ideas of harmony may differ. How can I help you?"

"There have been times of harmony in the history of the cities. Our beginnings were in great strife, and there was much death. Then that time passed and we began to understand that to kill each other was to destroy everything. We declared an end to war.

"That time continued for many generations. The small cities were established. We grew and we prospered. Over the years, over the generations, over the centuries, we grew stronger and more secure. There were divisions among the clans, but mutual need kept these in check. There were always those who sought to destroy the harmony, but they were kept in their place.

"It is that attempt at harmony that you see when the guntai face each other. Long ago we abandoned the terrible weapons of the past. Some survived, like those you see driven across the fields. But they are our champions.

"No group could totally subjugate the other, no one win a war, and so the battles continued. The forces of the designated cities would meet on the field. The champions would face each other. There would be battle. Honor would be served; farmland, mines, forests would change hands, but the basic harmony between the three cities was not disturbed.

"Now the Usugumo have obtained weapons even more powerful than the ones we had in the far past. We once had knowledge of such weapons, but it has passed into the realm of legend. We know about them, but we no longer understand their use. And now people will die on the field. It will be more than the champions. There will be a violation of the harmony that held our small world in balance. This will be very bad. I come to you, sent by some of my friends, to see if harmony can be restored."

Takuda listened in silence as Hushiko Miburi explained the situation. "I understand the necessity of harmony, and I understand that the Usugumo have obtained a weapon system that will destroy the balance of power, but I do not understand how my intervention will restore that harmony," he said.

Miburi pressed his fingertips together over the untouched cup of coffee. "We have been led to believe that you possess weapons equal to or superior to those of the Usugumo. We know that you have been attacked, that you have won the battles. Perhaps you could use those weapons against those of the Usugumo to redress the balance. All harmony is balance, a balance between the good and evil that begets harmony. Those who travel too far to one side or the other, either for good or for ill, will upset the harmony of the situation. The forces of the Usugumo are now in the hands of those who could bring evil, even chaos. You have the power to tip the scales back toward the center."

"Would it not be better to end all this?" asked Takuda. He eyed the slowly cooling cup of coffee in the hands of his visitor. It was the last cup that would ever be available. If his guest didn't want it, he hoped to find a way to preserve it for some future time. His harmony would be terribly upset if the cup were taken away and the liquid discarded.

"There is no reason," continued Takuda, "why this divisiveness should continue. You can settle any disputes you have. You need not do it with force. Renounce your weapons. If there are those within your cities who need the excitement, the adventure, that war provides, let them instead use that energy to explore and develop the land. There is so much land.

"When the conflicts have been settled, we can establish a formal society, as envisioned by our common ancestors. We can go back to the ideals of the great founder of House Kurita. We can return to the dream of Shiro Kurita. Then shall we know harmony."

Hushiko smiled at the naive gentleman who sat across the table. "We had problems before you arrived, Yubari Takuda, and we will have them after you and I are dead and gone. We had problems and yet we had harmony. But

they were *our* problems. It is you who have arrived to upset the harmony of our lives. It should be your responsibility to redress the situation. You can restore the system
to what it was. You are *obliged* to do so. Take your forces
and strike at those of the Usugumo."

"But there is a better way. We can move the situation
into the future rather than the past. Why should you return to the bad times when good days can be ahead of
us?"

"It is only you who see them as bad times. Few among
us would agree. It is the future that appears as a time of
trouble, and the future is something that you can set
right."

Takuda saw that he could say no more to the visitor
from the Amatukaze. Miburi did not see the possibilities.
He bid the man farewell, then sat down to contemplate
the situation. At least the coffee was still there. Cold but
still there. Takuda sipped slowly at the dark brew, savor-
ing the taste even more because it was the last.

There had to be other people within the enclaves who
could see a future not dominated by the past. Takuda
would have to send out additional patrols to find them.
And if they should seek him out, he would be easy to
find. The Tetatae were beginning to congregate in greater
and greater numbers, the DEST members acquiring more
and more followers among the aliens. Even Takuda, who
tried to discourage them, had numerous Tetatae following
his wake. And still they kept coming. Takuda could not
make the Tetatae stop treating them as demigods, and
most of his people had given up trying.

The commander's concentration was broken when Pita
came into the room to indicate that another person was
waiting to see him. Pita had not learned many words in
the language of the humans: coffee, chair, and visitor
were his big ones. Now he eyed the last of the coffee,
wondering what he would serve to this next strange human who sought to speak with his leader. Takuda nodded
assent, and Pita went to fetch the man.

The visitor, announced by Pita as Toge Omori, stepped through the curtain and examined the room and its contents. His face was impassive, but his eyes showed clearly that he didn't approve of the spartan furnishings. This was a man who was used to being in charge, used to being taken care of. He waited expectantly.

Takuda was too tired to go through the ritual. He gestured the man to a chair. When Omori didn't move, Takuda fixed him with his eyes. "You may sit or stand as you wish, Toge Omori. No one in this headquarters will stand for you. In here I am in charge, and I do not have the time or the energy to cater to you."

Omori sneered at the remark, but when no one moved to present a chair, he sat down. "Yubari Takuda, I represent a rentai of the Osio. It is not a regular, official regiment. It is secret, and some of the best in the city are among its ranks. They are not especially pleased with the current situation or the change your compatriots will bring. I have been authorized to approach you for your thoughts. And perhaps you would be so kind as to listen to ours."

"I know very little about your aims, Toge Omori. Perhaps you should speak first."

"Very well. We in Osio believe that the best of all worlds is the model designed by our ancestors and reflected in the structure of the army. There is a natural order in life, with the strong at the top. We are that group. We will win.

"That has always been the way of things. The strong are not only strong in force, they are also strong in their ability to see what the future holds and to seize it. You are the future. We wish to have you with us.

"That is why we invite you to join the forces with the Osio against the others. We know that you have twice defeated the new weapons of the Usugumo. You are the more powerful. With your guidance, the Osio can benefit from the equally terrible weapons that you possess. We can become supreme and bend the others to our will."

Toge Omori held up his hand to still the comment that was forming on the lips of the DEST commander. "I understand that you wish to know how this would be of benefit to you and your people. That is quite simple. You and yours will become the leaders of the rentai. You have the strength and the ability to use it. You should be our leader."

"All this is quite interesting," said Takuda. "But what happens if, as the leader, I decide that all weapons should be eliminated? What happens if I wish to see an older, more formal, more harmonious society evolve? What if I wanted to do away with the great weapons?"

"You can't! It is the only way we could dominate the others. We can rule the sekai! With your weapons we could strike out against all the enemies of the true Draconis Combine. We must remember how the legendary Shiro Kurita expanded the boundaries of our empire. We must be prepared for contact with the Inner Sphere. It will come. We must be acceptable to them. We must use force."

Takuda stared through the man as though the chair were empty. This Toge Omori, like Miburi before him, did not understand what the future might bring. They were all too interested in making themselves the supreme rulers. And to what purpose? None. Domination. Force. Was there no other way? Perhaps the people of this planet had become so divisive because of the rebellion that had been tearing at the seams of the Draconis Combine when their ancestors had crashed on this unknown planet some five hundred years ago.

"Toge Omori, you have said many interesting things. I have heard other proposals from representatives of all three enclaves. I must withdraw to make my decision. You will please excuse me. Make sure you leave word of where or how we can contact you. Leave the information with Parker Davud, my aide. I will contact you with my decision."

"I leave you to your deliberations, Yubari Takuda. I

leave you for a while, but remember this: there are others who will also want to hear your decision. There are others who will not wait long. There are others who will demand action. Decide quickly."

═══ 36 ═══

The room was small and overheated. Even with the gas jets turned down to a minimum, they still produced enough heat to make ventilation important. The secrecy of the meeting, however, was such that the participants would not allow even the smallest access to the room. The main door was locked and barred. Beyond the portal was a guard who would allow no one to pass without permission from those already within. The only unbarred door was the one to the serving area, but the servants' station was as secure as the main room.

Five men were present at the meeting: Hushiko Miburi, Toge Omori, Achira Kochira, Deau Kanso, and Pinto Geppu. They sat cross-legged around the inlaid table, which was set with the cups and a pot of a simple tea service. Around the perimeter of the room, josh sticks wafted the smoke of incense into the motionless air. Kochira, host of the ceremony, tapped softly on the table, and as if by magic a small Tetatae appeared from the serving quarters to replace the empty teapot with a full one. Then the alien vanished as quietly as he had come, returning to the serving area. Three other Tetatae remained, but the only humans within the secure rooms were the five at the table.

Kochira wiped his mouth with a small cloth, carefully tapping his lips with a single, cloth-protected finger. "We are all of one mind," he said, his voice so soft that it carried only to the other four. The others sat motionless, wooden statues carved and silent. They heard, but there was no reason to answer. "And since we are of the same mind, and since we have discussed this before, we need only review what we have planned and what we have discovered within the past five days.

"When first we met, we discussed the situation presented by the arrival of the other humans. We did not know then, and I am not sure we know even now, from where these people come. They have said, and they continue to say, that they come from beyond the stars to arrive here by accident. I accept the story, yet there is still the nagging doubt. They carry the symbol of our own legendary ancestors. That could be mere coincidence, but I think it not likely.

"But let us pass over that for now. They are here. They bring a level of technical ability far beyond what we possess, a level even beyond what the legends of our forefathers tell. They can do things that we have not dreamed of. They walk in great machines that are invulnerable to our weapons. I know this to be true. We have tested it."

"It was that information which spurred me to call the first meeting, and it was that knowledge that has made me so interested in what the rest of you have to say. We first met five days ago, because of our guest from the Amatukaze, Pinto Geppu. I note with interest that he has brought another of his brothers to visit us now. We welcome Hushiko Miburi of the Amatukaze. We understand that he has had direct negotiations with the leader of the forest force, as has Toge Omori. We will be interested to hear their reports." Kochira passed the teapot to his right.

Omori poured a serving of tea into his tiny cup and passed the pot to the right again. The pot made its way around the table to come to rest again in front of Kochira. No one spoke during the passage, and none of the participants lifted his eyes above his cup until the ceremony was complete. Then Miburi raised his eyes and spoke. "It is true, I have met the leader of the forest forces. He is

Yubari Takuda, and he is a most dangerous man. He does not understand the position of the enclaves. He does not see that we have attained a measure of balance. He does not understand that the best thing he can do is to go away with all his brothers. I approached him with these thoughts, but I think he wishes to remain. He plans to impose some structure, a concept of his own, on all of us. I challenged him, but it was no use. I suggested that he destroy the forces currently within the walls of Usugumo and that he then leave. This he did not accept."

"I, too, have spoken to the named Yubari Takuda," said Omori. "I believe I visited him some time shortly after Hushiko Miburi's visit. I proposed a different solution to the current problem, but I was also rejected.

"I suggested that Yubari Takuda join a rentai that is already in existence in Osio. I suggested that our forces combined with his could destroy the new Usugumo forces, and then destroy those of the other cities.

"Yubari Takuda refused my offer. He said that for the Osio to become dominant would not be a harmonious solution to the situation. He proposed that we unite. That we destroy our weapons. That we form a new society.

"This information is of great embarrassment to me now. That I would have suggested eliminating all of you, with whom I now have agreed to act in concert, is a terrible stain upon my honor. My only hope is that my actions will benefit all in the future. My actions were taken with the best intentions, and though they were directed against some of you, I trust you will see that I was attempting to perform with honor."

"Toge Omori," said Kochira, "We act in honorable ways. For you to have suggested a course of action that would be detrimental to those of us at this table is not without honor. You did what you saw as the correct course. Times change, and then the opposite way becomes the true one. That is the teaching of the tao, but it is not without honor." Kochira nodded to Miburi.

"It is what I had foreseen would happen," Kochira

went on. "That is why at our last meeting I put forward a plan to deal with these problems to our mutual advantage. We are not"—he let his eyes make contact with each individual at the table—"the most powerful members of our societies. We are not the leaders of our respective cities. But each of us wields certain power, and working together we are stronger than any one of the enclaves.

"It would seem strange that with only five people, we could be stronger than an entire city, but it is true. Each one of us brings to this convocation significant strengths. We must remember that if we unite, not only do we bring that strength to our dantai, but we also make our former cities weaker by that amount.

"Toge Omori brings to us an organization of young officers and lords. With those we can organize a force that is loyal to our leadership. Of them we will be able to ask any sacrifice. Hushiko Miburi of the Amatukaze has the skill of a negotiator and contacts within the elements currently positioned in the forest. He has already spoken with Yubari Takuda and understands the kind of a man he is. Pinto Geppu is a sanyu in the Amatukaze. He is already a member of the fifth pillar of knowledge. He can become the spiritual guide of us and all those who will join us. He has a following within his enclave, and he understands the vulnerability of the Sanyu Subash Chi himself.

"From the Usugumo we welcome Deau Kanso, the city's wealthiest man, and perhaps the wealthiest man in all our cities. Not only does he understand the power of wealth, but he also understands how others react to it. It will be through him that we will be able to reach, and have reached, the various members of the new humans. He has already made great progress."

Kanso smiled. It was a shy smile, the smile of one who has great power but prefers not to demonstrate it through ostentatious display. "I have already approached one of the new humans, with a proposal. It was not a direct approach; I had my agents accomplish it. The one called

Seagroves wishes to acquire gold. I am not sure what he plans to do with it, but he does love it. I have already ensured that he has a continuing supply of the metal. He is very busy accumulating it. I will be able to control him by the volume of its flow. He was very easy. Two of the people who work for his group, they are named Guardine and Sabine, are also busy acquiring metal and jewels. Both of them, I am sorry to report, are females. They, too, will be very easy to control. Women like interesting baubles. They are ours.

"I have even had agents make contact with those in the woods. I did not approach your Yubari Takuda, but my people did contact some of the others.

"There is one who will join our camp. He has been without wealth all his life, and the thought of being rich is an unbearable stimulus. He will join us if we can continue to make it worth his while."

Kochira tapped the table again and the Tetatae replaced the empty teapot once more. The Usugumo host paid no attention to the ancient alien who performed the service. The wizened figure might have been no more than another piece of furniture, for that was how the Usugumo viewed the Tetatae. Kochira knew that this Tetatae, an old one named Pōpae, had been in some form of service to the councilors of the Usugumo for as long as anyone could remember. He had no friends in the city except for his own family. A piece of furniture.

"It is time for us to begin the plan with real objectives," Kochira announced. "It is time. We know that these people are mercenaries, driven only by individual greed and hope of personal gain. We need to discover what each one wants and then fulfill that need. Some of them we know. We need to find the others.

"There are those whom we will be able to convince. There are those whom we will not. Those we control, we must bring together into a single force. Those we cannot convince must be eliminated. That is as it must be. Join us or die.

"There will be some opportunity for the mercenaries to carry out eliminations of their own. That would be better for us because treachery to their own would make them ours completely. But we must not insist on this. Remember that these people are driven by certain desires. We must not tread too heavily on their possible dislikes and lingering loyalties. If they will not terminate their own people, those who will become their enemies, then we must do it. I am sure that Toge Omori or Sanyu Pinto Geppu will be able to find those who will do it.

"Deau Geppu smiles at the thought. I have no doubt that he also has people who can perform the function. He has, I would also venture, already inquired into the possibility.

"Once we have the forces of the mercenaries either under our control or eliminated, we will be the masters of our own destiny. We will approach the enclaves with a force at our backs. We will dictate the future. Gentlemen, we can be the new order. We can be the future."

There was general assent and excitement. Now the plan was before them. Each had an assignment. They would meet again, and when that time came, each would have assets under his control. They filed out of the room and past the silent guard just as the first blue-amber light of dawn crept over the eastern horizon. Põpae cleared the table, washed the dishes, and went home to his family.

=== 37 ===

"I hate being treated like a slab of meat." Elizabeth Hoond shrugged off her jacket and hung it over the back of a chair. She flopped down in the chair, threw her feet onto the table, and accepted a goblet from Seagroves.

"Vost been after you again?"

"Not Vost. It's these damn people in the city. Every time I go somewhere, and even when I don't, there's always someone lurking around trying to make a deal. I don't know what they want. I just wish they'd leave me alone. All I want is to do my job, get paid, and be left alone."

"You don't understand the situation, do you, Beth? You're a mercenary now. You do things for pay. And it's the pay that's important." Seagroves gestured around the room, whose every surface glowed with gold. "Just look at how well I'm doing. I've got an agent out there getting me all the gold I can handle. I'll be so rich when this is over that no one will be able to touch me. They want to know what you want? Decide what it is and get on with it."

"Gold doesn't have any value here, you fool. No wonder they give you all you want. It's iron they want, not gold."

"But they will. Trust me. Everyone wants gold. Maybe not today, maybe not tomorrow, but sooner or later they'll want gold, and I'll have it. Then I'll be rich."

Suddenly the door to Seagroves' sitting room opened violently to reveal Vost and Pesht, who entered unbidden. Seagroves made a mental note to lock the door after anyone came. He hated being surprised by visitors. He rose now and threw the bolt with pointed significance. "To what do I owe this surprise visit?"

"We've got to talk," said Vost as he dragged a chair next to Hoond and sat down. "You got anything to drink here, Seagroves?" The mercenary looked around the room. "My, my, this place looks like a temple to avarice."

"I'm no more avaricious than you are, Vost. It's just that we're interested in different things. We all have our way of keeping score. Money is mine, especially gold. I don't carp at you for your way. At least I won't get some disease from the gold."

"Neither will I. And as far as a disease goes, you've already got it. It's a disease called stupid greed. If it doesn't kill you, it could kill one of us. Why don't you just dump this stuff and collect something else? Sometimes I think you're numb as a pounded thumb. I can't even remember why I hired you."

"You hired me, oh exalted leader, because I'm the one with the LAM."

"Fine. 'Nuff said. Let's deal with the real problem." Vost drained the goblet Seagroves had poured him, and grimaced. This city didn't have one decent alcoholic beverage in its entire inventory. He sat back and gazed at the other three.

"I suppose you've all been approached by someone or other about our status. I know I've been so popular with different people that I can't even crawl into or out of bed without finding someone waiting to talk to me."

"I thought that was what you wanted," said Hoond with an evil look. "I didn't know you ever went to bed alone—if you could help it."

"I don't, Beth. But I want to choose who that person is. How about you?"

"Get stuffed, Vost. Maybe it'd be you if you were the

last man on earth, but even then I'd probably choose celibacy as a more viable alternative."

"Stow it," interrupted Seagroves. "You said there was something important. Let's get on with it. I need to fumigate my rooms."

Vost waved away the sarcasm. "There's something going on, and we need to talk about it. Like I said before, people have been following me around for the past few days. They all want to talk deal. Do we want to talk deal?"

"Same here," said Pesht. He didn't want to elaborate on the subject; he'd been talking deal almost since they'd arrived in Usugumo. But these offers were different. "From what I understand, it's a consortium of businessmen from all three cities. They're outside the normal channels of power."

The others confirmed Pesht's words. There was another group, a gaggle of financiers, religious leaders, and officers, who were willing to pay for the services of the mercenaries. The contact with this group was tenuous; none of the mercs was quite sure who was in charge. Pesht raised an even bigger issue. He wondered if it wasn't all a trap on the part of Sirayuki. Perhaps the Usugumo shidosha was trying to trick the mercenaries.

The others thought about it and then discarded the idea. They could see no reason for Sirayuki to try to trap them. The only motive would be if he had reason to believe the mercenaries were not loyal to him. Everyone at the meeting assured everyone else that they'd never considered cutting another deal after the first few days. On this point all were quite adamant.

"Well, it looks like Sirayuki has competition," Vost said. "So, let's see what the others have to offer. It can't hurt."

Pesht contemplated the toes of his boots. "What about beating the bushes for the others? I mean, if we can sit here doing nothing and still find competition for the Usugumo, how many others might be out there? Why not take a look? Maybe we've been too sedentary. Maybe we need to do some looking."

Everyone fell silent for a moment. They'd all been thinking the same thing for at least half the meeting, and now someone had verbalized their thoughts. They agreed. Perhaps, said Vost, they should stage a demonstration to show exactly what the 'Mechs could do. Smiles and agreement.

The following morning, even before the first rays of the sun rising had touched the glacis of the mercenary bastion, the full team assembled. They came as individuals, each one drifting through the predawn darkness to rendezvous at the entrance. Silently the ground crew took up defensive positions within the covered way. Silently the pilots conducted the last pre-op checks on the great BattleMechs. As sunlight began to dapple the forward slope of the bastion, all three monsters came to life. In an explosive roar that reverberated within the fortress and then from the walls of Usugumo, all three 'Mechs cleared the walls and began their violent sales pitch to those interested in absolute power.

They cruised north at forty kilometers per hour, an easy pace for all three 'Mechs. They bypassed Amatukaze in the early dawn, the guards at the gate agape as they watched the metal monsters stride past. An hour later they assembled before the walls of Osio.

The fortifications were laid out as regular works: bonnettes, ravelins, lunes, and demi-lunes protecting the main rampart. The works were unmanned because there was plenty of time to reach the works before any adversary could storm the glacis and counterscarp. It was a perfect place for a 'Mech demonstration.

Vost did not want to kill people, just destroy property. Killing would only lead to hard feelings on the part of the survivors. A vendetta might follow. That was not the point of the exercise. Vost merely wanted prospective employers to see what 'Mechs could really do. He wasn't even interested in having the LAM go airborne. They'd already demonstrated the LAM's abilities; doing so again would serve no purpose. Besides, Seagroves was already cocky enough, already being hailed as a hero. The LAM would walk.

Seagroves was not happy about the situation, but he accepted it. He was perfectly aware of the fuel gauge on the dashboard, and didn't want to waste fuel if it wasn't necessary. He mused idly about re-routing the energy from the Allied 250 fusion core into the AVRTech 125 jet propulsion system. Tami Wilson, the chief tech still with the mercenaries, had been thinking about the problem, but she'd need help from Yaputi and perhaps even Mark Jacobs. Unfortunately, both had decided to remain with Takuda. Seagroves shrugged. Yaputi and Jacobs would be on the team once the real bidding for services began. He settled into the cockpit seat and traversed the wall section looking for a good target.

As planned, Pesht and the *Javelin* began the demonstration. All the 'Mechs stood within range of the 'Mech's short-range missile systems, another decision by Vost. He was not interested in demonstrating the range of the lasers and PPC. It would be more spectacular for the 'Mechs to work together on a target. They could save range as an added fillip for when it really counted

Pesht began by making single shots with the left SRM pack. There was an explosion and then the blast of an arcing missile. The first one struck square on the glacis of a bastion, exploding like a bright flower against the stonework. Pieces of the outer face peeled away, hurtling through the morning air. The second missile struck the exposed under-surface and burrowed deeply before detonating. A muffled explosion, a fountain of rubble. Another missile struck home. Another cascade of flying debris.

By the time the sixth missile was on its way, the parapet had disintegrated. A gaping breach had been blown through it, turning it to smoking rubble. The *Javelin* waited for the clouds of dust to settle. As the smoke cleared, Pesht ripple-fired the other SRM system, the *Javelin*'s chest exploding in a ball of continuous fire as it launched its six short-range weapons from their internal racks. The back blast of the launch swirled around the cockpit.

The incoming missiles passed through the breach and struck, one after the other, the rear wall of the bastion. A continuous roar as missile after missile hit the churning, boiling, glowing chaos. Great slabs of stone hurtled through the clouded air. A shower of debris pattered down over a radius of several hundred meters. Then silence.

Vost waited for the last bit of dust to clear. The bastion was a smoldering heap of rubble. Fiery pockets still glowed along the wing walls, erupting into sudden columns of flame as some portion of the gate, ladders, or hoardings took fire. The place was uninhabitable. Even to the untrained eye—and there were many now gathered on the main parapet—it was a sure and certain fact that no one could have survived the attack. Vost pushed forward on the throttle and let his *Panther* step over the covered way and into the bastion.

He swung the 'Mech's torso back and forth, raising the right arm. He let the PPC traverse the top of the parapet, watching with satisfaction as the crowd of onlookers scattered for safety. Then he steadied the cross hairs on a small ravelin standing at some distance, yet too close for the PPC to really demonstrate its ability. He swung the sight system to the right. There, outlined by the rays of the slanting sun was the upper tower of the Osio castle. He checked the sensor system; someone was in the tower. He watched. The person didn't move. Too bad, he thought. But it wasn't his intention to injure anyone who might yet become a client, so he let the cross hairs drift to the right and triggered the PPC. An incandescent streak shot past the edge of the tower, nicking, ever so slightly, the flaring roof.

The effect was immediate. The figure in the tower

failed morale. Vost could see the glowing mark descend from the tower. A very fast descent. Probably running. Vost let the figure disappear beyond an intervening rooftop, then swung his sights to the center of the tower. The PPC roared again, ripping the tower apart in a shower of stone and dust.

38

The explosion could be heard as far away as the DEST headquarters. Takuda had received a report that the mercenary 'Mechs had passed his location at dawn, but he hadn't followed them, assuming they were moving to another enclave as part of some deal. Now he could hear the chatter of Tetatae voices outside his door.

The curtain of the command post was swept aside as Parker Davud burst in. "There's a lot of shooting at Osio, Commander. They must really be tearing the place to pieces. You can feel the force of the explosions through the ground. Could be a full-scale attack."

"But why Osio?" Takuda asked, rhetorically. "They've never attacked the Osio before. Until now they've always hit the Amatukaze, and always with the ground forces. They've never attacked an enclave. Something's changed."

The two men pushed outside to find the camp in a state of confusion. The Tetatae were running for the shelter of the deeper woods, the members of the host tribe trying to maintain some kind of control. Over the thundering sound of hundreds of running Tetatae feet could be heard the screeching of those in search of ... something. Takuda watched in amazement. Why, he wondered, were people in panic always interested in getting to the other side of the area? Those who were on the left wanted to seek shelter on the right. Those who were on the right wanted to

seek shelter on the left. Front to rear, rear to front. It
never seemed that those in one area were willing to seek
shelter there. And why were the children always separated from their mothers by the greatest distance at the
moment of panic? The DEST commander stood and
watched. At last the scattering Tetatae reached some kind
of stasis and the movement came to an abrupt halt.

"I have them on the IR sensor, sir," said Ariake Sanae.
She gestured to the long-range I/R scanner system she'd
rigged to a salvaged 'Mech secondary screen. She and
Mark Jacobs, the inveterate tinkerer and former JumpShip
engineer, had bashed together the rig. By cross-feeding an
anode with the divergent screen-sorting matrix, they'd
built a crude, long-range system that could sense infrared
spectrum out to the horizon. They'd set the array on top
of a hill behind the DEST position, which put all three
enclaves at the limit of its range. It wasn't a portable
piece, and it required constant fine-tuning, but it did at
least give them early-warning capability. Its primary use
was against possible attacks by the LAM. With the
LAM's top speed of nine hundred kilometers per hour, it
could be on them from the city in five minutes or less.
Not much time to react, but certainly better than nothing.
Sanae swung the screen down so that Takuda could see
the developing action.

Amorphous glowing dots, the 'Mechs were faintly visible on the screen. The blast of the PPC, obviously from
the *Panther,* streaked the phosphorescence of the surface.
Takuda stared at the display. The 'Mechs weren't doing
anything rational. They were just standing outside the
walls of Osio and proceeding to blast them to rubble. He
could see the outline of the destroyed targets still pulsat-
ing with heat from the beating they were taking. The
LAM was in its 'Mech mode, stalking back and forth in
front of the walls. A great section of the outer works
leaped into relief as the laser hosed down a section. The
'Mechs weren't even attempting to enter the city.

"Looks like they're selling something to the Osio,"

mused Davud. "I'd say they're trying to convince them to be good boys in the future. I wonder what got them so bent out of shape?"

"Nothing! Nothing did!" exclaimed Takuda. "You were right the first time, Parker. They're selling something. Look! None of the Usugumo forces had moved. Not a sign of them anywhere. The 'Mechs are just out demonstrating their wares. They're looking for another bidder. They're up there advertising their abilities." He stepped back from the screen and shook his head. "This could be unfavorable. We know that there are bidders in the other enclaves; some of them have already approached us. Vost and his people are trying to see what they can do. Unfavorable. Unfavorable for all of us."

Takuda knew that he wasn't the only one among the DEST group who'd been tapped for a deal. Knyte and Arsenault had reported being contacted by humans who'd offered to hire them to fight for one or more of the enclaves. He also knew from talking with Sanae that at least one group was willing to freelance the situation. Evidently Vost was beating the brush to see what else he could scare up. A bidding war was about to start, and the losers would be ground to pieces by the winners.

"We've got to stop them!" exclaimed Takuda, punching his right fist into his left palm. "If Vost accomplishes what he set out to do, the whole situation will be out of control. Vost goes to the highest bidder, and he can hold all the enclaves hostage. It will set everyone against everyone else. It's the perfect mercenary environment. Mister Davud," he said, turning toward his aide. "Call up the *Locust*s. Let's see what we can do to slow him down."

Ten minutes later the two *Locust* 'Mechs strode into the clearing around the command bunker, the Tetatae scampering and scurrying around them, oblivious to the danger of being squashed by the foot of a twenty-ton 'Mech. Goodall and Jacobs opened their emergency hatches and looked down at their commander, both pilots grinning with excitement. This was the first time they'd been in action since the disastrous attack by the combined Usugumo-'Mech force more than a week before. Jacobs was confident of his ability to control and fight his *Locust,* and happy that now he'd get the chance.

They'd debated whether to train Bustoe up to operational standards, but Goodall had finally convinced Takuda that Jacobs was the best choice. Bustoe had other duties, responsibilities, and assets that Jacob could not duplicate. Now Jacobs was ready for a demonstration of what he had relearned. All the old training, gained so long ago from his father, would be put to the test. The last thing Goodall had said to him before closing down the hatch had been the timeworn reminder to 'Mech pilots: "There are old pilots, and there are bold pilots. But there are no old, bold pilots." Jacobs had shrugged off the injunction and fired up the 160 LTV fusion drive system.

There was a sudden roar at the edge of the clearing as a machine churned its way into the tiny space. Exhaust fumes and steam boiled from the device, and its wheels flayed the ground, throwing up great clods of dirt. The thing rumbled to a stop between the two 'Mechs. Panting and wheezing, it stood there trembling like a wet dog. The hatch opened and out popped the grinning faces of Parker Davud and Topi.

"I've brought reinforcements!" shouted Davud above the whoosh and whine of the engine. "Topi and I have been working on it ever since she stole it from the Usugumo. Not much firepower, but Sanae can give us the missile launcher for the top. She can even come along to fire it. And Johan, too, as a sniper. You never know when one really great shot might make a difference."

Takuda stared in amazement. He had forgotten all about the vehicle that Knyte had used in his escape from Usugumo. There was no way it would be of any use in the upcoming fight. It could only make the casualty figures on the DEST side that much higher. He shook his head in disbelief and as a negative response. "I cannot allow it," he said to the sorrowful Davud. "It wouldn't add much to the fight."

"Sure it will," said Davud brightly. "They won't expect it, and we can get in close. We can do it. Really we can. Please let us try." Davud looked around the assembled DEST members. "We won't take anyone who doesn't volunteer."

There was a chorus of response from those around him. Everyone, it seemed, wanted to go. Better, reasoned Takuda, to send them out in something like this than to risk them out there as individuals. He nodded his assent.

Vost had placed his forces in front of the main gate to Amatukaze. The demonstration at Osio had gone better than he could have expected. The population had been duly terrified, fleeing like panicked chickens before the advance of the 'Mechs. After the *Javelin*'s volley of short-range missiles and the PPC fire from the *Panther,* the LAM had walked into the dry moat, using its laser battery to destroy selected targets with pinpoint accuracy. It had all been both spectacular and appalling to those unfamiliar with the modern firepower wielded by a 'Mech.

Rather than continue destroying Osio, Vost moved off to deal with the Amatukaze. There was no use, he knew, in destroying so much that any possible employers wouldn't have any money left over after the task of repairing their city. The religious enclave was next on the list. They had plenty of money and the will to spend it.

Once they arrived, the *Javelin* stepped forward first. As at Osio, a vacant bastion would be the target of their demonstration. The main rampart was thick with people, and the white-light vision screen showed the flash of religious artifacts. The first short-range missile smashed into the glacis, the explosion sending slabs of stone scything through the air. Vost watched with satisfaction as he settled back into the command seat and waited. The screech of the intruder-warning klaxon suddenly broke his short-lived reverie. He glanced at the secondary screen to see where within the enclave a hostile force had been detected. At first, nothing. Then he saw it: a series of three I/R signatures approaching from the rear. The DEST team had come out to play.

Vost snapped a series of orders over the commlink, and his people turned away from the walls of Amatukaze. They had range and firepower over the advancing DEST forces, and he planned to use both. The LAM would again be grounded, over the strenuous protests of Seagroves. But fuel for the jet propulsion unit was still a problem, and they currently had no need for the additional speed and maneuverability of the airborne version of the 'Mech. Better, thought Vost, to just slug it out on the ground.

Takuda's two *Locust*s had been counting on surprise to get in close enough to do damage before the mercenaries' armor and the volume of fire could turn the tide against them. But the moment Goodall had cleared the edge of the woods and had the enemy 'Mechs on her I/R screen, she saw that the *Javelin* and *Phoenix Hawk* were moving toward her instead of facing the walls of the enclave. The *Panther* outranged the *Locust*s two to one, which gave the *Locust*s scant hope of doing significant damage to the 'Mech before the others closed.

The *Locust* was a light 'Mech that relied on speed and surprise. With surprise lost, its only hope was to move fast and keep moving, hoping to throw off an enemy 'Mech's targeting computers. The great advantage of the BattleMech, commanded by an experienced pilot, over the circuitry of the computer was that the human was completely unpredictable. But as the range dropped, there came a time when a mere point-and-shoot system was deadly. No matter how erratically the *Locust* moved, the *Panther* would be able to bring the heavy PPC to bear before the *Locust* could reach its maximum range. Then it was all over for the *Locust*. Goodall called for a swift retreat.

Though she was able to make the transition from attack

to retreat in a single step, Jacobs was not so swift. Whether it was inexperience or foolhardiness made no difference. Before Jacobs could swing the 'Mech behind the trees, the *Panther* PPC caught the light 'Mech square in the torso. A fountain of incandescent armor boiled off the front of the smaller machine, and the *Locust* staggered backward under the ferocity of the hit. As Jacobs and the *Locust* toppled to the rear, his career as a pilot would have come to an abrupt end had Parker Davud not driven the tank against the back of the falling machine's legs.

The shock of the PPC hit and the weight of the tank twisted the *Locust* completely about, and by the time Jacobs regained control of his staggering 'Mech, he was headed in the right direction. He jammed the throttle against the forward stops, and the *Locust* bounded off into the woods dripping molten armor and trailing servo coils.

39

As taught by the philosophy of taoism, in all things is their opposite. The defeat of the DEST forces in open combat was the gateway to riches and control for the mercenaries commanded by Vost. Yet from the defeat came resurrection, and from victory came fragmentation.

In the soft falling of night, Takuda sat dejected in his command post. He realized that he'd committed his 'Mechs to a hopeless battle, and for that they were paying the penalty. That Jacobs' *Locust* had not been destroyed was a stroke of luck, but luck was a fickle goddess, and the next time she might not smile upon his efforts. Hope and time for his people were slipping away like sands in an hourglass. For the second time since they'd landed on this planet, Takuda considered seppuku.

The curtain of the command post was pulled aside and Parker Davud entered. "I've got some good news and some bad news, Commander." Davud pulled a chair back from the table and settled into it. "The good news is that we've just picked up some recruits from the enclaves. The bad news is that only some of them are armed."

Takuda looked at his aide. Surely this man had drifted from reality to fantasy. Recruits? There couldn't be recruits after the fiasco of the morning. But it turned out that Parker Davud was right on both counts. A steady stream of people was making its way from the enclaves to the DEST location. They came for many reasons, but all wanted to offer their services. There was also a smattering of soldiers from each of the enclaves, equipped with whatever weapons they'd been able to carry. By the time the huge, mottled, gibbous moon broke the rim of the eastern horizon, Takuda had almost a full platoon. The force was a mix of people from all three enclaves, more than half of them women and children. Their weapons ranged from swords and muskets to light pistols and non-standard bolt action rifles. Neither was there any standardization of ammunition, but it was a start.

The people came, they said, because they believed the new humans on the outside offered a better future than did their life within the enclaves. Some were drawn to Takuda's philosophy of a better world; others were seeking dominance. A few were looking to even a score with those they had left behind. In all cases Takuda welcomed them into his ranks and began the task of organization.

In the enclaves, there was a feeling of euphoria among the leadership. The demonstration of 'Mech firepower had led each faction to decide that their future lay with Vost. They knew that by hiring the services of the mercenaries, they could achieve whatever goals they held in their deepest dreams. They knew that whoever employed those services would be the one who controlled the destiny of the enclaves. To assure that future, they poured out their promises to Vost and the others.

But the leaders of the enclaves were not the only ones impressed by the demonstration. The entrepreneurs represented by Achira Kochira and his associates found themselves part of a crowded field all clamoring for the services of the mercenaries. So fragmented were the groups and their offers that the aspirants found it easier to deal with the individual pilots in private than as a single entity. Vost, Seagroves, and Pesht were regularly besieged by enthusiastic buyers. It was a seller's market.

Each of the pilots reacted to the offers in his own way. Vost was most easily approached by those with soft, sinuous bodies, luminescent eyes, and fulsome lips. Never in his life had such opportunities come his way. The women of the mercenary team, Wilson, Sabine, and Guardine as well as Hoond, were no longer the focus of his attention. Now that he had no time for the mundane or familiar, they were left to sit alone in their simple rooms or splendid quarters while he enjoyed the charms of enclave society.

As for Seagroves, he became so saturated with gold that his room was like a shrine to Midas. Gold, in all its shapes and forms, continued to pile up around him. Though the planet's artisans were accustomed to working in metals such as iron, copper, and silver, they had been hastily recruited to create objects of splendor in the baser metal.

Then there was Pesht, who almost had to pinch himself to be sure all the marvelous offers were more than just a dream. No longer was he getting offers merely to become AN important person; now the offers were for him to become THE important person in any coalition or single group. One offer piled on top of another until it was almost impossible to tell the difference. The last was always the best, but there was no reason to take it because the next one would be better.

The leaders of the enclaves soon became aware that they were being outbid by the individual groups. They also understood the two factors that was making the market crazy: the existence of the separate enclaves and the presence of the DEST force still lingering in the forest beyond. They decided to solve both their problems in one fell swoop. For the first time in almost four hundred years, the three declared a truce among themselves—achieving, ironically, Takuda's single, most important objective. He had inadvertently welded the enclaves together in a common purpose. Unfortunately, the purpose for which they come together in truce was his destruction. The leaders of the enclaves decided that by eliminating the forest force they could reduce the need to hire the mercenaries. With Takuda gone, the enclaves might be able to get rid of the mercenaries in the same way they'd eliminated weapons of mass destruction so many centuries before. Takuda was first on their agenda.

The organization was patchwork at best, but by dawn they had hammered out an agreement that would set the forces of all three enclaves against the human intruders and their Tetatae friends now hidden in the forest. The enclaves would redeem their honor and resolve a problem at the same time.

The plan called for their combined forces to make a concerted attack against the forest group. Each enclave leader would contribute his entire mobile group, supported by infantry and weapons, to the attack. Secretly, however, each one was also planning to hold back a portion, just in case things did not go as planned. With much hand-shaking, back-slapping, and feigned good will, the leaders departed for their respective cities to make more plans.

At dawn the forces rumbled out from the gates of the enclaves. The mercenary pilots were too exhausted to take any notice, and only the technicians, still on lonely guard at the 'Mech bastion, saw them go. None made any attempt to notify their commander.

The three columns, a confused assortment of underpowered vehicles and clinging infantry, joined up in the open fields between Amatukaze and Usugumo. There was a momentary delay and fear of treachery when the Osio were late, but then everyone realized they had farther to travel and had suffered a delay in getting started because of a communications breakdown. Unwilling to lose face at such a critical time, the commander of the Osio column pushed his people hard to make up for the error. Because of the delay, the Osio commander demanded the right to redeem his honor by leading the attack with his forces. The commanders of the Usugumo and Amatukaze finally agreed. The attack went in, a little late, a little ragged, but in.

Takuda's people had seen the amalgamation of the forces coming. At first they thought it must be some climactic battle among the enclaves, but when they saw the troops coming together peacefully, they began to worry. The recruits who had joined during the night had no idea what was happening because they'd fled the enclaves before the decision to combine forces had been made. They were just as surprised as Takuda and his men by the assemblage. Any doubts about what was happening evaporated when the Osio rentai turned to face the forest and then came on.

The combat group was led by the lighter vehicles. These were small, wheeled affairs with exposed engines and troops on their rear decks frantically working the pumps that forced fuel to the engines. Clouds of thick, dark exhaust rose from the tall stacks, belching forth more and more violently until tongues of fire could be seen from the crowns. The roar of the motors was deafening. As the scout cars came forward, their great wheels churned up the soft dirt. In the front of each one rode the commander in a perch high above the prow; a tall, wooden latticework tower was his post. He used a long prod to direct the driver, hammering on the unfortunate's shoulder whenever he wished to make a turn.

Behind them came the heavier forces, enclosed vehicles that were covered with riding troops. These were armored forces and their infantry support. Great clods of dirt spewed from under their thrashing, spiked wheels. The infantry hung on, inspired by the terror of being thrown under one of the behemoths. It was all very grand.

Trotting behind the vehicles came the regular infantry formations carrying their assortment of muskets. Archaic though the weapons might be, they were equally deadly. Takuda had the advantage of firepower, but he lacked numbers. No matter where he deployed his thin forces, there would always be enough attackers to work around his flanks. To defeat this alliance would call for more than just bullets. The short-range missile launcher fired first, its arcing vapor trail streaking toward one of the second-line attack vehicles. The missile passed through the laminated wooden armor plate of the prow and exploded against the engine block on the inside. The vehicle staggered momentarily and then burst apart in a cloud of fire, steam, pulleys, belts, gears, and people.

The Osio rentai did not hesitate. A long, high-pitched scream rose up from the ranks of the jogging troops as they broke into a full run. Off to the right Takuda heard the staccato stutter of a DEST light machine pistol, followed almost at once by the steady thump of the weapon section's machine gun. Some of the volunteer recruits were getting into the action. He couldn't hear it, but he was sure that the DEST laser rifles were working their way through the horde of rushing enemy. Then he saw that someone must have targeted a scout vehicle with a laser. First, the exterior of the engine produced a bright red spot, and then the whole cylinder—piston, smokestack, and manifold—rose from the chassis like a rocket. It flared off into the smoke-shrouded sky with an infernal howl before crashing some distance away behind the supporting troops.

Commlink chatter. Unidentified but urgent.

"Too many. Have to pull back."

"Recruits breaking on my left."

"Bustoe hit. I'm withdrawing."

"Give me fire to the left. I have to pull back. Too many of them."

"Damn! They're like ants. Can't crush them fast enough."

"Watch out for that next vehicle. Looks like a slug gun in the front."

Takuda considered ordering the *Locust* up in support, but he didn't know where the LAM was. If he committed the 'Mech too early, the LAM could be on the scene in a few minutes and destroy it. Until he discovered the mercenaries' location, he could not commit the 'Mech.

Then a great crash drew Takuda's attention. It was on

of the second-line vehicles erupting in a cloud of smoke
and coolant steam, probably from another missile hit.
They were going to have to be careful; those missiles
would soon become more valuable than life. Then the vehicle emerged from the smoke, and Takuda realized that
it had fired at his troops. A sudden trembling in the
ground under his feet startled him. Looking off to the
right he saw a boulder the size of a large trash can bounding away into the forest. The vehicle was firing ball ammunition. Archaic but deadly. You'd be just as dead if
that fell on you as if from a hit by a laser, he thought.

The Tetatae allies were fighting with spears and
wicked, short kogatana that were sharp enough to slice
through an unarmored man. In fighting them, the Osio
forces seemed to redouble their ferocity as though they
wanted to exterminate the aliens rather than defeat them.

"Machine gun's gone. Had to pull back. Low on
ammo."

"My right. My right. Someone support my right. I can't
hold them."

"Pull back. Pull back. I can't get there. Pull back."

"The tetties are taking it in the shorts. They're getting
slaughtered."

Takuda followed the course of the battle over the
commlink. His lines were collapsing all across the front.
From what he could hear, the DEST members were doing
all right, but the recruits and Tetatae were bearing the
brunt of the casualties. The short-range missile launcher
was loading and firing as fast as Sanae and Miranda
could slap rounds into the launch tray. Its I/R guidance
system had no trouble locking onto the overheated tanks,
but sooner or later the SRM would run out of ammunition. At Takuda's signal, his troops began to give ground.

40

The light sections of Takuda's force covered the retreat, though it wasn't much to cover; the front line of recruits and Tetatae had broken under the weight of the assault. Those who'd had the presence of mind to think of the future had taken their weapons with them. Those recruits who'd been overcome by fear had abandoned their equipment in flight. Knyte and Arsenault kept their teams spread out and under control. They retreated in short jumps, returning fire as the confident forces of the enclaves came up against them. In the woods the lasers were at a distinct advantage over the simpler slug-throwers because they were the perfect ambush weapon. The rifle emitted only a sibilant hum when it fired and did not betray the operator with a muzzle flash or cloud of explosive gas. In many cases a DEST member was able to get off several, killing shots before being discovered.

By mid-afternoon they'd broken off all contact with the attacking forces except for the single vedettes that Takuda had left in touch. The ranks of the attackers had become so badly mixed up that they were equally willing to let the battle subside while they reorganized. In the excitement of victory they did not stop to count the cost or mourn the dead. They were on a roll and wanted to finish the job. There would be time enough later to deal with the lost and injured. Now was the time for celebration and victory. Someone broke out a bottle of budoshu and the party began, but the revelry was confined mostly to the support troops. The men in contact with the sentries understood just how deadly the forest could be.

To the rear of the scattered front, the heavy equipment began to gather. There were great gaps in the formations, and some units had simply ceased to exist. Not just as effective combat forces, but as entire units. Some had no survivors.

The leaders reorganized the mobile units as fast as they could. They knew that the battle was not over. They also knew that they were winning. Based on the enemy dead they'd discovered, based on the exotic weapons they'd encountered, there could not be many more of Takuda's troops in the woods. The bulk of the forest force had been broken. Victory was just a grasp away. They felt a driving need to finish the job before dark.

Takuda also spent the lull in reorganization. In addition to the casualties suffered by the recruits and the Tetatae, there were casualties among all the DEST teams. Bustoe had taken a soft lead slug through the chest. The slug had so wandered its way through the chest cavity that the only way to get it out was to cut through his back, where the object betrayed its presence by a great bulge below the man's rib cage. Bustoe would live, but he certainly wouldn't be in any shape for combat for some time. Takuda might have to use him as a last resort, but he wouldn't want to commit the *gun-so* to a mobile action.

Andi Holland had been struck by a flying object of some kind that had laid open her back to the shoulder blade. The wound was bad, but they could bind and support it enough to keep her on the line. It would mean she'd be firing weapons with only one hand for a while—and her off hand at that—but she could still move, shoot, and communicate. Johan Miranda had gotten burned when one of the short-range missiles, loaded before the launcher was fully cooled, had prematurely fired in the launch tube. He was out of action for good, his face and hands burned beyond immediate hope of repair. And even if they could find a way to relieve his pain, the expert shooter would never draw bead on another target: he was blind.

Takuda called the leaders of his disparate force together at his temporary command post. Davud was there to represent the DEST team, Dakodo spoke for the Tetatae, and Robert Fullerton, a recent arrival from Osio, spoke for the recruits. As the meeting progressed, they were joined by Holly Goodall.

Takuda glanced around the assemblage. There was no need to tell them that they were losing ground and the battle. So far, the DEST members had managed to survive the worst of the damage, but that would not last forever. Fullerton reported that of the forty-five recruits who had gathered in the forest the night before, only nine were unhurt. A dozen of the others were wounded, some seriously, and the other fourteen were gone—either dead, captured, or deserted. In any case, they were no longer part of the force. Fullerton estimated that he could put twelve people on the line, but his weapons were short of ammunition and his people were short on hope. They would stay, but they weren't enthusiastic about the future.

Dakodo reported much the same. More than two hundred Tetatae males had volunteered to fight with Takuda, representing slightly less than half the adult males in the assorted tribes who had gathered around the DEST group during the past week. Of that number, fewer than a fourth were in any shape to continue. Takuda estimated that he could put a force of perhaps fifty Tetatae into the next defense, a far cry from the two hundred at the start of the battle. There might be more, but that was a faint hope.

The last report came from Goodall. Both *Locust*s were operational, but Jacobs' 'Mech was less than half effective. Not only had the frontal armor been virtually destroyed, but the main gyrostabilizer servos had been burned out beyond all recognition. She had traded 'Mechs with Jacobs on the assumption that a good pilot in a bad

'Mech and an inexperienced pilot in a good 'Mech was a better option than Jacobs in the damaged *Locust*. Goodall would be able to fight the damaged machine, while Jacobs certainly would not. It took at least ten years to train a good 'Mech pilot, and although Jacobs showed great natural ability, he was nowhere near qualified enough. His past training was no substitute for experience. He could pilot the 'Mech and fight it, after a fashion, but it was almost impossible for him to do both.

Thus the reports to Takuda. The universal recommendation was to break contact and make the best retreat possible. By nightfall they should be able to cover enough ground to leave behind the forces allied against them. They would be faster than their pursuers because they could traverse the woods without having to deal with an enemy to their front. Never knowing where the DEST force might be hiding, the enclave regiments would have to be more cautious. Takuda still had his I/R technology available, which let him detect any enemy movement long before the danger of making contact. Despite all that, both his flanks had been turned by the assault, and the center was in danger of being breached. There was nothing to do but break contact and retreat into the deep woods.

Takuda listened to the litany of defeat. They were right, of course. The situation offered little hope. But if they retreated now, his force would fall apart. He already had two DEST members beyond recall as fighters, and a retreat would strain the fabric of command, perhaps beyond the limit. He knew that every one of the DEST members had received offers from some group in the enclaves, and a retreat now might encourage some of them to break ranks and join what they saw as the winning side. He could even understand how that might happen. They'd fallen onto this planet for eternity. It wasn't so difficult to understand that some of his people might want to leave a family name and traditions.

The recruits were in much the same condition.

Fullerton and a few of the others might be willing to live in the woods for the rest of their lives, but most of them had come to Takuda in the hope of finding a better life. Eating nuts and berries in the deep woods would hardly be their idea of that.

And then there were the Tetatae. No matter how much Takuda hated their viewing him as some kind of savior, no matter how he had protested, he did bear some responsibility toward the little aliens. To retreat into the woods to save his own skin would be to condemn them to the unrelenting wrath of the people of the enclaves. That would not be any justice as he saw it.

It would also be difficult for Takuda to abandon his high hopes of solving the dilemma faced by the leaders and inhabitants of the enclaves. To abandon that hope now was almost unbearable. There had to be some way, he thought, to redress the situation. He turned to Goodall. "Holly, do you think you and Jacobs can provide fire for us?"

"Certainly, sir," said Goodall. "We can still move and shoot. Not well, and I wouldn't want to fight their 'Mechs, but in the present situation I think we can do it."

"Good," Takuda said, rising to his feet. "There's only one solution right now. With the left in ruins, the right collapsing, and the center in danger of being breached, the only thing to do is attack, and attack at once."

The plan was simple. Knyte and his section would hold all across the front. They'd divide up into three teams, each with a DEST member and a few recruits and Tetatae for support. They would not engage attacks by the enclave forces, but would give ground, inflicting casualties and drawing the enemy in on themselves. The deeper they got into the forest, the better for Takuda's plan. Knyte and his people would try to separate the infantry forces from the supporting vehicles. If they succeeded, the strategy would also render the long-range fire of the riflemen and machine-gunners much less of a problem.

With the enclave forces being pulled deeper and deeper

into the trees, all of Takuda's people would work around the flank of the enemy. Once well to the side and rear of the armored force, they would attack. The medium lasers of the *Locust*s would out-range anything the enclaves could muster. The first charge would have to carry all the way.

By mid-afternoon Takuda's forces were in place, and none too soon. The probing by the enclave forces was becoming more and more vigorous, and it wasn't long before every member of the Knyte section was reporting pressure building to his front. Small enemy parties were working around the flanks of the strong points, and Knyte's section members were being forced to pull back.

Takuda acknowledged the information but issued no specific orders. He wasn't the type of commander to micromanage a battle. With the front extending over several kilometers, there was no way to truly understand each subordinate's problems. He gave mission orders and advice, but he left the battle up to those who were in contact. As long as they kept him informed of the changing tides of battle, he left well enough alone. His subordinates responded with enthusiasm and initiative.

Meanwhile the *Locust* 'Mechs and the rest of the force drifted off to the left flank. By the sounds of the battle and the reports from his people, Takuda could feel the line of combat pass across his front. He waited, waited, waited, and then sprang the trap. The *Locust*s rose from their hiding places and fired. The DEST members, recruits, and Tetatae charged.

The enemy's armored forces and some vehicle-mounted infantry were slowly traversing a broad, open area, so confident in their superiority that they hadn't even bothered to post security. Bad mistake.

With the motors chuffing happily away, they were perfect sensor locks for the I/R targeting systems of Takuda's 'Mechs. Goodall watched the targeting cross hairs flash red on the side of a vehicle, then toggled the firing button. So confident was she of a hit and target destruction that she didn't even wait for confirmation. She switched to the next vehicle in the line.

Both she and Jacobs had started with their engines at the limit of range so that the smoke and debris of the explosions would not interfere with the sensor locks or the laser fire. And it worked like a charm. The enclave forces thought they were being attacked from the other flank and turned away from the 'Mechs to fight the hidden foe. Nothing but rear armor faced the *Locusts*, and they took advantage of it. Before the enclave troops could realize that the attack was actually coming from the right, the field was littered with the remains of a dozen fighting machines. By then it was too late.

The DEST people, the recruits, and the Tetatae were among the survivors, closing with a ferocity that surprised Takuda. He too was swept along in the charge, forgetting to command, becoming once again merely an assault trooper. It was like old times. He fired the laser rifle from his hip as he ran, pausing only momentarily to snap aimed shots at fleeing enemy troopers. Over the commlink he heard, but did not comprehend, that Knyte and his section had joined the attack as well. All along the enclave line, front to rear, side to side, the enemy was on the run. Not just running, but fleeing in terror, abandoning their weapons and armor as they tried to get clear of this sudden assault.

By the time the sun sank in the west, the sky turning red with the drifting smoke of a hundred fires that rose like tombstones from as many vehicles. Takuda was back in his original headquarters bunker. Gathered around him were the wounded, smoke-stained, exhausted survivors. Exhausted perhaps, but happy in the knowledge that the day had been theirs.

=====41=====

Nothing but a battle lost, an ancient commander once said, can be half so melancholy as a battle won. And the truth of that had continued for centuries. Now, here on this unknown planet, it was true again that night for Takuda and his people. While the exhausted, dispirited survivors of the enclave force made their desultory way back to their compounds, the equally exhausted, dispirited victors dropped to the ground and slept, or moved over the shattered battlescape in search of surviving friends, or booty, or just because they were too tired to do anything else.

Takuda, as begrimed, blood-spattered, and hollow-eyed as any of his people, sat inside his command bunker and listened to the reports from his subordinates. The attack had been more successful than they'd even dreamed it could be. The most serious damage had been to the servo on the left leg of Goodall's damaged 'Mech. The joint had frozen in mid-stride, but she'd continued to fight until there had been no more targets in sight. The *Locust* could still hobble along in a crazy-gaited away, but it couldn't be called combat-worthy by any stretch of the imagination. All three techs were working on it now, and there was just the slightest chance that it would be mobile by first light.

Fullerton reported two recruits wounded, both slightly, in the counterattack. He also reported that some too badly wounded to fight in the afternoon had suddenly recovered enough to search the scape for wounded or, more probably, loot. Dakodo's Tetatae had taken no casualties.

The adrenaline rush that created the high of combat was rapidly fading into the low that inevitably followed. This was the time when a counterattack could be the most dangerous, though the likelihood was scant. The enclave forces were so thoroughly beaten that it would be days before they again ventured into the woods. Vost's 'Mechs were still in Usugumo and not likely to come forth until he'd made a better deal for their services. This last piece of information came from Fiona Sabine, one of the techs who'd originally gone with Vost and the others.

Creeping into the Takuda camp just after dark, she carried a tale of fragmentation among the mercenaries. Disgusted with the situation and the 'Mech pilots' lack of concern for the welfare of their technicians, she'd decided to leave. No doubt she also felt a deep bitterness at how quickly Vost had discarded her in favor of greener pastures.

Takuda gave orders for the establishment of security along their broad front. The DEST members were stretched thin, each one now commanding what amounted to a full squad. That would have been fine if those squads had consisted of battle-hardened troopers but just the opposite was true. Instead of experienced soldiers, the squads consisted of enthusiastic but undisciplined Tetatae and raw recruits from the enclaves, neither disciplined nor too enthusiastic. It was not that they didn't want to do the job, just that they didn't know how or even why. The concept of staying awake to watch an empty field for a possible enemy everyone "knew" would not be back did not seem reasonable to such as these. What was second nature to a soldier was anathema to a civilian. Whoever heard of staying awake all night to guard your house? Thus the DEST members and the Tetatae, who could sleep while awake, shouldered most of the responsibility.

The need for security was very real, however. The excruciatingly thin forward edge of outposts was under constant pressure. Not from the forces of the enclaves but from civilians fleeing the cities. They came for the same reasons that the originals had come: in search of something better. From the front came reports of numerous individuals and families seeking asylum within the Takuda lines. All were welcomed, with Fullerton and his original group taking over the task of bedding them down.

Takuda terminated the truncated staff meeting and sent his people out into the night. Though they needed sleep as much as the rest, the staff had to work while the others slept. Parker Davud and Holly Goodall had their work cut out for them with the damaged 'Mech, and Fullerton and Dakodo had their own people to look after. Takuda followed them out into the dark.

The moon was almost directly overhead, its mottled green and blue surface reflecting the light of the departed sun. The body wasn't really a moon, but another planet in its own right within the star system. Takuda looked longingly at it, wondering if there were life on its surface, if it might not be a better place for his experimental society. But the distance was impossible; it would remain a dream.

Single glowing eyes, the campfires scattered through the trees stared unblinking into the night. Takuda walked among them, listening to the muted conversations all around. For the most part, those speaking were the recently arrived refugees, still too excited about their trek to settle down. Their attitudes were as varied as their backgrounds.

"I just wanted to get away. I want something better for my children. The thought of being under some religious . . . well, some religious leader. They don't even give you a chance to think."

"You should be in Osio. It's so regimented you don't get a chance to raise your kids at all."

"It would be better to crush them all. Then we'd be in charge. We could tell them what to do."

"I'm so tired and hungry. I'd do anything for a little ocha."

"Crush 'em all. That's what I say. After today, we can do anything."

"You ought to try living in Usugumo. Only the rich have a say in anything. The rest of us are left with nothing. And it'll only get worse."

"Just leave the whole bunch to rot, I say. We can go somewhere else and get a new start. All we have to do is work together."

"Burn 'em out, I say."

Takuda found himself at the edge of the fire line, faced with the impenetrable darkness of the trees beyond. He turned aside and looked back across the orange dots of the fires. So many people. None of this was the way he'd planned it. The situation was getting out of control. Sensing movement behind him, he turned quickly, his right hand resting on the holster that slapped his thigh.

"Good evening, *Sho-sa* Takuda," came Dakodo's voice from the darkness. "You from your headquarters are far tonight."

"Good evening, Dakodo. I wanted to walk for a bit. I need to think. But I had to get away from the headquarters so people wouldn't keep coming to me with questions I can't answer." Takuda was surprised that it came out this way. Commanders, especially samurai commanders, did not complain. Perhaps, he thought, the situation was changing him even more than he'd realized. He wondered, silently this time, if the change was for the better.

"Come to our circle, *Sho-sa*. Tonight our meal we have late. We so busy have been. You are welcome to sit with us. None will question you among the Tetatae. Already you have done so much. Given us a future you have."

"It's not much, Dakodo. For all I know, the future I've given you is worse than your past or your present will ever be or could be."

"No, a future you have given us. To dream about. That is worth much. Come sit with us and listen."

Takuda let the little alien lead him by the elbow into the darkness. The Tetatae moved easily through the night, skirting boulders and hidden traps as he directed his less able guest through the trees. It was with surprising suddenness that they came upon the circle of squatting Tetatae. The leaves overhead created a stygian darkness that suddenly revealed the circle of figures crouched around a tiny fire. Dakodo indicated a place, and Takuda also squatted down. He chose to sit with his knees pulled up to his chin rather than in the traditional lotus position.

None of the Tetatae acknowledged his entrance in the circle. No change occurred in the conversation or the demeanor of the aliens. Takuda watched them, knowing they were far beyond his understanding. He shook his head; he'd have to stop thinking of them as aliens. He was the alien, they were the natives.

Beak protruding into the circle, Dokaepi crouched behind him, translating what the shaman was saying to the group. Dokaepi was speaking in a low, sing-song voice, his eyes closed, his body rocking slightly to the rhythm of his words. "He tell about the legends that came with the first ones who fell from the sky with fire," whispered Dakodo. "Of the arrival he has spoken. How like the children were they exploring their surroundings. Killed the Tetatae they did at first, understanding not the respect we felt them. Then came time when almost dead were they. Helped them with food did we, and them taught to live with land. We learned to speak as they. Even friendship there was.

"Then all changed. Became strong they. Took land of Tetatae and cut it deeply. Made things to grow. Hunted they in grass and woods and hills. Drove Tetatae out from lands they wanted, saying that they would govern all. Again they killed the Tetatae and drove them away. Other Tetatae they took within their walls and made them to work. So many of our people went to cities, never to return.

"But legend there is that others fell from sky with fire

at same time as these. Legend say they fell far away beyond the mountains that are only a blue mist in the distance. These ones not like those of the cities you see.
These ones peaceful were, and kind to all around them.
They wait for the Tetatae beyond the mountains, waiting
to lead us to the promised land."

Takuda leaned toward Dakodo. "Do you think that
what he says is true? Not about what happened here, but
about the other incident. About the people beyond the
mountains?"

"True is. It must be so."

Takuda was lost in thought. Somewhere, he thought,
there must be another group of humans. Perhaps there
was a real future. In all legends, he knew, was a grain of
truth, some hard nugget around which the tale had been
spun like the layers an oyster creates a tiny grain of sand.
The layers became a pearl, a thing of great beauty and desire, but inside was the grain of sand. Whether the pearl
came from the oysters of a Terra or the giant canropods
of Albiero, there was still the single grain. So must it be
with these stories of the others who fell from the sky with
fire. There had to be another settlement, a place for them
to be safe beyond the mountains. All of them: DEST
team, human refugees from the enclaves, and their friends
among the Tetatae.

The DEST commander remained lost in thought until
Dokaepi had finished his story. The other Tetatae sat silent in the circle, each one also deep in his own thoughts.
Dakodo touched Takuda gently on the shoulder; it was
time to go. The *sho-sa* levered himself to his feet and
made his way alone through the fading darkness toward
the glowing fires of the human camp.

42

They were all there, the leaders of the enclaves as well as the merchants and power brokers who had been negotiating with the mercenaries on an individual basis. Each had received a secret message to meet with Vost, and each had come expecting to be the only one. The message had said that Vost was calling this meeting to finalize the deal with the 'Mech pilots. Now the various enclave leaders found that it was not to be private.

"You have been dealing with these people behind our backs," snarled Risu Toho, shogun and leader of the Osio, at Sanyu Subash Chi. "But it is no surprise to learn that the high priest of the Amatukaze would stoop to dealing with mere mercenaries."

The sanyu of the Amatukaze turned to face his accuser. "What a surprise to meet you here, exalted shogun. You whose troops were routed at such great loss could do nothing less than crawl to the powerful for your salvation. As has always been said about the Osio, you are either on your knees before your betters or at their throats. And if you are at their throats, it is always from behind. As it is now."

Toho went red in the face, as much from anger as shame. It was true that the forest forces had routed the Osio troops in the woods, a defeat he felt most bitterly. "Our forces suffered more than anyone else's," he said in choking rage. "But it was the others who ran first. At least the Osio stayed together long enough to cover the cowardly withdrawal of the rest. And I note from the reports that the Amatukaze did not send all the strength they had committed to the plan. Neither did the Usugumo. Perhaps treachery was always on your mind."

"We did not plan treachery," interjected Homma Sirayuki, overhearing the exchange between the two leaders and feeling bound to enter the discussion. The Usugumo stood to lose a great deal in the current negotiations, and he was determined to minimize that loss. The Usugumo had been the first to cement a deal with the mercenaries, but the council hadn't been quick enough with the contract. Just when they thought they had the deal tied down, the mercenaries had slipped away. And now this chaos was the result. "Nothing of the kind was in the minds of the Usugumo. You know that we always honor our contracts to the letter. We agreed to pledge all forces, except those required for internal security, to the attack. The Usugumo sent all we could."

"Yes," said the sneering Toho. "We all know that the Usugumo honor their contracts to the letter rather than the spirit. The Osio and the Amatukaze, on the other hand, care more about the spirit of an agreement. Perhaps that is why we both hate you so much."

Sirayuki snorted at the statement. "If you hate us, it is because we are successful, profitable, while you cling to form rather than substance. And I have never heard that the Osio and the Amatukaze were such great friends." Unable to stand it any longer, Sirayuki lunged at the sneering face of Toho. It was only the rapid intervention of one of his staff that prevented an exchange of blows. The two men were dragged apart, still hissing at each other.

Nor was the incident an isolated event within the meeting room. Other groups were knotted together, trading insults in much the same manner. The focus of the hostility was on a group of five headed by Achira Kochira of the Usugumo. The others claimed that it was he who had started the bidding war for the services of the mercenaries. They all knew, of course, that this was not true. Kochira might have been the most persistent, and his consortium may have upped the ante, but he was not the first offender. It was just that they needed to blame someone and Kochira was the handiest target.

Matters had almost come to blows again by the time Vost entered the room. In calling the meeting to order, he had to shout over the rising cacophony that threatened to turn the assembly into a melee. When things finally quieted down, he made his offer: the mercenaries would go with the best offer. He didn't care who put the deal together, he didn't care what the dealers wanted. He and his force would supply the 'Mech muscle, the consortium would supply the compensation. When he announced the base fee for his services, the assemblage gasped almost as one. Then he walked out, leaving his guests in stunned silence.

Vost had reason to want the negotiations to drag on. Although his 'Mechs had successfully achieved a demonstration of their power to the enclave leaders, the *Panther* had taken three hits from the *Locust*'s medium lasers in the fight against Takuda's people. The damage was not serious, but the left knee servoactuator had become troublesome. Vost wanted to give the technicians, reduced now by the disappearance of Fiona Sabine, every opportunity to repair it. He was certain that the *Panther* was still the dominant machine on the field, but it was better to be completely safe than just marginally operational.

There was also the problem of short-range missiles for the *Javelin*. Pesht had started with six SRMs in each launcher, with an additional fifteen reloads for each rack. But he'd fired a full volley at the Osio and another at the Amatukaze. And then there was the ammo he'd spent in battle against the Takuda 'Mechs. All told, Pesht had used up five volleys from each launch system. Based on the one plus fifteen, and five gone, that left each launcher with only ten in the bins. And eventually they, too, would be used up.

The only possible resupply could come from the *Panther*'s SRM 4 packs. Counting reloads and the volley in the launch racks, the *Panther* carried 104 SRMs. Vost could give those to the *Javelin,* but with the light 'Mech's problem of resupply, he wasn't planning to do so. The *Javelin* and Pesht would become superfluous for long-range combat once the ammunition was gone. The 'Mech would still be capable of ripping things apart with its hands, which still made it better than anything the enclaves could field, but it would be no threat to the *Panther*. All the better for Vost.

But there was a danger lurking behind the advantage. If Pesht saw that he was losing importance because of problems with his ammunition supply, he might try to steal from the *Panther,* a confrontation Vost did not relish. The little rat-faced man was devious enough to engineer an encounter that would turn out badly, perhaps fatally, for one of them. And that "one of them" could just as easily be Vost.

The mercenary commander left the squabbling citizens to figure out their best offer. He smiled to himself at the scene he'd left behind. By the time he cleared the entrance to the building, they'd be at each other's throats. He had an appointment of his own to keep in his quarters. Marika, a lovely little negotiator from the Osio, was there to help him choose the correct path. She did not know, could not know, that he had dropped a bomb on the others. After all, she was merely an agent, however talented, of one of the factions.

Vost stepped into his room, expecting to find the soft scent of pengrya blossoms and the flickering light of a single oil lamp. Instead, he found a trio of three females waiting for him: Michelle Guardine, Tami Wilson, and Elizabeth Hoond. Seated and hostile. Vost smiled at the triumvirate. "You're probably wondering why I called this meeting," he said.

"You didn't," said Hoond evenly. "We did. And no one's got any doubt about why it was called. Have a seat and have a listen."

Vost took the chair that Hoond indicated. Guardine and Wilson were regular technicians, but Hoond had only been pressured into service when the team lost Sabine. Vost was still not sure what had happened to her. Perhaps he should have mentioned her disappearance at the meeting. Perhaps he could have made her return a condition of employment. Too late now, he thought. "And what can I do for you three lovely little ladies?" he asked, winking at Michelle as he spoke.

"We're not little ladies to you or any one else," said Hoond, her voice as level as it was chill. "And we want you to understand that. No. I take that back. We're not interested in whether you understand that. You either accept it or you end up with no support for your 'Mechs. We could all go the way of Fiona. What would you do then?"

"What happened to Fiona? What do you know about her that I don't?"

"Answering that question could fill a book," said Tami Wilson, the chief tech and usually the spokesman for the support element. "Unfortunately, there would be no pictures for you to color. Maybe we could add some so that the reading wouldn't be quite so tedious." The women snickered.

"I don't know what you're so sore about, Tami. You never complained about my finger dexterity or my hand-eye coordination."

Wilson dropped her feet to the floor with a crash and leaned forward into Vost's face. "Keep up that kind of talk, keep up that kind of attitude, Garber Vost, and you *will* find yourself without tech support."

"That's enough, both of you," said Hoond, pulling Wilson back. "We've got more important things to talk about. Think of us as your technical staff rather than conquests or almost conquests, Garber. We *are* the technical staff."

"All right. I respect that. Now what's this meeting all about . . . sweetie?"

"That's it!" snapped Wilson. "You can use that on Michelle or Fiona, but not on me!"

"Cool down, Sergeant Wilson," said Vost in his condescending tone. "I'll listen to what you have to say. At least you're better-looking than Seagroves or Pesht."

"You just can't leave it alone, can you, Vost?" demanded Hoond. "But it doesn't matter. We want to talk as techs and not as anything else." She settled back in her chair, throwing a leg over the table and staring at Vost over the tips of her steepled fingers.

"The problem as we see it involves the business of negotiations. So far it's been you pilots doing all the talking, but down here at the bottom, down here in the septic system where all the work gets done, we haven't gotten squat. We're tired of being treated like mushrooms—covered with manure and kept in the dark. We want to see some of the sunlight. We want to get our needs met too. What's in all this for us?"

"Beth, you've got to trust me. Of course you'll get your share of the loot. We wouldn't leave you out of all this. You three are an important part of the team. Without you, nothing would get done. By the way, who's guarding the shop? Is there anyone looking after the 'Mechs?"

"I have no idea. We told Pesht and Seagroves that they were in charge while we took a night on the town. Security is their problem for the evening." Hoond leaned forward. "Here's what we want. Each of you will either get an individual contract or you'll get it as a group. Half of what you get, we get. Either that, or we do no work. A signed contract. That's the deal."

Vost looked into the eyes of the former navigator of the JumpShip. They were like flint. This time she meant business, but he couldn't do anything about it right now. He'd have to think of a way around the situation later. Just wait until he got some of the locals trained as techs, he thought. Then he realized with a flash that, of course, that was the solution.

"Fine" he said mildly. "But you'll need some help. Three techs are hardly enough to keep one 'Mech in operation. The original contract called for the lance to be supported by assistant techs after we got down. That necessity remains. Get some of the locals to volunteer as astechs to help you. They can do the heavy lifting and stuff like that. Each of you will become the senior tech for one of the 'Mechs. I don't care who works on what. You choose."

Vost turned to Michelle Guardine, trying to make eye contact. She lowered her gaze and turned away. "I'm surprised at you, Michelle," said Vost, his voice oozing restrained passion, the tone he always used just before the climax of the chase. "I thought you were with me?"

"She was, Vost," said Hoond, her voice icy. "Like other people, she's seen the error of her ways."

Standing in the shadow of the bastion, Vost explained the mini-revolution to the other pilots. In the light of the setting moon, the three 'Mechs stood stark and pale. Pesht shrugged at the thought of having to give away half his share to a tech. The techs probably hadn't thought about how much they'd have to pay the astechs to keep them working—and that would serve them right. No one was stupid enough to work for free, especially if the locals got wind of how much money was to change hands.

Seagroves listened and said nothing. He'd go along with the deal, but there was no way some tech was going to get half his loot. As long as the LAM had jet fuel—which he planned to be a very long time—he would make his own deals. The techs could have half the base amount, but Seagroves would give nothing of the incentive bonuses he planned to add to his contract. If the locals wanted something that flew, they'd pay him more and

like it. It was the law of supply and demand. He had a
limited supply, a quantity of one, and they had a large demand, an infinite amount. He'd make his own bonus
deals.

43

Têopõ staggered into Takuda's headquarters, limping from the slug gun wound and trembling as much from fatigue as from being in the presence of the great leader. She chattered a long string of chirps and clicks, but Takuda caught no more than the word "BattleMech," even though he was beginning to get a grasp on the Tetatae language. Nothing he did would make her slow down or choose other words. By the time Dakodo arrived, she was shaking with frustration as well.

Dakodo settled the little alien into a nest of cloaks to ward off the evening chill and soothed her with strokes and words. He continued speaking in soft tones until the little one's violent trembling had passed and she was almost still. Only then did he begin to ask questions. At first the inquiry brought the words out of her in a rush. Dakodo held up his hands to slow the rush, but it was to no avail. She poured out all she had to say in what sounded, to Takuda, like a single sentence.

Dakodo gave up trying to control her and just listened. When at last she subsided into the cradle of cloaks, he turned to the DEST commander. "She is Têopõ named, daughter of Pikaete, a resident of Usugumo. Pikaete has been passing information on movements of mercenaries and leaders of enclaves. He for the shidosha of the Usugumo works, and Têopõ works sometimes with him.

For past three days she to us has been trying to get. Important information she has.

"Much has changed in past week or more. Leaders of cities and mercenaries now have resolved their disagreement. The 'Mech people and the owners of the money now speak together. Now will come the 'Mechs to fight.

"All of the fighters of the cities, like the ones we vanquished ten days ago, will also be involved. The little one does not understand what they plan to do, but Pikaete heard some words and made her memorize. The words are "hammer and anvil." Not understand does she, but her father said that you would. Pikaete said 'Mechs would be the hammer."

As Dakodo finished the translation, the curtain of the command post was thrust aside. Even before it had dropped back into place, Parker Davud had stepped through and begun to speak. "Enclave forces moving out of all the cities and coming toward us. It looks like the same deal as last time. They're forming right across the entire front. They don't look too enthusiastic."

"They don't have to," said Takuda, rising from his desk. "According to this very brave young lady, they aren't going to be very aggressive. The real attack will be coming from elsewhere. The flank. Probably the left flank. It's got to be the Vost 'Mechs, with the conventional forces to pin us in place. Pass the word. Here's the plan."

It wasn't a complicated one. Takuda knew that the enclave forces were mainly supposed to pin him into place and so would not advance too aggressively. In addition, they had been severely hurt only ten days before, and most of them would remember that. And even if human nature had dimmed memory of the disaster, the hulks of the burned-out vehicles should help remind them. They would be cautious. It was the 'Mechs, attacking from the flank, that represented the real danger.

But Takuda would have his own surprise waiting. During the past ten days his force had grown to more than five times its size in the last engagement. Disgruntled soldiers and others from the enclaves saw that a victory by the forest forces could give them a chance at a better life, to rise to the top via one simple change of allegiance. Takuda's one heavy vehicle had also expanded to a full company of twelve after his people had salvaged the wreckage of the battlefield. Alone, such a force couldn't stand against 'Mechs, but with the *Locust* to back them up, they would be a force to reckon with. And the Vost 'Mechs would not be expecting either a reverse trap or an armored force. Granted, the "armor" of the enclave vehicles was nothing but copper-laminated wood. But it looked good, and that alone would give the rebels more confidence.

The Arsenault team, reinforced by Davud and his 'Mechs as well as the heavy weapons, would hold the line against the enclave attack. As before, they would give ground rather than become heavily engaged. The Tetatae platoons, now rearmed with muskets, could provide long-range fire to delay and confuse the advancing troops. The rest of Takuda's force would concentrate on the left flank, the side nearest Usugumo. It was a calculated risk, but Takuda believed that if the 'Mechs moved to the other side, he would be able to react quickly enough. The two *Locust*s would support the armor, making quick shots where they could. With any luck at all, they'd be able to inflict enough damage to discourage the 'Mechs.

One of the problems with a mercenary force was that it had to be victorious to justify its employment. Buyers of merc services did not take well to expensive defeats. The mercs would either win or they would die. There was no in-between for the employers. And Vost knew only too well that he couldn't count on replacements. What he had is all he would have forever. That would tempt him to husband his resources, creating a conflict of objectives. The buyers wanted victory or death, the 'Mech force wanted anything but death. It was here that Takuda saw the opportunity for a victory.

Panting in anticipation, the armored engines stood like great bulls at the edge of the woods. Exhaust belched from their single and twin stacks to hang low among the overhanging foliage and then spread out like a great blanket. Drivers released their brakes, the armored drive wheels of their machines ripping at the ground. They laughed and pointed, making rude, obscene gestures to each other. The infantry riders and weapons operators took up the pantomime and expanded on it. They were READY!

To their right and rear they heard the snap and pop of combat. There was a brief spatter as the forces came into close contact, and then the sounds became more desultory as the forces arranged themselves. Probing, falling back, coming on, counterattack—the deadly ballet of strife. Men dead, shot through by wooden shafts, immolated in flaming coffins, dying from a single, well-placed shot. However it happened, the outcome was irrevocable. Death.

Then over the thin line of trees, hazy with distance and the gentle obfuscation of feathery branches, came the shiny monoliths of the BattleMechs, stalking, searching, giant machines with death in their arms and bodies. Slowly they came on, jerky and disjointed for all their humanoid shape and movement. Great, deadly, fragile things that measured human progress and regression. They were the future and the past. Nothing of human design could stand against them except man himself. Then they were breasting through the trees like metal towers, heads turning as their sensors reached out beyond their range of death.

The men in the armored engines saw them come, cheerful in their determination to do great and glorious battle. The feeling was like waiting for the starting gun at a race. Huge wheels flailing the ground. Gobbits of sod flung back and up. Howling engines straining against pistons and cylinder heads. Jets of steam screeched outward to mingle in a thick mist.

Like a herd of wild, intemperate beasts, the armored forces rushed at the oncoming 'Mechs. Takuda saw them go, made one ineffectual attempt to call them back, and then gave up. They were a wild, green, enthusiastic mob. He would have to bring up the *Locust* in support.

This wasn't as he had planned. He'd have preferred to let the mercenary 'Mechs get closer. Before revealing his surprise, he wanted them fully engaged with the armor. Now the green troops had sprung the trap too early. He toggled the boom mike and contacted Holly Goodall.

She responded at once as the two *Locust*s began to move from their hide position in the tall trees to the rear. They came striding through the woods to support the careening armored vehicles. They were a little late, but there was still time to do some good.

High above the battlefield no one saw the single, glistening reflection of sun on metal, the single flash that represented the position of the LAM. From four kilometers above the trees, Seagroves rolled the LAM back and forth to let the static sensors sweep the broadest possible path below. Tiny I/R returns showed the movement of the heat-generating targets. That was what he wanted. He rolled the LAM over into a broad split-S and powered down through the intervening kilometers of space.

The targeting computer centered on the first of the heat sources, the targeting cross hairs flashing red on the screen. Good read. Sensor lock. He let the LAM drift off the center line while the target hung like a fly in a spider web. As the LAM pulled up from its dive, Seagroves was forced back into the command seat. He watched the range indicator digitize the distance, watched the numbers scroll downward toward the sweet range. The target showed no evasive action. Closer, closer, closer. Green board! Fire!

The laser hummed in the armored right torso, the column of aligned light leaping through the carbon dioxide crystal that channeled the energy into a pencil-thin beam.

The computer I/R sensor blossomed into a ball. Hit. Target destroyed. Seagroves rolled the LAM over and let the search and lock system play across the field.

Almost immediately the cross hairs flashed. Green board. Fire. Target hit. Target destroyed. He rolled the LAM into a tight turn and came back across the field.

The first vehicle exploded, and then the second, even before those on the ground knew the LAM was there. Takuda saw it dive, shouted a warning into the boom mike, but it was too late. The men in the charging armored vehicles did not listen, did not want to listen. They were too intent on closing with the towering 'Mechs beyond the trees. Then it was too late. Caught in the open field, the LAM swooping down on them like some demented bird of prey, one by one they burst into incandescent balls of fire. And still they came.

Takuda wept to see them die. He called for support from the *Locust*s, but the medium laser in the *Locust*'s lower torso could not elevate enough to engage the swooping LAM. Then the BattleMechs were inside the range of the armored vehicles. A cloud of fire enveloped the *Javelin* as it rippled both racks of short-range missiles, hammering vehicle after vehicle into the yielding ground. No survivors. No survivors from those immense explosions that combined high explosives with flashing fuel.

The *Locust*s were in close, Jacobs with his good 'Mech firing blindly into the melee. Holly Goodall pranced and danced, trying to draw the *Panther*'s fire away from the vulnerable armor. Leading a charmed life, she dodged one PPC blast after another. Inside the rearward 'Mech, Jacobs watched his displays light up with information he couldn't understand. He only knew that Goodall was out in front, drawing the *Panther* and the *Javelin*'s attention away from the others.

They were in retreat. The armor had had enough. Careening tanks rushed past the long legs of his *Locust*. It was time to go. His screen bloomed with the heat signature of Goodall's 'Mech. Hits on the outer armor were pushing the heat warning system beyond the safe range. He saw the legs freeze, saw the warning circuits fry under the hammering of the PPC. The *Javelin* was closing from the rear, a full dual six pack of short-range missiles loaded and locked on target.

"Run, Jacobs! Run!" came the scream over the commlink. "RUN!"

He watched transfixed as the red danger light blossomed on his heat scale. It was time to go, and still Goodall did not move, did not move, did not move. There was a cloud of fire from the chest of the Javelin, then Goodall's 'Mech vanished in an explosion of titanic proportions. With tears streaming down his sweat-streaked face, Jacobs turned the surviving *Locust* toward the woods and ran.

44

Seagroves rolled the LAM over again and swept down over the smoke-shrouded field. The environment was no longer as target-rich as before. Though he could see the I/R signatures of dozens of targets, it was becoming increasingly difficult to tell the living from the dead. A steam-driven vehicle had such a significant heat return that a burning one was actually dimmer on the screen. There was no use hitting those destroyed or abandoned, so he switched from I/R to motion-sensitive. At least now he'd be able to tell what was moving and what was not.

He checked the fuel readout and noted that soon he would be down a third of a tank. All the aerobatics and high-power runs were sucking up his fuel. He pulled back on the joystick and let the LAM rise in a gentle arc. Time to break off. The land 'Mechs could deal with the remnants of the Takuda force; he was headed home. Nice thing about flying was that you could do your job and be home by dark for a shower, a hot meal, and clean sheets. Let the ground-pounders deal with the stragglers.

Takuda, meanwhile, stood in the woods and watched as the rabble that had become his force streamed by. Some still carried their weapons, but many did not. One recent refugee from Amatukaze came to an abrupt halt in a copse of trees and began to fire his weapon at his former comrades, probably in hopes that he would be mistaken for a member of the victorious troops when they arrived on the scene. Takuda raised his laser pistol to put an end to the little treachery, but he couldn't find the heart to pull the trigger. Instead, he walked quietly up behind the man and disarmed him. The trooper offered no resistance, just sat down heavily with his back to the tree and began to weep. Takuda secured the musket, patted the man on the shoulder, and walked away. There was nothing he could do for the sobbing recruit.

Andi Holland hobbled past, still nursing a wound from the previous battle, but now with an injury in the left leg as well. The left side of her face had been savaged by some weapon, droplets of blood dotting the space from the jaw to just behind one ear. She could still walk, but only with great difficulty and only with the support of two Tetatae helping with her weapon and pack. Takuda would later learn that Holland had suffered three broken ribs as well as kidney damage and a broken right hand.

Swalen Horg was not far behind her, also showing signs of battle damage. Something heavy had struck him square across the upper chest, crushing the armor and faceplate of his helmet. He staggered past where Takuda stood rooted to the ground, waiting for the advancing enemy. "It only hurts when I cough," was Horg's sole comment on his injuries.

Knyte was the last one past. Stopping alongside his commander, he waited expectantly for orders. It was as though he could read Takuda's mind, and he began to prepare their tiny plot of terrain for a last defense. "Keep going," said Takuda, but the *gun-so* continued to fortify the ground.

When Takuda protested again, the noncommissioned officer looked his commander in the eye. "I will stand with you, sir," he said, "or I will accompany you to the rear. But I will not leave you to this fate. There is nothing dishonorable about flight at this time. But we cannot lose you when we need you most."

Takuda felt the weight of command slip back onto his shoulders. It wasn't comfortable, but it was familiar. He looked at his section leader and nodded his head. "Correct, *Gun-so* Knyte. Yes, you go on ahead and choose a place where we can rally. I'll stay here just a little longer and see what I can do. I'll move from here in one hour. Less if the enclave troops begin to push." The statement was that of a commander taking charge of the situation. Knyte saluted and moved off.

Takuda found the rally point well after dark. He used the I/R glasses to discover the hidden fires in a deep ravine completely covered by the triple-canopy foliage. Even the supersensitive I/R devices carried by the LAM and the *Panther* would have been hard put to find them except at very close range. By the time the hostile 'Mechs got that close, they themselves would have been seen, and the fires could have been doused.

As Takuda came in, he was aware of activity in the undergrowth around him. Dim figures moved to sweep away obstacles and hold back hidden branches. It was the Tetatae, looking out for their commander but allowing him to find his own way home. Clucking voices as soft as the darkness itself.

Parker Davud was there, waiting for Takuda to arrive. He had become the complete staff officer. Gone were the days of independent command as enjoyed by a DropShip commander. Now he thought in terms of the unit rather than himself. Not only had he been able to cobble together the first piece of mobile equipment, but he'd also managed to build additional ones from parts scrounged on the battlefield. His talents didn't seem to stop when the battle started. Even during the retreat, with the situation falling apart all around him, Davud had found the time to secure a desk, two chairs, a cot, a cook stove, and a can of coffee. Where the coffee had come from was complete mystery because Takuda knew that the last of it had been consumed weeks before. Yet there it had been, and now a hot cup of dark brew was waiting for him as he entered the tiny camp.

Davud reported that Ariake Sanae was dead and Johan

Miranda with her. Sanae had died at the SRM launcher position when the *Panther*'s PPC finally obtained a target lock on her. Miranda had had no business being there, but he'd convinced the Tetatae assigned as his personal servant that he could be of some value with the weapon. The two had died as the last missile was firing. Dana Lost, griping to the very end, had stood against the forces of the enclave until it was too late to withdraw. Complaining that he would never have placed himself in this position, that he would have pulled out long before, he charged a block of musket- and bayonet-armed infantry, firing his laser rifle from the hip. Still complaining, he'd been swallowed up in the melee.

Robert Fullerton came to the fire to report the status of his refugees. Out of the five hundred at the start of the day, fewer than two hundred remained. Where the rest had gone was a mystery, but he had his suspicions. There had been fewer than a hundred in the armored forces, and some of those were accounted for. The main losses had been among people manning the main line. Most of them, suspected Fullerton, had drifted back to their enclaves when the retreat began, probably disenchanted at the prospect of actually having to fight for their freedom. Interestingly enough, it had been the most vociferous, the most aggressive talkers, who had disappeared. "Small loss," Fullerton commented.

Even the Tetatae ranks had thinned. Dakodo reported that the survivors of the original tribe were still with him, but there had been defections among the newcomers, especially those from farthest away. They had been the last into the group, and perhaps they'd decided that the trek had been in vain. In any case, they were gone.

The reports in, the staff members fell silent, each one harboring his own thoughts of what daylight would bring. "Our choice, as members of a Draconis Combine Elite Strike Team," said Takuda, breaking the silence, "is quite clear. It is less so for the rest of you. We have the honorable way of liberating ourselves from the dilemma. Our honor is important to us, and we know that to die in battle for a greater good is to die well. We have established our position, and now we must die by it. As did the forty-seven samurai of legend, we have an honorable way to end this. We must remember that we will not die unremembered or unsung. Those forty-seven warriors made the ultimate sacrifice for their lord and their honor. We can only do as well. The DEST team will stay here and finish what we have started. Those of you who are not of DEST, and that means you, Parker Davud, are not invited to attend the ceremony."

Stony silence greeted the announcement. What could be said to a man who had just announced that he and his compatriots were about to commit suicide? There was an uneasy stirring among the company as though someone had just stated that he was dying from a terrible, deadly, highly communicable disease. They all wanted to be somewhere else, but none was willing to break the bond of loyalty.

"The men who fell from the sky with fire will continue," said Dakodo softly. "It has been this way for as long as I can remember. It will remain that way for those who come beyond."

Takuda looked at the face of the little alien, his bulbous features lit by the fire. There was a long silence, and then Takuda said, "What about the others who fell from the sky with fire? Tell them the story I heard last night."

Dakodo rose from his crouched position and closed his eyes. He began to rock back and forth as he spoke. "When the first men came from the sky with fire, there were many Tetatae who hid in fear. And well they should, for those who came had sticks that brought death. The Tetatae were driven from their lands and enslaved. Thus it was with the men who came from the sky with fire.

"But there was another group that came from the sky at the same time. Their machine fell well away from the others and it did no harm to the Tetatae. It is said that at this place, beyond the blue mountains that lie on the land like an aoi mist, there is another group. It is said that they will rise to defend the Tetatae and then lead them to a land that is open and free. In this land the Tetatae will be able to live in peace with those who came from the sky with fire."

"Is it true, Dakodo?" asked Takuda.

"We so think. We thought you were of the same group. The legend says that there will be those we know who will lead us to those we know not. You are the ones to lead us to that spot. You cannot here stay and die."

Takuda shrugged. "I think, Dakodo, that you know how I feel about that. I don't want to become part of your legends. Being a DEST commander is responsibility enough for me. I would act as your advisor and your leader, but I don't intend to become part of your legendary past, present, or future."

"I fear, *Sho-sa* Yubari Takuda, that you have no choice. No matter what you choose, some in the tribe have already made that decision for you. Now you must decide whether to accept the task they would give you. For better or for worse, already you are part of our legends."

"So now I have the choice of dying here in an attempt to defend you, and thus give you the chance to escape, or I can lead you out while the mercenary and enclave forces destroy those too sick, too old, or too injured to move quickly. And what do I do with the refugees from the enclaves? They are also part of this equation, and I have heard nothing from them."

Robert Fullerton had been listening to this conversation in silence. He took some time to answer. "As far as I'm concerned, and I think I speak for the rest of my people, we'll go with Takuda, wherever he goes. I think I'd like to try Dakodo's idea. Let's go to wherever it is he thinks the other humans are. I liked what Takuda said when I joined up, and that dream hasn't changed. I'm willing to let him lead us."

Takuda felt the weight of command pressing down upon him. Now he would be responsible for the DEST team, the Tetatae, and the humans on a trek to some place only the Tetatae knew of, and only that from a legend. But it was something. It was a chance. It was a future that would continue for more than one morning.

45

The response among the humans was not so universally positive. A variety of responses ranging from acceptance to outright revolt greeted the announcement that they would be heading for the mountains in search of another civilization. The most strident protesters suggested that all things must pass. This would pass away as well. All they had to do was return to their enclaves. They didn't want to make a big deal of it, just go home. With all the fighting and turmoil caused by the BattleMechs, there would be massive confusion in the cities. No one would remember who had done what when. And the 'Mechs would be like a bad dream. The ones who piloted the 'Mechs would not be around forever, and after a time they would be no more than a bad memory. They would pass into the realm of legend as had all the others. Nothing would change. The extremes of today would even out. Everyone's life would return to normal, and all would again be quite simple. Better to give up and go home now while they had a chance.

There were others who were not about to stake their lives on anything that a Tetatae might say. The little bug-birds were stupid subhumans who had no culture and no value. The whole bunch should be exterminated by the more powerful humans. To believe some bogus legend about another human settlement was as foolish as wishing that humans could fly. Even without the evidence of the

LAM, these people still believed that the stories ranked as pure foolishness.

Half the people were willing to give the plan a try. Either they were too tired to think of any other response or they actually believed in the possibility of another settlement. In either case they accepted Takuda's leadership and were willing to make the trek across an unknown distance to a legendary destination. Was there, they asked, a better choice?

Then Holly Goodall stumbled into the campsite. She sank down by the fire and gratefully accepted a steaming cup of coffee culled from the last of the supply discovered by Davud. The others stared at her, waiting until she'd recovered before besieging her with questions. She drained the cup in three deep swallows, not seeming to notice the scalding heat of the liquid. Then she looked at the others and began to speak. She'd been able to eject from the damaged *Locust* just as the whole thing cooked off under the pounding of the *Javelin*'s multiple SRM hits. She'd been captured and turned over to Vost. The mercenary commander had been absolutely charming, just as he always was when he wanted something. Which he did now.

Vost was making an offer to any of the deserters, as they were now being called, to join him. There would be a base pay of fifty monme per day. The offer also extended to any of the human refugees who had fled the enclaves, although the amount of monme was lower. Vost, it seemed, was willing to accept the rebel humans on the assumption that they would be loyal to him out of fear of retaliation if they returned to their homes.

The offer was simple; it would satisfy every need of those who chose to accept it. For Takuda there was nothing. And the Tetatae, of course, were not even mentioned.

Goodall told her story in a voice so low that those around her had to strain to hear. She spoke slowly, carefully, with long pauses between the sentences. And yet by the time she had finished, the story, in varying degrees of accuracy, had spread through the entire camp. The results were immediate.

The campfires began to blaze more brightly, despite who or what might be watching from the deeper darkness. People moved from fire to fire to gather in animated knots that coalesced and then fragmented. Voices were raised. People ran through the darkness. Occasional blows were exchanged. Through it all, Holly Goodall sat by the small fire where she had told her story, sat staring into the undulating luminescence of the coals.

Robert Fullerton approached Takuda, backed up by a throng of his own people. The DEST commander, sitting with Goodall and staring at the same moving light, heard him coming. He could tell by the sounds that trouble was brewing. Fullerton came to a halt at the fire, some of those behind him also pushing forward.

Takuda looked up at the leader of the refugees. "You have something to say to me, Robert Fullerton?"

"We've been thinking," said Fullerton, refusing to make eye contact with Takuda. He scraped the toe of his boot in the ground, making intricate swirls in the forest duff, examining the furrows with deep interest. "Some of my people have heard about Vost's offer. Some of them, actually, quite a few, think it is a fair one. Most joined you in hopes that you would come out on top. Now it looks like Vost will win."

"They've heard the whole story? They understand that this contract would not last forever? Have they thought about what happens to them then?"

"More or less," said Fullerton, still making designs in the loose turf. "I guess they really don't see much of a future here. I mean, you gave them the option of crossing the mountains to some legendary new settlement. There are still those who want to try that. But there are others who don't want to leave what they know, what they understand. They just want to go home."

"So do we all," said Takuda. He thought of the little koya beside a small lake on Yumesta, far from anything even remotely military. He had seen the cottage while on a forced convalescent leave, at a time when he'd been hating every moment of his enforced idleness. But he had been struck by the place at once. It needed repair, but it still seemed to represent an alternative future. He had kept the image in his heart, but now he would never see the spot again. He jerked himself back to reality. "Have you made a decision? Have *you* made a decision, Robert Fullerton?"

Fullerton stood in embarrassed silence for a moment. "Yes, I have," he said in a small voice. "I think I'd like to accept what this Vost has offered." He raised his eyes to look at Takuda for the first time.

Mark Jacobs had joined the circle around the fire. "We all have our reasons for doing things, don't we? Some of us put a lot of store in money, more or less. And the amount we get paid is a way to keep score. I was paid pretty well as an engineer on the *Telendine,* and I haven't gotten a C-bill since we landed. But I'll tell you what, I've never had as much fun in my life since Holly and Takuda put me into that *Locust.* I think I'd rather stay with them."

"I'm just a mercenary," said Goodall, speaking for the first time since finishing her story. "And I was the one who got the best offer, so I suppose it makes sense for me to go with Vost. I suppose I should."

Goodall dropped her head to stare into the fire again. "But I just can't do it," she said quietly. "It's not so much that Vost's nothing but a bucket of slime. It's not just that he's a self-centered, megalomaniacal, egocentric bastard. I guess I just don't like the options. There's something wrong with the whole idea.

"Being a mercenary is all right. There's nothing wrong with fighting for money. But I guess I've got something else inside me. There's got to be more than money, and there sure has to be more than Vost. Since we've been together, me and Takuda and the others, I've found that I'm fighting for something more, fighting for an idea about my own future. I kind of like it. All things being equal, or even not equal, I guess I'll make the foolish decision and go with Commander Takuda. If that's all right with you. Sir."

"Nothing would make me prouder, Pilot Holly Goodall." Takuda felt a swelling happiness. Things were going to work.

"Well, Robert Fullerton," continued Takuda. "You have given me an unpleasant task. You want to throw in your lot with Vost, and that's your decision. But you now know what the rest of us are going to do, and that puts me on the horns of a dilemma. What am I going to do with you?" The crowd behind Fullerton shifted nervously.

"If I let you go, someone will tell Vost about our plan. Our only real hope is to break contact and get away. We'll have to move soon and move fast. But if you and your people go now, you'll never be able to keep our plans a secret. You'll have us gored by one horn or the other. Do you understand what I'm saying?

"On the other hand, I could have my people try to disarm you. I'm sure we could do it; we have the weapons and the training, but that would be just as bad. We'd have to round you all up, even those who might be planning to stay with us. We wouldn't be able to trust any of you at that instant, and we'd never be able to trust any of you after that. And there'd be some casualties. Both on your side and ours. That's no way to build loyalty."

Fullerton looked up. "It's true, sir. We don't win if we fight and you don't really win if you disarm us. We'd get some of you, but you'd probably get more of us. That's not what we want. All we really want is just to be able to go our own way. Get away with our skins and our people Some of these men have families that they need to protect. I don't want anyone hurt any more than you do."

There was a strained silence between the two men, bu both could hear the muted conversations taking place be hind the back of the refugee leader. They could also hea the movement behind Takuda, the sibilant sound of lase rifles being readied for action. Fullerton waited for the talking to subside before he spoke again. "If you'd let us get our things together, kind of split the camp, letting people know what's happening, your people could just slip away in the darkness. I can keep mine here until it gets light. After that it'll be wide open."

Takuda looked at the man who would destroy the organization of his unit. Robert Fullerton had been as loyal as any subordinate could have been. He had stayed through the bad times, but now he had a decision to make. As with any good commander, he was thinking of the welfare of his own people. Takuda nodded. "All right, Robert Fullerton. We'll try that. Get your people together. Split the camp. Make sure everyone, *everyone,* understands what's happening. Then we'll move."

46

Takuda wanted to assign the *Locust* as part of the rear guard for the column, but Dakodo advised against it. With the Tetatae so emotionally attached to the 'Mech, it would have to lead. Otherwise, said the spokesman for the Tetatae, they would probably huddle around the vehicle and refuse to move. Some of them would understand the necessity of getting a move on, but emotion was likely to be stronger.

Thus the *Locust*, piloted by Jacobs and/or Goodall, would be up front. The DEST members and any refugees who volunteered would form the rear guard. The Tetatae and the other humans would mix into the column. The Tetatae could help with the wounded as needed.

The only real problem with the retreat would be the Tetatae themselves. This was birthing time for them, and the eggs were very fragile. They could be carried, but were susceptible to damage if not treated with great care. That would slow the march. In addition, the Tetatae wanted to reach the new location, wherever that was, before the birthing took place. They seemed to think it was very important for the young to come into the world at their new home rather than on the march. This would make the Tetatae insistent about moving, even though the humans might get tired. And, of course, it would be better to resolve these problems before the march began rather than later. They would have to explain the situation to the refugees, a significant number of whom had opted to follow Takuda and his vision of a better world.

It was several hours before first light that the *Locust* rose from its crouching position and began to move. Goodall sat in the command seat, with Jacobs crammed into the rear of the cockpit. There was so little room that he had to half-stand, half-crouch behind the seat, trying not to kick any of the spaghetti-like bundles of cables from their moorings. His presence wasn't particularly needed in the cockpit. He had come along simply because he'd rather be with Goodall than anywhere else. Dakodo rode perched on the sloping carapace of the center torso, from which he could direct the movement of the *Locust* toward the far country that was their goal.

At the rear of the extended, straggling column were the DEST members and the refugees. Takuda's unit had been small enough when the operation had begun, and now they had taken over 100 percent casualties. All but Parker Davud had been wounded at least once, and some like Holland, Bustoe, and Horg, had been hit twice. Six of the original members would never take another hit. All were stiff with fatigue. The human recruits from the enclaves were not in much better shape. The only thing that made them better able to cope with the strain of the march was that they hadn't been involved for as long a period.

Takuda had been very careful not to give details about the route or direction of the march to Fullerton or anyone else who chose to stay behind. The location of the refugees—which is what they all were now—would become known sooner or later. Takuda preferred that it not be too much sooner. If Vost came after them with the *Javelin* and *Panther,* the column might be able to hide. But if the mercenary used the LAM, its altitude and speed would make discovery a certainty. Takuda hoped that Vost would be trying to conserve both the LAM's and the *Javelin*'s assets from running out too soon. That might make him prefer to hold the LAM in reserve. At least so Takuda hoped.

The Tetatae with the rear guard addressed the task with their usual exuberance. They were masters of the woods, and they cheerfully constructed dead falls and pits to catch the unwary enemy 'Mechs. They were encouraged to create more and more of the infernal devices when the *Javelin,* overconfident in its armored might, actually tumbled into one of them with a resounding crash.

From his own cockpit, Vost saw the *Javelin* go down; one moment it was there, the next it was gone. He knew immediately what had happened, and began to send a continuous string of venomous remarks and sarcasms over the commlink until he saw the 'Mech climb out of the hole. Vost had already had his own problems with a pit, and he was glad to see Pesht also looking like a fool.

The presence of pits made Vost call for ground support as well as the LAM. The fleeing column would be difficult to find in the triple-canopy rain forest, and he didn't want his valuable 'Mechs damaged by some over-enthusiastic infantry type. He had plenty of foot-sloggers available, especially since the influx of those who had recently defected from Takuda. With these people more than willing to show their loyalty to their new master, he sent them in on their prey. If they got killed, Vost reasoned, there would be fewer to pay. And more to split among the survivors.

The new recruits fell on Takuda's rear guard with a will that bordered on desperation. They knew that this was their chance to go for the bonus money. Do it now or lose out completely was what Vost had said. They attacked the screen with desperate courage, apparently ready to tear each other apart to become part of the mission.

Takuda and his people saw them coming as Vost's new recruits crashed through the trees in their untrained, blind urgency to find and destroy their enemies. It was easy, too easy for trained warriors like the DEST team. First, Holland, Horg, and Knyte fired quick warning shots with their lasers into the trees above their heads, but that was

worse than a killing shot. The attacking foot soldiers took
it as a sign that their enemy was not a good shot and so
presented little danger. They became more bold, shouting
to each other in their excitement. There is nothing more
invigorating than to be shot at with no effect. That truism
had been around for thousands of years, and it was just as
valid in these deep woods of this uncharted world. Those
who had been missed now felt themselves invulnerable,
immortal. On they came.

That was when Takuda's men got down to some serious shooting. The DEST members were superbly trained
marksmen who could drill an enemy through the eye—
you choose the eye—at a hundred fifty meters. But the
killing did little to reduce the enthusiasm of Vost's soldiers. Those who'd been shot at and missed had been
quick to report that fact to their hidden friends. Those
drilled through the eyes did not report the fact to anyone.
And so the foot soldiers came bounding through the trees,
all the while the DEST members continued to take them
out.

The human refugees were not as successful. A few had
subguns and pistols, but most were armed with the same
archaic, muzzle-loading weapons as their attackers. When
those groups came into contact there was much bloodlet-
ting.

The refugees and the DEST people had worked out
their tactics for dealing with the vanguard of the Vost
troops. When one of the rebels saw an enemy, especially
if that enemy were in danger of closing, he would shout
a warning. The nearest DEST member would react at
once, arriving, with luck, in time to provide fire support
for his side. Then the DEST member would drop back
and await the next encounter.

It was not so effective when a Tetatae was involved.
The little aliens, caught while digging a pit, could not call
for support. Most of them had not mastered the language
of the humans, and the humans could not tell one Tetatae
cry from another. The result was that when a Tetatae en-

countered the vanguard, he or she usually died before help could arrive. The refugees with Takuda were not accustomed to helping Tetatae, in any case, so the only help the bird-like creatures could hope for was from Takuda's people. When a DEST member was close by and knew of an encounter, he was quick to react. But mostly the Tetatae suffered casualties.

While all these bitter little skirmishes were being played out under the canopy of the thick forest, Seagroves and his LAM were out looking for the head of the column. The LAM cruised through the tall canyons of clouds, its twin Allied AVRTech 125 jet propulsion units throttled back as low as they'd go without sending the LAM into an uncontrolled stall. The I/R sensor and motion-detector systems were set on high area-scan so that they swept back and forth over the broadest possible area. Seagroves had also turned the sensor warning klaxon up to its greatest sensitivity, so that he didn't have to pay attention to the plot. This was flying the way it was meant to be; almost silent, almost like being a piece of the clouds themselves. Knowing that he was alone in the vault of blue and white, he could go anywhere without fearing hostile activity. He slid between a pair of towering white columns and butted his way through an errant vaporous arm that reached out across the gulf like a gigantic ethereal arch. The cotton whipped past the canopy and the LAM drifted out over a vast chasm that fell away to the green carpet below.

Then, suddenly, the klaxon went off with an insistent screech. Both I/R and motion sensors had discovered something six kilometers below. Seagroves sat forward against the restraining harness and adjusted the tuning dials to bring the digital scan to finer scale. The plot plan reduced to a smaller and smaller area until the twin sensors indicated the same target. Red corners descended on the single blip until they converged as a single reading. Target identification scrolled across the HUD. A *Locust* moving at a walk. Fully armed. Seagroves studied th eight-digit coordinate readout and called Vost with the information. He waited for a reply and then rolled the LAM over in a gentle dive.

The pilot's problem with the LAM had to do with target location. Deep in the trees, the I/R and motion detectors gave accurate information, but there was no chance of visual lock and identification. That would mean that he would be firing the laser battery on instruments only. That was an acceptable procedure, but in this case Seagroves knew there was intervening terrain. The trees, triple-thick with overhead cover, would have been easy for a multiple short-range missile system or PPC. The heavy weapons would pound through the crud and bore in on the target. The lasers, however, would strike the leaves and make them flash into steam. With enough laser energy directed at the leaves long enough, the same thing would happen. But diving on a moving, even a slowly moving, target at nine hundred kilometers per hour did not allow enough time for the lasers to bore through. He could scare the target, but unless it stood still and fought, there was no way he could get to it.

The LAM came screaming over the trees, and Seagroves triggered the full battery as his screen went green. There was a flash of steam and a momentary glow as the laser energy bit into the foliage. Then the LAM was past the target and into a gentle climb. He checked the sensors; the target was still moving, putting new foliage between it and its attacker.

As Seagroves pulled up into a gentle hammerhead stall, the fuel-expenditure light flashed and began beeping. The light came on when the fuel load reached half value, and the tone would continue at thirty-second intervals until the tanks were dry. He still had plenty of fuel for this mission, but now there was something else to think about. He didn't need either the light or the noise. Seagroves reached forward against the harness and twisted the light from its bayonet socket, silencing the beeping at the same time. He would replace it after he landed. It went against his training as a pilot to allow the light to remain out, a known gig on the maintenance report. And Elizabeth Hoond, his senior tech, would be all over him like a blanket if he didn't report it. But, then again, even if he ran out of fuel, he could always glide in and walk the 'Mech home.

═══ 47 ═══

The retreat continued through that night and into the next day and then the next day and the next until the periods of daylight and darkness melded together in a blur of fatigue and fear. Some people dropped out and were captured. Some were killed by the thinning cloud of their comrades who had now joined Vost. Some just drifted away from the column and never returned. And still the retreat went on.

They began to climb away from the broad river that had been home to the humans and the Tetatae. The triple-canopy rain forest gave way to mixed deciduous/coniferous growth. The heat of the great valley gave way to cool air by day and sharp chill at night. And still the retreat continued.

Dakodo rode in his place on the *Locust*'s exterior, Jacobs and Goodall in the cramped cockpit where they could change places to keep the 'Mech in continuous operation. They disregarded all but the most serious warning lights, knowing that redundant systems would keep the 'Mech going for at least a little longer.

In daylight the length of the column shrank under the pressure of the pursuers and the prodding of Takuda and the rest of his DEST team. More and more of the Tetatae crowded to the front where they clustered around the *Locust*, remaining there when the cavalcade ended during the night. They became a source of inspiration to the

'Mech pilots. They got to know, on an intimate and familiar basis, many of the Tetatae who plodded along beside them. They watched as the aliens became more and more fatigued. They watched as the little bird-humans shared the burden of the trek. They gave many of them nicknames like Bouncy, Happy, Springboard, Dumbo. They watched as some collapsed and were laid to their final rest, covered by whatever flowers grew in the area.

When Arsenault went down with a spear thrust through his hips, the Tetatae carried him. Paul Tessarak, a refugee from Osio, picked up Arsenault's laser rifle, but found that the full charger rig and rifle were too heavy for him. A Tetatae carried the charger. Together the two, human with rifle, Tetatae with power pack, became inseparable. And always the Tetatae would move ahead on the trail, clearing it of sticks and rocks to make the passage easier for the humans. By the time the last member of the column passed a point, the trail was as smooth as energy and imagination could make it.

Takuda pointed out that a trail so well marked might make it easier for the humans to travel, but it also made it easier for their pursuers to follow. The Tetatae then rushed to cover the trial with the sticks, branches, rocks, and boulders they had so laboriously removed only moments before. Takuda gave up. It looked like he was going to be an avatar to the Tetatae, and there was nothing he could do about it.

On the seventeenth day they crossed from the forest to an area of scrub. The temperatures dropped and the winds howled down out of the gray northern sky to bite through the party's light, warm-weather clothing. It became impossible for them to travel after dark because of the cold. The refugees, the DEST people, and the Tetatae huddled around tiny fires that gave more visual comfort than real heat. On the twenty-first day they encountered the first snow.

* * *

The LAM came less often, even as the ground became more o*~ ~*. The flight time from Usugumo to the head of the column became a real consideration as fuel and maintenance began to wear down its capabilities. The trekkers were three hundred kilometers from the river, and even at nine hundred kilometers per hour, the time out and time back began to eat up the craft's precious fuel. The other 'Mechs hung at the rear of the column, but they too began to feel the strain of the trek. It had been days since their technicians had been at them, and Seagroves spent much of his precious fuel shuttling people and parts from the base at the Usugumo bastion. He began to complain about being used as a truck driver. Vost was not amused.

As far as the commander of the mercenaries was concerned, Seagroves was getting what he deserved. The pilot was too big for his britches, and it was nice to see him knocked down a peg or two. Vost decided that the LAM would remain with the other 'Mechs on a regular basis, returning to the Usugumo base camp only as needed. Seagroves, as a reaction to his less and less frequent visits to the city, made each one count. He began to move his gold from its hidden storage caches around the bastion into lockers in the LAM. The pilot wanted to be sure that at least part of his stash was safe. The extra weight in the forward portion of the LAM meant that the pilot had to re-trim the craft for every flight, but a slight manipulation of the trim tabs took care of the problem.

Late on the afternoon of the twenty-second day, Seagroves brought the LAM in for a rougher than usual landing near the other 'Mechs. As the days dragged by, the rest of Vost's people had become less and less willing to smooth out landing sites for the LAM. It wasn't so difficult to bring the fifty-ton machine down into a clearing, but it was always better to know that the ground had been swept of rocks and any unseen holes filled. The LAM was a heavy, solid, well-armored machine, but the landing thrust was liable to pick up loose objects and hurl them around with significant violence. Foreign-object damage to one of the AVRTech 125s would be just as fatal as a direct hit from a PPC. Seagroves complained about the lack of diligence on the part of the enclave forces still in pursuit. Vost had told him to take his FOD and stuff it.

"Your problem," said Vost with the sneer that had become a permanent expression on his face, "is that you're afraid to fly. All you ever do is gripe. I don't know why, but it seems that the longer you guys fly, the more your guts turn to water. I'm surprised they don't issue you pilots diapers to keep your uniforms clean. I'll bet Hoond spends more time cleaning your pants than she does maintaining the LAM."

Seagroves clenched his fists in frustration. "I'm a professional pilot, and I plan to stay alive as a pilot. When you're four kilometers above the surface of a planet, falling can be very permanent. It's one thing to fall over in one of your land-bound machines, but in the air, any mistake can be fatal. Having some FOD break a fuel lead or damage a heat sensor or trim control can be fatal. All you guys on the ground have to do is clean up a bit. Is that too much to ask?"

"Flying a computer-assisted, fly-by-wire LAM isn't all that hard," Vost scoffed contemptuously. "Remember, I'm LAM qualified, too."

"You think so? You think so? Having flown one once doesn't make you qualified. Here," said Seagroves digging into a trouser pocket. "Here, take the security decoupling system. If you think it's so easy, you fly it." Seagroves flipped the interlock disconnect control pack into the air.

Vost snatched it with an evil grin. "I will. And just to show you what a good guy I am, here's the interlock to the *Panther*. Have a good day." Vost turned on his heel and made his way to the access ladder. Seagroves watched as the other man climbed up the side of the LAM and crawled through the hinged port in the belly of the *Hawk* portion of the combination. The deposed pilo jumped clear as Vost fired up the propulsion unit and let the twin turbos wind to a high whine. Seagroves listened with an experienced ear, criticizing the revs as being too high for the needed maneuver. Vost had a lead foot.

Then the LAM blasted clear of the small field. Seagroves watched it rise in a near vertical climb, the AVRTech 125s screaming at full power. As he reached up to his right breast pocket to put the *Panther* interlock code package away, his fingers found something already there. He poked them in and withdrew the fuel-warning light bulb. He shrugged and snapped the tiny globe into the bushes. Too bad.

Inside the LAM's cockpit, Vost began to remember what it was like to fly. He'd been a MechWarrior more than half his life, and he knew the surge of raw power that came with driving a fifty-plus-ton articulated fighting BattleMech across the terrain. But this feeling he hadn't experienced in years. To be absolutely free of the ground. To be able to do anything he wanted. To be a bird, a bird of prey. Wonderful. Rapture of the air. He rolled the LAM onto its back and then brought it back to level, upright flight. He got the feel of the controls. He could fly by the seat of his pants. Instruments were unnecessary. Not for him the artificial horizon, the climb and dive indicator, the compass. He could feel the movement of the LAM under him. It was the good old days all over again.

There was a sharp beeping from the secondary screen, and Vost adjusted the controls. The screen wasn't identical to the one in the *Panther,* but it was close enough. He twisted the tuning controls until a clear picture appeared. There below him, clear against the stark rock of the mountain, stood the rebel *Locust.* Vost eased the LAM over into a shallow approach, watching as the sensors scanned the stationary 'Mech. Information on the status of the enemy machine scrolled across the corner of the secondary screen as well on the main screen HUD. Vost concentrated.

The first information was the target type and identification. He knew all that. Then came propulsion information and heat status. The 160 LTV plant was fully operational, and heat was well within normal operating levels. The sensors scanned the Bergan VII chassis; a glitch! Now Vost really concentrated. The 'Mech wasn't moving, not even twisting or elevating its torso. It was a sitting, dead, duck. He felt the surge of adrenaline pour through his body. A sure kill. he let the LAM drift into a wide circle to approach from the rear, and then when he was almost directly over the crippled *Locust,* he slammed the joystick into the left-front corner of the cockpit. The LAM rolled over into a neat split-S and came down like a thunderbolt.

Inside the *Locust,* Jacobs and Goodall had seen the LAM on their own sensors as soon as it cleared the edge of the mountain. They'd worked frantically to free the jammed servoactuator, but the cold, the travel, and the limited maintenance made the effort futile. Given time and some judiciously applied heat, they'd be able to free the joint, but they had neither at this instant.

In the cockpit of the LAM, Vost let the targeting computer lock onto the *Locust*'s center top. He jammed the throttle full forward, and the AVRTech engines responded. Jet exhaust leaped thirty meters to the rear of the screaming LAM. Inside the computer monitoring the status of various systems, the low-fuel warning matrix registered the last of the jet fuel pouring through the massive turbos. It responded by sending electron impulses to the warning light on the dashboard directly in front of the pilot. One pulse a second, sixty to the minute, more than three thousand in an hour. It would continue to respond this way until the fuel was replaced.

Vost didn't see the light. There was no light. But he did feel the last of the fuel rush through the screaming engines. The control panel went red. Warning lights and klaxons howled in his ears, so loud that his teeth vibrated. He pulled back on the joystick, saw the target computer lose its lock on the *Locust.* Then the ground was rushing at him with incredible speed. The storage compartment over his left shoulder snapped open and a golden goblet dropped against the dashboard. Then another and another. He stared in disbelief.

Five kilometers away, Seagroves turned when he heard the engines shut down in mid-dive. He didn't see the impact, but the rising fireball and the shock waves a moment later told him what had happened. He reached into his pocket for the Panther interlock.

Seagroves and Pesht talked over the unfortunate and untimely death of their leader, though neither mercenary was particularly heartbroken at the loss. Seagroves was a bit put out at the destruction of the LAM, but lacking jet fuel, and without propulsion, the LAM was just an overweight machine. And neither man was completely aware of the contract Vost had made. They decided to make the long hike back to Usugumo and start over. After all, the contract had been fulfilled. They'd driven the rebels over the mountains and destroyed their 'Mechs. Though they couldn't be completely sure of that, there was no one to dispute their report. If natural predators and starvation didn't get them first, the Tetatae and the deserters would probably freeze to death in the high mountains. The *Panther* and the *Javelin* turned west toward the distant plain.

In the high mountains to the east, the ragged band of refugees staggered upward. The *Locust* had been pampered and coaxed into activity once more, but it moved with the unsteady gait of a tired man. It was no longer a smooth, even ride, but made rolling, halting steps that threatened to throw Dakodo off his perch on the carapace.

Service in and around the *Locust* was prized duty. Under normal conditions the heat generated by the power plant was a danger to the operation of any 'Mech of its class. Now, with the wind howling through the canyons with enough force to stagger the twenty-ton 'Mech and pluck the unwary from the narrow path, being near that warmth was a lifesaver. At night, when it became too dangerous to travel, the body of the *Locust* would squat low, the survivors huddling in its lee.

At last they found and crossed the high pass. There was a celebration in the ranks, despite the difficulty in eeking enthusiasm out of their chilled, exhausted bodies. There were those who thought it meant the trek was over, but the long, winding rifts that fell away promised more hardship and starvation. The chargers for the laser weapons continued to draw power each night from the fusion core of the *Locust,* so ammunition was no problem for Takuda. Horg discovered that the rifle, set on low power, could be drained into the rock strata, heating the stone to near-incandescence. Around its heated surface the frigid refugees could huddle until the most violent spasms of shivering passed. With the *Locust's* unlimited power, there was no worry about running out.

The only worry, as expressed by Goodall and Jacobs to Takuda, was that the 'Mech itself might fail. It was in danger of simply falling apart. In any other lance, it would have been consigned to depot maintenance for a good, long rest, but they had no such luxury. Goodall commented that if she were in the real world, wherever that was, she'd be severely reprimanded for the condition of the 'Mech.

At last they found the trees again, the same mixed forest through which they'd passed almost a month ago. Food became more plentiful, and the Tetatae happily began to forage for the others. Now the humans began to understand how valuable the bird-like aliens could be to their survival. The Tetatae knew what the humans could eat and what they could not, and they brought in a bountiful supply of edibles. Movement had become faster, and the *Locust,* no longer freezing in the joints, made good time. Dakodo kept them headed in the direction he alone seemed to understand. Even when some of the Tetatae complained that this area or that area was good enough, he refused to settle. Somewhere, perhaps not too far, was the far country of the other settlement. There was no stopping him now.

The *Locust* staggered to the top of a sharp ridge where Dakodo could view the broad grass and forest land that lay beyond. At last he seemed satisfied. Here, in the broad valley, was the far country he sought. It was here, he said, that they would find the others. Jacobs and Goodall activated the sensor system that had been shut down and ignored for so many days. There was an immediate response.

Jacobs and Goodall stared at the secondary screen. There was no doubt about the target reply—a solid metallic response from beyond the normal limit of sensor range. The sensors could send an inquiry and receive a response faster than the secondary screen could "read" and analyze the reply, but the screen would still show that there was something beyond its maximum scan. And it could only be something very large. It could only be a 'Mech, and the only other 'Mechs on the planet were those of the mercenaries. Somehow the mercs had swept the flank and were now waiting for them in the area Takuda's people planned to call their home. The whole trek, the fighting, the dying, the starvation, freezing, and exhaustion had been for naught. There must have been an easier way to reach this plain than the high passes over the mountains.

Takuda climbed stiffly into the cockpit to confirm the sensor target. There was no doubt about the nature of the signature; only a huge metallic object made a response like that. He examined his resources and began to plan.

The original DEST team had been reduced to seven, counting Parker Davud—which everyone did—and all had been wounded or injured in some way. Frostbite was a common denominator. Then there were the crushed fingers, swollen joints, sprains, and muscle pulls. Arsenaul was being carried by four Tetatae, the spear wound never having received the medicine to speed its repair. At leas gangrene had not set in. Paul Tessarak was still carrying the laser rifle, with his trusty Tetatae power-pack bearer close behind. Andi Holland still hobbled from injuries taken more than a month before. She too had suffered from the lack of time and medicine.

Takuda was too tired, too disappointed by the signature, to come up with any plan other than going straight at 'em. The others agreed. It would be all or nothing. With the *Locust* in support, the DEST members spread out over the terrain and began to sweep forward. It would take a full day to reach the rebound point of the response, unless, of course, the enemy 'Mechs came toward them.

The forest was high climax, and the going beneath the branches was easy for the infantry. It was harder for the *Locust* because it was right up among the tops of the trees. Finally, Jacobs climbed out of the cockpit to sit where Dakodo had spent much of the last month. Under his direction, the *Locust* was able to maintain its supporting position behind the infantry.

Goodall kept the return centered on the screen, using it as the guiding star for navigation. The constant return was a mesmerizing dot that drew her eyes until it became all she could see. She did not even notice the scrolling information that appeared shortly after noon. Finally she snapped herself out of her trance and paid attention. She brought the *Locust* to an abrupt halt, a stop so sudden that Jacobs nearly lost his handhold on the outer hull. He crawled back inside the cockpit after his complaints drew no response.

Goodall was transfixed by the data screen. She turned to Jacobs as he squirmed his way into the tiny space. "Get Takuda," she said without looking up. "He's got to see this."

Jacobs moved quickly to find the commander and bring him to the *Locust*. When Takuda had made his way into the cramped cockpit and taken the seat relinquished by Goodall, he watched the identification information scroll over the display. He, too, was astonished.

The target they had been stalking was not a hostile 'Mech. It wasn't even a 'Mech. The information on the screen identified the rebound as coming from a *Vulture* Class DropShip. The name that flashed onto the screen in reply to the electronic query identified the vessel as the Combine DropShip *Hideyoshi Toyotomi,* registration number DC445/157-AKA. A computer scan of the *Locust*'s limited information bank could not identify the *Vulture* Class. As a best guess, based on the radar and I/R sensor scan, the computer gave the *Seeker* as the closest possibility because the size, mass, and propulsion were close. The *Seeker* had been introduced in 2762, but the *Vulture* was obviously a much earlier model if it had been in operation in the 2500s. There was no sign of life around the ship.

By evening the refuges had closed on the target. It sat like a huge metal egg, one hundred thirty meters tall and one hundred wide. In solitary splendor it dominated a broad expanse of chest-high kusa. Knyte tapped on the interlock of the ship's personal access door, and the portal opened at once. The smell of stale air rushed over him, and he paused for a moment before entering, almost expecting someone to protest his breaching of the seal. Only silence greeted him.

Takuda and his troops poured into the DropShip, eager to discover all they could about what it was and where it came from. And where the people who had once crewed it? Almost immediately they came upon the human remains. These had been so well preserved in the climate-controlled environment that they were almost like unwrapped mummies, rigid at their stations or in their bunks. The computer log would hold the key.

Takuda called all the DEST members of the command bridge of the *Hideyoshi Toyotomi,* where they would unlock the ship's mystery. He waited until all were gathered then pressed the pressure-sensitive log-screen to bring up the most recent entry. The screen glowed to life, and the face of a handsome man, his features strained by fatigue and resignation, filled the square. "This is the last entry in the log of the *Hideyoshi Toyotomi,* which departed from the planet Salford in the year 2510. We were docked to the Draconis Combine JumpShip *Raiden.* The JumpShip encountered a cosmic accident of some kind, and we misjumped into this system. With the *Raiden* breaking up, we abandoned the JumpShip and made our way here. We believe that we are the only survivors. A breach in the pressure hull killed many of those on board, but we were able to land safely.

"We have survived for one year at this location, but our commlink inquiries were never answered. We have discovered no sentient life with whom to communicate. It has become obvious that we will die here, for we have no way to reproduce. There were a dozen women aboard ship when we made the jump, but the breach in the pressure hull took the lives of all of them. Thus we are a society of twenty-five men. We will not survive.

"Rather than die old and useless, we have decided that seppuku is the honorable way to depart this life. We will close the ship against the indignities of the environment, and we will reduce power output to the lowest point. We trust that at some time, when we are discovered, the *Hideyoshi Toyotomi* will be in a condition to bring honor to its crew.

"This is Captain and Master Pama Tohoku of the Draconis Combine DropShip *Hideyoshi Toyotomi* wishing good luck to those who find us. Signing off."

Takuda and the rest stood in silence as the transmission ended. This was the nugget at the heart of the legend. It was one of those who had fallen from the sky with fire. The survivors had not become a society that would save the Tetatae, at least not by their action. But perhaps they had, in their own way, given the little bird people a chance to live a life of freedom and security. Here, far across the mountains, it would be years, perhaps decades, before the humans of the vast plain ventured this far. Here they would have the fresh start they so needed.

But there was now the question of the humans themselves. Here, sitting silent and barely alive, was a transport that could free them of this planet. Perhaps it would be possible to reach one of the stranded JumpShips now hanging as orbital junk above the planet. Perhaps there was a way off. And even if they could not reach the ships or get them operational, there was another habitable planet within the star system. They could go there.

Rick Harris
93

=== 49 ===

Davud and Jacobs began a detailed examination of the ship. It wasn't that they were looking for something, they were looking for everything. There were so many questions that had to be answered before they could even come up with an intelligent option. The first question, of course, was whether the ship could fly. After that would come the question as to whether or not the ship should fly. And if it should, where would it go? But first Takuda needed to know if they could even get off the ground.

On that score there was some good news and some bad news. Parker Davud had never been on the command bridge of a *Vulture* Class DropShip. He'd never piloted a *Seeker* either, but he'd had simulator training on the type. The *Seeker* was an ovoid design rather than the aerodyne configuration that he had brought down. That meant the ship would land on extending legs, settling straight down onto the target. His ship had operated more like an aircraft, requiring a strip for takeoff and landing maneuvers.

Davud settled himself into the command seat and ran through the computer simulation sequence. It would take a day or two to become familiar with the instrumentation and access programs. That shouldn't be a problem, for the ship had ample reserve power in the storage capacitors. Any additional power requirements could be supplied by the *Locust*. There were power access ports on both the 'Mech and the DropShip, and even though there were n common cables, Jacobs could cobble something together. The bottom line was that neither man saw any reason why the ship shouldn't be able to fly. Docking was another question.

Davud took a good look at the exterior of the egg-shaped craft. Though the interior had been sealed for the five hundred years it had sat here, the ship's exterior had not been so protected. Five hundred years was a long time for metal to resist the attacks of nature, no matter how well protected it might be. In addition, the weight of the DropShip, which was about ten thousand tons, had also affected the DropShip's situation.

By its own weight, the ship had settled into the ground until the entire lower hull arc had pushed below the surface. The six landing legs were embedded to a depth below the access doors, and the doors themselves had buckled under the weight. They would not close, and there was some doubt as to whether the legs would retract.

There were also signs that, aside from the ruptured area that had killed so many of the crew, the ship's outer skin had lost some structural integrity. Davud ran a pressure test on the vessel's interior, and the results had neither condemned nor vindicated the strength. The frame was still straight, the laser designator and mirrors confirming that the columns and spokes that formed the skeleton had remained true.

The quad thrust V450s were completely buried. There was no way to test whether they would actually fire on demand. Davud had gotten a green reply from the several diagnostic programs he'd run on them, but he still couldn't be sure that they would fire. That was Jacobs' problem.

The result of all this inspection was a "maybe" to the question of flight. Though they found no obvious reason why the DropShip couldn't fly, suspicions lurked that it would not. The only way to be absolutely sure was to try, but that was probably going to happen only once. It might fly the first time, but the chances of it being able to do it more than once were a gamble Davud was not thrilled about taking.

Jacobs' news was not as good. Getting the fusion core restarted would be a problem because it had died long before. They could create a magnetic vessel to contain the reaction from the energy of the *Locust*'s own reactor. It had enough power, assuming the 'Mech didn't need to move, to generate the bottle. The second problem was supplying the tritium for the reaction core. Tritium was produced by a neutron flux passing through water, which could be produced by breaking up the shielding also found around the *Locust*'s reactor and filling the cavity with water. So far so good. They could then extract the water and use electric current to split it into hydrogen and oxygen, then dump the raw hydrogen into the fuel stream. The reaction could then be triggered by firing a laser through the tritium inside the bottle. *Voilà*, reaction.

The *Locust*'s medium laser had more than enough kilojoules to initiate the process. But the biggest "but" was the impossibility of getting the laser energy into the center of the reactor housing. The only way would be to separate the laser from the *Locust*'s chin mount and carry it into the DropShip. If all those tasks could be accomplished, the DropShip would have power. That was fine for the energy requirements of the vessel, but none of that would get it off the ground. For that they needed hydrogen fuel.

Under normal conditions, the DropShip would be fueled with liquid hydrogen from holding tanks at a spaceport. The *Seeker/Vulture* Class carried enough fuel to get off the ground, land, get off, and land again. That allowed the DropShip to land on some planet as part of an assault force and still have enough fuel to get back to the mother JumpShip and then return planetside. The *Toyotomi* had been fully fueled when it departed Salford. They'd landed hard but safely without rupturing the fuel cells, but time and the tiny hydrogen molecules had taken their toll. The fuel cells were less than half full. There would be enough to get the *Toyotomi* off the ground under normal circumstances, but neither Jacobs nor Davud considered this launch normal. They would have to generate hydrogen.

Again, water could be charged to produce the hydrogen needed, but liquifying it would be a trick. The *Toyotomi* had compressors, but it would take days to create enough hydrogen to fill the tanks. Fueling was a dangerous job, and five days of it was something no reasonable pilot would want to undertake. Too many risks of an accident—a liquid hydrogen accident was usually the last one anyone would have.

The two men explained these problems to Takuda and the other refugees. Seeing the magnitude of the decision necessary, Takuda did not believe it should be his alone. It was fine for a commander to make tactical choices affecting the life and death of his unit, but this choice would affect the future of an entire civilization. It should be made by those most affected. The little society listened in silence as Davud, Jacobs, and Goodall made their reports.

Paul Tessarak was the first to respond. Ever since Fullerton's defection, he had become the spokesman for the humans from the enclaves. "What do we gain or lose if we leave?" he asked. "What do we gain or lose if we stay?"

"What we gain if we stay," said Goodall, "is the absolute certainty that we will be the gods of the Tetatae for the rest of our lives. It was all right at first, but I'm not sure I want to have an entire society hanging on my every word, my every action, for the rest of my days. I want the chance to be wrong for a change. I want to be able to make a mistake without having to wonder if it will kill someone. It's getting so I can't do anything without having some loving little fur ball at my feet or at my side. I'm tired of it."

"It isn't that I don't like them. Dakodo, Totito,

Dokaepi, and Têopõ and the rest have all been good to me, to all of us. But I don't want to be the head shove for their society. As far as I'm concerned, I'd rather go somewhere else, and leave them in peace. Let the memory of us be enough. We'll have fulfilled their legends. We'll have led them to a better place. The legend doesn't say anything about having to stay around. I say let's go and be done with it."

Goodall's opinion was echoed by many others. They were willing to try for the other planet, the one they now called Toku Kuni, the Tetatae word for "far country". There was nothing for them here, and if they were to start afresh, it would probably be better done somewhere else. Toku Kuni was the choice. The total human population of their group was close to fifty strong. They were enough to survive in a strange, new world. If it was possible to make the DropShip mechanically safe, if it was possible to fuel the drives for the liftoff, they were willing to make the trip.

Tessarak had a request if they were to go. He wanted to make sure everyone knew the rules before they went aboard the DropShip. Once on board there would be no turning back. The request was seconded by all.

This was a new experience for Takuda. Never before had he been involved in the creation of a government. The officers, Takuda, Davud, Goodall, and Jacobs, huddled together with Tessarak to cobble together a form of government, but the task was monumental. An absolute dictatorship with Takuda as the chief involved a whole series of problems, the most difficult of which was that of transition. Who would take over when Takuda's reign ended, and how would that time be determined? The DEST commander wanted to be important in the government, but he did not want to BE the government. The lights burned late in the DropShip bridge as they hashed over the dilemma.

It was the body of refugees and the rest of the DEST team who finally solved the problem. They were willing.

they said, for Takuda to have absolute power in the government for at least one standard year. After that time, they suggested, the people should meet again. Yes, this would put absolute power into the hands of the military, but having seen Takuda in action in both combat and administration, they felt they could trust him. Besides, no one else in the group seemed qualified, so why not set up a government like a family with a *pater familias*? Their group was certainly small enough for that. According to the refugees, Takuda's greatest assets were his contemplative nature and his unwillingness to use his power in an arrogant or selfish manner. If he would lead, they would follow.

Takuda took the news with resignation. He was proud that the members of the little society believed they could trust him, but sitting alone in his sparse quarters on the *Hideyoshi Toyotomi,* he wondered if he would be up to this new and immense responsibility. Now that the chain of command had been formalized, the weight of responsibility was even greater.

There was also the problem of the Tetatae. Takuda sought out the leaders of the combined tribes. He called together Totito, Dokaepi, Dakodo, and Pikaete of the Usugumo enclave to discuss the situation. The decision that the humans, especially Goodall, Jacobs, and Takuda, were about to depart threw the aliens into a panic. They had only just decided that the humans were the symbols of their new life, and now they would be deserting them.

"No," said Takuda, "we are not deserting you. There was the legend that other humans would come to lead you to a better life, and that part of the legend has been fulfilled. There is nothing in the myth that says that the humans will remain to rule or guide. The ruling and the guiding must come from your own ranks. You have been through a great ordeal that has shown your own ability to work together, no matter what your tribe of origin.

"No one will come here to trouble you for some time. The leaders of the enclaves will be at each other's throats;

they will not come looking for you. And even when they do, many more of your people will have joined you by them. They will hear of you and they will come. Your force will be strong. From here on, you don't need us anymore."

Mark Jacobs let the hydraulic pressure rise against the piston. The shining steel slug moved forward into the cylinder, and Jacobs watched the pressure indicator scroll upward as the kg/sq cm rose toward the liquification point of the captured hydrogen. This was the forty-seventh time he'd gone through the process, and every time he felt his palms grow wet with nervousness. The snaking hoses that led away from the pressure pump to the fuel storage tanks had been checked and rechecked each time the procedure was completed, but it still made him nervous. Jacobs was well-versed in the theory of statistics, and he knew the first rule: if there exists any chance of a disaster occurring, no matter how slight, it will happen if the procedure is repeated often enough.

Although a liquid hydrogen leak would cool itself as it expanded, a hydrogen-rich atmosphere was not pleasant to contemplate. Any spark—ANY spark—would set it off. The only good thing was that if it happened, Jacobs wouldn't be in any condition to worry about it. He tried to console himself with the thought that he wouldn't suffer from horrifyingly disfiguring burns.

He watched the kg/sq cm scroll to liquefication and held the pressure to let the piston and cylinder cool. Then he opened the valve and saw the hoses stiffen with the liquid hydrogen. The piston crept forward as the hydrogen rushed through the hoses to the tanks. The pressure dropped, and Jacobs began to breathe again.

Outside the DropShip, Parker Davud had crews excavating the landing pads and thruster ports. The pads were easy compared to the difficulty of digging all the way under the ship's ovoid body to open the venturi. Finally the workers resorted to tunneling under the DropShip to reach the openings, which permitted Davud to squirm through to inspect the conic thruster exhausts. They seemed undamaged by the landing, although the number five cone showed some distortion.

Inside the hull itself, Goodall supervised the placement of the *Locust*'s medium laser in the fusion generator. The other techs had salvaged enough tritium from the coolant water of the *Locust*'s core to initiate fusion if enough heat could be applied. The magnetic containment bottle was ready. Now it was only a matter of throwing the switches, which were, at the moment, in Mark Jacobs' pocket. He had insisted, and reasonably so, that all circuits be absolutely dead while he generated the liquid hydrogen. The only assurance he would accept was to have all the switches with him until fueling was complete. Even then, he demanded that the area be swept for pockets of hydrogen before they went any further. The more fuel he created, the more paranoid he became. As did they all.

Sagiri Johnson took over the dismantling of the *Locust*, though there was little of any value still on the 'Mech. The machine guns and ammunition were stowed aboard the DropShip, although the vessel itself had plenty of inherent firepower. They would also keep the medium laser or at least the guts of it, onboard the ship. The three-meter-long barrel would remain where it was, at the request of the Tetatae. They wanted to keep the *Locust* as a reminder of what they had been through and as a visible symbol of their legend fulfilled.

Takuda had granted their request, as long as the Tetatae let the humans salvage all usable equipment. He did not know what he and his people would face on Far Country,

nor did he think it a good idea to leave the Tetatae with
advanced technology they didn't understand. All it would
take was for one of them to figure it out to unleash a
chaos they could probably not control. The fusion core
would be the last thing they would shut down. It would
remain in the *Locust,* mainly because it would not be of
any value. If the DropShip's core failed, two cold power
plants wouldn't do its passengers and crew any good.

The refugees continued to work on the DropShip, now
re-named *Noah's Ark,* until the supervisors reported that
they were ready. All systems had been checked and rechecked. All reparable damage had been repaired. The fusion generator was up and functioning, the fuel tanks
were full. It was time to load.

But what to take? There was no telling what kind of
environment they would face or whether they would find
anything edible on their new homeworld. Yet they didn't
want to upset a functioning ecosystem by introducing alien species. They chose carefully those plants and animals that seemed most benign. Choosing plants was easy
enough; it was the animals that proved difficult. They decided to take neither fish, nor fowl, nor beasts. If they
found any of those on Far Country, fine. If not, the humans would just live without them. But insects and
worms were another kind of problem. Any vegetation
they took would require pollination and fertilization, for
which they would need the bugs and stuff. The "two of
each kind" idea proved more difficult than anyone at first
imagined. DEST members, techs, and humans scoured the
fields and woodlands for insects that crawled, burrowed,
and flew. For days they wandered about with thin mesh
nets in hand, leaping after any tiny thing that often flitted
maddeningly away.

But finally the task was accomplished. Without a biol-
ogist on the team, the refugees had needed to observe the
plants they wanted to take to learn what kinds of insects
played around them. That also took some time. They'd
also had to catalog and store the specimens, tucking them

safely away for the journey. The plants also had to be fed. They had to be watered. Tessarak's people even claimed that they had to be sung to sleep at night.

Jacobs and Davud collaborated on the *Ark*'s navigation. Lacking a true navigator, they were making it up as they went along. The huge surface of Far Country was an easy target, but since it was pointless trying to choose one point over another, they simply picked the center of the mass and hoped for the best. The general coordinates of the proposed landing zone were plugged into the computer and then checked for three consecutive days. The computer would get them somewhere within the center of a hundred-kilometer circle. After that it would be up to Davud and Jacobs to get the ship down.

The loading doors swung shut and sealed. Personnel doors were closed and dogged down. Checking for leaks, Davud let the pressure rise inside the hull. He held the pressure there for a full ten minutes; there was no decrease. The hull was sound. He started down the computerized check list.

"Inertial guidance?"

"Check."

"Initial firing sequence?"

"Check."

All computer systems and back-up. Landing hydraulics. Secondary firing system. Primary thrusters. Directional vanes. Everything checked. Davud touched the internal commlink panel. "Now hear this. Now hear this. *Noah's Ark* prepared for liftoff in five minutes. All personnel to stations." The last order was unnecessary. The crew and refugees were already securely strapped into their flight stations.

Davud took a deep breath and began the countdown firing sequence. Fuel valves were opened and checked. Green board. Ignition sequence was checked for the last time. Green board. He rocked the landing legs to help break the vacuum under the *Ark*. Everything still green. He watched the clock scroll backward as the sensor panels came on line. In the adjoining seat, Jacobs was opening the engine ports. One last diagnostic of the systems. Green board.

"Ten, nine, eight, seven, ignite initiators, six, five, open fuel outlet ports, four. . . ."

"We have ignition."

". . . three, two . . ."

"Full burn."

". . . one. Power valves open."

"Power valves open. Green board."

Flame blasted the ground away from the venturi mouths, creating great chunks of sod and stone under a white-hot cloud. The *Ark* trembled as the thrust from the six engines struggled to break the legs free. "Liftoff!"

Davud thought he could hear cheering from the personnel bays as the *Ark* drifted slightly in its rise above the surface, though still without enough thrust for rapid acceleration. Then the power began to take hold, and the DropShip lifted on a pillar of flame many times as tall as the ship itself. With a shattering roar it climbed straight into the sky and vanished from the sight of those on the ground below.

At the forest edge a kilometer away, the Tetatae watched the fire rise into the sky. The humans, those who came from the sky with fire, had gone again in the same way they had come. Someday they might return, but that would be another legend.

Beneath the *Ark* as it passed westward, gaining altitude with every millisecond, the circle of the planet grew rapidly smaller. The ship's navigator and commander were too busy watching their destination to see the circles of fire that outlined the enclaves or the smoke that hung over them. In the great open plain of the Usugumo, the *Javelin* and *Panther* stalked each other.

JAVELIN

PHOENIX HAWK

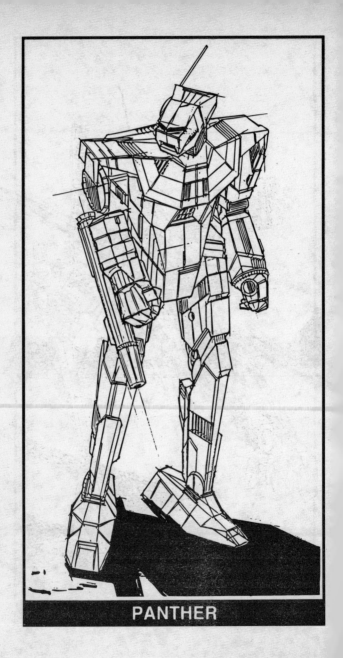

PANTHER

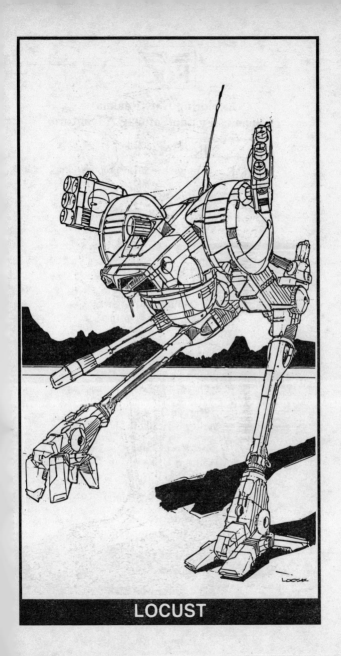

LOCUST

RoC

**Exploring New Realms
in Science Fiction/Fantasy Adventure**

Battletech®

Titles already published or in preparation: